Demon's Consort
By Lori-Anne Cohen

Paperback: 1-7370838-1-7
E-book: 1-7370838-0-9

Edited by Anya Weber
Cover art by Damonza
Printed by Kindle Direct Publishing in the USA

---

*For my mother, who always believed I could do the thing.
Love your guts. I miss you.*

PROLOGUE

Declan had been late to marry. What with one thing and another, seeing his sisters wed after their mother's passing, taking care of his aging father, and working the farm, there hadn't been time. So, when he met Alice, he was ready to settle down. Falling in love with her at first sight had been a happy bonus for him. With a bit of luck and a good deal of natural charm, he won her heart, and they were married. Two children, a girl and a boy soon followed. He was happy and felt that his life was as perfect as it could be, or as perfect as he'd let himself hope for. He was a smart man and while he often found himself wondering if there was more to the world than his small farm, it never really occurred to him that he'd know anything beyond his village. So, when the doctor told him that his wife and five-year-old daughter would most likely die from the sickness spreading through their town, he would not believe it. He prayed to God over and over for them to get well, but they got worse. A day came when he could not take it anymore and he ran out in the rain, railing at God. He ended up at a large rock outcropping at the edge of his land, where he wept. "Declan," said a voice, "Declan, stop crying."

Declan looked up and saw he was being watched by a very odd-looking man. With his height, his white hair, and eerie eyes, he looked otherworldly. Declan was frightened by the man's appearance but refused to show it. The man had spoken Gaelic, but Declan did not believe he was Irish. "Who are you to tell me what to do or not to do? My wife and daughter are dying and there is naught that anyone can do!"

"Well, no human can help. But I can."

"Human?! Are you mocking me?! Who are you?" The man was obviously crazed, thought Declan.

"I am not mocking you, Declan."

Declan's eyes narrowed. "*What are you?*" Declan began to shake with fear, but also with anger, and grief.

"Declan, what do you think I am?" Anaranth had been watching Declan for years. He knew the young man possessed a keen mind, one wasted on farming and small-town life.

Declan had always heard talk about supernatural beings, the priest referred to them as devils, but Declan wasn't sure he believed any of that. This man didn't seem human, that much was true, but what was he really?

"You are a devil," he said flatly, getting his emotions ruthlessly under control.

Anaranth smiled a bit at the control the young man was exhibiting. "Not a devil. Well, not as your priest says. But I am not human."

Declan sucked in his breath. "Are you evil?"

"I can be either, just like humans."

Declan pondered this. The priest had been very clear on this point. Devils, or demons, were evil. Still, Declan had never been one to follow blindly. "How do I know you are who you say you are? What you say you are?"

The man looked up at the sky and the rain stopped immediately.

Declan went to cross himself and this made the other man laugh. "It's just a trick, boy. It will start again soon enough."

"Who are you? I want to hear you say it."

"I am Anaranth."

"That is not what I meant."

"I know. I am a demon. And that," he put up his hand before Declan could say anything else, "is all I am going to tell you for right now about what I am."

"What do you want Anaranth?" His voice hard now.

"No, it's what you want, son." Anaranth had to admit that Declan was providing a bit of a challenge. A welcome one.

Declan narrowed his eyes at the demon. "What I want?" His voice held suspicion.

"Yes. Right now, what do you want above all things?"

"I want my wife and child to be well."

"And then?" The demon prompted.

"I want my children to live happy lives."

Anaranth started. "You do not want them to be wealthy, their coffers filled with riches?"

"No. Happiness, and their health. Why would I want them to be rich? Wealth won't save you if the plague takes. And it won't make you happy." Declan still didn't see what this had to do with anything.

Anaranth examined the man. Declan was demon born, and Anaranth had taken a chance coming to him now, instead of waiting. One of the Ancients had told him that this man would be important, powerful. Anaranth had not believed it of a simple farmer, but over the years he'd seen Declan's strength. He worked hard, he took care of his family, and he showed all kindness and respect. He could be hard when it was warranted, but the people in the town looked to him for advice. They trusted him. Power would not corrupt this man. Anaranth wanted access to the power that Declan would yield. And being honest with himself, he liked the man. He thought one day, he might be able to call him a friend.

"I can do this for you."

"You can?" Declan was skeptical.

"I can. Your wife will not be able to give you more children after this, though."

"I just want them well."

"That is a simple request."

"You're a demon though, you must want my soul in return." Declan stared at the strange man. He still showed no fear and was approaching this with his usual logic. He was Irish, believing in the unbelievable was never that much of a stretch. He'd always felt different, that he didn't quite fit in perfectly. Somewhere, deep in his soul, he'd always felt a bit out of step with the village. He felt it keenly those times he had looked to the horizon. He knew he would not grow old.

"That is not strictly how it works. You will become a demon upon your death. I will not take you now though. I will give you time to see your children grown and settled." It wouldn't do to sow seeds of discontent with this man. Anaranth was patient. When you were as old as he was, a decade or two didn't make much of a difference. "Once you die, your soul is promised into my service. But you do not 'lose' your soul. You will serve me solely for a time, and then you will be able to take direction of your immortal life. Do you understand all of this?" Declan thought for a moment and then nodded. Anaranth hesitated, this is the part where he had lost many a human. "But your family will wither and die. You cannot be with them. I am sorry, but that is how it must be. They will believe you truly dead."

Declan looked shocked, then resigned. His wife and daughter could not be allowed to die. His son must grow to adulthood and take over the farm. But he took a few minutes to think about it, nonetheless. "I accept." He finally announced. He would have the best life he could with his family, for as long as he was able to and that would have to be good enough.

Anaranth hid his surprise. "It is done."

"Now what?"

"Go back to your home. You will find your wife and child on the mend."

"Will the townspeople…"

"Their suspicions will not be aroused."

"I would thank you, but I think you are getting exactly what you want out of this."

"I am." Clever lad. "You and I will do well together, young Declan. You are meant for great things."

"I never wanted great things. I just wanted a family and a home."

"Sometimes our destiny is not what we would want it to be." With that alarming statement, he disappeared, and the rain started again.

When Declan arrived home, it was to news that his wife and daughter's fevers had broken. "Your prayers have worked." Exclaimed the neighbor who had been tending them. Declan knew this to not be true. He had gotten his wish, but it was also the day he stopped believing in God.

There would be no more children though, as Anaranth had said. This was fine with Declan, but Alice was worried about the farm. "If we don't have more sons…"

"We will be fine, my love. I am a happy man." And this was true. He loved his wife and his children. He insisted that both of his children learn to read and write. He saw them to adulthood. His daughter married a good man, and his son was ready to take over the farm.

On a warm spring day in 1218, when Declan would have been around forty-two, he met his end. Trampled by a scared horse. He would have lingered, but Anaranth had taken pity on him and allowed him to pass quickly. Declan was never really buried, but the townsfolk would talk about the funeral in years to come as an actual event, an easy demon's trick. Anaranth brought Declan back to life at night, on the rock where the two had met. "What now?" Declan asked.

"Now, we get to work, my boy."

CHAPTER 1

"Gwendolyn, please stop doing that." Anya looked over at Gwen, exasperation plain on her face, her voice sharper than she'd normally be with her friend.

"Doing what?" Gwen feigned innocence.

"Drumming your fingers on the taxi door."

Gwen looked chagrined and stopped the drumming. "Aren't you nervous? This is weird."

Anya was working an old coin, flipping it between each of her fingers, something she'd been doing since she was a child. It was a trick her father had taught her, and it was something she did when she was feeling out of sorts. This was the only sign that she might be a little agitated. "I am a bit nervous," Anya admitted. "But your tapping is not helping. Can you not do something quieter?"

Gwen pointed a finger at Anya's hand and made a flicking motion. The coin sailed neatly over to Gwen, who held it suspended midair. A flick of her wrist and the coin started flipping over, and then back again.

Anya smiled at her friend, even though she really wanted her coin back. "Gwen….my coin, please." She paused, wanting to soften her tone. "Though, you're really getting quite good at that."

"I've been working on it. It makes a nice change from spell work, though that is what I should be concentrating on. If nothing else, Methuselah is entertained by it."

"I'm sorry, who?"

"Methuselah. The cat."

"I thought the cat's name was Morrigan?"

"It felt too Irish."

"You *are* Irish." Anya looked at her friend, exasperation warring with affection.

"I know. But it felt too on the nose honestly. I am enough of a stereotype, being an Irish witch with a black cat."

"So, you changed it to Methuselah? Before this, he was Morrigan. And before that, Maximus. Why do you keep changing the cat's name?"

"Because it's not right. Neither is Methuselah, but it will do for now." Anya rolled her eyes. "Names are important."

"Whatever you say, you tiny weirdo."

Gwen knitted her brows at her friend. "Just wait, he'll tell me his name eventually."

"Uh-huh. Sure"

Gwen made a face at her friend and sat back in her seat, looking out the window as they slowly made their way towards the Marais.

"My coin, please? It was a gift from Natalia. She insists it belonged to the last Tsar of Russia." She grinned. "I don't believe that. But it is as old as she is."

Gwen flipped the coin back to Anya, who caught it, without looking and began working it through her fingers again. "If Natalia is Russian and not really your grandmother, why does she insist you call her that? In French?"

Anya smiled. "Natalia is very affected and likes the sound of it. She likes being called *'grand-mère'* because it makes her feel matriarchal and frankly, it's just easier when talking about her to people who don't know what she is. I called her *babushka* when I was very small, and she was not pleased. She lectured me very soundly in both French and Russian for about an hour. I owe my early French language skills to her. She thought shouting in French sounded classier. I prefer shouting in Russian."

Anya's own accent was mostly Russian, though she occasionally sounded French from having lived there for so long. Most people she met found the accent, coupled with the deeper timbre of her voice, exotic. Anya found this annoying and would get prickly anytime it was brought up. She didn't put stock in many people and as such, didn't give a damn what anyone thought of her accent. She was not an exotic creature and it irritated her that anyone would think this. She didn't let people get close as a rule. Well, until Gwen. When she'd realized the blonde could drink most men twice her size under the table, she'd known they would be friends. Anya had opened up to her in a way she'd never done with anyone else. Anya had not realized that she had been lonely, until Gwen came into her life and had filled it with friendship.

When Anya had decided to come clean to Gwen about their task tonight, she'd been hoping that with her being a witch, she'd be more open to the fantastical. Gwen had been shocked, but in the end, she'd come around. It had taken two bottles of wine and a lot of questions to get there. Witches were one thing, but demons were apparently a bigger stretch. Gwen still had so many questions whirling around in her head, she didn't know where to start sometimes.

But what stymied her the most, was how parts of Anya's life had been mapped out for her since she'd been born. Natalia had seen to that. It was both fascinating and a little horrifying.

Gwen smiled. "Does Natalia do that imperious thing with her voice that you do?"

"What imperious thing? I do no such thing!"

"Anya, I've heard you lecture." Anya was a literature professor.

Anya looked affronted. "That is just not true!" She thought for a moment and shrugged. "Well, ok. That's fair. I suppose I do get imperious sometimes. Maybe." Anya huffed out. In Anya's case, it was a defense mechanism designed to keep people away. Gwen knew that Anya was, at heart, warm and loving, but she rarely let anyone see that side of her.

Gwen sighed. "Why tonight?" she asked, bringing it back to the task at hand. "What's the rush now?"

Anya rolled her eyes. "Apparently the Council has been badgering this demon about it being time for him to take a consort. They met with him recently to hammer it home some more. Natalia is absolutely sure that it is destined to be me, so she wants me in there before someone else gets there." Anya paused. "I am still not really fully convinced to be honest. She has said that it was an ancient demon who told her this, that it was part of some prophecy or something. It's just...well...it's just that it's always felt so far away. Something I didn't have to worry or think about. And as I've been looking back at my life, I see how Natalia has been pushing me in the direction she's wanted me to go. This has been informing my decisions as an adult, even if I haven't realized it, hasn't it?"

"Annie, come on." She thought about it, but she owed it to her friend to be honest with her. "To a certain extent, possibly. Yes. But you're a strong person. I don't think in the end that you do anything because you're expected to. Did Natalia really want you to be an academic?"

"Not really, no."

"But you are one. Because you love to learn and study."

"True. Though teaching is another story entirely. In the circus, she wanted me to do high wire. I didn't want that. I wanted the knives."

"Exactly!" She paused. "You know, we don't have to do this."

"I am forty-two years old and my whole life has been wrapped up in preparing myself for this. Or at least it feels that way to me. So, I am going to do this and see what happens next."

"So, you don't believe you were meant for this?"

"I am not sure what I believe. The closer I've gotten to it, the more my doubts have ramped up. And beyond telling me his name and where to find him, Natalia, that old bat, has refused to answer any more questions. Something that is really pissing me off, by the way."

"What if he's awful?"

"Then I walk. Period. I am not tying myself to some kind of tyrant. And Natalia can just fucking deal. I am fairly sure she's worried about newer demons wanting to take over Eastern Europe, so she's trying to protect Vlad and herself. The one thing she did tell me is that he can't come into his full power until he takes a consort." Anya shrugged.

Gwen didn't really get the whole Council thing, and she was more interested in the demon himself. "What does it mean? His full power?"

"Well, he's destined, so Natalia tells me, to be a much more powerful demon one day. He will likely sit on the Council, sometime in the future."

"Oooookkk. But doesn't he need to rule a larger area than just Paris."

"He rules all of France. And Belgium currently."

"My question still stands though." Anya gave Gwen a pointed look and light dawned. "Western Europe?"

"Western Europe. But I also really don't get how. There is already a Demon of Western Europe, but our guy rules both France and Belgium. It's got to be weird demon politics."

Gwen smiled. "This is a puzzle. And you want to figure it out."

Anya started to deny it, then sighed. "Yes. It's a puzzle and I cannot just walk away from a puzzle."

"No, I know you can't. You'd be powerful then?"

"Well, he would be. I assume I would also share in that some."

"Would you be more powerful than Natalia?"

"Possibly." She thought for a moment. "Oooh, she'd hate that."

"Hmmm, this whole thing is a bit shady."

"You think? She and Vlad must have some kind of plan here."

"You're being awfully casual about this whole thing."

"It's not me being casual, Gwen. It's just something I need to figure out. And I need to figure out why I've been guided here. Natalia tried to make me into a little mini her. Which failed spectacularly."

"Did she think the highwire was a more feminine pursuit?"

"One can only assume. I think she thought high wire would be a more romantic story. More...dramatic maybe. Knives are messy and she doesn't like messy. She has been very good to me in a lot of ways, but I suspect in the end it was to her own gain to do so." Anya and Gwen never really discussed a lot of her childhood, and she had never told Gwen about what happened in Russia and why she'd left when she was still a child. She needed to tell her soon.

"Does he know you exist?"

"Not that I am aware of. I am not sure how he's going to feel about it. About me. It could be a non-starter. He could see me and run the other way."

"Why would he do that?"

Anya smiled indulgently at her friend. "Because he doesn't want this whole thing, he doesn't like tall women, or redheads, or Russians. Maybe he already has someone. Any number of reasons."

"He'd be a fool. And then I may have to curse him."

"Pretty sure you cannot curse a demon."

"Pretty sure I'd try anyway."

"How have we gone from you doubting I should do this to cursing a man who may not want me?"

"Loyalty knows no logic."

"You may also be a wee bit biased."

"Naturally. But honestly, I don't think the issue is going to be him not liking how you look."

"What do you mean?"

"Oh my God! Are you fucking serious? Do you not see any of the attention you get?"

Anya was 5'9' and curvy, with large breasts and generous hips. Her pale skin and dark auburn hair made her naturally violet eyes stand out. Her nose had been broken and that kept her face more on the interesting side. She looked soft but looks could be deceiving. Anya had a lot of strength, and she was quick. She was also lethal with a knife or dagger.

"Ridiculous!" scoffed Anya. "You are much prettier than I am."

"Yes, I am pretty." Anya looked at Gwen. "What? It's true, and I am not going to deny it. I am also smart and funny and have magic coming out of my pores. I don't deny what I am. You do. All the time."

"I own my brains."

"But you've never owned your looks. You may not be traditionally pretty, but you are someone people look at. And who has violet eyes? Not deep blue, violet!"

"Are we having this conversation to get my mind off what we're doing tonight?"

"Maybe? Is it working?"

"A little, actually." Anya thought she was weird looking, same as when she was a kid.

"But he's old timey, right? He may like how old timey you look." Gwen grinned at her friend.

The taxi screeched to a halt, causing Anya to smack into Gwen. "Was that really necessary?" Anya asked the driver in French.

He shrugged. "Not the easiest address to find," he replied in English, causing Anya to roll her eyes. That was not a reason, to her mind. But she let it go.

"*Bien, merci.*"

"We should get out," Gwen said.

"We should." Neither moved. The driver started tapping his fingers on the steering wheel and staring at the two in the rearview mirror. Anya sighed, pulled out some bills and paid the man. She had added in a healthy tip and he smiled at her. Always a bit of a soft touch, thought Gwen.

"*Merci, madame!*" She nodded at him and got out of the car, followed by Gwen.

"Where exactly are we?" asked Gwen.

"His club."

"Nightclub type club?"

"Yup. He owns and operates this one, and a handful more so I'm told." She paused and looked at the awning and unobtrusive entrance. A large man, demon most likely, in a dark suit stood out front. Security, by the look of him.

Gwen leaned into Anya. "Is that a demon?" The man was over six feet and was built like a square block. He had a large scar running down one side of his face and when he saw Gwen looking at him, he winked at her.

"Yes."

"They look like people."

"Gwen, they are people. Well, they were."

"Point taken. Well, at least we can get a drink."

"We can." Anya didn't move.

"So, how do you know...how will he know…"

"If we're meant to bond, he should be able to feel a bit of a tug."

"A tug?"

"Apparently. Look, I don't know. I know what I was told, but I have no clue how any of this really works. I am just as much in the dark as you, at this point." Anya was very agitated. She had put the coin away and she wished she hadn't.

"Annie, it's ok. You're nervous now."

"I am. Natalia told me we'd recognize each other, if indeed we are destined to be mated, but that's about it. I am not even sure how we've managed to avoid each other."

"Run in a lot of demon circles, do you?"

"Fair point well made. It's just…"

"What?"

"Something is niggling at me about this whole thing. Something odd. Not bad, just off. "

"Do you want to go?"

"No."

"Ok, then let's go in."

"I don't even know what he looks like!"

"He's the owner, it won't be that hard to find him. What's his name?"

"Declan O'Shea."

"Oh, An Irishman! That's nice then! Ok, let's go in and get this Declan O'Shea." Anya breathed and pulled out a card. "What's that?"

"We need this to get in. It's a really exclusive demon club. Humans need to have this card. Natalia sent it to me."

"Fine." She began to propel Anya towards the large demon standing at the front door of the club. "We're going in. You're buying."

***

Declan sat brooding in his office. His meeting a few days ago with the Council hadn't gone as planned and he was still pissed off about it. They had insisted that he find his consort and begin the bonding process. It was ridiculous and archaic, but so was the Council of Demons.

The Council was run by eight Demons, who each ruled over a part of the world. The de facto head of the Council was Anaranth. He was the ninth, non-voting member, and was sometimes called upon to break ties. He could also overrule a vote he didn't agree with. That was something he rarely did though. All Council took a human consort who ruled with them. The consort became immortal, so they lived as long as their demon. Even Anaranth had one from when he had been a voting member. Only demons destined for the Council were *allowed* consorts. The whole thing sat badly with Declan. It felt elitist and he hated that. Why should he be allowed to mate because he was meant for bigger things like the Council? It was appalling that class distinctions were still a thing with the demons.

"Declan," Anaranth had said, "You are eight hundred years old. It is well past time that you found your consort. You will never come into your full power until you do. And now is the time. She is out there and it's time you found her." The threat was clear. Western Europe would never belong to him otherwise, he'd never hold it. Declan didn't really care about that. He never had, and this ironically, was why he had done so well. He didn't rule his territory like a monarch on a throne. He ran it like a business. He valued loyalty, but that and respect were earned. And he paid his employees, both human and demon, very well. He would not rule from fear, ever. He was not one to cross, but as long as you did your job and followed the rules, there was never a problem. Betray him or steal from him and you would pay. Dearly. It was how he had amassed so much wealth over the last several hundred years. Matthew, Declan's number two man, called him the demonic answer to Bill Gates.

"What if I don't wish to mate. What if I don't care about power."

Anaranth had laughed. "My boy, there is no such thing as not caring about power!"

Declan sighed. Another of his inner circle Dougal, had referred to the Council more than once as a "bunch of old farts." That wasn't entirely unwarranted.

There was a knock at the door. "Come in!" he barked.

Christian, his general manager entered. "Someone is in foul humor this evening, I see."

"Christian, my patience is thin right now, please just tell me what you want."

"I just have some papers that you need to read and sign. Updated supplier contracts."

"Leave them." Christian stared at him. "I will sign them, but not at the moment. I am just as likely to incinerate them right now."

"I will nag you tomorrow about them, then. And cheer up…the club is packed, and we have some very lovely new blood in the building."

"The last thing I need right now is a woman."

"There is nothing so wrong that a night in the arms of a soft female, or a hard male for that matter, cannot cure. But have it your way, be a misery." And he swanned out of the room.

Declan rolled his eyes at his manager's words. He liked women; he liked the idea of having someone. But he didn't like the idea that he was going to consign someone to immortality as the consort of a demon. It seemed selfish just to have some company. And who knew what he may end up with? She may be a lunatic, like Liliana. Or, have no backbone like Mikhail. There had not been a new consort in hundreds of years. The elders on the Council were bored and wanted some new blood. And some good gossip fodder. Declan was in no mood to give it to them.

He sighed, got up and left his office, making his way downstairs to the heart of the club. The closer he got, the louder the music and noise got. He had learned to let it wash over him and not concentrate on it, otherwise the buzz of human energy would get to him. And with that, came their thoughts sometimes. He really disliked that it was one of his special Demon gifts. He kept it under tight control, but the initial blast when he hit the club was always a bit of a problem.

He stopped at the top of the last set of stairs leading down. He could immediately tell something was different. He frowned. The energy was off. Not bad, different. But it was jarring to him.

Something…someone was down there, throwing it off. There was a witch down there, but they weren't the problem. They had some power, but it wasn't threatening. It felt almost gentle. He stood stock still and opened himself up to find the cause. It took no time at all. His eyes flicked to the bar where a redhead in a deep eggplant dress sat with a petite blonde, who was the witch he had felt. But the redhead was the issue here. The back of his neck started to tingle, as did the tips of his fingers. Slowly, the redhead turned towards him, knowing exactly where to look. Their eyes locked and she smiled, smirked really. *Well fuck*, he thought. There she was—his fucking mate.

***

Anya and Gwen had made their way into the club and found seats at the bar. Or rather, the bartender saw them coming and cleared two places for them. Gwen was leaning over to talk to the bartender, a giant of a man who was already putty in her hands. "I am curious though…who owns this place? It's amazing!" she ran a golden hand down the bartender's dark arm. She lingered though; Anya noticed. Once, twice and then she almost went for a third before she stopped herself. Interesting, thought Anya. Gwen hadn't actually flirted with anyone in months.

"He's not down here at the moment," the bartender said. Gwen frowned and the man forged on. "But he should be down soon."

"Gwen…"

"What's he like? What does he look like?" Gwen was anything but subtle.

"Gwen…"

"One hears so many things after all."

A sigh. "Gwen!"

"Shit! What?!" Gwen kept her eyes on the bartender.

"It's fine. I found him."

Gwen looked at her friend finally. "But…" She saw Anya was staring off into the distance and followed her gaze until she found the man on the stairs staring back her friend. "Oh fuck me. No, seriously! That's him? She pivoted back to the bartender and pointed her head at the stairs. "Is that him?"

"Yes. That's the boss."

"Wow! Hey, what's your name?"

"Donovan."

"Is that a first or last name?"

Donovan shrugged. "Whichever."

"I'm Gwen. So, does he always look that pissed off?"

"Not usually, no." He looked over at Anya and wondered. "Is it you, then?" Declan had related his conversation with the Council to Donovan and Matthew when he had returned. And Donovan had wondered if something had been set in motion with that meeting. He hadn't expected her so soon, but he felt the charge when the two looked at each other. Declan was looking incredibly pissed off at the moment.

Without moving, she replied. "It does seem so." She was fairly sure about that now. The back of her neck and fingers had started to tingle. When she had turned around, she had found him easily.

"How do you know what he means?"

"What else would he mean?"

"Good point."

"And he's been with his boss a long time."

"How can you tell?"

"It's a hunch." She hadn't taken her eyes off of Declan. "Ask him how long it's been."

Gwen asked. "Well?"

"Three hundred and ten years."

"Ask him how old he is now."

"How old are you?"

"Three hundred and eleven."

"Well...hell!"

"Nah, that's a myth." He winked at her and she huffed out a laugh.

"Donovan, can you keep an eye on Gwen now, please?"

"No one needs to babysit me!"

"Gwen," Anya replied, "You ever been in a demon club before?"

"No. But..."

"Demons like to siphon off human energy. You're a witch, so your energy would be exceptionally potent to them. You won't know it's happening. So, do me a favor and let Donovan keep an eye on you and then you two can continue to flirt. Ok?"

"Fine. I will have questions later."

"Naturally."

"What about you?"

"I'll be fine."

"Do you have a knife?"

"That was rhetorical, right?" She had a sheath strapped to her thigh.

"Of course, what was I thinking?"

Anya got up and started walking towards the stairs. Declan sighed and started down the stairs and towards a fate that he was determined would not be his.

They met in the middle of the dance floor. "Anya," she said by way of introduction.

"Declan."

"I like that. It suits you."

He seemed startled by this. "Thank you?"

"You're welcome." She was unsure where to go from here. She was more nervous than she thought she would be, and her instinct was always to babble when she felt like that. She was working overtime to make sure she didn't do that.

"I don't mean to be rude..." he started.

"In my experience, people who say that, absolutely do mean to be rude."

He pulled up short and almost grinned. "Well then, I do mean to be rude. I know who you are, and I know what you're doing here, and you've come for no reason. This will not be happening. Now, or ever. So, I'm sorry you got dressed up for no reason. You can take your friend and go now."

"You're a bit of a dick, huh?" Her lips quirked upwards. Honestly, she couldn't blame him. This wasn't going as she'd planned. I mean, she didn't expect him to fall at her feet, but she had expected a bit more civility, but she appreciated his bluntness. She found herself excited by the prospect of him. She found banter sexy and his outright refusal to buy into this whole thing actually made her feel better. She also had not expected him to be so gorgeous. The pull she felt could have just been attraction, but she didn't think so. The tug, with the tingling, felt distinctive. That said, she would not mind climbing him like a ladder one day. She liked to be in control of situations, but right at this moment she wondered if she wasn't punching above her weight. "I take it you are not happy to see me?" She could see it on his face. His really, really gorgeous, chiseled from marble, face. She could feel the heat pooling in her belly.

"Very perceptive," he answered sarcastically. Jesus, she was beautiful. Not your standard pretty like her friend, but she was everything he had always liked in a woman. Curvy, redheaded, with a bit of bite to her. He had never liked a pushover. Her accent was also doing things to him that he'd rather not be thinking about right now.

"Why?"

"Why what?"

"Why are you not pleased to see me?"

"I am not taking a consort."

"Are you so sure about that?" The huskiness in her voice went right to his groin and he almost groaned.

Declan smiled, despite himself. "You are not going to change my mind."

"I am meant to be your consort. Are you going to deny you felt the tug?" She felt the pull and knew also had felt it. Even if there'd been no mutual attraction, they'd both still feel that tug and the tingling. "The wheels are in motion and the pull is going to get stronger. We recognized each other straight away. This is not something you can ignore.

I am not just going to go away," she said this with a hell of a lot more bravado than she was feeling right now. False confidence, a big mouth and tenacity had gotten her through life, why change that now? Truth be told, she really didn't understand why she was pushing for this so hard. In the end, she'd never force his hand. Not that she thought she could, really. But man, she wasn't sure she'd ever been this attracted to someone she'd just met before, and she kind of wanted to see where it could go. Maybe she just liked playing with fire.

Declan grabbed her hand and they both gasped at the charge that shot through both of them. "Oh, for fucks sake!" Declan muttered as Anya grinned, slowly. Ok, so not only did they have the classic mating pull, but they also had some actual personal chemistry here. There was an absence of sound though and at first, she wasn't sure why. Then she noticed that they were standing still but the world was going on around them in silence. "Nice trick," she said, her voice sounding raspy. "What did you just do?"

"I pulled you out of time a bit."

"You can do that?"

"Obviously."

"Huh. Very cool" Could she learn to do that? "Can all demons do that?"

"Not necessarily. It's one of my manifested powers."

"Very flash. I like it. Did you do it for a specific reason though?"

He hadn't. It had just kind of happened when he touched her. He had felt electricity move through him and it had stunned him momentarily. He'd lost control and had pulled them out of sync with the room. He rarely used this power, which might be why it had manifested right then, but it was a lack of control, and he was damned if he was going to admit that. "Look around, what do you see?"

"Is this a trick question?

"No. It's not. What I did not only pulls us out of time, but it also pulls us out of the glamour over the club. You can see it for what it is. A demon's hunting ground. We siphon energy from humans." Declan didn't and neither did his inner circle. If you had discipline, you didn't need to. He needed her to take this situation seriously, even if it meant frightening her a little.

"These demons are not siphoning any more than usual and frankly, I think they're all taking less than is generally allowed."

"How the fuck can you be aware of all of this?"

"Don't know, just am. The glamour doesn't work on me."

"How is that even possible? Your friend is a witch, so I know it doesn't work on her. Did she do something for you?"

"No, she didn't. I don't know why, but I can smell it. The energy siphoning."

"You are shitting me."

"I am not. I can generally pick out demons from humans. I don't know how I can do that either."

"And you can really just smell the energy being siphoned?"

"I can. I'm used to it." She hadn't been at first and she'd hated it. Now it barely bothered her.

He sighed. "It would be a mistake to romanticize me. Or this situation. You don't know me. I don't live a normal life. This isn't a fucking fairytale. This life can be brutal. I can be brutal. I've taken lives."

"So have I. What's your point?" Anya had not meant to share that, but she knew when she was being handed an excuse over an actual reason. Students did it fairly often, so it was something she was good at seeing through. He was just trying to convince himself and put her off at the same time.

Her reply brought him up short. He changed strategy. "Why would you even want to saddle yourself with a demon?"

"A normal life is not something that would work for me. Why not a demon?"

He dropped her hand and pulled them back into sync with the rest of the room. "This is what you want for yourself? A demon who owns a handful of nightclubs?"

"I think we both know that you are so much more than that." She felt the loss of his touch and it discomfited her more than she was willing to admit.

"You could do much better. Look at you."

"What about me?"

"Do you actually not see it? You glow. You're like a big ball of golden light." He could see it so clearly. "This is on top of being stunning."

"I have no clue what you're talking about with this light business. I am one of the least light people I know. But I thank you for the compliment, your eyesight is obviously going."

"I am not even dignifying that with a response. But you have to go. I am not taking a consort, not even one with your assets."

Anya had to stifle the urge to laugh. Or scream. Or kiss him. She wasn't sure which. She gestured to the dance floor. "You think I don't know from your life? You think I don't get darkness and violence? Trust me, if there is anyone who was meant to be the consort, a very equal consort, of a demon...it would be me. Every demon in this club knows I'm something different. No one even tried to siphon energy from me, or my friend."

That was true. He could see other demons giving her a wide berth as she walked towards him. "I would still like to know how you know so much about demons."

"Natalia Krasnova"

He looked shocked. "How do you know the consort of the Demon of Eastern Europe?"

"She's family. A number of generations back, but still family."

She was telling the truth; he could see that. "Are you fucking kidding me?"

"I am not. She comes down from my father's bloodline. Demons are not a new concept for me."

"Most demons and consorts give up their human families after a time." Declan hadn't realized that Natalia, and Vlad it would seem, still kept up with her family.

"She didn't. And that is only to make it easier when the families die. The demon moves on. Natalia did not. She is a formidable woman."

"Despite your family connections, this is still not going to happen. I am sorry. But as I've said, you've come for nothing." He took a deep breath. "We will never happen." Saying that was causing him actual physical pain. This was mostly due to the connection. To deny it would cause pain, but he had to admit that his attraction to her played into it as well.

Then she smiled. A genuine smile, filled with sweetness and sadness, and he nearly came undone. "I am sure you think that's true. But Declan," she said his name softly, like a prayer. "It's simply not." And then, against her better judgement, she put her hands on his chest, leaned up and nipped his lip. She then ran her tongue over where she had nipped. He opened his mouth in surprise and she began kissing him in earnest. Before he could think about it, one hand grabbed her waist and the other, grasped the back of her neck as he leaned into the kiss. The shock of his hands on her caused her to gasp and he used the opportunity to sweep his tongue into her mouth, meeting her tongue with his own. Her hands curled into his chest, and she sighed into his mouth. They kissed for a few moments. Then, with much difficulty, she ended the kiss and stepped back. "I will see you soon."

He started to answer that no, she wouldn't, but she was gone. Lost in a sea of people now and he felt the loss keenly. He had to force himself to not go after her, like a randy teenager, and carry her up to his office. *Well fuck*, he thought.

***

Anya raced over to the bar, slapped some money down, grabbed Gwen and started to quickly make her way out of the club. Gwen was trying to ask her what was happening, but Anya was not answering. On their way out, Anya got jostled by two demons and a human dancing together. Well, not dancing, she thought as she growled and shoved them out of the way. "Goddammit! They have rooms for that here!"

"They do?" Gwen asked in surprise.

They were a block from the club when Gwen ripped her hand free and stopped. "Anya, I am much shorter than you and wearing heels, please fucking stop!"

Anya pulled up short. "God, sorry!" She blew out a breath. "Holy shit balls…that guy is intense. And hot. And intense…and really hot. He said I was stunning. And then I kissed him." Now she was definitely babbling. Must be hormones.

Gwen's eyes widened. "I am sorry…what did you say? Did you say you kissed him? On the lips?" Anya nodded. "You don't kiss anyone. You stabbed the last guy who tried to kiss you"

"He deserved it."

"I know…but still. What happened?" Gwen hadn't been able to see them and was annoyed she'd missed the kiss.

Anya told Gwen what had happened, and Gwen made her describe the kiss…twice. "Was it nice? Was there tongue? Does he have good lips?"

"Yes, very. Hell yes. Fuck, yes."

"What do we do now?"

"I need a drink. And maybe food. And a cold shower."

Twenty minutes later they were sitting at the back of The Tsarina's House, a Russian restaurant in St. Germain De Pres. The place was owned by distant relatives on her father's side, and if the name of the place was a bit silly, Anya ignored it because they treated her like a long-lost daughter. Something she wasn't used to, since her own family hadn't treated her like their child, much of the time. Her father had, as much as he felt able to. But he was often cowed by his wife. Anya wasn't allowed to order from the menu here, they just brought her food, a lot of it and she was never allowed to pay. Every time she walked in, she was enveloped in hugs and truth be told, she didn't hate it.

A bottle of vodka and two shot glasses appeared on the table. "Thank you, Sascha."

"Food will be out soon. You'll eat, getting too skinny. Both of you!"

Gwen grinned up at him. "You're my favorite!"

He grinned back and walked away muttering in Russian about how thin they were.

"He's adorable. What is he to you again?"

"Uncle? Maybe? It's a bit convoluted."

"Ok, so what's next?"

"We eat. It'll be borscht, I bet."

"You know what I mean."

Anya shrugged. "I have no idea. I suppose we do the dance."

"The dance?"

"Yeah. We dance around each other until the pressure gets to be too much. Which it will, I assume. I mean, the thing is, it's now complicated for me as well."

"How so?"

"I didn't expect to have such an… intense reaction to him. It's more than him being a ridiculously dishy demon. There was that pull. Something else, under the surface though. I expected we could handle this like a business transaction and now, I know that won't do. It will never be just business with us. Which is going to make it even harder for him to accept. We had definite, legitimate chemistry. Like normal people."

"What happens if the pressure gets to be too much?"

"Well, if I am honest, I am hoping it means a lot of sex."

"Will you try and see him again?"

"Not sure. I am going to give him some time to process and hopefully come to terms with the idea. Time for me too. Though, I am not holding my breath. Where we were tonight is where he spends the most time. He doesn't visit the others as much."

"Do you know why?"

"The nature of the other clubs is apparently vastly different. Natalia wouldn't tell me any of this, I had to corral one of her staff to tell me. There are demons, older generally, with certain much unhealthier appetites. It's not uncommon either, but the demon was loath to say much more than that. But I got the feeling it wasn't your usual kink or fetishism, like you and I might know them. Way darker stuff."

"But...why allow that?"

"I've thought about that. I think it's about balance and protecting the bulk of the population. They aren't out in the general population harming humans to take all of their life energy, or worse. They aren't causing chaos or drawing unwanted attention to themselves. The clubs give them boundaries, but also lets them explore what they like, with humans who consent to it. The demon who gave me the info was very clear that the relationships are consensual or meant to be. Clubs elsewhere may run differently, but I suspect Declan, after having met him, works to ensure that those clubs stay on the right path. How demons handle relationships with each other, I cannot say, nor did the demon. Again, dark shit." Anya thought for a moment. "And I am going to venture a guess that it also allows humans to indulge themselves with demons and know they're safe. You know, a little danger can be exciting sometimes. It's not unlike all those humans who have a thing for vampires in books."

"Ok. I need to process that. But balance?"

"When you have light, you have to have something dark. I mean, there's light magic and dark magic, right?" Gwen nodded. "And you practice magic that does no harm, so it's considered light magic. That means that someone out there is likely practicing dark. You bring balance into the world, in your way. Demons serve a purpose by, in theory, keeping the worst of humanity's appetites and darkness at bay."

"Ok, I am following you. But the world is a pretty fucked up place."

"Agreed. I am not sure I can speak to that specifically. It does not always work, nothing is perfect. Not being a demon or a consort right now, a lot of what I think is conjecture." Anya shrugged. "We think about demons as devils, so we have a certain idea about them. Some of that may be true, most is myth because of the Bible. They keep control of the dark, so that it doesn't overshadow the light. It's why there is still happiness and joy in the world, even though there is also a lot of shit happening. You have to have both. So, they're kind of like a sin eater."

"A sin eater?"

"Yes. Sin eaters would generally absorb the sins of the recently dead. It absolved that person, and they were able to rest in peace and go to heaven. Mind you, that's also a myth. But I kind of think of demons like that. My theory is that the energy that demons siphon from humans is mostly their dark energy. It feeds the demon, while helping the human. I could be way off base here."

"Would this demon siphon energy from you?"

Anya shook her head. "I am going to say no. He didn't try to. And Natalia told me it's not generally done."

Would you be in danger of becoming dark?"

"Some would say I already am." She'd certainly say it about herself.

"Some have never seen you cry while watching animal videos on the internet."

Anya smiled. "I don't think I'd be in danger, also...never mention that again!" She winked at her friend. "Donovan is a demon, what do you feel about him?" Her friend was asking good questions and it was helping Anya settle, which she knew was partly Gwen's aim.

"Well, I liked him. He didn't feel...evil." Anya nodded encouragingly. "So, wait. There's a difference between regular dark and evil dark?"

"Sure. Like chaotic good and chaotic evil. Dark doesn't mean evil. I can be dark, but I am not evil. I believe there are demons that are evil. Just like there are humans that are evil. But demons are not inherently evil, they just exist in the dark, or in the cracks of the light. That's a poetic way to put it, I think. And I believe that they likely do have a Hell of sorts, despite Donovan's joke. So, they understand evil."

"Huh. That's interesting. I love when you go into lecture mode."

Anya laughed. "Sorry. Habit. But you still look concerned."

"I just...I just worry about you."

Anya reached out and grabbed her hand. "I know. And I won't say you don't need to, you will anyway. But I know who I am, and I know I can handle a lot more than the average human. And I will always have you to pull me back in."

"What if...what if you have to kill someone or something."

"Then let's hope it's a righteous kill." Anya cringed inwardly. Gwen didn't know that Anya had already taken a life. Three to be exact. She just hoped when her BFF did find out, that it didn't change how Gwen felt about her. Anya wasn't sure she could bounce back from that.

CHAPTER 2

In the end, it was two weeks before she saw Declan again. She'd been busy grading papers and giving midterms; but Declan and that damned kiss lurked in the back of her mind. Why? Why had she kissed him? And why didn't he come after her? Her hope that he'd come find her quickly was embarrassing. The whole thing was making her very grumpy. She'd think about the kiss or how his hands had felt on her, how green his eyes were, and her blood would heat. Anya had always been unsentimental when a romance had run its course. She never looked back wistfully at any relationship. In truth, she had been the one to walk away most times. It had nothing to do with what awaited her; she just got bored and decided to move on. She suspected that Declan would never bore her. Both in and out of bed. And she found herself longing to see him, and that made her even crankier.

She was just finishing up a lecture on Female Empowerment in Victorian Literature when he stepped into the room, standing in the back, against the wall. He just watched her, not taking his eyes off of her, even when another student spoke. It was very hard for her to concentrate with him standing there looking like sex on toast. She raised an eyebrow at him, all the while just taking him in. Tall, well over six-foot with wavy hair that was both gold and brown. Ridiculous green eyes. They made her think of Ireland, which seemed appropriate, given his obviously Gaelic roots. He was very well proportioned. Not overly muscled, but he had strength. She could feel it when she had her hands on his chest. He was solid. She was betting he had great biceps. Oh, and forearms, she really wanted to get a look at those. Dressed in all black, he didn't even look real.

Her student had stopped speaking and there was a small pause while Anya brought her attention back to the rest of the room. "Thank you, Nicole. That is an interesting way to look at Wuthering Heights, although not conventional. I suppose you could argue that Cathy was a feminist, but I am not sure everyone would agree."

Nicole huffed and responded in her French accented English. "Well, all I know is that she wanted what she wanted and didn't let anyone stand in her way. Not even her husband." Anya groaned inwardly. That was not what being a feminist was about. Something must have shown on her face because she caught Declan smiling at her slightly, as if he'd read her thoughts.

This kind of thing always tested her patience as a teacher. She was overly opinionated and it's not something that serves one well in her profession. Anya merely raised an eyebrow at the twenty-year old's pronouncement. "I am not sure if her husband would have seen it that way. She and Heathcliff caused a lot of pain for people." She glanced at her watch. "OK, that's it class. I will be having office hours tomorrow, but not Friday this week. And if I do not have the topics for your final papers, get them to me by the end of the week. Or I am assigning your topic to you." Groans. "Well then, decide on your topics so we avoid that."

The class filed out, and most of the girls and at least half of the boys shot Declan interested glances. The one young demon who was in her class inclined his head to Declan, who stopped and spoke to him quietly for a moment. The young man nodded, smiled, and left the classroom. Interesting

"Anya." He drew her name out, causing her to shiver.

"Declan. To what do I owe the pleasure?"

He stared at her and then grinned. "I have no idea. I just needed to see you. I waited as long as I could and then, my car just seemed to make its way here."

She smiled at him. Two weeks was his limit it seemed. "How did you know where I worked?"

"I did a little research on you." She looked at him. "I asked Vlad."

She nodded. "I'm flattered. You know Luc?"

"Yes." He looked at her. "You know what he is?"

"I do. Why don't you come down here?"

"I am not sure that's a good idea."

She laughed. "It's probably a terrible idea. Do it anyway."

He shrugged and started down the stairs. She was really grateful that there was no other class here today. He stopped about two feet from her. "Better?"

"Yes. And no."

"Anya, you're killing me. I don't suppose I can convince you to leave Paris?"

"I've been here for fifteen years, so no. Nice try though."

"Fifteen years? How did I not know you were here?"

"You weren't looking for me and I don't frequent demon nightclubs or other businesses that cater directly to them. Natalia also impressed upon me that I shouldn't see you before the time was right." Anya rolled her eyes with this last statement. She was annoyed she hadn't questioned, not only that, but a whole host of other things. She and Natalia may be having a long talk soon. "Or I am just really good at staying under demon radar."

He looked at her for a minute. He couldn't imagine someone like her staying under anyone's radar. She was wearing black jeans, a purple t-shirt and black high heeled boots. Her dark red hair was in a long plait down her back, except for some stray tendrils that had come loose, and he found he wanted to touch those tendrils. "What am I going to do with you?"

"I have a list." Her voice sounded hoarse to her own ears.

"Anya…" He closed the distance between them and reached for her. He leaned his forehead onto hers and put his hands on her waist. She placed her hands on his forearms. Yup, they certainly felt nice and solid. Would it be weird to roll his shirtsleeves up? Yes Anya, it would.

"Declan, fighting it will make it worse. I know this is not what either of us expected. But we need to figure it out and deal with it. I have not stopped thinking about you for a solid two weeks. I am not built like that, and I don't think you are either. This is weird, too quick and I don't like it, but I also really like it. Probably too much."

Her honesty both surprised and pleased him. "Mine is not a normal life." He sighed and also opted for some truth. "And I can't stop thinking about you either." Ten short minutes had changed everything.

"I told you that I've never had a normal life."

He sighed and dropped a kiss on her nose. "You will be my undoing."

"And you'll be mine."

There was a small sound at the back of the room and they both stiffened. "What was that?" she whispered.

"No idea, but I don't think it's anything good. Can you casually look towards the door and tell me what you see?"

The noise, which now sounded like flapping, got more insistent. Anya moved closer to Declan, wrapping one arm around his waist, and looking through hooded eyes over his shoulder. The thing hissed "Dddeeccclllaannn…."

"It's ugly as fuck. It's winged, long claws, longed pointed ears, sharp teeth, red eyes. Walking on spindly legs that look like…well, flamingo legs? It looks both oily and dusty. All black. Coming towards us."

"I know what it is."

"Can it be killed?"

"It can, yes. Why?"

"Do I need to aim someplace specific?"

"Chest. I repeat, why?"

Anya didn't answer. She reached down to her boot and before Declan could say anything had a dagger whizzing past his head at a ridiculous speed. There was an ungodly scream, a good amount of writhing as the thing went into its death throes. Declan and Anya watched impassively until it finally died.

Declan turned to look at her. "So? What gives?"

"I am really good with knives." She shrugged.

"Apparently."

"What was that?"

"Hell wraith."

"No shit?! I've read about these." Anya looked excited and not all freaked out about the wraith and the fact that she'd killed it.

"So many questions. I will ask my top three. You've read about them? How is this not freaking you out? And finally, where the hell did you learn to throw like that?"

"Yes. I've studied demon culture some. Not much freaks me out. I've been able to throw knives since I was a kid. My question is, why was it after you? Also, how do we get rid of it?"

Declan waved his hand and the wraith crumbled to dust and then the dust disappeared."

"Cool." Anya leaned down and grabbed her knife, putting it back in her boot."

"I have to admit, that is kind of sexy."

She grinned at him. "I know. So again, why was it after you?"

"I don't know."

"So, hell wraiths aren't really demons? You can kill them?"

"They are the lowest class of demons and are born as hell wraiths, never having been human. They just are. At this point, they tend to be the bastion of the eldest demons. They're, well not in style really. They are no more than foot soldiers who can't really think for themselves. They need to be set a task. They are meant to cause havoc or as a warning."

"But you don't use them."

"No. I don't need a hell wraith to do any of those things. I prefer people who can think for themselves. Mindless foot soldiers hold no allure for me." He frowned. "That said, I find this worrying. You may not be safe with me."

Anya rolled her eyes. "Oh really now?"

"I wouldn't want you to get hurt."

"Hurt?! Really?! I just killed that thing! I am not some fragile flower who is going to wilt when the shit hits the fan. I can handle myself and have done so for most of my life. What nonsense! Fuck you and your stupid patriarchy!"

He gaped at her and then couldn't help himself. He grabbed her and kissed her. She wrapped herself around him, moaning into his mouth. "Dammit Declan. I am mad at you. Don't kiss me!' She knew she should disentangle herself and explain modern feminism to him, but damn, he felt good. She could lecture him about his attitude later.

"Do you want me to let you go?" He would if she said yes, but he was really hoping she didn't say yes.

"Don't you fucking dare!" He picked her and carried her over to her desk while she wrapped her legs around him. He nipped her bottom lip. "Turnabout is fair play."

She laughed and planted kisses along his jaw, while he loosened her braid, so her hair tumbled over his hand like a waterfall. She arched back and he planted kisses on her neck while writhed under his touch.

"Woman, if you do not stop moving around like that…" he fisted his hand in her hair and pulled her head up and kissed her again. Her tongue met his, while her hands roamed over his back. He moved one hand over to breast and tweaked her nipple through her t-shirt. She yelped and nearly came off the table. "You'll pay for that!"

"More lectures about the patriarchy, I hope." There was a commotion outside the door and the couple broke apart, breathing hard and trying to put themselves back to rights, quickly.

The door opened and two students walked in. "Oh, oh sorry Professor. We were going to study here. But only if you're done with the room?"

"No worries, we were just leaving."

***

Once outside in the fresh air, the two started to laugh. "Well, that is a bit more excitement than I usually experience at the end of my workday."

"I try." He twirled a lock of her hair around his finger. "Anya…" He was frowning again. She didn't like when he frowned, as adorable as he looked doing it.

"Let's just table the mate thing for today. The bigger issue is…."

"The wraith and why was it after me? *If* it was after me"

"Yes, that. Who else could it be?"

"You."

"Why?"

"Who's to say? Could be random too. I piss humans and demons off regularly."

"This does not surprise me. But I don't think it was random."

I don't think it's random either. Please be careful. And that's not the patriarchy. It's me, a guy who's groped you, asking you to please be careful."

"Well, when you put it so romantically, how can I refuse?"

"You can't. Obviously. Let me drive you home."

"It's not necessary."

"No. But it's polite. I don't mind." And truthfully, he wasn't quite ready to let her go yet.

"Well…ok, then." She wasn't sure how she felt about being in a small, enclosed space with this man, despite the fact that they'd just had their hands all over each other. Or, maybe because of that. She wanted more, that was for certain.

In the car, she gave him her address and he peeled away from the curb. "So? Knives then." He tried to sound casual. "How?"

She sighed. "I told you I have been able to throw since I was a child."

"Anya don't be difficult. You know what I mean."

"My family had a traveling circus. My mother's family was Roma. Well, I suppose they still are. My dad's family are Circus folk. Russian. They performed over much of Eastern Europe, and they were performing in the States when I was born. They wanted me to do something like high wire, but the minute I held a knife…I knew that's what I was supposed to do."

"How old were you?"

"I first picked up a knife when I was six. I could out throw my cousin by eight. Well, really by seven, but I held back for a while."

"Why?"

"He was a real shit and liked to throw a punch my way."

"How old was he?"

"Fifteen."

"To your seven?! You were a child! What the fuck was wrong with him?" Declan's hands gripped the steering wheel tight enough that it was in danger of cracking. Wanting to kill someone he didn't know was not a rational reaction.

"A lot, apparently. When I was eight, he tried to…well, he tried to…" She hated talking about this and she wasn't completely sure why she was telling him something that she hadn't even told Gwen. They'd really just met. It was unfathomable to her, but she didn't feel able to stop herself.

"I get it, it's fine. You don't have to say." Declan removed one hand from the steering wheel, flexing it. Then repeated it with the other hand. It wouldn't be the first time he'd cracked the steering column of a car, but he didn't want to do it with Anya sitting next to him.

She breathed out. "I managed to get away from him and I grabbed a knife. I didn't think. I turned around and threw it."

"What did you hit?"

"His eye."

"Were you aiming for his eye?"

"Sure." She didn't sound convincing.

"Anya."

"Ok, no. I was aiming for his heart, but he moved, and I got him in the eye."

"What became of him?"

"One day, I didn't miss." That was the day she'd found him trying the same thing with her much younger cousin. She'd been thirteen and had taken to having a knife on her at all times.

He was silent. Taking it all in. She looked over to see if he was horrified, but he looked thoughtful. It was silly. Thinking a demon would be horrified over what she'd done. "Are you disgusted?" she asked quietly, not sure why it mattered to her that he wasn't.

"No. I am amazed actually." She let out the breath she'd been holding. "And the rest of your family now?"

She paled. "I do not want to talk about that, just now. If it's all the same to you. You got one secret from me today and that will have to do."

"That was a secret? Your friend doesn't know?"

"No. She doesn't. Not sure why I told you, but now you know."

He picked up her hand and kissed her palm. "Thank you for trusting me. Your secret is safe with me."

He pulled up in front of her apartment building. "I am not going out again tonight. You don't have to worry. You can even call me later." She took his phone and added her number. She then leaned over and gave him a quick kiss and was gone before he knew it.

He sighed. Could he have her without her becoming his consort? His mate? He didn't know. But he wasn't sure how much longer he could hold out. She was becoming a need ticking away inside of him. He pulled out his phone and dialed. "Donovan?"

"Declan?" Donovan's big, booming voice came over the phone.

"So, Anya and I just had a run in with a Hell wraith. Have you heard anything?" Donovan was his eyes and ears. It's why he often tended bar; he could see everything going on in the club from that vantage point.

"No one's mentioned Hell wraiths. But I will keep my ears open tonight."

"Thank you. I'm also going to ask Matthew to do some checking around the city tonight." Declan drummed his fingers on the steering wheel. "Anya and I meet, and a Hell wraith shows up? That's too much coincidence, and I don't like it."

"Agreed. I don't think it's a coincidence."

"I also need you to arrange someone to watch Anya's place."

"She'll hate that," Donovan said.

Declan thought of the berating he had just received. "Yes. She will. And she will likely yell at me, but I'd like to do it anyway. I'd feel better." He also found that he kind of liked it when Anya yelled at him.

"Ok, I am on it. What about Gwen?"

"Who?"

"Her best friend."

"The wee blonde? Donovan…."

"Declan listen to me. It'd be a way to get to Anya. If something happened to Gwen and Anya felt responsible, I think all hell would break loose. They're sisters, plain and simple."

Ah fuck, points to Donovan. "You're right. We protect her friend as well."

"It's done."

"Thank you. I am going to sit here until someone else shows up."

"Of course." said Donovan with a knowing smirk in his voice. "I'll have someone there soon."

Declan hung up, called Matthew, and relayed what had happened.

"We haven't seen a Hell wraith around here in a number of years. That, in and of itself is suspicious." Matthew's clipped English voice sounded both concerned and irritated.

"No, we haven't. And it's got to mean something."

"Oh, it absolutely does. And I think it has to do with your redhead."

"Why does everyone keep calling her 'my redhead'?"

"You're joking, right?" Matthew didn't wait for an answer. "I will roll through the city tonight with Michel and see if we can find out anything. If they won't talk to me, they will talk to him. The charmer."

"Thank you."

"Made it two weeks and you just had to see her, huh?"

"And?"

"She's your consort."

"Matthew, she is not my consort."

Matthew snorted. "Really? Then why did you feel the need to go and see her?"

"Because…to talk some sense into her." It sounded ridiculous to his own ears.

"How did that work out for you?"

"About as well as you'd expect."

"Did you kiss her again?" There was amusement in Matthew's voice.

"I do not kiss and tell," Declan said primly. "And what do you mean 'again?'"

"We all saw you two kiss at the club. We're not blind."

"Ah, fuck!"

Matthew laughed. "You did kiss her again! Declan, I think you're running against the tide with this one."

"Matthew, I can't invite anyone into the life I lead." Even someone who could take care of herself, the way he now knew Anya could. The bodyguards were there to make him feel better about things, but also because he knew he knew that he would never be able to lock her away. The guards would give anyone second thoughts about attacking her.

"I don't think you're going to have much of a choice. You've been a real asshole the past two weeks. Despite your concern over today, you sound much calmer. Calmer because you've seen her. She is obviously your mate."

"I don't like what it means."

"Declan, for chrissakes, the only person that has any issue with your burgeoning powers is you. Why?"

"I didn't ask for them. You'd be better suited to the Council."

"Well, that's nonsense and you know it. You're being a coward."

"Oh, fuck off, Matthew."

Matthew laughed. "Yes sir! I'll check in later." And with that, he clicked off.

Cheeky bastard, Declan thought. But he was getting the sinking feeling that Matthew was right, he was fighting a losing battle. He looked up to see Anya silhouetted against her window, typing on her phone. Probably texting her friend. She straightened, looked out of her window, and caught sight of him. She raised her hand in acknowledgement and walked away. *Goddammit*, thought Declan. *I am in real trouble here.*

***

When Anya got upstairs, she sent a text to Gwen. *Things happened today. We're having a girl's night. I am ordering pizza. Get your ass over here.*

Gwen replied quickly. *Was there kissing?*

Anya laughed and responded: *Ayup*

Gwen hooted in her apartment: *There in 15. With my eating pants on*

Anya smiled and looked out and saw Declan sitting in his car. So, she waved at him. He rolled his eyes at her but smiled. She suspected he was arranging a babysitter for her and was waiting for them to show up before he left. Predictable. She wasn't sure how she felt about getting a babysitter, but she'd expected it. They'd have to discuss this later. Anya was used to coming and going as she saw fit, and that wasn't going to change.

She was taking off her makeup when it hit her. He knew that. Declan knew that he'd never get her to stop living her life as she saw fit. She might be wrong, but she suspected that he was trying to stack the deck in her favor. They'd still have a talk about the heavy handedness of doing it without discussing it with her, but she'd let it go for tonight.

The doorbell rang and Anya let Gwen in. "Demon McHottypants is outside in his car."

"I know. He's waiting for my babysitter." She thought for a minute. Should she tell her? "I am not going to be surprised if you get one too."

"What? And why me?"

"Give me a minute to open some wine and I'll explain." Over wine, she explained what had happened that day. Being Gwen, she cared more about the kissing and groping than the actual danger. "I hope there is more kissing. That said, I am going to check the wards on your apartment before I go tonight." She looked abashed. "I don't think I told you I did that."

"I can feel them, don't worry about it. I'm not mad."

Gwen grinned. "But why would I get a babysitter?"

"You are my only friend to be honest. Anyone who was trying to get to me, could use you. Though I don't think that's going to happen." Well she hoped it wouldn't.

Gwen looked a little freaked out at that but powered on. "Too bad it won't be Donovan."

"I know. I'm betting you could call him at any time though. If you get a little scared."

Gwen grinned. "And I just might! Oooh, I am so scared and are you so big!"

"Does anyone fall for that?"

"You'd be surprised. I managed to get his number."

Anya looked at her watch. "Ugh, it's late. Just crash here?"

"SLUMBER PARTY!"

"So, that's a yes?"

"YES!"

Anya looked outside and saw two cars sitting out there. "Ok, hang on a sec." Anya went running outside and knocked on one of the car windows. The demon on that side rolled down his window. "Erm...yes, ma'am?" Gwen opened one of the windows and positioned herself to try and hear what was going on outside.

"Hey there, fella. Do me a favor...tell your boss that my friend is spending the night. So, you can follow her in the morning. I am nor leaving until noon."

"Ummmm…"

"Ok, thanks. Good talk...bye!" Anya ran back into the apartment where Gwen was on the floor laughing so hard that she was crying.

"Now, let's see if I'm right." She stared at her phone. "5...4...3...2...1" The phone rang. "Hello?"

"Anya, what the actual fuck are you about?"

"I just didn't want them to worry. And now they will wonder if we're acting out some lady-on-lady porn up here and it will give them something to talk about during the night. I have provided a much-needed distraction for those poor guys!"

Gwen snorted wine out of her nose at that. "Jesus Anya...warn a body first.".

Declan sighed and tried not to laugh. "How did you even know?"

"Men are predictable. Even eight-hundred-year-old demons. We will be discussing this further though; you're not getting away that easy. Now tell me I'm pretty and go to work."

"You're pretty and go to bed."

"Hmmmm...night." She hung up the phone.

"Planning on taming your demon?"

"God, no! Though we're going to have a talk about a few things." Anya grinned. "OK, more wine then!"

As Anya was opening another bottle of wine, Gwen was perusing her books. She pulled one out. "You have a book on angels?"

"I have books on lots of things. I am an academic you know."

"But angels? Are there angels?"

Anya shrugged. "Anything is possible, but it's not probable. I'd believe Fae are real first." She stopped herself from going on.

"Go ahead, lecture a bit. You know you want to. Also, the Fae are indeed real."

Anya stuck her tongue out, but it was true. "Wait? The Fae are real?"

"Of course they are Anya. Everyone knows that."

"Everyone does not know that." She shrugged. "That said, if Angels do exist, I doubt they bother about humans."

"But demons do? What about that balance thing you talk about? If there are demons, there must be angels?"

"Well, that tracks only if you believe demons are supposed to be evil. Or the opposite of angels."

"The Devil is a fallen angel though."

"But that's a story, really. The reality of demons is much different. Though, my guess is that the story of demons has morphed into the Biblical idea of the Devil. That said, angels would not flit about on a cloud, playing a harp and being benevolent and singing hymns. There were warring archangels. Flaming swords are not benevolent and friendly. Ancient Greeks cast demons as divine but not necessarily evil. So, what's to say that this is not a more accurate interpretation of demons?"

"Ok, I am following this. But how did we get both Angels and Demons?"

"Paganism to Christianity. People needed explanations for things."

"So, angels may really be demons?"

"No idea honestly, but it's a pet theory of mine. I have read extensively on the subject demons. No one really knows where they came from, how long they've been on Earth and their history is not all in one place. So, I am piecing it together the best I can. There is some talk, in some of the histories about some demons being bringers of light. Not sure what that means. I think it's about a prophecy, but it makes no sense to me right now."

"Light? Didn't Demon McHottypants say you had a glow?"

Anya rolled her eyes. "I assume it was just lust making him say that."

"Hmmm...maybe." But Gwen wasn't so sure. "So, Donovan is pretty dishy, huh?"

"He is." Anya looked at her friend closely. "You really like him."

"I do."

"So, not just some harmless flirting?"

"I mean, I do love to flirt, but no. Not just that honestly. He is gorgeous, yes. But he feels...steady. I know what he is and all, but he feels safe." Gwen blushed a little.

"Anya smiled. "You have quite the crush!"

"Oh be quiet and drink your wine, you lush!"

***

Declan turned to Donovan after the call ended. "That woman is going to be the death of me."

Donovan grinned. "You already died."

"Good point."

"What are you going to do about it?"

"Take a cold shower and then drive her to work tomorrow."

"You know what I mean."

"I have no fucking idea."

Donovan grinned even wider.

<u>CHAPTER 3</u>

Gwen left early in the morning to get ready for work and was going to let her keeper drive her around. "If he's going to lurk, I am going to put him to some use," she said, ever pragmatic. Anya spent the morning checking email and planning out lessons for the next semester's classes when the doorbell rang.

"Yes?"

"It's Declan."

Anya looked down at her old yoga pants and her t-shirt that read 'I like big books and I cannot lie!' and groaned. Figures, she thought, opening the door. He looked good enough to eat and it was all she could do to not jump him. He was wearing black pants and a black jacket, but a dark green shirt, that made his eyes look even greener. This man ought to be against the law with those looks.

He smiled. "Well, aren't you a sight?" He took in the yoga pants, t-shirt, and messy bun and his smile widened.

"I was not expecting company."

"I can tell."

"What do you want?"

"I thought I'd drive you to work."

"Are you protecting my body this morning?" She stepped aside to let him in.

"Yes. And I know you aren't pleased, but I am also not sorry." Cards on the table.

She stared at him "I can take care of myself."

"I realize that, and that is great. But Demons are different, and I don't think you've fought any?" She shook her head. "So, this is just a way to make sure you have a bit of an assist if you need one."

"For someone who keeps saying they aren't interested in having a consort, you seem to be going to a lot of effort here."

"True. But there is a chance that you are a target because of me, so I feel some responsibility to see to your safety. This way, the deck is stacked in your favor," he said, echoing her own thoughts. "I feel better. And when I feel better, I can relax and work. Demons are different from humans, and you know it. You can't fight them the same way. My guys know what to look for, they've got more experience with demon threats than you do."

This was a much more logical and progressive explanation than she expected. "It's hard to argue with that kind of logic. And you are correct that I have never fought a demon. But it's the heavy handedness of you doing this that most irritates me. If you are going to make decisions about my life, you need to talk to me first. Ask me. I am a reasonable person and will listen to a well laid out argument. This includes just assuming I'd just let you drive me to work." Of course she was going to let him, not the point.

"Apologies. May I drive you to work?"

"You may. And do not think that I didn't notice that you're only apologizing for that. We will discuss this further. When I am not wearing ratty yoga pants."

He grinned. "You did promise me more lectures about the patriarchy." She looked at his face trying to determine if he was patronizing her and decided that he wasn't. He seemed to like her argumentative side.

"Yes, I did." Make yourself at home and I will go get ready."

In a minute he heard the shower go on and he tried very hard to not think about Anya wet and naked and failed miserably. He tried to think about any of the Elders, the year 1323. It was a terrible and violent year and nothing he tried went well. His mind kept wandering back to her and that spectacular body, and brain, of hers. Those breasts though, enough to make a grown Demon weep for joy. He winced and tried to get more comfortable. He heard the water go off and sighed. Then she appeared at the door to the living room wrapped in a towel. "Alexa, play my Pop mix."

"*Playing Pop Mix.*" Music filled the apartment.

"You are in a towel." He crossed his legs and Anya grinned at him.

"Yes. Did you want me to take it off?" She reached up to undo it.

"Yes. But please don't."

"Lucky for you, I have places to be." She moved back into the bedroom, throwing the towel out into the living room and Declan groaned again. It was stupid to continue to deny it. He wanted to be balls deep in that woman and there was no getting around it. But it really was more than that, and that was the problem. He liked her. She was smart, funny, tough. He just liked being around her. If it were just lust, he could have dealt with that. But the fact that he actually liked her was an unexpected problem. And also a little weird considering this was only the third time they'd seen each other in person. Consorts did not have to love each other. It was a fairly rare occurrence. Wait? Love? No, but he could feel it was more than lust, more than just friendship. Time would tell if anything else developed. She peeked out into the living room, dressed now in a long black skirt and deep red tunic with a V-neck. She grinned at him and moved back into the bedroom. Yeah, he was screwed. He stood and started to pace around the room, paying attention to the music for the first time. "What in the fuck are we listening to?" he said popping his head into the bedroom.

Anya was seated at a vanity, putting on makeup. She listened for a moment. "Roxette. Joyride."

"Why?"

"Because I like it."

"You cannot possibly like this."

"I do. I like pop music. Deal with it."

He moved back into the living room, pacing the floor. Two minutes later he popped back in. "You have terrible taste in music."

She looked affronted. "How dare you! Pop music is the glue of the world, my friend. Everyone loves a good hook."

He rolled his eyes and left the room. A minute later, baroque chamber music filled the apartment. "Oh fuck, no!" She bolted to the living room. "Alexa! Stop! You whore!" The music stopped. "Really?"

"It's better than whatever the hell that was."

"At least I listen to music from this century!"

"Terrible music!"

"Your opinion and frankly, I do not think Demons are known for their musical taste."

"Brat! I should put you over my knee." He didn't really mean it, he didn't think.

"You want to spank me?" It wasn't the worst idea, really.

"I just might, you keep this up."

"Promises, promises," she said blandly. They stared at each other. "Declan…" This conversation was getting completely out of control.

"If you do not go back into the bedroom and finish getting ready, I am going to strip you naked and have you on the floor."

"You say that like it's a bad thing."

They stared at each other another minute before he spoke. "We both have places to be right now."

She waited a moment and decided to not mess with him any longer, turned on her heel and went back into the bedroom. She sat at her vanity and tried to calm her blood. Shit, she thought, squeezing her thighs together. She'd really been messing with him; with the towel and coming back out into the living room dressed and then flirting with him about the spanking thing. Though she needed to make sure he wasn't actually serious about that as a form of control. She didn't think so. But then it had just gotten much too intense and now she had to go teach turned on like a Christmas tree. It was going to be a long car ride and a long day.

***

Ten minutes later they were on their way. "I am not going to apologize," he said petulantly.

"I am not asking you to."

"About any of it."

"Again, not asking you to. But I am going to be very honest here. Shit or get off the pot. I understand that it's only been two weeks since we met and this is only the third time that we've seen each other, but the intensity of this is, well, a lot. You've managed to kick my libido into overdrive."

"Ditto."

"There is nothing to say that we have to seal this mating deal right away. We can take some time. Although one of us is not getting any younger. It's me by the way. I am the one not getting any younger." He cracked a small smile at this. "But your continued resistance coupled with the fact you just keep showing up is sending mixed signals. And that is not fair. For either of us. But mostly me."

"You don't know everything I am," he said quietly, parking across the street from her work.

"Then show me. If I don't run screaming, you'll have your answer. There is shit I am not ready to tell you. Afford me the respect to give me a fuller picture of what you're about. I told you about my cousin."

He sighed. "Anya…."

"No. Do it or go away and leave me to find someone else."

"The hell you will!" he growled, pulling her onto his lap, plunging his tongue into her mouth while yanking them both out of time like he had done at the club. He didn't want any students to walk by the car and see a professor making out with someone. She gripped his shoulders and moaned into his mouth. His hand found its way to her breast, and she just sighed, nearly undoing him. He pulled away, put her back in her own seat and pulled them back into the timestream.

"Fucking hell, Declan. I have to go teach now and I am not sure I can walk. But again, mixed signals."

"That was my way of saying you're right. Let's see how this goes." He grinned at her. "Friday night?"

"A date?"

"Yes. Sure. A date."

"Done." She leaned over to kiss him on the cheek and her hand grazed his hard on and she squeezed, just a little. "I just want you to have one piece of information before you make any rash decisions."

"Yes?"

"I have absolutely no gag reflex." With that, she was gone. Declan sat in stunned silence for about ten seconds before he started laughing helplessly. Well, no matter what happened, it wasn't going to be boring.

***

She opened the door to her office and almost missed the envelope on the floor. Setting her bags down, she knelt to pick up. It was addressed to her, but her full name, Anya Bohdana Lelyah Orlova. She frowned. She didn't use Bohdana. Lelyah was her paternal grandmother's name, which she didn't mind as she had been very fond of that old woman, but she generally only used the initial. And Orlova? Really? She used Orlov. She wanted to distance herself as much as she could from, what she felt, was an archaic convention of language. So, this…this was troubling.

She stood, eyeing the envelope like it was going to explode and opened it. Two lines in Russian, handwritten:

You are an abomination.
You must be destroyed.

She sighed and snapped a photo of the note and one of the envelope sending both photos to Declan, along with the translation. It might or might not have anything to do with what happened yesterday. But if it did, he should know. That was the reason she gave herself at any rate. It took him about ten seconds to call. "Anya?"

"Declan?"

"Where was the note?"

"Slipped under my office door."

"Is that your full birth name then?"

"Yes."

"It's pretty. But it upset you." It wasn't a question.

"Yes, actually it did. Very few people know my full name. This smacks of family, but that doesn't make sense to me." She took a breath. "But I thought I should send it along on the off chance it had something to do with yesterday and not with my family at all."

"Your instinct was good, no argument there. What do you have for family?"

"I have two brothers and a mother who are still alive. My father and one brother have passed on. I have assorted family on both sides in Russia and Romania, but I am only moderately close with my Uncle Tomas' family, my father's brother."

"Anyone closer?"

"I have some distant relatives here, also on my father's side. They are really distant family, but they are also really lovely people. They run a restaurant that Gwen and I eat at a lot."

"Are you close to your mother and brothers."

"No, I am not."

The way she had said that made him sad, but he decided not to pursue that right now. But he made a note about the family she mentioned here so he could look into them further. She'd be pissed if she knew, so he wasn't going to mention it. "Three brothers?"

"Yes. I am the oldest. Pavel and I were close for a time. He used to stand up for me with the other, but that changed. He changed."

This broke his heart a little. "Fucking morons. I never let anyone bother my sisters." He hadn't thought of them of years. Purposely. But Anya's sadness had brought back memories of them. The need to make her feel better was strong.

She smiled. "You had sisters?"

"Two. They were younger. They made good marriages. I made sure of it. And by good, I mean they married decent men."

"That's lovely," she said quietly. "About the note…"

"Hang onto it and I will send Donovan over later to get it, if that's amenable to you."

"That's fine." She didn't want it, so it was fine if he held onto it.

"Are you worried for your safety? I know you can take care of yourself, but…"

"I think between my cache of knives and the bodyguard you'll have here in about ten minutes; I should be fine."

"Please...he's already there."

She smiled. "Declan! I should be mad, but I'm not."

"Which only proves to me that this note has upset you quite a bit. You call me if you need me, or want me, for anything. Ok?"

"Ok."

"Good. Now, tell me I'm pretty and go to work."

She burst out laughing. "You're pretty and thank you."

***

Donovan found Anya during her last class of the day. A freshman composition class that the faculty took turns teaching. It was a 4pm class and no one was interested in it, including Anya. Donovan walked in and she dismissed the class early, threatening them with a pop quiz if they weren't a little livelier next time. Donovan bounded down the stairs and before Anya could give him the letter, he had enfolded her in his massive arms. No one but Gwen had hugged her in ages. She didn't invite it, but Gwen was right, Donovan felt safe. And there were no weird conflicting emotions there, as there were with Declan. Anya just leaned into the hug and rested her head on his chest, wrapping her arms around him. Donovan broke into a huge smile at this show of trust.

"Gwen told me to give you a hug, because you were sad."

"Gwen?" She had talked to Gwen earlier in the day and went through the entire thing. Gwen had decided they should go out dancing to cheer Anya up.

"Yup. She texted me after you all spoke and told me if I was coming to get the letter, to give you a hug."

"Why a hug?"

"Hugs make people feel better. Even I, a demon, know that. Do you feel better?"

She thought. "Actually, yes I do. Thank you, Donovan."

"Most welcome!" He held out his hand and she placed the letter in it. He glanced at the envelope. "Bohdana?"

"Gift from God."

He burst out laughing. "Oh, they didn't know what you'd become at all, did they?"

"Hah! No, I guess not. I don't use the feminine form of my last name. Because it's dumb."

He grinned at her. "Yup, a poor choice for a middle name. Ok, are you done for the day?"

"I am."

"Cool. I will drive you home. Declan didn't ask, but I'm here and you're here and it seems polite."

More polite demons. "Ok, that's fine."

"I hear you are going out dancing."

"Yup. Will you be there?

"Nope. You get Matthew tonight."

"Will I like Matthew?"

"You will. And he is very handsome. Not as handsome as I am, of course. But he's no slouch."

"Is he as modest as you?"

"Much more so! Let's go."

***

In the car, Anya decided to assuage her curiosity a bit. "May I ask where you and Declan met?"

"So formal! But you may. In the States, in the South. Georgia, eighteen hundreds. "

"Oh. Oh, I see." She paused and wondered how to phrase this, so it didn't sound rude.

"Go ahead and ask. I am hard to offend, and I can hear your brain working."

"You were a slave?"

"I was. A slave, then a demon and for a bit of time, I was both. A new demon who had no clue what he'd gotten himself into really."

Anya was dying to know how he'd become a demon, but she felt that was too personal to ask. He'd share when or if he wanted to.

"Declan was there with another demon and took a liking to me."

"Jesus Donovan, tell me he didn't...purchase you?" She'd be cancelling the date if Donovan said yes.

"Good lord, woman! No! He helped me escape." She let out the breath she'd been holding. "The only thing he asked was that I stay with him until he had taught me what he thought I needed to know, and that included learning to read. I mean...can you imagine? The only thing he asked of me was for my own benefit. Don't get me wrong, he can be a real bastard, but his human sense of fairness has always stuck."

Anya cleared the frog in her throat. "Why did you stay?"

"How could I not? He only had Matthew and me as friends. And Matthew is about as lonely as Declan and closed off to boot. They both needed someone in their lives who was more open. And we had some fun. We still do." He smiled to himself, obviously remembering some good times. "Declan also pays really well. But they were the two loneliest people I'd met, until I met you."

"I am not lonely. I have Gwen!" Anya knew it was bullshit the moment the words left her mouth.

"Anya, you are about the loneliest human I have ever met. And this is only the second time I've met you in person. It's coming off of you in waves, that's how lonely you are."

"Is that one of your special demon gifts?"

"I can sense emotions, yes. But I don't need the gift to see that in you. I bet even Gwen feels it. She is your best friend, and I know you love her, but you also haven't let her in completely have you?"

"How could you know that?"

"I saw her face at the club the other night. I could feel deep worry coming from her. We chatted a little and she mentioned that she thought you were still keeping things from her."

"She told you that?"

"She did."

"Well, shit!"

"She thinks that you think she'll reject you if she knows all of your secrets. Anya, she's a witch and your best friend. She can feel you're hiding stuff."

"Why did she talk to you?"

"Same reason you let me hug you and didn't kick me in the balls. Some people are scared of me, the people who aren't, feel safe with me and trust me."

"She did say you felt safe."

"Yup. But the holding back is the thing that keeps you lonely. And it will do so with Declan as well. So, just think about it. That said, I know if I so much as hurt one blonde hair on her head, you will gut me like a fish."

"Also true," she said smiling. "You wouldn't hurt her."

"No. I never would. Declan has that same vein of loyalty running through him."

"So, you stayed out of friendship?"

"Yes, I stayed out of friendship. I am very fond of him and Matthew. And the others. You'll meet them soon, I'm sure."

"You ARE for sure more than a bartender though. But it benefits you that people don't look beyond it much, doesn't it?"

"Even demons can be racist assholes. They see a large black man and they may think I'm an idiot. Which means they talk freely. And that is their downfall."

"But why put yourself through that kind of behavior from people? Doesn't it burn you, especially having been a slave? How do you do it and not tear people apart?" Anya bit her lip. "I am sorry. This is none of my business. The last thing you need is some white lady all up in your business."

He smiled at her. "No. I'd rather you ask. To be clear, Declan didn't ask me to do any of this, and for much the same reasons you note. I am good at this work. When I was still mortal, I was a spy in the slave quarters. For whatever reason, even with my size, I was exceptionally good at observing, at being able to stay still and hidden. And I was also particularly good at getting information from people without them knowing it. I knew how to blend in."

"Donovan, really?"

"Really! And to answer your first question, yes, to some extent it does bother the fuck out of me. But that is the job. If you did it, you'd resent that they ignored you because you were a woman, but it would help you too, because it would be easier to do your job. It's their weakness that you'd be exploiting.

I know who I am, and I know I can outthink every one of those fuckheads. I'm very secure there and I know that what I do is important, and it helps Declan and ultimately keeps the population safe. I am a demon; I can play the long game."

They pulled up in front of her apartment. "Here," he said. "Let me put both my number and Matthew's into your phone. You can call either of us if ever you can't get a hold of Declan." She handed him her phone and he added the numbers, handing her phone back to her with a huge smile.

She leaned over, kissed him on the cheek and said, "You are already one of my very favorite people." And with that, she was gone.

CHAPTER 4

The demon that picked them up that night looked like he was carved out of marble. He had picked Gwen up first and he was standing against the car when Anya came out. "Have mercy," she said under her breath. He was tall, dark hair, dark eyes with full lips and pale skin. Build wise he was similar to Declan, but she thought Matthew might be a bit bigger. But he flat out had the most elegant hands she had ever seen on anyone, male, or female. He exuded very controlled power.

"Anya? Matthew. It's very nice to meet you." He held out his hand and she shook it. His accent was British, a bit posh but his voice was like honey. He was no Declan, but man...he looked good!

"So, does Declan only hire gorgeous men?"

This unexpected statement caused Matthew to bark out a laugh, something he didn't do often. "Thank you for the compliment, but I fear I pale in comparison to Declan."

"Well, obviously. But that's only because I saw him first." She winked at him.

He opened the door to the backseat, and she climbed in next to Gwen, who looked gorgeous in a short red dress and strappy gold sandals.

"Is he not beautiful? He's like a painting!" She breathed at her friend.

"He really is like a painting."

"You'd think he was cold, all that seemingly British reserve," Gwen said. "But I don't think that's the whole story."

"It's not. Donovan told me he was lonely, closed off. I think though, if he works for Declan, he's probably a decent guy, with a good sense of honor. I don't think Declan would have anyone near us that he didn't trust completely."

"Agreed!" Gwen grinned at her. "You look great!" Anya was wearing a sleek long-sleeved button-down shirt in black, short skirt, sequined black booties and a sequined black belt. The long sleeves on Anya allowed her to wear her spring-loaded knife sheaths. She wasn't taking any chances.

"As do you."

As they walked into the club ahead of Matthew, he let out a low whistle of appreciation. Anya turned and gave him a saucy grin. "Where will you be, handsome?"

He pointed to the far wall. "Standing right there. Give me a sign if you need anything. Otherwise, have fun."

"What did Declan tell you about me?"

"To let you do your thing without interference. But if there is a demon threat, I am to get involved. Some guy gropes you, that's on you, unless you specifically ask for my help. Then, of course I will gladly step in and help."

She nodded. "Fair." And with that, Gwen dragged Anya onto the dance floor.

Declan texted to ask how it was going.

Matthew responded quickly. *Fine. They're dancing. Ignoring everyone else. Loveliest ladies in here, I might add. I like her. If you don't take her as a mate, I might.* He didn't mean it, he just wanted to see Declan's reaction.

Do not touch that woman, Matthew.

I mean if you aren't interested...

Don't make me kill you, I don't want to train another second.

She's safe from me, don't worry. Anya just strong armed someone who was trying to get handsy with Gwen. It was great.

Declan sighed but smiled. Of course she did.

Matthew surveyed the room and found the men had placed around the club as extra security. Good, he thought, as he settled in to watch the ladies.

***

It happened so slowly that it took Matthew an hour to notice that not only had the energy in the club shifted, but that his men were gone, along with a number of people on the club. The floor itself was just starting to empty at an alarming rate. Something hadn't wanted him to see it. He pulled out his phone to dial Declan as Anya caught his eye. He held up his phone and she nodded at him.

"Gwen?" she asked. "Are you…"

"Yup. I feel it and see it. Now."

"Keep dancing but keep an eye out."

"Will do. I feel it. The energy is getting very bad here." She waved her hand lightly in a way that would look like a dance move. "Oooh, this was some dark magic. And strong if it took us this long to see and feel it."

Meanwhile Matthew spoke two words into the phone. "Here. Now." and hung up. He walked around looking for any of his men. Nope. Gone. "Fuck!" Strong glamour to make sure he hadn't noticed. It was rare that someone got the drop on Matthew, and he was pissed. And concerned. That was kind of a magic he really hadn't seen before. Given that Gwen was a witch, and she hadn't felt it, either the magic was very strong, or she wasn't. The club still had people milling about on the dance floor. They looked confused. Anya and Gwen were dancing, or moving around more accurately, back-to-back. Smart, he thought. They kept shifting around so they could keep an eye on things. Gwen was muttering under her breath as they came in contact with humans on the dance floor. Slowly, those people started to move off the dance and out of the club. So, she had some good magic if she was able to do that. The music was still going though, and it was all really creepy. Matthew made his way down to the dance floor, using compulsion, his own special power, to get the last of the people out of the way. He reached Anya and Gwen and was about to ask Gwen if she could do something about the music when it cut out completely. Looking around, they saw a number of demons surround them at the perimeter of the floor. Well fuck, he thought sourly.

***

Declan had raced downstairs and out of the back of his club where a motorcycle was waiting. He hopped on it and raced away, breaking every single traffic law to get to the club. Worry turning his blood to ice. When he walked into the club, the place was virtually empty. Only Anya, Matthew and Gwen were there, on the dance floor. They were standing in a tight circle, back-to-back. They were surrounded by a group of demon foot soldiers.

He stripped off his jacket and let out a deafening roar.

Everyone's eyes went to the door. "Your man is here," Gwen said quietly.

"It would seem so."

The voice that came out of Declan was unearthly and should have frightened her. "Who are you to invade not only my city, but to insult my consort?" Huh? Anya thought. That was interesting. In the blink of an eye, he was on the dance floor. "Hey," she said weakly.

"You know, if you wanted to see me...you could have called."

"I like to make an impression."

"Oh, you do." They were all back-to-back now, each keeping an eye on one area of the club. No humans seemed to be lingering. Which was good. To have killed them would have been an outright declaration of war, someone was trying to avoid that, for now. But this was bad enough. You just did not walk into someone's domain and shit all over it like this. There were rules and this broke them. "Well?! I am waiting for an answer! These people are under my protection."

The demon in Declan's line of vision answered him. "We just want you and the consort. The other demon and the tiny woman can go."

"Tiny woman! Of all the...sorry," Gwen said, chagrined.

Declan tried hard not to grin. "It's fine." He leaned over to Anya "Can she fight?"

"She has magic, but beyond that, I don't know. I don't think so, but I could be wrong. She's tough though."

Declan grimaced. "Ok, good to know."

Another demon. "I want the little blonde…" he hissed.

"Really, I've had about enough of this shit." Gwen rolled her hands as if she were forming a ball and threw a globe of white light above the demon's head. It hit a light and set off sparks to rain down on the demon, burning him a little. The demon howled in pain.

"She has a temper, that's promising," said Matthew.

"It is at that," answered Declan.

"Shit, that was cool!" Anya said. "You've gotten really good at that!"

"It was pretty...cool," Matthew said.

"Fire is my bitch," Gwen said with a small grin.

"Are you having fun?" asked Anya, incredulous.

"Well...I mean, maybe a little. I am also taking this perfectly seriously though. Really."

"So, while they are still menacing from afar, what's the plan? Can they be killed and, should we?" This was from Anya.

"A direct hit to the chest or head will cause them to evaporate into dust. They won't be back anytime soon as they need time to re-form into their bodies. They're foot soldiers, born like Hell Wraiths are but able to think up to a point. They are slightly higher up the demon food chain. They're quick though. In some ways, quicker than Matthew or myself because they are bred for this kind of thing."

The demons began to advance on them. Anya sighed, made a downward motion with her arms and two deadly looking knives slid into her hands. As the demon advanced on her, Anya threw a knife and hit the demon right between the eyes, he burst into dust and she ran to catch the knife, spun into a roundhouse kick to another demon, and lodged a knife into his chest. Declan was suitably impressed. She was absolutely the perfect woman for him, in so many ways and all of a sudden, he just wasn't sure why he was fighting it so hard. Later, he thought, as he punched a demon with one hand and reached into his chest, yanked and the demon erupted in a dust storm, as he spun around and kicked another in the head.

Matthew was fighting three demons and not even breathing hard. Completely calm. One on his back, and two in front. Gwen enchanted a chair and threw it at the one on his back. The demon fell off, slightly winded and Gwen used the opportunity to pick up a piece of chair and stab it in the chest with it. It was Anya's turn to be impressed. "Gwen!" She yelled at one was about to attack from behind. Gwen spun and threw a bolt of fire through his head. Matthew grabbed the two he was fighting and crushed their heads together.

"How does he do that?" Anya asked Declan.

"Remain that calm? I have no idea. Honestly, he is scarier than I am. It's why he's my second." He punched a demon in the head and shook the dust off of his arm. "Gwen uses her magic well and she's helping. I think with training, she'd be fine at hand to hand."

Anya knifed a demon through the head and grunted. "Gross. I think you're right. I have to say, her glee at this is a little startling."

Declan was fighting with a large demon who had grabbed him by the neck. Anya threw a knife right at the demon's head and exploded. Matthew was blocking Gwen as the demon who professed he wanted the tiny blonde headed her way. "Mmmiinneee" the thing hissed. "Like fucking Hell!" Matthew growled as he punched through where his heart would be. Donovan had hemmed and hawed enough about the blonde that Matthew had gotten the hint that he liked her. That meant Matthew was going to make sure she stayed absolutely safe for his large friend. This was the last one though. Too easy, thought Matthew.

"That's it?" Declan asked. "That hardly seemed worth it. What's the point?"

"I would assume to prove that they can. And maybe they thought I would be easy pickings," Anya said.

"And you've proven you can handle yourself. Someone is playing the long game here. But who? And why?"

Gwen was standing in the middle of the floor, looking shocked now that it was all over. Anya rushed over. "Gwennie? Are you ok? Are you hurt?"

She shook her head. "No. No, I'm fine. I mean, I know what Declan said but I've never caused harm like that before, and I am just processing it now."

"You could have fooled me." Declan snorted.

Anya shot him a dark look. "Gwen, you didn't really kill anyone. The foot soldiers don't stay dead."

"Oh, I know. Let me see if I can be clearer. Yes, I am processing actually being in a fight, but I am also kind of processing my reaction to it. It was kind of exciting, even though it was scary. That being said, I am also dealing with you."

"Me?"

"You acted like fighting was second nature to you." She sounded almost accusatory. She'd seen her friend pull a knife but then it had all felt like a game. Having seen Anya's face, her deadly concentration, and her skill, she thought she knew what her friend had been hiding all this time.

"I don't know what to say Gwen. The knives aren't just for show. I thought you understood that. You've seen me throw them."

"Not in this kind of setting. You meant business." She looked at Anya, then at Declan. "You too, which I'd expect. Of course. Christ, if any two people ever belonged together, it's you two."

"Gwen," Anya began but Gwen interrupted.

"Have you ever killed anyone?"

"You just saw me…"

"No! A person. A human." She wanted the truth from her friend.

Anya took a deep breath. "Yes. Yes, I have."

"What the fuck?! Why didn't you ever tell me this?! I know other people like to treat me like I'm some kind of doll, but I didn't think you would ever do that!" And that was the crux of it. Not that Anya had murdered someone, but that Anya had thought her friend had needed to be coddled and protected. Gwen had expected better from her, thought Anya.

Declan spoke this time. "Gwen." His long-forgotten brogue, more pronounced in the presence of Gwen and her own brogue. "I suspect she didn't tell you because she was afraid, you'd reject her."

"Like her family has?" She faced Anya. "Like your family, right? They rejected you. Is that why you don't like to discuss them much?"

"Yes."

"But how could you even think I would ever turn on you?" Gwen was hurt, but a part of her also understood. So much about her friend suddenly made sense to her.

"Because everyone else has. My family, other friends, boyfriends. Anyone who has ever known anything about me has left me or rejected me. And I *should* have trusted you. I know that. But I was scared. Caring about other people, including you, is kind of new to me."

Gwen walked over to Anya, reached up and took her face in both hands. "I don't care about what you did in the past. I don't even care about what you do now. I am your friend through everything. Including this. I see you, Anya, I see you. You can tell me when you're ready. But you have to drop the walls and let people in. Even if it's not me, even if it's Declan. Shit, even if it's Donovan, or Matthew here...you have to talk to someone. Don't carry it around anymore, it's going to eat you alive." And then she gave her friend a big hug.

"I'm sorry."

"You're forgiven."

Declan cleared his throat. "We really need to go." They made their way outside and got into Matthew's car. Gwen immediately got in front with Matthew, so Declan had to climb into the back with Anya. Slickly done, thought Matthew. Declan sent a quick text to get his motorcycle picked up and said to Matthew, "We need to drive for a bit, make sure we're not getting followed.

"You got it."

"There's something…" Gwen said. "Something I am not remembering. It struck me in the club, but now it's gone. It's so irritating. I'll remember it." She then swore profusely in Gaelic. It was really going to bug her until she remembered.

"Gwen, where are you from?"

"County Cork, Skibbereen specifically. Where were you from?"

"Cashel. Tipperary."

"Your brogue is coming out," Anya said.

"I think it's because of Gwen."

"I like it." Anya smiled at him.

"I will try and let it come out to play more often then." He moved closer to Anya, putting his arm around her shoulders, and leaning down to sniff her hair.

"You called me your consort."

"You said you cared about me."

"That is not exactly what I said."

"It's what you meant."

"Yes, it is. You're right. But I am not trying to hide anything. You, Mister dig your heels in, went from denying it would ever happen, to confirming the relationship."

"I know. I shouldn't have. But…" he trailed off.

She looked at him, her hand brushing his check. "Oh," she said quietly. "You fool."

He leaned down and gave her a soft, but quick kiss on the mouth. "Truth. And in thinking about it, confirming it may help us discover who's behind the attack."

"True." She kissed him quickly, sighing and then rested her head against his shoulder, looking out the window as they sped past the Eiffel Tower. She snuggled against him, and he knew he was in deep trouble here.

He cleared his throat. "Gwen, are your people witches?"

"Good lord, no. Actuaries. Very salt of the Earth Irish, but lovely people. I am the only witch in the family for hundreds of years. And I only discovered it by accident. I found an old spell book and tried one for shits and giggles. I may have been a little drunk at the time. It worked and tried another. And then another. I had a natural inclination, but no training. I did find an older witch at some point, but she was pretty dotty. I am mostly self-taught, which is why my magic isn't as refined as it could be. But I am naturally good with spells."

"Huh. Interesting. I have met a few witches throughout the centuries, but they have gotten fewer and farther between. Your natural talent is very good. You're just going to get stronger."

"I think they're mostly keeping a low profile. Lot of charlatans out there. And thank you!" She thought a moment. "Anya doesn't think the Fae are real."

"Gwen!"

"Of course they're real, lass. To think otherwise is just silly."

Anya sighed. "I never said they weren't, I just said…oh, never mind."

"Good. Because they are real, and you don't want to make them angry by saying they're not," Gwen said.

Declan tightened his hold on Anya, and she moved to lay against his chest, sighing. "Anya?"

"Hmmm?"

"I'm sorry, I have to postpone our date. "

Anya sat up and frowned. "Why?"

Declan gently tugged her back down to him. "I have to go see Anaranth and do something for him. He's the head of the Council. It's not a request, it's a command. It'll take me out of Paris."

"Well, I suppose if the boss needs you, we can reschedule."

"Good. I still want to do it." He started rubbing her back gently, in circles and she sighed happily. "I'll miss you."

"I will miss you too." She looked up at him and he leaned down to kiss her again. Gently, sweetly.

"Will you be careful while I'm gone? If you want to go dancing, maybe come to my club?"

"Declan…"

"I know you can handle yourself. I have no doubt about that. But you do not have wide experience fighting demons, and you could possibly get in over your head." Also thought of it scared the shit out of him, but he wasn't going to say that.

She thought about it. "Ok, that's reasonable. If we go out, we'll come to your club. We don't go out a ton, really. We're more movie and pizza night kind of ladies."

"Thank you." He dropped a kiss on the top of her head.

They drove around for another hour before the ladies could go home. Anya had fallen asleep on Declan, who had not minded one bit. He felt peaceful for the first time in several hundred years. He stroked her back gently. He was beginning to see the appeal of a consort. No, of a mate. A true mate. It felt nice, the weight of her on his chest. Her hand was curled around his waist. The car eventually pulled up in front of Gwen's apartment and they all got out of the car, stretching a bit.

The two women hugged. "You will be careful Annie?"

"Of course. And we will talk about things soon. I promise." She turned to Matthew who was taking her upstairs and was going to wait for her guard to get there before he left. "You take care of my friend, buddy!"

Matthew smiled. "You got it, boss." Declan side eyed him, and Matthew laughed. "She is also the boss, and you know it."

Declan rolled his eyes. "I'll see you back at the club later. Please be careful."

"You know me."

"I do. It's why I am telling you to be careful."

Declan took the car and drove Anya home. "Matthew likes you. He doesn't like a lot of people. But he's taken a shine to you. And to Gwen."

"I like him." He looked at her. "Not like that and you know it. But I do like him. See me upstairs?" She asked quietly. He nodded, knowing that once he did, there was no going back.

CHAPTER 5

She flipped on the lights in her apartment and bent to take off her shoes, while Declan did a check of the apartment before coming back into the living room. She flipped around to him and wound her arms around his neck. "Kiss me."

"Anya…"

"I don't care. It's been a long night, I am tired, and I want a proper goodnight and goodbye kiss since you're going away."

He looked down at her and knew he was going to comply. "OK, then." His hands wound around her body and cupped her ass, pulling her closer to him. She groaned softly. He leaned down and ran his tongue over her lips. She gasped, opening her mouth, her hands moving into his hair to pull him down more. "Don't tease. Kiss." she breathed. He laughed softly and took her mouth. His tongue swept in, and she met it with her own tongue, a soft moan escaping her. He was gentle at first, then grew more insistent, taking more. His hands started rubbing circles over her back and her own hands lowered to his shoulders, squeezing. He picked her up and she wrapped her legs around him, and he groaned this time. He carried her into the bedroom and laid her on the bed. He dropped down next to her and then rolled her over until she was on top of him, his hands back on her ass and his tongue back in her mouth. "Declan, please."

"Please, what?"

"You know I want you, I can tell you want me, why are we waiting?"

He didn't answer but rolled her over until she was under him, and one hand moved to her breast and he squeezed the nipple. She gasped. He unbuttoned her blouse and then his mouth replaced his hand, taking her nipple in his mouth through her bra as he began to suck on her nipple in earnest. She started to arch under him. "Sssh, baby…be still for me." With a flick of his finger, a long claw descended, and he sliced open her bra, pulling each side back to expose her breasts fully for his view. He raised some to look down at them. "You," he said, "have amazing breasts." He started to lick her nipple again, taking the tight nub in his mouth. He gave her a quick nip and moved on to the other nipple. "We're not fucking tonight. Because when we do, I don't want it to be a quickie. I am going to take my time with you, and I am going to make you scream when you come."

"Sure of yourself aren't you?" she breathed.

"Always."

"Then what are you doing?"

"Giving you something to think about while I'm gone." He undid her pants and slowly worked them down. Anya was breathing hard, but her eyes were on him, watching him. He saw desire there and he smiled. He raised himself up to look at her, their eyes met for a long moment before he raised himself to kiss her again. He used one leg to move her legs apart and touched her, stroking his finger back and forth. "Oh, someone is very wet, aren't they?"

"Mmmm, see what you're missing?" she murmured. He nipped at her bottom lip. "Behave yourself now." His brogue had gotten thicker as he had gotten more aroused. He started rubbing her clit, while he took 2 fingers and moved them inside of her, causing her to gasp again as her head fell back on the pillow. "Declan." she breathed.

"Come for me, Anya. Come, *malysh*." He had called her "baby" in Russian. Did he already know Russian, or had he looked up a few words to impress her? "You're so wet Anya, you feel so good, I can't wait for this to be my cock and not just my fingers." He was pumping her with more insistence now, faster, while he still rubbed her nub. He could feel her tighten around his fingers and he pinched her clit gently and she exploded in his hand with a small scream. "Sssh, sweet...sssh" he said leaning over, kissing her. Kissing her was like a drug. She put her hands on his chest and wrapped a leg around him. "Stay tonight, stay."

He pulled back. "If I could. I am already late to meet Anaranth, but I couldn't help myself. You smell far too good for me to have just left."

She smiled and kissed him again. "Are you sure? I could…." she reached down and rubbed her hand over his crotch. He put his hand over hers to still it.

"No. Absolutely not. This was about you. I can wait."

"There's not…is there anyone else?" she asked, nervous to hear the answer.

He looked down at her. "Absolutely not. I am way too enamored with a Russian knife thrower to even look at anyone else." He kissed her soundly on the lips.

She smiled. "Ok. Ok, then. Let me walk you out." She shimmied out of her shirt and bra, making him groan, and pulled a robe on. "You ripped my bra."

"I will buy you twelve more. In all different colors."

"Not necessary."

"Oh, but I want to," he said, pulling her robe apart and bending down to take one nipple, then the other into his mouth.

Anya put her hands on his shoulders. "Declan, if you keep doing that, I am going to fall over." He chuckled and stood up while Anya re-tied her robe.

They walked to her door, and he looked down at her. "Call Donovan if you need anything. Matthew if you can't reach Donovan. You do have someone, um, looking out for you. It just makes me feel better" he said when she started to open her mouth. "I am eight hundred years old; you have to cut me a little slack there."

"Fine. I will try not to torture him too badly."

"That's my gal." He kissed her one last time and then he was gone. Having finally gotten the last word in.

"The bastard," she said, laughing.

As Declan drove away, he was now certain of one thing; no way could he walk away from Anya. Aside from the fact that she wasn't safe, he just didn't want to. He didn't even want to fight it anymore. But he was going to show her who he was and hope like hell she didn't run the other way.

***

After Declan left, Anya wasn't really tired, oddly enough. She was still kind of pumped, not just from the fight, but from the ridiculously great orgasm. Probably more from the orgasm. She should shower but she could still smell him on her, and she didn't want to lose that. "UGH! You asshole." she rolled her eyes at herself. She was not going to go all mushy and sentimental now over a guy. She liked sex, a lot. She was monogamous though and had mostly had sex in the confines of a relationship. Which she now saw as a means to end. She wanted sex, didn't want to sleep around, so she dated someone fun, who she'd never get serious about. It pissed a lot of her boyfriends off. They liked that to be their role in the relationship, not hers. The few men she'd let in close had disappointed or rejected her. One of them even said she enjoyed sex too much. That her eagerness was unappealing and slutty. She'd thrown a steak knife at his head and told him to get out and to lose her number. She hadn't been emotionally involved in that relationship, but he had been good, if uncreative in bed. But a large penis couldn't cover the fact he was a misogynistic asshole. And all this thinking about penises made her think about Declan again. She didn't think they'd be having any issues in that department. Not helping, she thought. Ok, time for a cold shower and sleep.

***

The next morning, Anya and Gwen checked in with each other and decided to go easy on the babysitters, even letting them drive the ladies to work. Michel seemed shocked when she climbed into the front seat. "Mademoiselle Orlov, I think you should sit in the back. *Peut-etre?*"

She snorted "Perhaps," she said, enunciating the word, "you should call me Anya and no, I am sitting in front with you."

"I do not think Declan would like that. I would not want him to be angry." He looked a bit nervous; he'd heard about Anya and what had happened last night and while he knew Declan liked him, he didn't want to fuck this up. Declan made it very clear that this woman was to be respected and protected and if anyone thought about touching her, he'd rip them apart. Michel, generally very easy going was not feeling easy going about the consort right now. He'd worked for Donovan for a century but had only been with Declan himself for about twenty-five years. He was pretty sure his boss trusted him completely, or else he wouldn't have gotten this assignment, but he wasn't sure he wanted to chance it.

"Michel, he's well aware of what a pain in the ass I can be. I wouldn't worry about it."

"If you are sure, then. I am still not sure I can call you by your first name though."

"What do you call the boss?"

"Declan, *bien sûr.*"

"Then you call me Anya. Both Donovan and Matthew do."

"Yes, but they have been with him longer." Michel looked at her and she grinned at him. He couldn't resist a grin back. He was a charmer by nature, and he was always ready with a smile for a pretty lady, even if she was off limits. "Fine! I will call you by your first name and I don't really mind if you sit in front. I like the company."

"Good!" She settled in. "Michel, how did you pull this detail?"

"Oh, Declan called me this morning and requested I do this." She knitted her brows at him. "*Pourquoi?*"

For some reason, she found it really charming how he peppered his speech with French words. "Curious. He must trust you then. But you seem more nervous than Matthew or Donovan. I wondered why."

He glowed at the implication he was trusted. "Ah, I see. I have been with Declan for twenty-five years, Donovan for a number of years before that. I am the newest. But, yes, I believe I am, maybe...inner circle? Donovan always seemed happy with me, so I got the opportunity to move up." He wasn't going to fuck this up. He'd fucked up enough in life, he wasn't going to do it again. She nodded at him to continue. "I am nervous though. I've not had to guard someone before, let alone someone so important. I am mostly considered an enforcer. Muscle. Or someone...." his brow furrowed. "*Dans l'ombre?*"

"In the shadows?" He nodded. "I see. So, this position is a lot more visible?"

"*Oui! Exactment!*" He paused. "But it does appear that Declan is keeping your protection within his circle. Matthew last night, me today, I suppose. Even the people you cannot see..." He blushed at this.

"It's fine Michel. I can't see them, but I assumed they were there."

"Whew! Even those guys, Donovan chose them very carefully."

She nodded. "I thought so. So, what makes you such a good enforcer? You seem very charming."

"I am good at putting people at ease, and then if need be, putting them through a wall." He grinned at her and she couldn't help but laugh.

She widened her eyes at the slight demon. "Really?"

"Indeed. I get the job done." He shrugged, almost delicately. Anya should have known better. Neither Declan nor Donovan would give her to someone who couldn't handle themselves. "I will likely be your day shift for now. Take you to work, bring you home, tail you for the day."

"That seems very boring for you."

"Are you kidding? You are the consort, there can be no work more important." His dark brows knitted together at this.

He was completely serious, she saw. "I am not the consort yet."

"Pshaw. Details. I like learning different parts of the business and being able to protect you is an honor."

"Ok, but look, I am a casual person. None of this 'consort' business. We are going to be friends."

"Will you listen to me if there is danger?"

"If I think what you say makes sense."

He nodded. "This is fair. Declan said you were smart." He also told Michel to pick her up and carry if need be, but he really hoped he wouldn't have to do that.

"How old are you?" She thought. "Is that a rude question?"

"Would it change your mind about asking?"

"No."

He laughed. "It's not. I am older than Donovan, four hundred and fifteen years or so."

"You use a lot of French, but you are not French." It was not a question.

He laughed. "You hear something in my accent?" She nodded. "I am originally from Mongolia actually. So, closer to your um…neck of the woods really. Michel is not my birth name either." His face closed off. "I was taken in by a demon who, as it turns out, was powerful but corrupt. They were not kind to me." This, he knew, was a vast understatement. "I felt the need to reinvent myself when I left him and came here. So, I let people think I am French."

"I'm sorry."

"I thank you for that. Do you wish to know what I was in life?"

"Desperately!" laughed Anya.

"I was a monk."

"I'm sorry? Say again? You were a…monk?"

"Yes. Tibetan Buddhism. It was introduced to Mongolia in…"

"The sixteenth century."

"*Oui*! You know Buddhism?"

"I do."

"*Bien*!"

"What would be rude to ask you?"

"How I came to be a demon. But I think you would ask anyway, no?"

"I might. But not today." She paused. "But I will not ask you about your early days, ever. Not unless you choose to share it. I promise you that. But one day, I would like to talk to you about your life as a monk."

A dark look passed over Michel's face. "I can talk you about being a monk. But not the other. I do not like to think about it."

She patted his shoulder. "Then let's not think about it then."

Michel pulled into a parking spot and got out. "I am your shadow, if you remember. *Je suis désolé*." He sounded formal, but his dark eyes sparkled.

"You don't need to be sorry. But you do need to fade into the background. I don't want the students or other faculty upset. Can you do that?"

"*Oui!* This is another reason why I was chosen. I blend in well. You go on ahead, you will not know I am here." She didn't know how he could blend in. He was very striking with his burnished skin and mass of curly dark hair and the eyes set off by the longest lashes she'd ever seen on another person. The students were sure to notice him. Michel was true to his word though. She actually forgot he was there over the course of the day, and no one else caught wind of him. Anya was beginning to see just how and why Declan chose the men he did.

***

Over the next few days, life was quiet. She and Michel got to know each other on the rides to and from work each morning. She found out he liked a certain kind of tea that she also sometimes drank and brought him a travel mug of it each morning, along with her own coffee. Declan texted her with *"Stop making your bodyguards fall in love with you."*

"I can't help it. Their boss is away and not here to pay attention to me."

"Their boss does miss you though. Behave, malysh." She smiled through a really boring staff meeting after that.

She wasn't going out much at night, unless it was dinner with Gwen. Gwen preferred to come over and Donovan generally picked her up and brought her home. Anya usually had Matthew out front for a goodly portion of the evening. And even if she was alone, he still would not come in, preferring to sit in the car. This made Anya suspect that she had demons positioned around her apartment. But she always made sure he had dinner or coffee. He was always very gracious, but a bit distant.

"Gwen, I can come to you, you know," she said one evening as they were having dinner at Anya's small place.

"I have roommates and they are annoying."

"They're your cousins."

"The point still stands. They are young and irritating and think I am cute with how I can move things with my mind." Gwen looked disgusted.

"You asked them to move in with you."

"Because my mother asked me to."

"She asked you to look after them, she didn't ask you to move them in."

"She would have. She's like that." Gwen replied darkly. "Have you heard from Demon McHottypants lately?"

"Yes, he texted this morning to tell me to stop flirting with Michel."

"Are you flirting?"

"No. I'm bringing him the tea that he likes."

"I cannot believe that you are charming demons right and left. Michel with the tea, Matthew, and his coffee. What next?"

"It's just the decent thing to do. Matthew is still a tough nut to crack. I'll get there though. I also have it on good authority that you made Donovan some cookies, so you are one to talk. I have another fan, one of my students, Luc. He's starting to wander into lectures he isn't even supposed to be in. He keeps giving me brown puppy dog eyes. Michel says he's harmless."

Gwen shrugged. "Yes, I have Donovan, but you seem to have charmed everyone you've met. Which is not like you at all. And you realize Luc is sitting out in the car with Matthew right now? They both drove me here tonight. Donovan was busy."

Anya looked out the window and saw that to be true. "Ah well, that's interesting. Hmm. And hey! What do you mean charming people isn't like me?"

"You generally don't like anyone enough to charm them. These demons, you seem to like a fair bit. So, who are you and what have you done with my misanthropic friend?" Anya stuck out her tongue at Gwen. "Oh, that's mature. But come on, am I wrong? Since when are you friendly?"

"Well, that's true. But I do like them and if they like me, maybe that will soften Declan up."

"Donovan told me that your place as Declan's consort is well known now, after that night at the club. As is your prowess with a knife. The younger demons are all agog to get a good look at you."

"But Declan and I haven't even come to an agreement on it. We may not stay together. He is not even sure he wants me."

"Oh, he does. I saw how he looked at you. You are a known entity now, so it's going to be tougher on Declan if he backs out. He's not going to back out.

"He might. I am nothing that extraordinary."

"Christ, you're an idiot."

"Huh? Why?"

"You are the first consort in hundreds of years…."

"I am not an official consort yet!"

"Oh please…that man is so besotted with you that he doesn't even know what to do with himself."

"Come on, Gwen! That's storybook shit!"

"No, you come on! It's a matter of *when* and not *if.* Because it's going to happen. If you want it to." She paused, looking worried. "Do you want it to?"

"I do," she said softly, looking at Gwen. "I can see there's something you want to say, so say it."

"I mean, are you absolutely sure? Because if you're not…that's ok. It's going to be different and not necessarily always safe, and I worry. And I know I'm harping on this, and I am sorry, but I am really not sorry. Anya, who did you kill? I really want to know. Please tell me," she said this in a rush. Gwen couldn't help it. She was wildly curious about this.

Anya went to her friend and enfolded her in a hug. When they pulled away, Anya answered. "I am absolutely sure. I know it won't be safe. But I had a rough childhood, and my life has always been a little non-standard. I am not going to tell you the second person right now, but the first person I killed was my cousin. I took out one of his eyes when I was eight because he tried to molest me. At thirteen, he was trying to molest a cousin, so I threw a knife right at his heart. And I will tell you that I am honestly not sorry. He was twenty-one, trying to molest a child and he deserved to die."

Gwen gave her a gentle look. "Yes, Anya. Yes, he did. Thank you for telling me. You can tell me about any other people you killed later." Gwen poured Anya some more wine. "Now, tell me something really important…like about this amazing orgasm that Declan gave you. And spare no detail!"

"I believe I told you all of that already. And you really don't care that I have killed someone?"

"No, I don't. And yes, you did, but tell me again. It will help me sleep tonight."

Anya grinned at her friend, and they settled in for the night.

<u>CHAPTER 6</u>

The next day Anya had a full day of teaching and was also running a workshop on PhD preparation. so, she didn't get back to her office until the end of the day. She had no classes the rest of the week and had cancelled her office hours, saying she'd be available via email. All she needed to do was gather some materials so she could do some work from home and call it a week. She walked into her office and kicked an envelope, her full name visible. Her hand shook as she bent to pick it up. She was a little scared, but mostly absolutely furious. She opened it carefully and read it.

"You and your demon lover are monsters. You cannot be allowed to live. Your death will be a cleansing."

In Russian again. And horribly over dramatic. Typical, she thought. She took another photo and typed a message to Declan and Donovan. She had no idea if Declan could get messages in…well, wherever he was but she wanted him to see it when he was able to. So, it was a surprise when he called her about twenty seconds after she hit send.

"Anya, are you ok?"

"I am. You have service at, well, wherever you are?"

He laughed. "I do when I'm in Belgium."

"Oh!" She also laughed. "I wouldn't have expected Belgium. I'm sorry. I should have just texted Donovan but…" she stopped talking. She had texted Declan because she wanted him to make her feel better.

"You can always text me. Even if it's for no reason. I will always respond if I can. And I usually can. Are you upset again, *malysh*?" Yup, that made her feel better. What a dope.

"A little. But I am mostly just mad. Declan, could these notes be connected to what's happening?"

He thought. "It's possible. It's also possible it's a coincidence. But I don't necessarily believe in those. Though, this seems very personal."

"It does. I do have an uncle in Russia I could call. He may know something."

"Do that. Let me know. Or let Donovan know." He paused a moment. "No, let both of us know."

"I will." She paused. Ah, fuck it. "Thank you. I feel better having talked to you."

"I'm glad. I feel better talking to you."

"Are you ok?"

"Yes, don't worry about me. Take care, knife thrower."

"Take care, demon."

She waited until she was home to call her uncle. *"Dyadya? Eto Anya."*

Her uncle Tomas yelled into the phone. "English Anya! I want to practice!"

She winced at his volume, then smiled. "Yes uncle, how are you? How is auntie?"

"We are all fine, but missing you, my little assassin."

She winced again, though she knew he meant it affectionately. He and auntie were the only two who had agreed with the assessment that Cousin Pascha had needed to die. But the little girl she had rescued was Tomas' daughter, so that stood to reason.

"You should come to Paris and visit me then!"

"Maybe one day. What can an old man do for you?"

"You aren't old! But I do have a question for you. I have received a couple of startling notes addressed to me, my full name, in Russian. They are ugly and that is all I wish to say about them specifically. But have you heard anything about Yuri or Nik being up to something?"

Tomas sighed. "Your brothers are a menace to life. Mama's boys, and your mother...I am sorry, she is still your mother, but Anya, she is a bitter, vengeful woman. How she can live with so much anger, I do not know."

She liked her uncle because he didn't bullshit her, but he wasn't cruel. Her mother was all of those things and more. Doina thought all of her problems were Anya's fault, and she never missed an opportunity to tell her this when she was growing up. Doina would never be mother of the year. "I know uncle, but is there anything specific going on?"

"Well, your brothers," he spat the word, "do seem to be a little more agitated and aggressive lately. They have heard some talk about you, it seems, and it's gotten them riled up. I am not sure if they are behind the notes though. Should I see if I can find out?"

"No! Absolutely not. If they are behind it, I'll know soon enough." Her brothers were dangerous and even though this was their father's brother, she was sure they wouldn't hesitate to hurt him if necessary.

"If you are sure…"

"I am. But, if they leave the country, or you hear anything else, please let me know."

"I will do so." He paused. "Are you ok, little one?" That's what her father had always called her, and she melted a bit at hearing a voice so similar to her dad's call her that. "I'm fine, *dyadya,* I am just annoyed."

"If you need me, you have only to call."

"I know. How is Irina?" Her cousin, grown now. She knew this would distract her uncle and she settled in while he talked about Irina and the rest of his children. After she hung up, she texted Donovan and Declan about her conversation. As an afterthought, she added *"Neither of you go to Russia, please. At least without me. I prefer to terrify my own brothers, thank you very much."* Donovan replied with a laughing emoji and Declan replied with the eye roll emoji. She had not expected emoji replies and it delighted her more than it should have.

***

Anya had managed to doze off on the couch, a book laying open on her chest, when the phone startled her out of sleep. She opened her eyes a bit, reaching around until she located her cell. "Hello?" she said sleepily, not even bothering to look at who was calling.

"Anya?" Declan's voice came through the phone, warming her. "Did I wake you, *malysh*?"

Her toes curled at the endearment. "You did, but I had fallen asleep while doing a little research." She didn't want to admit that she'd also been dreaming about him.

"Research?"

"For a book, I am thinking of writing. It's about time I thought of publishing again." It's what she preferred to do over teaching.

"Are you published?" The thought, he was ashamed to admit, hadn't occurred to him. But she was an academic, so it stood to reason that she would also be a published author. He leaned over to type her name into the search engine on his laptop, seeing if he could bring up her books.

"Yes. But unless you're in Academia, you'd not have ever seen them. Though I am told they are available if you look." He'd managed to pull up her author's page that listed her books, so she was correct there.

He read for a moment. "Anya, you're a PhD!" He smiled to himself as he put each of her books in his shopping cart.

"Well, yes, I do hold a doctorate in English Literature. And I have two masters: in Russian and Comparative Religion. Oh, and a B.A. in Archaeology. That one was for shits and giggles."

"Isn't Russian cheating a bit?" he laughed. He placed the order and closed his laptop.

"Sssh, don't tell. But yes, if I want to, I can throw in 'Dr' before my name."

"You are an astounding person."

She blushed some. "Oh well, thank you. I'd say it was nothing, but it was a lot of hard work."

"I've no doubt. Brains are sexy."

She blushed at that. "Well, thank you."

"I didn't go to college."

"Yes, but you have first-hand historical knowledge. I mean, you are eight hundred years old. I am not going to hold the lack of a college degree against you."

"Appreciated."

"But this can't be why you're calling."

"No. Soooo...I am not really sure how to ask you this…"

"Just ask."

"Ok." He took a breath. "Anaranth has taken a bit of an interest in you."

"He knows about me?" she asked nervously.

"He does. Not from me."

"Ah, I see. I did mention to Natalia I had met you when she asked. The blabbermouth. Shit!"

"It's nothing bad, I promise you. We were talking and he mentioned he knew about you and yes, from Natalia. I told him that I wasn't happy with Natalia having told him our business. It's not an official request by any means. It would be, well casual is not the right word for it, but as casual as he gets. He's just curious, it seems. And since he knew about you, I did bring him up to speed on recent goings on. But to be clear, you are under no obligation to do this." Declan was very firm with Anaranth about this. He was not forcing her to make an appearance. "He is very eager to meet you it seems and has impressed upon me that I should use all of my powers of persuasion to convince you."

Anya thought for a moment. Her first instinct was that Anaranth had a lot of cheek thinking she would drop everything to meet him. But he was a demon and very likely a millennium in age at the very least, and in his world, that kind of thing would be normal. "Was it genuinely a request?"

"Yes, and I made it clear that you have responsibilities. For someone of his age and power, he can be remarkably reasonable about certain things. But were you my consort, your appearance would be expected as a general rule. I am expected to come when called most of the time. That said, I'd try to make sure it didn't interfere with your work."

She made a face. Not a deal breaker, but a possible problem down the road. Even if she stopped teaching at some point, this would rankle.

"Question. Do you have a problem with a consort who works?"

"Anya, I would never even think to ask you to give up your work. It wouldn't occur to me. I would never ask you to give up family or friends or even a pet if you had one. The world is different now. Were we to officially mate, I would want something different."

She smiled to herself. He was such an odd mix of modern and old fashioned. "That is all I care about. As it happens, I am clear. Most of my students are working on papers and I have cancelled office hours for the rest of the week." She was also experiencing some serious teaching ennui that had set in long before she met Declan. She had been considering taking the next semester off, but she didn't want Declan to think it was because of him. "Wait, are you still in Belgium?"

"Yes. Brussels. I can send a car for you in the morning to go to the airport."

"I need to book a flight."

"You're adorable. No, I have a plane."

"You have a plane? You have one at your disposal, or you own one?"

"I own one, that is always at my disposal."

"You own a plane." It was a statement.

"I own two actually. Anya, I'm fairly wealthy."

"Fairly? Or disgustingly so?"

"Disgustingly so."

"I don't really care about your money, but it's nice to know. Ok, I can be ready by seven a.m. Good?"

"It is. And Anya, thank you. I realize you don't have to do this, so I appreciate it."

"I get to see you, it's all good. Good night, Declan."

"Good night, Annie." he hung up and she was left staring at her phone. It had not escaped her notice that he had used Gwen's nickname for her. She didn't mind. It was alarming how much she didn't mind.

***

The flight to Brussels was about an hour and she was amazed at how quickly they managed to get in the air and on the way. She took a quick nap on the flight but was wide awake on the drive to the hotel. As they pulled up front, she let out a whistle. "Swanky!" she said quietly to herself. The concierge came out to meet her and instructed the bellhop to take her small bag. "Dr. Orlov, Mr. O'Shea is waiting in the suite for you. I will take you up." The use of her title both touched and amused her. He was obviously a big deal if she was getting a personal escort. They stepped onto the elevator and didn't quite go to the top floor, but close. The concierge knocked, then opened the door to the suite "Mr. O'Shea, Dr. Orlov is here."

He turned around and stared at Anya as he spoke. "Thank you, Marcelle. Gustav, you can drop the bag there, I'll take care of it."

Once the two were gone, Anya just walked into Declan's arms and put her own around his waist, laying her head on his chest and sighing happily. His arms came around her back and tightened, holding her there. He rested his cheek on the top of her head and started to rub her back lightly. They said nothing for a long while. "It's so weird to hear your last name used, I don't know why." Anya asked, a small laugh in her voice.

He pulled back. "I do need a last name sometimes. This one works when I need it, Dr. Orlov."

"That was a sweet touch."

"It pleases me that you're not an idiot."

She laughed outright then. "I highly doubt you'd want a stupid consort."

"You'd be right about that." He looked down at her and kissed her lightly on the lips.

She shook her head. "More," she said.

He grinned down at her. "More?"

"Yes. More." He complied by kissing her in earnest, his hands rubbing much more insistent circles on her back. "I missed you." She murmured against his mouth.

"I also missed you." he moved her hair out of the way and began to kiss her neck. Someone cleared their throat and the two broke apart, both of them irritated at the interruption. "Anya, this is Lucien, he runs things for me here. Lucien, Dr. Anya Orlov."

Lucien had a lightly accented voice. "I am pleased to meet you, Dr. Orlov."

"Anya. It's very nice to meet you. Swiss?"

He looked pleased. "Yes, I am. Declan, I am sorry to interrupt but Anaranth is waiting."

"Of course he is." Declan sighed.

"Oh! I need to change quickly."

"You look fine."

"I absolutely do not! Twenty minutes, max."

Declan picked up her bag and walked her to a room. Opening the door, he said "This is your room. Mine is down the hall."

She made a noncommittal sound and shooed him out. And in exactly twenty minutes, to the surprise of both men, she walked out of the bedroom. She was wearing a soft looking forest green wrap dress and sky-high black heels. She'd managed to tame her hair into a bun and put makeup on. "You look beautiful. That is an amazing color on you."

"Thank you. I thought all black might seem, I don't know, aggressive somehow."

He shrugged. "Maybe. One thing though…" he eyed her a bit.

"What?"

He walked over and took her hair down. It tumbled over her shoulder and down her back. "Hey!" she cried. "That took me most of the twenty minutes to do!"

"Your hair is too pretty to be up and hidden."

"For him, or for you?"

"For me." He leaned down to whisper in her ear, "I cannot wait to see how that hair looks laying against your naked breast."

She shuddered. "Ok, you win." she whispered back, nuzzling him slightly. He growled low in his throat at her but took her hand gently. "Shall we?"

"May as well."

CHAPTER 7

They drove through the streets of Brussels while Anya tried to calm her nerves by flipping her coin through her fingers. "Is that something you do when you're nervous?" She nodded. "Don't be nervous. He'll like you."

"Don't be nervous? Are you kidding? This demon is basically the boss of all demons, isn't he?"

"Well yes, so far as it goes. He is supreme head of the Council. There are older demons, who act as the elders, but no one really sees them, and they do not take part in demon politics anymore. Anaranth is truly our de facto head."

"So, don't be nervous of this extraordinarily old and powerful demon, who could probably kill me with his pinky finger."

"Nah. He'd have to use his index finger."

"Funny."

"Something you should know though, Anaranth is very old. He's so old that he appears as something other than human. He's somewhere between his human form and his demon form all the time now. It can be jarring. It certainly was when I met him eight hundred years ago, and it's more so now if you aren't used to it."

"Thank you for telling me. That absolutely does not freak me out even more than I already was." She started working her coin a little faster. Declan thought this was charming.

"I sense sarcasm."

"You think?"

They pulled up in front of a beautiful building in the Ixelles area of Brussels. "He lives here?"

"He stays here when he's in Brussels."

"In a house? Like a regular person? Really?"

"We have to live somewhere. Where do Natalia and Vlad live?"

"Well, a house obviously. But for some reason, I didn't think that someone this powerful would live in something as pedestrian as you know, a townhouse."

He laughed. "There is a netherworld, for lack of a better term. There are houses that are considered portals as well. We're still in the house, but we're not. This house is a portal...but also, just a townhouse."

"It's like a Doctor Who episode."

"What?"

"We really have to introduce you to some modern pop culture."

"Not likely. Are you ready?"

"I suppose."

"You look beautiful."

She squeezed his hand and smiled. "Thank you."

The driver came around and opened her door. She stood looking at the building with dread. Declan came to stand next to her. "Is there anything I need to know, or say, or do?" she asked.

"Not this time. This is a casual visit. If we proceed, then you will need to be introduced to the entire Council, and the other higher-level demons, like myself. An official presentation."

"Super."

The front door opened, and a tall female demon stood in the doorway. She had black hair, grey eyes and was wearing a short skirt, with a fitted black jacket. She also wore black heels. She was stunning. From the top of her silky hair to her red lips to the legs that went on forever. Anya tried really hard to not compare herself to this stunner. The stunner gave a Declan a very hot look which made Anya narrow her eyes, and said in a British accent, "Are you two coming, or are you going to stand out here all day?"

Oh, I do not like you, thought Anya.

"Yes Rosamund, we're coming." He leaned down to whisper to Anya. "Watch her, she is not to be trusted." He put a possessive hand on the small of Anya's back to spur her forward. Rosamund watched the gesture with flat eyes. Anya smiled broadly. *Oh, that's right girl...he's mine. Die mad about it.*

They stepped inside. The front hallway was much darker than outside with a dark marble floor and dark grey walls. It was a large space, but the dark walls made it feel smaller. Confined. Which she supposed was probably the point. To make people feel insignificant. It was a fairly typical tactic of the powerful.

"He's waiting for you in the main sitting room." Rosamund went to lead them when Declan spoke up. "I know where it is. Rosamund. I'll take us in."

Her lips turned into a flat line. "As you wish...Declan," she said his name in a soft, silky manner that would have had Anya going for a knife if she had one on her.

Declan caught the murderous look and put his hand on the back of Anya's neck and rubbed. "She is nothing to me. Nor has she ever been." He whispered as Rosamund left the room.

"Much to her displeasure. She's lucky I am not carrying any knives."

"You're not?"

"Of course not. That would just be rude."

He laughed. "You are a delight."

Anya had to stifle a gasp when they got to the room. It was sumptuous. But also...a lot. It was all Louis XIV furniture, with maybe some Louis XVI thrown in for good measure. She wasn't a particular expert, but it was very similar to how Natalia and Vladimir decorated their home in Russia. And this was all the real deal. Oh Christ, was this a demon thing? Was Declan's home full of this kind of thing? I mean, it was gorgeous, but it's not how she'd choose to decorate. It kind of made her itch. She made a mental note to ask him later. The chairs themselves were the most gorgeous chairs she'd ever seen. She couldn't sit in this room. She was out of place; she should leave now.

This wasn't money. This was power. This was history, this was way beyond her. It suddenly occurred to Anya that she was in way over her head. She hadn't actually considered her life beyond actually meeting her demon and how it might change, and what might be expected of her.

Her agitation must have shown because Declan leaned down and whispered to her again "You're fine. Relax. Breathe, *malysh*." The endearment had the desired effect of calming her down.

Standing by the window was an extraordinarily tall, thin man. He had the whitest hair she'd ever seen, and his skin was pale, almost translucent. The hair fell well past his shoulders and was held back in a long braid. His eyes were a light red. His face, somewhere between his human and demon form, cheeks sunken and a larger eyebrow ridge. His nose seemed fairly human, but the nostrils were enlarged. His mouth was purely human though and she had never seen a man with lips that red. Like all his blood was congregating there. His fingers were overly long, and he had talons, not unlike the ones she'd seen on Declan. He was the damnedest thing she'd ever seen. She could feel the power coming off of him in waves. He wasn't doing it on purpose, it just was. He was power. But he didn't frighten her. While she'd been looking at him, he'd been sizing her up. She met his eyes, waiting for him to speak first.

"Dr. Orlov, it is a pleasure to meet you finally."

She couldn't help it; she winced a little. His voice was too much for her human ears to deal with. It surrounded her and filled her at the same time, and it was an unpleasant sensation. "Anaranth, can you take the voice down?" said Declan. "She's not used to it yet."

"I apologize Dr. Orlov. I forget sometimes." His voice was still deep and rich, but bearable.

"You have nothing to apologize for, you are who you are. And please call me Anya."

He smiled at her then. It was a sincere smile, but his teeth were pointed, not at all human and she had to admit, they freaked her out some. "Thank you. Please sit."

He sat in a beautiful gold chair, that was covered in a lustrous red fabric. Anya and Declan sat on the matching sofa. "Refreshments?"

"Anaranth, you do not need to trouble yourself for us."

"It is no trouble and I think your Anya would benefit from a glass of wine."

Anya agreed there. "That would be nice, actually." Within twenty seconds, the door opened, and a small demon came in bearing a tray with wine and three glasses. He poured, handed out glasses and left, all without anyone saying a word. "What shall we drink to?" Anaranth thought. "Ah! Future days and young love." Anya choked on her wine a little.

"Stop teasing her."

Anaranth laughed then. "I am sorry. I don't get to meet new people very often. I have heard a lot about you from Natalia and from Declan, as of late. And so I was curious to meet you, see you for myself." Anaranth sat back, relaxed and the mood immediately changed. "I did want to see how you'd react to me. I am like this all the time, and it does put some of the newer demons off."

"Which I am sure you enjoy."

He laughed. "Yes, as a matter of fact, I do. This though, this is exciting. We've not had a new consort in so long."

"You still don't." Anya shot a look at Declan.

"Yes. Declan is being stubborn, but that is nothing new." He shot Declan a look filled with affection. And Anya immediately understood that Anaranth had been directly involved with Declan becoming demon-kind. She made another mental note to ask him about that at some point. Theirs was a long relationship, that much was obvious. He didn't think many demons spoke to Anaranth with such directness. "But trust me when I say that he is interested in you. And he's worried."

"Oh, for chrissakes," Declan breathed.

"Declan, no blaspheming." said Anaranth softly, but with no irony or humor.

This struck Anya funny, and she attempted to cover up her laugh with a cough. Anaranth was not fooled.

"I do understand the irony of what I just said. Anya. But our mythology is a religious one, even if that is not necessarily the reality. Some of us have chosen to not lose that mythology and to embrace it. And many of us were born into a time when religion ruled over science."

"Are you saying that God exists?"

He smiled at her. "I am very old; I am not sure I am quite old enough to verify the existence of God. That said, faith is real, at least for those that believe. And when it comes time for me to shuffle off my... immortal coil, I would like to think that there is a Heaven, and I may be welcomed there."

"So, you believe in God?"

"I believe in the possibility of God."

"In other words, you have faith."

"Yes, child. I have faith."

Anya found this fascinating. "But how can you believe in God? When religious dogma has said that your first demon, Lucifer, was cast out of heaven by Him? I know that this is only part of demon mythology, so, are you allowing that this may be your true beginning? That your entry into the world is more in line with Biblical teachings, than say how the Ancient Greeks view demons?"

Anaranth looked startled. "She has a master's degree in Comparative Religion," Declan said.

"Oh! I see we are going to have many wonderful conversations then. I will say that our view of what happened is not in line with the Bible's version. But I allow that there could be some truth to it all the same. That is me. Much of our earliest history is an oral one. But we believe that we were, that we are and that we are meant to be. Declan does not share my views on God. I believe you will find his leanings more with the Ancient Greeks."

She looked at Declan, who shrugged at her. "I don't think about it much honestly."

"But you also protect humankind, to a certain extent."

"Yes," said Anaranth. "We do what we can. I should say, we have done what we could. It has become much more difficult in the modern age. This is why Declan and those like him are important. The balance is now being able to manage demons, to make sure they have what they need so they do no harm to humans. And to protect humans from the worst of demon-kind, and the worst of themselves."

"So, to keep the worst of the darkness and violence at bay, contained."

"Something that has become harder and harder as the centuries pass.

"Agreed, but it surprises me to hear you admit it."

"Why does it surprise you?"

"In my experience, the very powerful and the very old tend to have tunnel vision."

"Do you mean arrogance?"

"That would be rude."

"But accurate?"

"I think with power and age comes a certain arrogance. I don't think that is a bad thing, in and of itself. So yes, it's likely accurate. I don't see arrogance as wholly negative. I mean, I can be pretty arrogant." Declan was enjoying himself immensely. He really loved this woman's brain. And he was delighted that she had forgotten how nervous she was and was basically calling Anaranth an arrogant old fart.

"As can Declan. He is one of the best of us though."

"Why?"

"Because he still cares."

That brought her up short. "Does he?"

"He does. Humans still matter to him. I think more than demons do."

Declan sighed. "My job is to protect humans and I take it seriously. Demons can take care of themselves for the most part. Humans do not really understand everything that waits in the darkness," answered Declan, causing Anya to shiver.

"Do you see?" asked Anaranth. "The best of us."

"How about the Council?"

"Some on the Council would deny that our purpose is changing, but I see more than they do. We need to take a more active role in protecting humans."

"There is only so much you can do, as humans have free will."

"Exactly so, Anya."

"But you can't harm humans. Or you aren't supposed to. So, your hands are tied? So, we are back to maintaining the balance then? That seems feeble."

"I would agree."

"There has to be a better way."

"Yes. And I believe that Declan will find it. Along with a consort who sees the bigger picture as well." The look on his face was gentle. "You, Anya. You are a completely worthy consort for my Declan."

"Is he your favorite?" Declan groaned at this. Anya always had more questions.

Anaranth roared with laughter that only hurt her ears a little. "He is actually. And well he knows it."

She smiled. "He's my favorite too. Though Matthew is beginning to run a close second." Declan gave her a baleful stare and she smiled at him.

"She's smart, Declan. You're lucky."

Declan rolled his eyes. "We haven't settled anything as of yet."

"You, my boy, are an idiot." Declan started to speak, but Anaranth put his hand up. "I know, I know. There is the worry about the attacks. And your letters, Anya."

"Do you know anything?"

"There are rumblings that there are those unhappy with how close Declan is to the Council and how his powers are growing. A consort helps those powers continue to grow, so there is animosity. It is also no secret that there are demons on the Council that I consider a liability. One of them is the Demon of Western Europe, Francois. He is old and he is complacent. Truthfully, it's more his consort, Liliana that is the problem. She is dangerous. She is a combination of canny and crazy and she's beginning to err more on the less sane side of things. Were I a wagering demon, I'd put even money on her. It's why I have brought Rosamund into my fold. For now."

Declan turned to Anya. "Rosamund and Liliana are related. Separated by a couple of hundred years but related."

"Just so," replied Anaranth. Anya really wanted to ask why France and Belgium seemed to be annexed to Declan but decided to let it go for now. She'd ask Declan another time. Anaranth continued. "As for your letters. I cannot say. I have a suspicion, but I can say no more. I am hoping that my feelings are incorrect. This would have far reaching consequences for our kind. I shall say no more."

Anya hated that answer, but she knew he wouldn't budge. "Thank you, then. Does Rosamund suspect though?"

"I do not think so. She is wily, but she has a great arrogance that doesn't let her see things for what they are." He smirked. "In her case, arrogance is not a good thing." Anya grinned at his comment.

They talked about far more mundane things for the next hour. Anya was convinced that Anaranth wouldn't be interested in the facts of her everyday life, but it seemed she was wrong. Or he was very good at pretending to be interested. She assumed he probably had to act interested when he wasn't a fair bit of the time. But the interest seemed genuine, and he kept asking her questions. He asked her about work mostly, staying away from her childhood. But did ask her about living in the States and about Gwen. At some point, his questions ceased, and he stood. Anya and Declan stood with him. "Anya, it was lovely to meet you, I look forward to your official presentation." He looked pointedly at Declan, who looked away. "I would like to speak to Declan privately for a few moments. If you would not mind?" It was phrased as a question, but it wasn't truly one.

"Of course." Anya put out her hand. "It was an honor to meet you."

He took her hand in both of his and said, "The honor was mine, young one."

She smiled and turned to Declan. "I'll be right outside."

"Don't hurt Rosamund."

"I make no promises," she said letting herself out of the room, as both demons laughed.

When she was gone, the two men sat and Anaranth spoke. "That woman is special."

"I know."

"No. She has great power. I can feel it. I don't know how, or why, yet. But it's there. Not only will she help you grow into your power, but you will also help her grow into hers. I didn't want to say anything while she was in the room, but this could be exactly why these attacks are occurring."

"I never wanted this power."

"Nevertheless, you have it. You always have. It's part of the reason we met. I had been watching you for years." Declan looked startled. "I could sense your power as well as the fact that you were demon born. You cannot deny what is to come."

"I…I have grown attached to her in a very short time. I find it discomfiting."

"You're scared."

"Yes," Declan admitted. "I am."

"So is she. And I don't think she fully understands what will be expected of her. You will need to explain it. But she's brave, and her heart is true. Once she loves, there is no going back. She is formidable. She and Graziela will get on." Anaranth still referred to his own consort by her given name, and not the more modern one she preferred now, Grace. But come, I have other business to discuss with you."

***

Outside the room, Rosamund oozed from the shadows. "Ms. Orlov, I trust your visit went well."

"It's Dr. Orlov, and yes. It did." Rosamund was much taller than Anya, but she wasn't put off by that. Height meant very little to her in the scheme of things. She knew how to size up an enemy appropriately. And Rosamund was most certainly an enemy.

There was silence for a moment. And then Rosamund overplayed her hand. "You are in over your head. You should leave. Leave him for those that understand him and our own kind!" Anaranth was right, her arrogance was a problem.

Anya raised an eyebrow. "I'm sorry? What are you babbling about?" Her voice was steady.

Rosamund's eyes widened, aware that somehow, she was being mocked. Anya never did like bullies. "I am talking about Declan. What could he possibly see in you? A human! And a fat, middle aged one at that!" She was warming up to her topic now. Anya adopted a bored expression. "He needs someone who can be a true partner to him. Not you!" she sneered. "You have no understanding of our ways. What it means to be a demon. You can never be his equal!"

Anya's fingers twitched. Good Lord, she wanted her knives. One right though the eyeball would silence this bitch. "Look, you jumped up little receptionist, I know you want Declan. I can see it. Jesus, I can practically smell it; and if he wanted you, you'd already be in his bed. But thanks to me, you never will be. As for fat, you can go fuck yourself. Just because I don't eat lettuce and misery, it doesn't mean you get to stand there, and fat shame me. As for middle aged, that's hysterical coming from someone who probably has centuries on me. No one will ever take me for a petulant child, like you. You will never be more than someone's errand girl. Sure, you serve Anaranth now, but how long do you think that will last? I'd watch it. He's very fond of Declan, which means I'll also have his ear." Rosamund was turning red with anger. "Now, do me a very large favor and fuck off before I decide to blind you with my stiletto heel."

Rosamund hissed and moved forward when a voice came from the direction of the study. "Rosamund, I would think very long and very hard before you threaten my consort. If you so much as take one step closer, I will tear you apart with my bare hands. And that would be a mercy. I could let Anya have you."

Anya was standing in a fighting stance, waiting. Ready, but loose. Rosamund paled, turned on her heel and left. "Stand down, soldier," Declan said.

Anya visibly relaxed. "Too much?" she asked him.

"Just enough."

"How much did you hear?"

"Enough."

"On a scale of one to ten, how big of a mess did I just make?"

"One, less than one. Liliana will be pissed, but she can't do much. And even she is aware that Rosamund has more mouth than sense."

"Ok, good." She let out a breath.

"Are you ready to go?"

"Absolutely!

When they got into the car, Declan hauled her onto his lap and kissed her. "What was that for?" she asked when they broke apart.

"Honestly? I found the whole exchange with Rosamund kind of arousing. You didn't back down at all. You're a hot shit."

She blushed. "Oh! Oh, ok. I'll make sure you're always around when I give people shit." She climbed off of his lap and began to chew her lip.

"Relax, Anya. He liked you. Very much."

"So, he didn't tell you to dump me at the nearest airport when I left the room?"

"No! He likes smart people and people who aren't afraid of a little friendly debate. I mean, don't get me wrong. You'll know when he orders you to do something, and you do not want to see him angry. But you were fine."

"I think it's because he cares about you. As much as he can."

"He cares about my power and how it can help him."

"That isn't fair to you. Or to him. I mean, all of that is true. But he does hold quite a bit of affection for you. And don't roll your eyes at me, buddy."

"Ok, ok. I give in."

She smiled at him. "No, but you will."

"Wench!" Then he kissed her soundly, getting the last word in for once.

CHAPTER 8

It had been a long day, so they opted to have dinner in the suite. Anya went off to change and take a shower, while Declan ordered dinner. He had no clue what she liked food wise, so he ordered up way more food and wine than was strictly necessary for two people, but so be it. He called to her when it was delivered, and her eyes widened. "Declan! It's just the two of us!"

"I wasn't sure what you liked."

"So, you ordered everything on the room service menu?"

"Not quite everything. But, close. I did order *Moules-Frites,* not sure how you feel about mussels?"

"Love them! Honestly, look at me...I am a woman who likes to eat."

"You are perfect." She blushed as he poured her some wine and then heaped a plate of food for her and put it on the table that was set up by the window. "Come eat. It's been a long day."

She sat down and tucked in. Well, he was never going to be like her college boyfriend who once told her she was getting kind of chubby. Things didn't go well for him after that. "This all looks amazing. Thank you! For the food, and for making me a plate. No man has ever done that for me."

He sat down with his own plate. "Most welcome. Sometimes it's nice when someone takes care of you, huh?"

"Oh, you've got my number. Ok, fine...yes, it is nice." She ate for a few minutes, savoring each bite and Declan found himself completely charmed by her all over again. No, he was smitten, completely smitten.

She looked at him. "What? Do I have food on my face?"

He laughed. "No. I just like watching you enjoy yourself."

She raised an eyebrow at him. "No one has ever told me they like watching me eat."

"You savor each mouthful, it's actually really sexy."

"Oh, foreplay then?" He laughed. She put her fork down. "Ok, I have some questions."

"I thought you might. But you keep eating while I answer." She rolled her eyes but nodded. He was hesitant to reveal what Anaranth had told him today about her power. He knew he should, but she'd already been through so much in the past several days, that he was loath to add to it. He decided he would keep that to himself for now. If they never mated, it wouldn't come to fruition. He didn't want to worry her, at least not tonight.

"Where do you live? Do you live above the club? Is it all gilt and Louis XIV?"

Not what he had expected. "I have rooms above the club where I stay sometimes, but I have a house in Paris. On the Ile St. Louis. There are a couple of formal rooms that are a bit gilt, but in general, no. It's contemporary."

She nodded. "Ok, that's good to know. All that gilt kind of freaks me out."

"Me too, actually. Those particular rooms are formal ones, for receiving Council members or older demons. They seem to enjoy it quite a bit."

"Can I see your place?"

"Absolutely. I will bring you over and wine and dine you when we get back to Paris."

"Great! So Anaranth says you do not believe as he does. Do you really not believe in God?"

"Does it matter to you?"

"No. I am honestly just curious."

"I don't. Anaranth is very old, and I think he feels his time may be waning, so he's getting sentimental. I stopped believing in God when I was still mortal, and that hasn't changed."

"Why did you stop believing?"

"It has to do with Anaranth, and why I became a demon. Let's hold on that if we can? Just for now."

She looked at him. He looked so sad, suddenly that she felt it inside of her.

"Of course, we can," she said softly.

He smiled at her. "Do you believe in God?"

"I... I don't know. I don't think so. I've studied religion, but honestly? I've never really thought about what I believe. If demons are immortal, how can Anaranth's time be...as you say...waning?"

"At a certain point in their immortality, demons can choose to either end their lives, or simply become non-corporeal. He hasn't done so because of Grace. She's not as old as he is and he wants to make sure she's satisfied with her life span."

"Explain, please." She commanded.

"Well, you know when you become the consort, you become immortal, yes?"

"Yes. Natalia told me that."

"Well, your life span, once that happens is only as long as your demon mate's lifespan. So, if Anaranth chooses to cease to exist, so does Grace, at least that is what we believe. But you need to be ancient, like Anaranth, to choose this. I couldn't, nor could Matthew. Therese, another of my core team, may be able to. But I am not sure even she is old enough for that. While we can't die like mortals, there are things worse than death. Though there are myths about weapons that can kill us. So, if something were to happen to me, and we were bonded, then you would likely die." He looked at her warily. He wasn't sure how she'd take that.

"Even if I haven't lived out my natural lifespan."

"I think so. But I cannot say for sure. It has never happened."

"Never?" she scoffed.

"Oddly, no. Demons, in general, are very careful. And not all of us can or do mate. But you see, while demons can, and do, marry, the process is different for what's known as a... I hate this term...highborn. Only powerful demons can mate. This means they are on the Council or serve the Council; those demons are considered aristocracy. I find it, honestly, kind of obscene."

"Is this why you don't want to mate?"

"It's partly why. I just think it's unfair and archaic. Donovan or Matthew could technically marry, but not mate. And this demon aristocracy feels very arbitrary to me. In my head, my people would be included there, if I were to sit on the Council. That is not how it is, and no one can really tell me why?"

She narrowed her eyes at him. "You're trying to find the reason so you can change it."

"Maybe. That said, Donovan could marry Gwen, but not mate with her in this current system. She would die like any mortal," he said this gently. It was important to him that she understand, but he didn't want to be cruel.

Anya blinked back tears at the thought of Gwen dying, ever, and Declan took her hand in comfort. "Could...could you change that? For her?"

"She's not meant to be a demon, Annie. I am not sure I could do anything," he said softly. "But this is something you will need to think about seriously. Because you will outlive her."

Anya looked down at her plate, tears swimming in her eyes. She knew that, logically. But she had held all the emotions that went along with it, at bay. "I knew that, really. But this is the first time that I have felt it. It hurts."

"Yes, yes it really does."

She looked up. "I'm sorry. You've also been through this. I am acting like it's never happened to anyone else."

"I have had eight hundred years to make my peace with it. It is new to you; your feelings are very valid."

"Have you really made peace with it?"

"Some days, I think I have. Others...not so much." If she chose to not bond with him, he knew he would mourn her when she passed. And it would hurt. A lot.

She smiled at him. "Thank you for your honesty." She sniffled and took a sip of wine. "So, you live while humans fade away, with time. Do you have human friends?"

"I have humans on my payroll and there are humans with whom I am friendly, but I do not have a human friend. I like humans, though there are demons that don't. It's just easier with other demons."

"Do they know what you are?"

"The ones on my payroll do. The others don't. I admit I keep them at arm's length. For their safety and mine. At some point, I may need to disappear on them."

"But you don't age?"

"Ah, we all employ a bit of glamour for that. They think I do. You will never have to pretend with Gwen, and that is a good thing."

"I am definitely feeling the repercussions of this now. I've been horribly naive about this. I thought because I had Natalia and read about demons, I knew what I was doing. It turns out that what I don't know is a lot."

He got up and went over to her, kneeling next to her chair. "This is hard. There are a number of reasons why there hasn't been a consort in several hundred years. It's difficult to leave friends and family. It can be a brutal life, but you're asking questions and that's good. And I will tell you everything and anything I know. You may well change your mind and I will never hold that against you. Ever."

"Would we stay friends?"

"I don't know. It would be nice to have one I don't have to pretend with. But you and I have a real tug to each other and that would cause issues. I am not sure I could ever stand to see you with another man."

"Oh. Well, that makes sense. I am also not sure I could stand to see you with someone else. Can that go away? That tug?"

He took a breath. "It can. No one has told you that, have they? Why would they? Us bonding benefits a lot of people. Including Natalia and Vlad. One of us would have to officially repudiate the other. That tug we feel would be gone."

She rubbed her hand over her heart. "I'd hate that." She already felt him in a way she'd never felt anyone else. It was odd, but nice. Like having someone with her all the time.

"It would be the only way. Or else we wouldn't be able to help ourselves."

"Has that ever happened?"

"Yes. Ergo, no consorts in recent history. This life isn't for everyone."

She put her hand on his cheek and he closed his eyes, enjoying how it felt, the heat of her hand there. "I don't want that. I know you are still undecided. So if it's going to be done, you'd have to do it. But I don't think I would ever forgive you for repudiating me."

He opened his eyes, looking into hers. She looked so sad at the thought. "I am not planning on repudiating you right now. And it is not something I would do without discussing it with you first. But Anya, if the only way to keep you out of danger is to do it, I will not hesitate. Even if you hate me."

"No. Promise me you will give us time to figure out who's behind this? Promise?!"

He put his hand against the one laying on his cheek, knowing he'd promise her anything she asked of him right now. "I promise, *malysh*." He hoped he would not have to go back on his word.

"Ok, I believe you." She gave him a brilliant smile and turned back to her food. Declan was left with the feeling that she'd made some kind of a decision, but he was too much of a coward to ask her about it just then. For now, he'd let it go.

***

Anya yawned loudly and Declan grinned at her. "You've had a long day."

"I have. I think I am off to bed now. Are you staying up?"

"I have a couple of calls to make, and then bed."

"Do demons sleep?"

"We can. We do. We don't need as much sleep as humans, but it helps to rest. Just like food helps us as well. And I enjoy doing both."

"Good to know." She stood and then leaned down to kiss him goodnight. "Sleep well."

"You too." He watched her walk down the hall and then turned towards the balcony to watch the streets below while he made his phone calls.

An hour later, he decided it was enough and headed towards his room. He stopped in front of Anya's room and cracked the door a bit. He just wanted to make sure she was resting easily. The room was empty, and her bag was nowhere in sight. "What the fuck! Where could she…." he backed out of her room and looked towards his own room. He walked to it, opening the door and came up short. The lights were off, demons had good night vision, he could see her in bed. She was curled up on one side with her hand under her head, fast asleep. Her breathing told him she was deep into REM. He wasn't sure what he had expected to find, but her sleeping comfortably in his bed wasn't it. He wasn't sure why this was more discomfiting than finding her in his bed naked and waiting would have been, but it was. He padded softly into the room and sat down in a chair, staring into space.

Ah! This was a level of trust and intimacy that went beyond sex. She had never planned on sleeping in the other room at all he realized. She'd always planned on coming in here, which is why she'd been noncommittal about the room in general. He could not remember the last time he had actually slept next to a woman. It had been at least a couple of centuries, probably more like four of them. He liked sex, but either he left, or the woman…always a demon…did. He found he was looking forward to sleeping next to Anya. He took his shoes and socks off and then stood to take off the rest of his clothes. He couldn't sleep naked like he usually would though. He pulled out a pair of pajama pants and a t-shirt and pulled back the covers on the other side of the bed. He laid down and pulled the covers up, sighing blissfully. Eight hundred years old and an exceptional bed was still a delight.

He flipped over to his side and very gently, so he wouldn't wake her, pulled Anya over to him so that they lay like spoons. He put his arm under her head and in her sleep, she dropped a kiss on his forearm. He rubbed his face in her hair and inhaled deeply. Here in the dark, he could stop lying to himself. From the minute he'd seen her, he'd been a marked man. He couldn't fight it, nor did he want to anymore. While he'd been trying to resist it, it had already been happening. When she walked into the hotel suite today and straight into his arms, he'd felt it. She had settled inside of him when she had settled her head on his chest. It had been the most natural thing in the world, her in his arms, holding her like letting go was unthinkable. And in truth, it was.

It had been mere days since they had met but they were a part of each other now. Trust, yearning, desire, and home. All there and all in one person. He had said he would keep her close, keep her safe, while they figured out who was out to harm them, but he just wanted her with him. How she smelled, how she felt, how she smiled at him and joked with him, it was inside of him now. He dropped a light kiss on her shoulder, feather soft. He wasn't sure if he could even give her the option of backing out now. No, he would never hold her, but it would break something in him if she decided to leave. Finding her sleeping in his bedroom had stripped away the last wall he had built around himself. Such a simple act, but one with so much meaning. In the end, he'd been undone by it. She stirred and turned around in his arms, her luminous violet eyes open, truly seeing him. "Stop thinking so hard. You woke me." She reached up and stroked his cheek, while her other hand settled on his chest. "I am not going anywhere. My decision was made when I boarded the plane to Brussels. I don't give a flying fuck what you show me or tell me. Because in the end, it's not going to change the fact that I am here to stay."

"How did you know what I was thinking?"

"I told you, I heard you while I was sleeping." She thought for a moment. "I suppose it's better to say that I felt you and felt what you were thinking."

"Really?"

"Hmmm. I have felt connected to you since I walked into the suite this afternoon.

"Same." He kissed the top of her head, awed. "We've begun the bonding process."

The hand that had been on his cheek, wrapped around his waist and she snuggled closer. "Jesus, you're nice and warm. Hmm, that does seem to be it."

"It's a process, you could still change your mind." He searched her face. "You are sure?"

She huffed in annoyance. "Yes. I am," she said with a finality he wasn't going to argue with. "Additionally, don't you ever make me sleep in another room, away from you again. Are we clear?"

He dropped a kiss on her nose this time. "Crystal clear."

"Good. Now get some sleep, *lyubov moya.*"

"What does that mean?"

"It means 'my love'. Go to sleep." With that, she closed her eyes and drifted off again. With the endearment in his heart, he fell into a deep, dreamless sleep.

***

About an hour before dawn, Declan woke up, his heart beating a mile a minute. He was on his back and had taken his shirt off during the night. Demons tended to run hot, which was partly why he slept naked. Anya was lying on his chest, her hair spread across him like a waterfall. Christ, his heart was hammering. He started to rub her back gently, something he realized he did for his own comfort, as well as hers. She wiggled a bit and then let out a raspy "Good morning."

"Good morning, Anya." It occurred to him that it wasn't only his heart beating fast, he could feel her heart as well, her blood inside of him.

She sat up and looked at him and his blood began to thrum. She smiled a little and said "My heart is beating so fast all of a sudden. And it's like I can feel your heart and your blood inside of me. It's weird, but really nice."

"Same here." He hauled her on top of him and kissed her, one hand on the small of her back, one fisted in her hair. Her hands were kneading his shoulders. He answered her low moan with his own growl. "Anya…."

"I can't explain it. It's like your blood is calling to my blood now."

"That is exactly what it is. It's part of the mating process."

"What are we supposed to do?" He raised an eyebrow and she barked out a laugh. "So, our blood wants us to have sex?"

"It does indeed." He sounded amused.

She raised herself up some, but Declan's hand would only let her get so far. "Does everyone go through this?"

"Something like it from what I've heard. But…" he stopped.

"What?"

"Well, Anaranth told me that consorts who form a blood bond are different. That kind of bond shows a true affection. Not all mates have a blood bond, but it seems we will. We will always feel each other through our blood. When you could hear me thinking last night, I should have figured it out."

"Affection?" She seemed a bit skeptical.

He sighed. "Love. Anaranth actually used the word 'love' when he described it. But I thought he was being sentimental again."

She grinned. "I was thinking maybe lust or desire, but I'll take affection. Or love." She nipped his jaw. "So, a blood bond is rare?"

"Rarer than you'd think really. There can be true affection between demon and consort, but it doesn't always translate to a love bond. I can only think of Anaranth and Graziela. Grace. She prefers Grace now. He also said we should hide it in the beginning. He must have suspected."

"Do you think we should? Hide it?"

"No, I do not think we should hide it."

"Good! Me neither." He started to laugh. "What's so funny?"

"Years ago, I thought to myself that if I were ever to have a consort, I'd want one like Grace. She is very formidable when she wants to be. And here you are!" He kissed her soundly and grinned at her.

She felt all kinds of warm and fuzzy from that. "That's sweet. You old softie."

"Soft, huh?" He shifted some, so she could feel how very not soft he was currently.

"Ok, not so soft then." He laughed at her comment.

"We obviously do feel something deep for each other, even if we don't want to call it love yet, or even if we do. That said, I am not going to hide what I feel for you, ever. I think for us, in the end, it will make us a stronger team."

She put her head on his chest to see if she could feel the blood call more. She could. "You have some very modern ideas for a very old demon. Considering I've had to scold you about the patriarchy."

"Well, in this, yes. I do admit to fighting my more archaic instincts where you're concerned. I won't always succeed there."

"Bodyguards."

"Yes. We will always fight about that because I will likely always do it. It's not about me not having faith in you, but I am what I am."

"As am I."

"Which is always why it's going to be a sore point. You will also chafe at some of the etiquette and rules in regard to the Council. We'll deal with those as they come up."

"Ok, I will polish up my speech on free will then."

"I look forward to it, *cushla machree*."

"And what does *that* mean?"

"Vein of my heart."

"Oh!" She blinked rapidly, to keep the tears at bay. "That's lovely." So stupid, she thought, to be emotional over that.

"And in our case, accurate."

"Agreed." She started stroking his chest, following the thrum of his blood, her own answering in kind. She started to rain kisses on his chest, her blood heating up and she could feel that his was as well.

"Anya?"

"Sssshh" she said. She lifted herself up into a sitting position and pulled her t-shirt off. His hands came up and he palmed both of her breasts, causing her to gasp at the contact. He stroked her nipples lazily. "Declan, question…"

"I can't get you pregnant, nor can I give you any disease, but I do have condoms if you'd feel better about it."

"So, that part of the bond goes both ways, you can tell what I'm thinking too." She hissed as he flicked one nipple, then the other, with his fingers. "Jesus, it's like I'm made of nerve endings. And no, I don't need a condom in that case." He sat up, shifting her some and replaced his hand with his mouth on her breasts. "Talons." She breathed.

"Really?"

"Yes. I like how they feel. Don't look so smug, you bastard."

He laughed and let the talons on one hand come to play. "I cannot get enough of your breasts."

"You really like curvy women?"

"I do." He nipped lightly at her breasts, causing her to yelp. "Mmmm, yes. I have a distinct preference for curvy women. One day, I will tell you about some of the artists I've known."

"Holy shit! Famous artists?"

"Yes, but I am too busy with your breasts to discuss this just now." He tongued her right breast while his left played with her other nipple, using a talon to trace a circle that sent shivers through her

"You really are very sensitive here." She arched her back as he continued to alternatively nip and then lick her nipples. He ran the point of his talon down the other nipple, and she gasped. She was sitting right on his erection and wiggled some. He used the hand without the talons to pinch her bottom through her sleep shorts and moved her a bit. "Aw, you're no fun."

"I will be even less fun if your wiggling makes me come before I'm ready."

"True" She put her arms around his neck and pulled his head down further, so it was nestled between her breasts. She could feel him, more than hear him, growl. She laughed and he came up for air. "Were I to die, that is how I'd wish to go." He rolled her off of him and stood.

"Hey!"

"Don't worry, I am merely taking off my pajama bottoms."

Her eyes lit up. "Oh! Huzzah!" She sat up to watch him and her eyes widened when she saw him naked. His erection was a wondrous thing. She had been right; he was incredibly well endowed. Before he could say or do anything, she'd bounded off the bed and was on her knees in front of him. She took the length of him into her mouth and began to suck and lick alternatively. "Anya, don't. Jesus!" He made a strangled sound.

She pulled back. "Just a little taste for now. I can't help myself." She licked the tip of his cock slowly, winding her tongue around the head. "You just taste good."

"I will get you back for this." His hand fisted in her hair, as he pushed her head a bit to take more of him. She took him down to the root. He almost exploded. "Holy shit, woman! You really do not have a gag reflex. I am going to come if you don't stop that." She pulled back and laughed. She stood and worked her sleep shorts down and off, then pressed herself to him. "You feel so good," she said. "I want you inside me. I need you inside me. Very soon." She stroked his chest.

He picked her up and put her on her back on the bed. He joined her there, but on his side, facing her. His head resting on his hand. He took the other hand and stroked the length of her torso, stopping just short of the curls at the juncture to her sex. Feather light strokes back and forth and she was sighing in bliss. She turned her head and pulled him down into a searing kiss. Her tongue, demanding and his answering the call. His hand went further and found her nub. He stroked her slowly.

"Declan!"

"Ah...patience, beauty. We have all the time in the world this morning." He pulled away and started kissing down her torso, all the places he had just stroked, one his hands still stroking her. "You are so wet. It's going to feel so good when I'm inside you. Is that what you want, *malysh*?"

"God, yes! Please!" He laughed. He moved down her body, kissing her legs and back up again. He spread her legs and where his hand had been before, his mouth was now. She yelled and started swearing at him in Russian. This delighted him so much that he began to suck her in earnest, his hands under her, kneading and bringing her closer to his mouth. His tongue flicked out, giving her a long, insistent lick and she came, yelling his name.

She lay there, panting and willing her heart to calm down. "What did you call me in Russian?" he asked, casually. Raising himself so they were eye to eye, but he still lay between her legs.

"I honestly have no idea at this point." she breathed. "Wow!"

He kissed her deeply. "We're not done here."

She looked at him innocently. "No?"

"Oh, my dear. No. There is no stopping now."

"What could possibly come after that amazing orgasm?" She grinned.

"I am going to make love to you. No, that is not accurate this time. I am going to fuck you, until you scream my name again." He grinned at her wickedly, and her heart lurched.

"Mmmm." She rubbed her cheek against his, reaching down with a hand and squeezing him.

He laughed and began to kiss her, even as she lifted her hips. He broke the kiss, grabbed her legs, hovering above her, just taking her in for a moment and then in one movement, he was inside her. "Fuck!" he yelled. "You feel perfect. You feel...right."

"We feel right." She wiggled some.

"Yes, yes. I know. I am just enjoying how you feel for a moment." He began to move slowly at first, setting a rhythm that she met stroke for stroke. Her hands went from his shoulders to his back, her nails raking down his back as she tried to make him go faster, harder. He eventually complied, pumping harder and faster as he took her mouth in a kiss.

"How does that feel?" he asked.

"You feel so good. God, you're really good at this!"

He laughed and went harder. He could feel she was close. "I want you to come sweetheart, I want to feel it while I'm inside you." He raised himself and her, grabbing her ass, pounding into her even harder. He looked so beautiful above her and she came looking right into his eyes, her eyes glowing gold. He came a moment later looking into hers, his having turned a deep red.

***

He rolled off of her but took her with him, so she was laying on top of him. Heart to heart. "Holy fucking shit!" she said.

"You're not kidding. I am not sure I have ever, in my life orgasmed that hard. And I'm old."

She dropped a kiss on his shoulder and smiled. "I'm glad it was me then. So, is it just that we have good sex, or is it the blood bond, making it stronger?"

"I am going to say maybe a bit of both. The chemistry is undeniable, but the blood bond makes it more intense."

"Good to know. Just to repeat, you are really good at that. It's nice to know that you know exactly what to do with that giant penis of yours."

He grinned and let out a short laugh. "I am glad it pleases you."

"Oh, it does. It really does. Your eyes went red when you came."

"Yours went gold."

"What?! Really? Gold? Is that…does that happen?"

"I have no idea. I feel like it means something. There's something niggling at the back of my brain. Something that's important. It's not bad," he said quickly, seeing her look. "It's just something I know that I should be remembering. Something about gold eyes."

"How did it look?"

"Honestly? Pretty cool. They glowed gold and then slowly faded back to that gorgeous violet of yours. How do you even have violet eyes?"

"No idea. No one in my family does. My mother thought I was a freak of nature."

"Your mother is obviously an idiot." She stroked his cheek at the comment.

"I liked the red. Do you have…I mean…I've read that demons have…"

"Other forms? More traditional demon forms. Yes, I do. I can control that pretty well. But with you, I lose a lot of control. It concerns me."

"Why?"

"If you see me that way, or I turn while we're having sex, you may get frightened, or I may get violent. I am not always in control in that form. I tend to not turn to it ever."

She looked at him. "I won't ever be frightened of you."

"You don't know that."

"Is that what made you hold back?"

"I shouldn't be surprised that you could feel that, but I am. And yes."

"Am I going to have another form?"

"No. You will stay in human form. Though you may get some powers, and of course, you'll be immortal."

He looked worried and a bit scared and she didn't like that. She kissed him softly. "There is time for all of this. For now, let's just try to enjoy it. Get to know each other, even if we've done this whole thing ass backwards. We'll fully bond when we're meant to. I am not worried. Ok?"

He looked relieved. "Ok."

They lay for a bit and then Declan sighed. "I don't want to get up, but I suppose we should. Sun is up now."

"Do we really need to? What do you have to do today?"

"I thought we'd play tourist today."

She raised her head, looking delighted. "Really?"

"Really. I think it's fair to take a day for ourselves."

"Yay! Ok, shower, breakfast, tourist stuff!"

"Shower, huh? What a wonderful idea." He raised himself to a sitting position, adjusting her so she was straddling him. They shared a kiss and he stood, holding her up while she wrapped her legs around him.

"We should definitely take a shower."

"You are really strong. No one can lift me."

"Pssh. You weigh nothing."

"Not to you maybe."

"Anyone who has not worshipped you for the goddess you are is a complete waste of DNA."

She cuddled into him. "You are going to spoil me. You are supposed to be a terrible, awful, demon."

"Oh, I am that. Not to worry."

"Ok, good. Because I don't want a wussy demon. It would be bad for my reputation."

"Well, you're going to pay for that in the shower." He walked them into the bathroom, turning on the water with one hand while he held her with the other. He then dunked her under the cold water. She yelled. "You complete bastard!"

He had to put her down as he was laughing too hard to hold onto her. She looked completely pissed off and gorgeous. She fixed the water temp and turned to him. "We are so NOT having shower sex now!" Hands on her hips, glaring at him.

"Oh yes, we are totally having shower sex." He stalked menacingly towards her, and she squealed and backed herself up against the shower wall. He placed an arm on either side of her head and kissed her neck, then nipped her ear lobe and reached for a breast. "I am pretty sure I can change your mind."

"I am an immovable object. I will not...oooh...what are you doing there?" She breathed out and started stroking his back. "Your hands are...wait, we are not having shower sex."

"Mmmm, let me warm you up, after that cold water." He turned her around to face the wall and started kissing her shoulder blades, her back...working his way down until he reached her bottom, he cupped it and squeezed. "Hands on the wall, Anya." She complied. His hand reached through her legs and up to her sex while he dropped kisses on that delicious posterior, one hand kneading soft flesh. He dropped kisses between her thighs while she groaned, loudly now. "Declan, Declan, please?"

"Please what, consort?"

"Please can we have shower sex?!"

"I thought you'd never ask." He stood up, pulled the bottom half of her back some and she automatically changed her stance, so her legs were a bit further apart. He massaged her breasts briefly while he nipped her neck. Her hands were lying flat on the wall of the shower, and he then put his hands over hers, their fingers intertwined. She wiggled her bottom against his erection, and he growled at her. "Behave yourself."

"Then, stop messing around and fuck me," she said.

"Your wish is my command," he said as he drove into her from behind, sending them both over the edge again.

CHAPTER 9

After an extended shower, Declan and Anya made their way out to the suite's living room. Lucien and breakfast were waiting. "Good morning, Lucien. How long have you been here?" Declan asked.

"Long enough," answered Lucien drily.

Anya laughed and said, "We won't apologize."

"Nor would I want you to."

Anya sat down, pouring herself and Declan coffee. Lucien had some already. She also began to uncover the plethora of dishes laid out. "God! I am famished!"

"I can't imagine why," Declan said wryly.

She stuck her tongue out at him and fixed him a plate of food, as he'd done for her last night. She fixed her own, then poured them coffee. Lucien didn't seem to need a refill.

"Thank you, love."

"My pleasure."

Lucien cleared his throat in what was becoming a bit of a habit with them. "I know you two are having a vacation day, but I have a few things before you go, if that suits."

Declan looked at Anya who replied. "Fine with me. I am just going to eat and text Gwen."

While the two worked, Anya texted Gwen. *Morning gorgeous. Guess what I did last night? Well, this morning really.*

Please say it was sex. If it wasn't, we can't be friends anymore.

Got it in one!

YES!! Gwen included high five emojis, heart emojis and finally eggplant emojis, causing Anya to bark out a small laugh. *It's about goddamn time. It also means I won the bet.*

What bet?

The one I had with Donovan. I said it would happen on this trip. He said it would not.

Good lord! What did you bet?

Winner takes the loser out to dinner.

Wait a minute? Is this just a way to get a date with him?

See? If I lose, I still win. It is a brilliant plan.

Anya couldn't argue with that. *It is. Have fun. We're playing tourist today. Be good.*

You're not the boss of me. Love you.

Love you too.

Anya waited until Lucien left before she told Declan about the bet. "Gwen and Donovan had a bet about when we'd have sex. Did you know?"

Declan set his coffee cup down with a clatter. "Are you kidding?"

"I am not."

"Who won?"

"Gwen. She said it would happen here."

"Wait? You told Gwen we had sex?"

"Of course, I did. She's my best friend. It's not like I gave her details." Ah shit, she'd need to rethink what she told him in the future.

He gave her a baleful look and asked, "Is she going to know everything?"

"Not everything. I promise. I was happy about it."

He smiled. "Well, I can't be mad now, so I am going to let it go."

***

At lunch, Declan knew he needed to bring something up, so he ordered a nice bottle of wine in the hopes she'd get a bit buzzed while they talked. "So, I need to tell you something."

She eyed him, twirling the stem of her wineglass around. "You're married" His eyes got wide. "Oh my God! Are you married?" She looked horrified.

"I was. Not now though."

She breathed out. "Well, when then?"

"Thirteenth century Ireland."

"Excuse me? Did you just say Thirteenth century Ireland?"

"I did."

Anya started to laugh. "I am sorry. It's not funny, I know. But that was eight hundred odd years ago. It was when you were mortal?" He nodded. "I assumed you had a life, darling."

"Well, I am telling my consort about my wife. It's weird. That was the only other woman I chose to share my life with. In all of this time, I've had lovers, but no one I ever wanted to be with permanently."

Her gaze was soft. "Then I must be in good company. Were you a father?"

"I was. A little girl and boy."

"Oh, that is lovely. Are they part of how you came to be what you are?"

"They are."

"Will you tell me now?"

He looked around. "Yes, I will." And for the next hour, he did just that.

****

When Declan looked over at Anya, she was crying. She had tears running down her face, and she didn't care who saw them. "You made a deal to save your family, so they would be happy and healthy." It wasn't a question.

"I did."

"And were they? And don't try to pretend you don't know. I know you checked in on them."

He smiled. "They were. And so were their children. And their children's children. And when I could offer help, I did. As the years wore on, they knew me for a stranger, so it made it easy." He took out a handkerchief and slowly wiped away her tears. "Don't cry, *cushla machree*. Don't cry."

"I am so mad at Anaranth right now. He could have just saved your wife and daughter."

"That is not how it works, Anya. You know this."

"Oh, bullshit! He could have done it." She knew she was being ridiculous, but she didn't care.

"I used to wonder about this myself. But it does no good. In the end, it would not have mattered; turns out I was demon born. And Anya, if he hadn't done what he did, we wouldn't be here now. I wouldn't be with you." He poured her some more wine. She was much more tender hearted than she let on, and he was honored she had let him see that part of her.

"True." She took a large sip of her wine and tried to calm down.

"Forty-five was a good age for the thirteenth century. I'd lived a full life by that point. I had hoped to live as long as my father, but it was not to be."

"But your wife…"

"Anya, I loved my wife. But I would not have missed you for all the world."

She looked at him. "Truly?" She looked impossibly young to him all of a sudden.

"Truly."

"Declan?"

"Yes?"

"Can we go back to the hotel now, please?"

He caught the waiter's eye. "Check please!"

***

They barely made it into the suite before Anya was pulling at Declan's clothes. She pushed his jacket off of his shoulders and ripped open his shirt, popping every button. "Sorry!' she said.

"Don't be!" he growled at her.

She began kissing his chest, his hands fisted in her hair. She nipped one of his lips, then the other, causing him to gasp. He pulled her up, pushed her against the door and pulled her sweater over her head, and once again, using a claw to rid her of her bra. "Declan!"

"I will happily replace every bra I ruin. I am going to ruin a lot of them." He palmed her breast and kissed her, his tongue sweeping into her mouth. He plundered. It was the only way she could describe it. Kissing him was like a drug. His hands left her breasts and pulled her skirt up to her waist. He slid his hands into her panties and plunged two fingers inside her, causing her to scream his name. "God, are you always ready for me?"

"Pretty much."

"I like it." He smiled at her.

"Me too."

He laughed, used a claw to slice the side of her panties open, even though she could have removed them easily and said "Yes, I plan on ruining those too."

"Maybe I should just stop wearing them."

"Fine by me."

She reached down, unbuckled his belt, undid his pants, and slid them and his underwear down. She stroked him slowly, he shuddered. He removed her hand, kissing it. "Hands above your head, on the door." She smiled slyly and complied. He lifted her and she wrapped her legs around him. "Don't move your hands."

"Oh, no sir." she whispered saucily.

He laughed. And then he drove into her. He stilled for a moment and then began to pump, hard. Her legs were gripping him, and he was doing little to hold her up, so he moved his hands to lay over hers, their fingers intertwining. She closed her eyes and arched her head a bit. "Look at me, Anya. Don't close your eyes, look at me while I'm inside you." She opened her eyes; a faint gold glow to them and nipped at his lower lip.

He moved his hands to cup her bottom. "You are so beautiful, my Anya." Faster and harder, she almost couldn't take it, it was so intense.

"Declan, God...please. I can't..."

"Are you close, *malysh?* Hmmm?"

Instead of answering, her hands came down to his shoulders, pulling him into her even more, fingernails raking his shoulders. His mouth met hers and he sent her over the edge, joining her a moment later.

***

A bit later, they were in the tub together. She was leaning against him and his arms were wrapped around her lightly. He was nuzzling her, purring into her neck. "That tickles," she said.

"Good. I like to hear you laugh."

"I didn't know I was even ticklish there.

"I hope it's only for me that you are.

"Vain."

"When it comes to you, yes. I do like it when you're compliant," he said.

"Don't get used to it, buddy. Only during sex and only sometimes."

"We'll see. I am used to getting my way."

"As am I. I have another question."

"Your mind never turns off, does it?"

"Just during sex."

"Good information to have. Ask away."

"Are all consorts humans?"

"Yes."

"Why?"

"You keep us humanized. That's the theory, at any rate. By the time any of us are ready to take consorts, we've been alive for hundreds of years. We start to lose touch with the world around us in some ways, you ground us, help us keep things in perspective. Many demons prefer to stick with other demons, romantically, but it's different than bonding with a human. I've had demon lovers."

Anya's eyes narrowed. "Who?"

He laughed. "Who knew you had a jealous streak. No, my love, they are no threat to you."

"Hmph! You mentioned that not all demons are allowed to mate? Or can mate?"

"It's supposed to be just demons on the Council or those that serve the Council. But I am beginning to question that. It's a way of saying that only demons who are part of the Council are good enough to mate. It's wrong. None of my people are less because they aren't on the Council."

"How is that decided? Being on the Council I mean."

"You have to be demon born."

But that isn't the only deciding factor. Matthew is demon-born, but he's not destined for the Council. It's something that is known when you become a demon and it's apparently a rare thing. Obviously."

"I mean, that's kind of stupid. It comes off sounding like it's hereditary."

"Exactly. Matthew is way more suited to it than I am." He looked morose.

"I am not sure that's true. I think you're exactly what the Council needs. And you'll be all the better for having Matthew and the rest of your team supporting you."

He kissed the top of her head. "And with the support of a badass consort."

"Damned straight! So, the bond has never kicked in with a demon, just humans. So, you've concluded that only humans can bond with you, because of our humanity. Yes?"

"Yes."

"Has a consort ever become a demon?"

"Yes. That happened."

"And?"

"The bond disappeared. The couple stayed together, but it was never the same."

"Did the original demon have to leave the Council?"

"Yes. The mate delved into some real dark magic to become a demon. But it broke the bond. This was a long, long time ago."

"Huh. Interesting. You don't seem to have lost touch though."

"In some ways, I have. Aside from world events, I could not tell you about much that has happened in pop culture or media in the last couple of hundred years."

"Do you not watch movies? Or TV?"

"Some movies I like, generally older ones. No TV really."

"Define 'older'. You're going to need a TV. I watch TV."

He looked at her. "Through the 1940s, maybe 50s. And really?"

"Yes, really."

"Wait? Let's back up...so, are you going to move in with me then?"

She stopped at that, made a face. "Um, I was mostly being facetious, but I suppose we do need to think about this."

They were silent for a bit. Declan opened his mouth to say something when Anya's cell phone rang from the bedroom. She started.

"That's Irina's ring!"

"Rachmaninoff?"

"She's a pianist and Russian so, he's her favorite composer. And she rarely calls unless there's a problem," she said as she leapt out of the tub and bolted into the bedroom, answering the phone.

Declan got up, grabbed a towel, and wrapped it around his waist. He grabbed a second for Anya and followed her back into the bedroom. He stood behind her and wrapped the towel around her. She leaned back briefly in thanks as she spoke in rapid fire Russian. She sounded upset, but she was obviously trying to calm her cousin down. She hung up and looked at him. "What's wrong?" he asked.

"Someone attacked my uncle, Tomas. He's in the hospital."

"This is the uncle you just spoke to, yes?"

"Yes. I told him to not poke around. My brothers are dangerous. He knows this. It sounds like he may not have listened to me."

"You blame yourself."

"I do. I know it's silly, he's an adult. But I did call him. It could be a coincidence, but I don't think it is."

"I understand."

"He...he reminds me of my father. My father tried very hard to not give up on me. My mother was, is, difficult though. It was always his nature to just get along. Tomas has tried to be a surrogate father."

"Are we going to Russia?"

She leaned against him, and he put his arms around her. "I am. You don't have to."

"Yes, I do. We'll use my plane."

"You really don't..."

"Do not finish that thought. I'm going. I want to go with you. I am very much looking forward to meeting your brothers. And your delightful mother." He bared his teeth.

"Declan..." she warned.

"I'll behave. But you won't be going alone. You are NOT alone anymore." He realized he hadn't brought up what he wanted to at lunch, they'd gotten sidetracked by talk of his wife. Now was not the time either. Anaranth's theory about Anya's power could wait a little longer. Right now, she just needed him to be there with her.

"We haven't completed the bonding process though." He could see she was worried about her family, but also worried about being abandoned again.

"We've started it, and that's the important thing."

She let out a breath. "Thank you."

"You are welcome." He let her go and went off to prepare for the flight to St. Petersburg. She dressed, dashed a text off to Gwen who sent her huge hugs back and then emailed and called the head of her department at the university. She'd need someone to cover her classes, as she didn't know when she'd get back to Paris. She hoped for a quick trip, but she was going to have to see her brothers and her mother while she was there. And she suspected she'd also need to see Natalia and Vladimir. Declan couldn't visit Russia and not see them. Oh, did they have to let them know they were coming now? That seemed the politic thing to do.

Declan came back into the room to get dressed. "Things are all set on my end."

"Do we need to alert Vladimir?"

"Already taken care of. If we visit the home base of a Council member, we let them know."

"Thought as much. I do let Natalia know when I am going to be in Russia, which is rare, but that's a family thing. She's the de facto head."

"It's still weird to me that your family knows about demons and consorts."

"It is weird honestly." She pulled on a pair of jeans and then a sweater. "I am really not looking forward to seeing my mother. I honestly used to wonder if I was really hers." She stepped into a pair of black flats and then pulled her hair into a quick braid down her back.

He walked over and gave her a quick hug. "It's her loss, Annie."

"Thank you." She kissed him lightly.

"Are you ready?"

"Just about."

***

In flight, she decided to ask Declan more questions, since she needed the distraction. "Question, how will we know when we are completely bonded? We'll feel it?"

Declan really enjoyed how she'd start each question by announcing she was going to ask a question, almost like she was warning him. "We will. And you will immediately feel different, like you are becoming something other. Which you are. Immortal. Your body won't change much to start, but you will feel clearer, stronger, your eyesight will get better. Little things." He paused. "Also, if what I think is true is indeed true, you and I will be able to fully feel each other. So, it's like we carry a small version of the other person in us at all times. Like, we're part of each other's blood, or heart. We'll know if one of us is in danger."

"Weird, but nice. Ok, how does it happen?"

He sighed. "We both have to drop our internal shields completely, while we're making love."

"And you haven't because you are worried about control."

"Yes."

"Explain."

"Not that you'd be sexing up a beast, but a beast is our other form." We can partially change. And I think that's what happens. I am still me, but also...a little bit not me."

"And you feel like I might freak out? Or reject you?"

"It's a possibility."

"It's not. That said, I am glad you told me in advance."

"It's not pretty."

"But it's part of you though." She thought for a moment. "This is a trust thing." It wasn't a question.

"It is. Have you dropped your shields completely?"

"No. Also a trust thing. For me, it's abandonment."

"That makes sense. I am not ever going to abandon you. But you have to feel it."

"Yes. Ok, this is all good to know. It'll happen."

"You seem very sure."

She took his hand. "I am." She forged ahead. "We also didn't settle the living arrangements."

"We don't have to do it now, love."

"I know, but it helps to distract me. If you don't want me to live with you now, or ever, I'd understand. I'd be sad, but I get it."

"Anya, I'd like you to live with me, but only if you want to. I know you have your own life."

"Do we need to wait to be fully mated?"

"No."

"Did you and your wife live together?"

"Of course."

"And if we were both human and got married, would we live together?"

"Again, of course. But..."

"Then why wouldn't we live together. I mean, I know we're not getting married, but it's like that, right?" He nodded at her. "My apartment is cute. But it's small, the plumbing sucks and my upstairs neighbor is an asshole. I am assuming your place is bigger and nicer. If my place were the larger of the two, I'd suggest we live there. Or get a new place. I am not the type of woman who is going to stand on principle when the principle isn't logical. If I didn't want to live with you, it would be different. Nothing on Earth could get me to move. And maybe it will hasten the final bit of bonding we need to do. Moving into a nicer place is not a hardship for me. But what if I hate the place?"

"I don't think you will. But if you do, we will either see if renovating will make you not hate it, or we'll move. But I've been there for two centuries, so I will be honest and say, I'd rather not move. And it will make me grumpy if we do."

"That's fair. Is there room for me to have an office? I have a lot of books, and things."

"Oh, just you wait and see what I have for you!"

She smiled at him. And for the first time in about eight hundred years, Declan felt at peace. "How about closet space?"

"Anya, my place is really big. Don't worry. Now, try and get a little rest. He put his arm out and she moved into it and put her head on his chest, wrapping one arm around his waist. "Ok, I will close my eyes, but I don't think I'll sleep." He started rubbing her back and she was out in a matter of minutes.

CHAPTER 10

When they exited the plane onto a small tarmac, unused tarmac, Anya spied two people standing near a black sedan. One very large person and one considerably more petite. "Anya!" yelled Gwen running towards her friend and jumping on her. Anya laughed and caught her with an "Oooph!"

"Oh, you weirdo! What are you doing here?"

"Declan thought you may want your knives and he thought I was the best person to get them."

"Great! Which ones?"

"All of them." Gwen thrust a bag at Anya. "I couldn't decide which to bring."

"But why didn't you just give them to Donovan?"

Gwen looked at Declan. He shrugged. "I thought you might like to have your best friend here, so I asked her to come. Donovan said he'd bring her, and I needed Donovan to bring me some things as well. It all worked out." He tried to look casual about this.

She stared at him, blinking back tears at his thoughtfulness. "Thank you, *lyubov moya,*" she said softly.

He kissed the top of her head. "My pleasure."

Gwen looked at both of them. "Aaw, you too are so cute! Aren't they Donovan?" She poked him in the ribs.

"The cutest ever." said Donovan, grinning.

Declan shot him a look as Donovan tried not to laugh. "Did you find what I asked for?"

"Indeed, I did."

"Excellent! Hospital first? Vladimir and your brothers will hold until tomorrow, I think."

It was a bit high handed, and she'd likely regret letting it slide, but for now, she would. "That sounds right." Besides, it's technically what she would have done.

They made it quickly through customs, as invariably, the customs agents were also demons and were on the way shortly. They drove to the hospital in silence for a while. Gwen sat on one side of Anya, holding her hand and Declan sat on the other, his arm around her shoulders. "You guys, I am pretty sure he's going to make it."

Gwen sighed. "We know. It's just that we know it's a bit rough to be back here for you."

It's true, she rarely came back if she could manage it. She smiled. "With any luck, we won't be here long.

When they got to the hospital and found out where Tomas was, there was a loud argument going on between the medical staff and the family in the hallway. Anya stood and watched it for a moment before letting out a booming "STOP!" and the place went silent.

The family rushed over to her, starting to talk all over each other. She held up her hands. "Everyone be quiet! This is a hospital and you're all acting like children. I am embarrassed for you and by you!" A young man tried to say something, "Alexander, if you open your mouth right now, I will put you over my knee, I do not care how old you are!" Alexander, all of fifteen and Tomas' youngest, stepped back, head down. No, thought Declan, Natalia was not the head of this family. Anya was. "Irina, and only Irina, what happened?"

Irina started to speak in Russian and Anya held up a hand. "English, please. I am here with non-Russian speakers and it's rude." Irina started to protest "I do not want to hear it; you all speak English perfectly well."

Irina went on to explain that Tomas had gone out the day before but wouldn't tell anyone where he was going or what he was doing. He just said he needed to check something. Several hours later they got a call from the hospital saying he had been found and brought in.

"Where was he found?"

"Summer Gardens."

Declan piped up. "They wanted him to be found. That's a fairly busy area." Anya nodded. "But my guess is he was attacked somewhere else and left there."

"I'd agree with that," said Anya. Part of her bristled at him inserting himself, but she knew he was just trying to help. She was just so used to handling this kind of thing on her own, that help was hard to accept.

Her Aunt, Lehyna spoke, "Anya, who are these people you bring here?" Her aunt was upset, so she'd let the tone slide. Her aunt could be intensely frustrating. She liked to pretend she didn't know what Natalia and Vlad were. Despite her love for her husband, it had never sat well with her, and she tried to keep her children out of it as much as she could. What had almost happened to Irina at the hands of their cousin and what Anya had done to him was family lore, but her aunt liked to gloss over the more traumatic bits. She loved the woman, but her aunt could be exhausting.

"Auntie, this is Declan, my…" she paused. How to manage this? Fuck it, she thought. "My mate." There were gasps and awestruck looks from her family, but she plunged on. "This is Gwen, my friend and this is Donovan, another friend. They are family." Her tone made it clear that no one should argue. She turned and saw the doctor standing a little ways away. She gestured and he came over. "Doctor, what kind of damage are we talking about?" The family started yelling again. "ENOUGH!" she bellowed as they moved a bit away from her family in order to talk quietly.

The doctor asked her a question first. He spoke in English. "You're Anya Orlova?"

"I am. But it's Orlov, please."

He nodded. "You are your uncle's healthcare proxy. That's partly what the yelling was about. They didn't know, it seems."

"I'll speak to Irina. Tomas likely didn't say anything so as not to cause a fuss. I doubt he thought it would ever be an issue. What else were they yelling about?"

"They want to take him home, against my orders."

"Absolutely not." The doctor smiled. "Now, what are we looking at?"

"Punctured lung, broken and bruised ribs, two black eyes, a concussion, a broken arm. I think that was from trying to fight them off. He also has broken toes on both feet. I suspect that's from when they dumped him. He has some other lacerations, contusions. He will be fine, but between the lung and concussion, we need to keep him here. The puncture is not large, so we don't think he will need surgery. And as yet, does not even seem to require a chest tube, which is good based on the condition of his ribs. But the lung still needs to fully expand, and we are working on that. But he is in a good deal of pain and needs to be monitored."

"Agreed. What's your name, Doctor?"

"Doctor Petrov."

"Thank you, Doctor Petrov." She pulled out a card. "I can be reached at this number should you need me. I am going to talk to Irina, his daughter, and make her understand the situation. I do not live here, nor can I stay long, and Irina should be the backup, if I'm not available. But, if there is ever a time where they want you to do something you don't feel is right, including Irina, you call me."

"Yes, ma'am. Your uncle is awake, but he's very groggy. We're keeping him fairly medicated so he's comfortable."

"Understood. I can see him?"

"You can, but not for long." He held out a card. "And this is my card, should you need me."

"Thank you, Doctor."

"Thank you," he said and walked down the hallway.

She turned to her friends. "Fair warning, I am about to berate Irina some. If you think you're going to try and stop me, you're wrong. So, walk away now if you can't handle it."

Gwen spoke first. "I am for berating."

"Me too" This was from Donovan.

"Oh, I am not missing this." Declan smiled.

She smiled at them and then yelled down the hall. "Irina, come!" her tone of voice brooking no argument.

Irina slowly walked towards her cousin, a wary look on her face. "Cousin…"

"No, you'll be silent until I am done speaking. I do not know what has gotten into you, but you are never to put on a display like that again. I expected better of you, of all of you, but mostly you. I don't live here, and as the eldest, I expect you to be calm and hold the family together when your father cannot do it. I am your father's healthcare proxy for a very good reason it seems, as none of you are capable of acting in a reasonable manner. Yelling at a doctor because you want to take a very injured man home is insanity. I know the family, much to my eternal chagrin, is mired in superstition, but you are not. I did not pay for your schooling or your music lessons, so you could turn around and act like an ignorant peasant. They live in St Petersburg at the whim of Natalia and Vladimir, and if you all continue to disgrace her, she will knock every single one of them back to the village they came from. You will listen to what the doctor says and follow his advice. If you are concerned with anything he says, you call me. Do not cause me shame. Am I being perfectly clear with you?"

"Yes, Cousin Anya, I understand." Irina said softly.

"Will there be further problems, Irina?"

"No, cousin." Head still down.

Anya folded her cousin into her arms, and they hugged. "Now, you go talk to your family. And you tell them if they continue to make scenes, they will be barred from the hospital. And that goes for your mother as well. I am going to see Tomas and then I am leaving."

"Yes Annechka." Irina said, walking down the hallway, squaring her shoulders for a possible battle.

"I fucking hate being here." Anya breathed.

Gwen spoke first. "I am so turned on right now, I don't even know what to do with myself." She winked at Anya to show she was teasing.

"You aren't the only one," Declan said, smiling.

"I am not saying anything, but it was seriously pretty great. You didn't even raise your voice. You did glow a little though, didn't she?"

"Yeah, you were glowing a bit."

Anya looked startled. "Declan?"

"It's true. I don't know why though. Maybe it's part of what's happening to us. I could feel the tight control you were keeping on your temper. My blood was humming." He was beginning to think what Anaranth said was the truth.

"Well, huh. So, look...it's evening. I am going to visit Tomas briefly. Then I think we should go back to the hotel, eat dinner and rest. Tomorrow, Declan and I can see Natalia and Vlad and then deal with my brothers. And maybe you all could, sightsee?"

"Cute. No, we stick together," Gwen said.

"But…"

"I was here in college for a school sponsored trip. I've seen all the things. I would really rather watch you and Declan kill your brothers."

"You've gotten really bloodthirsty. I am not planning on killing them."

Declan shrugged. "I mean, I might be."

Anya shook her head at him while Gwen spoke. "Those little fucks deserve it. We don't have to go in to see the grandparents. We can wait in a cold, but lovely room while demons watch us to make sure we don't steal anything. But no, we're with you." She looked at Declan. "Um, sorry. I am with you. Donovan does work for Declan." She grinned and he laughed.

"Good plan, Gwen." He winked at her.

"But…"

"Annechka, no arguing now," Declan said.

"I really also fucking hate that nickname."

He laughed and gave her a kiss. "Go see your uncle!"

"Come with me? I'd like to introduce you."

"Oh, of course." Declan was very pleasantly surprised by this.

"Good luck talking past that lump in your throat, boss." Donovan whispered to him and got an evil look in return.

***

They walked into the hospital room and Anya took a breath. Her uncle looked terrible, all bandaged up, arm in a cast. He looked impossibly old. "*Dyadya?*" she said quietly, wondering if he was up.

Softly. "English, Anya, English."

She smiled "Uncle, how are you feeling?"

"Like shit, frankly. And your aunt isn't helping. I heard you bellow at them." He smiled weakly. Or tried to.

"I do not bellow!"

"You bellowed." Tomas tried to sit up some and both Anya and Declan rushed to help. "Family," he coughed a little and she could tell it pained him. "Are a pain in the ass sometimes. Who have you brought for me to meet, *malen'kaya ptitsa.*" Little bird.

"Uncle Tomas, this is Declan."

"Your demon?"

"Yes."

Tomas looked Declan up and down. "He's handsome enough for you, I think. But is he smart and strong?"

"I was smart enough to take your niece as my consort."

Tomas laughed quietly. "He is smart then. And I suppose he looks strong enough." She could hear the exhaustion and pain in his voice, and it broke her heart.

"He is. Uncle, what were you doing?"

"Nothing. It was random." He tried to look innocent, fooling neither of them.

"That is bullshit and you know it."

He sighed. "Fine. I was worried, so I did a little poking around. Your brothers do a lot of strong-arm stuff out of the warehouse by the docks. The one all the circus stuff is stored at. I got caught."

"Did you see either of them?"

"No, they're too canny for that. But this has their sticky fingers all of it. One of them was a demon. I heard the other say, 'Don't beat him to death, demon, they just want the old man scared.' Which I am not. I am furious." Declan had stepped into the corner of the room and made a quiet phone call.

"Uncle," said Anya in a warning tone, "Stop 'poking' around please. You could have been killed. Then Auntie would call me all the time and that would be terrible."

"Don't make me laugh. It hurts."

She smoothed his hair. "I spoke to your doctor...and Irina. Things should quiet down."

"You take good care of us, Anya." Tomas never used 'Annechka', she thought. He must know she hated it.

Declan came back over. "Sir, I've called Vladimir and he's installing two guards at your door. Until we speak with Anya's brothers, it's better if someone keeps an eye on you." He paused. "Also, they can report back if your family acts up again."

Tomas frowned. "I don't need..."

"You do, sir. I am sure they know Anya is here, it's safest for you."

Anya nodded. "Take your medicine like a man, uncle. He's right."

"Fine. Irina and Lehyna?"

"They will also have guards. But Vladimir does not think we should tell them."

"He's correct. Thank you."

"I am glad to help."

"I assume you are not here long?"

"As long as you continue to mend, I am likely back to Paris the day after tomorrow. But I'm glad I saw you." She leaned over and kissed him gently.

The old man blinked back tears. 'Me too, Anya." He cleared his throat. "Anya, I'd like to talk to your demon for a moment."

"Why?" She frowned.

"Because I asked to."

She narrowed her eyes but agreed. "I will be outside."

When she left, Tomas pinned Declan with his gaze. "This may seem old fashioned to you, but I stand for her father, and I thought we should talk."

"I am eight hundred years old; this does not seem old fashioned to me." He liked the fact that someone in her family was thinking about Anya.

"Good. Good. Anya had a very rough childhood, none of it her own fault. Her father adored her, but he didn't know what to do with her. And the longer he was married to that harpy, the less he seemed to take up for his only girl. She suffered because he didn't protect her. And I didn't either because I was clueless. No, because I was not paying attention like I should have been. It is one of my biggest regrets in life. I should have taken her, I should have known, but I didn't. I say all this so you understand that this is the one thing I can do for her. You treat her right, you take care of her, you don't make her sad. I am an old man, but I will not stand for her to be mistreated."

Anya could take care of herself, but Declan knew what to say. "I will do all of those things. You have my word. I will treasure her."

"Good. Good. Now, go. And make sure she doesn't murder her brothers. She'd feel too guilty. She already...never mind. I am tired and have to rest now."

Declan let it go, but the slip told him something. Anya had had something to do with her brother's death. He was sure of it.

***

The car pulled up in front of a house south of Nevsky Prospekt. Anya whistled. "This is not a hotel, is it?"

"Nope. I managed to secure us a townhouse. I thought it was safer, there is a demon staff and security detail. And I thought it would be more comfortable."

"Is there dinner?"

"There is indeed dinner."

"Excellent!" The car door opened from the outside and a tall demon with raven hair stood by. Declan got out and offered his hand to both Anya and Gwen. Donovan got out the other side and spoke quietly to the two men standing by the trunk of the car. Anya looked at the demon holding the car door. "*Dobryy vecher*," she said, taking a chance.

He smiled and spoke in heavily accented English. "Good evening to you, Dr. Orlov."

"Oh, we're Doctor here, now?" Gwen asked.

"Yes, because Declan tells everyone I'm a Doctor."

"I am proud of my woman." He grinned. "Let's go inside."

"Your woman! What cheek!" But Anya had to laugh.

Dinner was a smorgasbord of Russian food and vodka. "I hate being here, but I do love the food. And" she said, downing a shot. "the vodka." She tasted the borscht. "Not as good as my cousin's, we'll go to his restaurant, but this is still really good."

"Anya, we didn't get the location of the warehouse your brothers are using."

"I know where it is. It can only be the one we use to store the circus equipment. I don't know why they used that one. Tomas would know it. I assume it's because they're morons. Or arrogant. Or both. Natalia holds that lease. I am going to convince her to sign it over to me tomorrow."

"Will she?"

"I think so. I hope so. Oh, what time are we due there?"

"Ten a.m."

"Good. Actually, I'll phone after dinner and see if she's willing. That way, I can sign the paperwork in the morning and then tell my brothers they are no longer welcome there." She rubbed her hands together. "That is going to be fun. I can't wait, I am going to call her now. Excuse me." Anya got up and stepped out of the room.

"I should check in with work while she's on the phone doing that, and then you can talk about us," Gwen said as she left the room.

Donovan got up and got a box from the table in back of him, handing it to Declan.

"Here's the book. It's in good shape for being so old."

Declan opened the box containing the book and could smell the old leather and the mustiness of the pages. The necklace he put in his jacket pocket. "Thank you, Donovan."

"May I ask, why did you want that book?"

"There's been something in the back of my mind about Anya, about our bond, since I first saw her eyes turn gold. Well, before that, but it's really begun to bug me since the gold eyes."

"This book though, it's not just about our history, it has prophecies in it."

"I know." Declan looked a little grim. "We're stagnating, Donovan. We're not moving with the world, and we should be. I think Anya is part of that."

"And you, Declan, and you."

"Yes, and me. But I think she may be the key. The thing that pushes us, all of us, to make changes in how we do things. And I believe that someone else thinks this as well."

"You don't think you're the main target, do you?"

"I don't. I did at first. But frankly, I've been pissing people off for years, so why would anyone try to dispose of me now? The only new thing that's happened is her."

"But we're immortal."

"For the most part. But as you know, there are ways we can die. And there are weapons, supposedly, that could accomplish that."

Donovan looked horrified. "What?"

Declan could hear the women talking and knew they were coming back in. "Don't worry, right now it's just a myth." He set the book down on the floor and hoped Anya didn't notice yet.

Anya and Gwen came back in, chatting about something only known to them. Anya dropped a kiss on the top of his head. "Natalia would be delighted to sign the warehouse and all of the equipment, etc. over to me. Papers will be ready for me to sign tomorrow."

"You are a bloodthirsty lass." Declan smiled up at her.

She leaned her head on top of his and wrapped her arms around him. "I am! And I am also tired. I am going to bed. You should follow shortly." She nuzzled him and winked at Donovan and Gwen.

"Goodnight, you two."

They both said goodnight as Anya left the room.

Gwen stood a few minutes later. "I am also going to turn in." She got to the door before she turned and addressed Declan. "I am going to be deadly serious here. Declan, if you hurt her, I will bring down the power of the goddess upon your head. And yours too, Donovan. I can put up with a lot when it comes to me, but not when it comes to her. Don't fuck this up." With that, Gwen swept out of the room.

"That was a little scary," Declan said.

"Just a bit. And I find I am really kind of turned on by it."

"What are you going to do about Gwen?"

"I don't know. She's...human. There is a lot to think about there. It's a big ask for a mortal. Aside from the obvious that I will outlive her, she's Anya's friend. It gets complicated because she's always going to be in Anya's life. I don't want to do anything to jeopardize their relationship."

"Coward."

"Gee, thanks."

"Most welcome, you ass. That said, I have some ideas about this whole mate and consort thing. If I am right, it could be huge."

Donovan was surprised at this. "Planning on making waves?"

"I am going to cause a fucking tsunami if what I am thinking is correct. I am just hoping I can keep Anaranth on my side. Now, I am going to join my lady in bed."

"Asshole."

"I know."

***

Anya rolled over when she felt the bed dip and felt Declan slide under the covers. "You aren't asleep," he said.

"Not yet. I was waiting for you." He stretched his arm out and she moved in, laying her head on his chest. "Declan?"

"Yes?"

"I killed Pavel. My brother," she said it all in a rush. It was something she'd never actually said out loud.

He sighed and kissed the top of her head. "I thought as much. Will you tell me why?"

"Yes. It was an accident though. He killed my father, also accidentally. He was trying to kill me. Pavel and I had been arguing a lot. He was insane, losing his grip on reality and it became violent when he finally found me."

***

Pavel had snuck up on Anya while she was going over one of the caravans to make sure it was still solid. She was in from Paris for a brief visit, and she had decided that she wanted to check some of the circus equipment while she was home. Her father was getting older, and she frankly didn't trust her brothers to do it properly. He had gotten her in a chokehold, hissing he was going to kill her. Anya went slightly slack, so he'd be fooled into loosening his grip, which he did. She used the advantage to wiggle out, giving him an elbow in the windpipe as she broke free. "What the fuck is wrong with you Pavel?"

"You. You're what's wrong. You are a blight on the family. You're...not right. You were born wrong."

"Pavel, how can you say that?" Anya was heartbroken that Pavel felt this, thought this. Her sweet little brother seemed to be gone. She didn't know what happened the last few years, but he'd been different with her. She had assumed her older brothers might have turned him, but he was barely with them, preferring to be alone.

"Because it's true. You are our bad luck. You are what's wrong with the family...you..." Pavel stopped and leaned over, his hands on his head. "It hurts, why does it hurt, Anya?"

"I don't know Pavel, but we can fix it. I'll help you!" she pleaded with him.

He roared and stood up straight again. "No! Not you, never you. I have to kill you!"

Their father came running in. "Pavel? Pavel, moy syn, you cannot kill your sister. This is wrong. Please, please let me help you. Let me help. Please son."

"I don't want to have to go through you batya, but I will. She's a monster. She's a murderer."

"Son, you know she had a good reason. You know this. She was only a child. Like you. You were so small then. You weren't even there."

"They said...they said I had to. Told me to." He pulled out a gun but seemed surprised to see it in his own hand all of a sudden. He was waving it around wildly. "I...you don't understand, I have to." He shook his head some, seemingly in confusion.

Nikolai Orlov walked slowly to his son. "Pavel, please give me the gun." He stopped about five feet from Pavel.

Anya moved in front of her father. "Batya," the familiar endearment holding no small amount of fear. "Please. Please let me take care of it. He may hurt you in this state." Anya couldn't let her father fight this battle.

"My little bird, it's beyond time that I protected you."

"I never blamed you."

"I blamed myself."

"Please don't. And please don't do this. I can handle Pavel."

"No, Anya," he said kissing her cheek. "No." He moved around her as Anya began to cry. She had a very bad feeling about this. "Pavel, my youngest. My little mouse, please put the gun down." Mouse and bird, that's what he called them. They'd been so close growing up, Anya always watching out for the youngest brother, the sweetest in the family. He'd had the same red hair as Anya, as their father. It was no secret to anyone that even though you were not supposed to have favorites, that Yuri was biased when it came to his oldest and youngest. They were his favorites.

"Batya, please...I can't control...if you're in the way, I won't be able to..." Pavel begged his father.

Anya spun around. "Batya! Move away quickly! He's not himself, someone is controlling his actions somehow. Please!" At the same time the gun went off and Yuri dropped. Anya screamed and ran over to her father. Pavel just stood there, looking shocked and breathing hard. "Batya, no! Don't you dare die on me! Please."

She shakily got her phone out so she could call for help. Nikolai raised his hand and said "Too late. It's too...late..." He coughed up blood. "Ya lyublyu tebya, malen'kaya ptitsa." I love you, little bird. "I am so sorry." And right there, in his daughter's arms, Nikolai Orlov died. Anya heard a scream and looked up to see her mother running towards her. "What did you do?" she yelled at Anya.

Well, that fucking figured, it was always her. "I didn't do this. Pavel shot him."

Yuri and Nik came running in as well, stopping short when they saw Anya cradling their father and Pavel standing not too far away with a gun.

"What did you say to make Pavel shoot him?"

Anya looked up and looked over at Yuri. "Call for help." Not a question, a command. "Doina..." she looked at her mother. "Pavel was trying to kill me. Batya stepped in front of us, despite me stopping him once and then Pavel shot him. So, take that poorly aimed blame and turn it in the right direction." She stood, covered in her father's blood, and stalked towards Pavel. "Pavel Mikhail Orlov, give me that gun."

"No…no…no…it wasn't supposed to happen this way. THIS IS YOUR FAULT! YOU MADE ME DO THIS!" He lunged at Anya and they went down, Pavel trying to subdue Anya while not giving up the gun. Anya had her hand on the gun and there was another shot. Both of them widened their eyes. "Pavel?" Anya said brokenly.

"Anya, oh Anya, what have you done?" said Pavel as he rolled off of her with the last of his strength. His eyes closed and his blood was seeping out. Anya started screaming and did not stop until her uncle Tomas showed up and slapped her. "Anya, this isn't helping." She looked around and saw Vladimir and Natalia were there. Tomas walked her over to the couple. "She needs to leave Russia tonight and no one can know she was here."

"But I killed…"

"No one." said Vladimir. "You killed no one. Pavel killed your father and turned the gun on himself. End of story."

"But…"

"No Anya, this is the way it has to be." Natalia spoke. "You need to leave before your mother gets back in here. And your brothers."

"I can't just leave. They'll hate me."

Vladimir looked sad. It surprised her. "They already do hate you, Anya. I'm sorry. But it's true. They blame you for this. Natalia and I will calm them down. But they can't see you right now."

She nodded. Vladimir nodded and handed her off to two of his men, and within the hour, she was on her way back to Paris.

***

"To this day, I remember nothing about the drive to the airport, or the flight or landing. I remember Gwen was there. I assumed Natalia or Tomas called her. She took me home, put me to bed and stayed with me for a week, until I felt almost human again. I know she doesn't look like a fighter, but she is. You had to hear her on the phone with my mother and brothers. She was like a lioness, protecting her cub."

"Well. she was in a way. You needed someone right then. I am horrified that Natalia or Tomas didn't go to the airport with you, or even Irina."

"It was such a mess, so much confusion."

"Annie, you were heartbroken. Your father was killed in front of you, protecting you. You shot your brother, not intentionally, but you did kill him, you loved him. You loved them both. You should have had company on the plane. I never would have left you alone."

She looked up at him. "You don't think less of me?"

"Why would I think less of you?"

"You pretty much died for your family. You protected them."

"My family did not blame me for being born. They loved me, as I loved them. It was a different situation. They don't deserve you. None of them. I don't either, but at least I know it. I swear to you, that you will never be alone again."

She kissed him deeply. "What a bastard you are. Turning out to a sweet guy, after all."

"Your bastard. And don't you forget it," he said when they came up for air. "Now, you get some sleep." She snuggled into him and was asleep within minutes. He smiled when he heard her deep, even breathing. They had all let her down. Natalia, Tomas, Irina, her brothers and parents. No one had ever just held her hand and told her it would be all right. Soon they would all realize that this had been their biggest mistake. Because there was one thing Declan would flat out not put up with, and that was any disrespect against his mate. They hadn't seen the beast yet, but if anyone stepped out of line, they would.

<u>CHAPTER 11</u>

When Anya woke up the next morning, she was alone in bed and heard the shower running. She got up, stretched, and saw the old book sitting on the night table on Declan's side of the bed. She opened it, because it was a book after all, and stared at a page. She had absolutely no clue what it said. She frowned. She had a feeling it was important, but she'd ask later. She padded into the bathroom and stepped into the shower behind Declan. "Good morning, *malysh*."

"Mmm, good morning," she said rubbing her breasts against his back. "Did you learn that word or did you already know it?"

He laughed. "I learned it for you. I taught myself a few words but haven't had the chance to use them." He sighed. "That feels nice. You can surprise me in the shower anytime."

She kissed the back of his neck and ran her hands down his sides, eventually landing on his really excellent posterior. "You have a really great ass, you know? It's perfect. I could stare at it all day and not get tired of looking at it."

"I rather think you would."

"Oh no," she said, her hands gliding over his flesh. "Not at all. I'd really like to take a bite of it. You know, I think I will." Her breasts slid down his back and over his ass and he groaned. "Anya…"

"Now, now…let me work here." She molded the flesh with her hands and then took a nip out of his left cheek, and then his right. Declan hissed as Anya laughed. "This is what you get for having such a lovely butt." She dotted kisses all over said butt and then rubbed her breasts over them again.

"That's it! There is only so much I can take, woman!" Declan turned around, leaned over, and picked Anya right up off the shower floor and pressed her into the wall. She wrapped her legs around his waist and put her hands around his neck, bringing his mouth close to hers for a kiss. He entered her while they were kissing, and she gasped into his mouth. He laughed low in his throat and Anya tightened her legs around him. "Oh no, Anya, I know what you want. But this morning, we go slowly."

"Dammit, Declan."

"It's going to be a long, difficult day, this is just for us, and I am going to make it last."

"You won't be able to hold me up for that long."

"I'm a demon darling, I can sure as shit hold you up for that long." Then, he proved it.

***

At ten a.m. exactly, two demons and two humans rang a doorbell and were let in by an old and distinguished demon, one much beloved by Anya.

"Alexander! It's so lovely to see you!" She gave the old demon a hug and Declan were surprised when the old one squeezed her back.

"It's lovely to see you Miss Anya. You're looking well."

"You as well."

He beamed at her and turned to Declan. "It's good to see you again, sir."

"Please Alexander, Declan."

"Yes, sir." Anya stifled a laugh as Declan rolled his eyes. "Natalia and Vladimir are waiting for you in the morning room." Alexander looked at Donovan and Gwen. Gwen smiled and piped up "Oh, you can just stick us in any old cold and impersonal room for now."

Alexander smiled at the blonde and said "We've set up coffee for you two in the study. Anya said you would all be here this morning."

"Oh! That's nice. I can always use more coffee."

As they walked down the hallway, Gwen poked Donovan and gestured to Declan and Anya in front of them, holding hands. Donovan looked at her questioningly and Gwen mouthed "They're holding hands." He mouthed back "I know." "Isn't it great?!" she mouthed again. He nodded at her and smiled.

When Declan and Anya walked into the room, Anya looked around at the furnishings, raised an eyebrow and mouthed "See?" at Declan, who tried very hard not to laugh.

"Annechka, come give your grand-mere a kiss." Natalia said. Only Declan heard the small sigh as Anya walked over to comply. "Hello, Natalia. You are looking well, as always." Natalia had been close to sixty when she became a consort. She had married, raised a family, and buried a husband before she and Vladimir met, and he made her his consort. They were both glamoured to look only a little older than Declan and Anya. They were both very vain. "Hello Vladimir."

"Anya. Declan, welcome." For some reason, Vladimir sensed she hated the family nickname as he never used it. "Please, sit. Thank you for taking the time to visit."

As if they'd had a choice, Declan thought. "Thank you, both." They sat and Natalia served them coffee. She handed an envelope over to Anya. "The deed of ownership for the warehouse and everything within it. I had the locks changed last night, so the keys are included. I also had the animals moved to the same farm your uncle uses for his. Additionally, the circus name only is turned over to your mother. She has the name; you have everything else. This means that I divest myself of all financial, legal, and familial responsibility for your mother's side of the family. She has to figure out how to keep the circus running herself, with no equipment and no animals. And good luck to her."

Smart, thought Declan. Anya had made sure her mother and brothers were no longer under the Demon of Russia's protection

"Wonderful. Thank you, Natalia."

"My obligations now only extend to your father's side of the family."

"And that will continue?"

"Yes. Even though I have heard about their behavior at the hospital. I've been remiss, how is Tomas?"

"He's pretty banged up, but fine overall. I spoke with the doctor earlier and he's coming along well. And how did you hear?"

"The nurses were discussing it in front of the guards. They told us."

"Anya handled it beautifully," Declan said. Anya smiled gratefully at him and squeezed his hand.

"She did," Natalia agreed. "You will be a worthy consort."

"Yes. I will be," Anya replied.

Vladimir's lips quirked but he didn't laugh. "We look forward to the official presentation. Soon, we hope."

Anya nodded. "We hope soon as well." And no one else's business, Anya thought.

"Anya, what are you going to do about your brothers?"

"We don't know yet."

"Anya wants to play it by ear until we see them. See what they do."

Natalia nodded. "What about your mother? Will you see her?"

"I'm hoping to prevail upon you for one last favor. Once we leave here this morning, we'd like you to call her and ask her to meet you at the warehouse. But we will be the ones showing up."

"You don't wish to go to her house?"

"Not particularly. She lives close enough. We'll drive a bit, give her and if I'm right, my brothers time to get there."

"I can do that. Once they're there, we can call or text you."

"*Spasibo.*"

"You are welcome. Good luck. Anya, your family are very unpredictable. Let us know if we can do anything else for you."

***

They drove around for a little less than an hour before Vladimir called and said that all three of Anya's family were at the warehouse.

"That was quick, even for them." said Anya.

"Why aren't we there first?" Gwen asked.

Declan is the one who answered. "Them waiting on us puts us in the power position. If we're waiting on them, the roles are reversed."

Gwen nodded. "That makes sense."

"It also gives my mother more time to get really angry," Anya said. "She doesn't know it's me showing up, but she hates to be kept waiting and she hates Natalia. So, we're letting her stew."

"And you want that?"

"Oh yes, I do. I want her absolutely furious at being called there, having to wait, and then seeing me, and not Natalia, get out of the car."

"You are straight up pissed off, aren't you?"

"I am so beyond pissed off at the moment. There is no way she didn't know about what happened to Tomas. None. She let her husband's brother be attacked, she likely was in on the planning. She'll leave before anything gets too violent, it's her way, but she'll get a few verbal licks in while she can."

"I can't promise not to kill her. I am just telling you that now. I am going to try really hard not to, but it's possible the demon may take over if she goes too far. Can you live with that?"

She looked at Declan. "I will deal with it if it happens. That woman stopped being my mother when I was eight."

"When your cousin attacked you?"

She paused before she answered. "Yes."

"Anya." His tone held a note of warning. "What aren't you saying?"

"Nothing." He was silent, just waiting, watching her. She sighed. "Doina knew what he was. He was my mother's kin. They are good people, but they couldn't handle him. So, Doina practically begged my father to take him in. She made it seem like he was an innocent, like her clan was being unfair to him, it was all a terrible misunderstanding and they had to give him a chance. You don't go to the authorities when you're Romany. So, Doina got her way, and he came to us."

Declan had started growling very low, his eyes went red, and his talons extended. "No *lapochka*, calm down." She took his hand and stroked his cheek. The deep growl continued, his eyes turning a deeper red. "Declan, please…please, don't. It's fine. I'm fine." Declan was having trouble getting control of himself. His beast wanted to tear that woman apart. No one protected Anya when she was a child, but he could protect her now...he could do that for her. But she was petting him, trying to calm him, and he knew he couldn't let the beast out now.

Gwen, wanting to help, created a ball of multi-colored light, it was a rainbow. She floated it over to him and then had it float gently around the backseat of the car and eventually back to Declan, landing on his knee. Declan was so startled by it and by Anya's gentleness that he finally managed to get himself under control. "What does *lapochka* mean?" His voice was still a bit hoarse. "Thank you, Gwen."

"Most welcome." She winked at him, and the ball blinked out of existence.

"It means 'sweetie pie.'" said Anya, relieved. She was not scared of him but scared for him.

"I'm sorry? 'Sweetie pie?' Really?"

"Yes, really. It's what popped into my head."

He laughed and kissed Anya soundly. "Thank you too."

Donovan watched the whole interchange with a thoughtful smile on his face. Like he had just worked out a puzzle. They pulled up to the warehouse and standing out front were Anya's brother and mother. Doina stood up straighter when she saw the car pull up.

Gwen realized that while Anya had gotten her looks and most likely her warmth and humor from her father's side, her bearing came straight from her mother. Ice wouldn't melt on that woman's ass. She was willing to bet that her spine of steel also came from her mother.

"Ok," Donovan said. "Everyone breathe. And let's just accept right now that this is going to go be a shit show." They all nodded.

Gwen got out of the car, followed by Donovan, then Declan. Anya waited a beat and then stepped out. She watched her mother stiffen.

Doina was wearing tall gray boots, jeans, and a gray leather jacket. On closer inspection, Anya realized it had been her father's. Inexplicably, this infuriated her. Yuri and Nik moved closer to their mother, closing ranks. It was going to be hard to not let Declan kill them. She could feel the rage just below the surface in him now. She walked towards them, and the others fell in behind her.

"Doina."

"Anya," her mother said in English. Which was good and bad. She obviously wanted to make sure she was understood by everyone. It meant she was planning to verbally flay her daughter. "What are you doing here? Natalia asked us to be here."

Natalia *commanded* was more like it. "Yes. She did. But she's not coming." She turned to her brothers. "Tomas is in the hospital. He was attacked. Do you two happen to know anything about that?" They stared at her, saying nothing, but Yuri shifted a little, right foot to left and back again. That was his tell for when he was uncomfortable. "No? Nothing?"

"No idea. Why isn't Natalia here? And why is our warehouse locked?" Yuri asked.

She looked at him briefly and took a breath. "It's not your warehouse. It is, as of this morning, my warehouse. I own it and everything inside of it." She handed the copy of the deed and the worth of the items to Doina. "You are now trespassing on my property."

"Anya, we're family. If you own this, we own this."

Anya laughed. "Are you out of your mind, old woman?" Anya looked over at Declan. "I think she may be losing her mind."

Declan walked up to stand next to her. "I couldn't say, she's your mother, *consort*." He placed emphasis on the last word and watched Doina's face darken. "So, this is your monster? Are these monsters too?" She looked at Gwen and Donovan.

Anya stepped very close to her mother and looked her directly in the eye. "I would be very careful what you say next. Any one of these three would kill you if I nod at them. And I'm very tempted to do so. Now, you will be quiet and let me speak." Anya stepped back. "I own this warehouse and the contents. The animals also belong to me, and I have retired them to a farm."

"*We* own the circus!" Nik bit out.

"That's funny. No, you never have. But as of today, you own the name only. I left you that. You do not own the equipment, including tents, caravans, ticket booth, costumes, etc. Just the name in case that was not clear to you. Natalia has owned this warehouse and all of the contents since she became a consort. All replacements over the years have been made with her knowledge and approval. It's all there," she said pointing at the papers. "I am actually fairly surprised, based on how mercenary I know you to be, that you did not realize all of this. Or maybe you did, and you were too arrogant or stupid to care. I suppose since it didn't affect the bottom line, you didn't give a shit."

"Excuse me?" Doina barked.

"I just called you a greedy bitch, basically."

"Open the doors!" Doina screeched, her face red. Anya had never really openly defied her in this way. She'd generally just walked away. Now, she was playing to win. Anya suspected her mother didn't give a shit about the circus. They hadn't even bothered to work it since her father had died. Too much real work for them. Tomas sure as hell wasn't going to help. No, Doina wasn't upset about the circus. This was about Anya's defiance, and Doina not getting her way. Doina was losing, and she hated to lose.

"No." Anya was calm.

"Excuse me?"

"I said no. I am not opening this warehouse. If you try to get in, I will have all of you arrested for trespassing. If you try to take anything, I will include charges of theft."

"You'd send your own mother to jail?!" Yuri asked.

"In a heartbeat. If you want the warehouse and the contents, you will need to come up with the money to buy it all back from me. But, since I am fair, I won't make you pay the full worth. 75% of the full worth is acceptable. "

"You ungrateful little bitch!" Doina was nearly purple with rage.

"Oh, I'm ungrateful? From the time I was small you belittled me, you hit me, you bullied me, you put me in a position where I could have been raped instead of just groped. You have called me a monster, evil, a bitch, the devil's spawn. You told me you wished I were dead. But I'm ungrateful?"

Declan was standing stock still. Doina was a dead woman walking. It was only a matter of time now. He'd always been a demon with more of a conscience than most of his brethren, but the fact he just decided to kill a woman in her sixties did not bother him at all. Hearing, out loud, everything that woman had done to Anya had sealed her fate with him. Anya glanced at him, her eyes widening, letting him know she had picked up on his thoughts.

She smiled softly at him, but her look said they'd discuss it later. He just shrugged.

She sighed, but let it go for now. He thought of his own mother, how loving she had been, how fierce she was when it came to her children, and he knew that Doina was the abomination here.

"You can't speak to her like that!" This was from Yuri.

"I can. And I will. You allowed my brothers to do all of those things to me too. You didn't deserve *Batya*. He would be ashamed if he had known everything you did to me." Anya was taking a chance that her father hadn't known the half of what Doina had been like. She was good at hiding her true self.

Doina walked over to Anya and slapped her once. She raised her hand to do it again, but she was plucked from her spot and held against the door of the warehouse by Declan. Donovan had moved to Anya's brothers and was holding them by the back of their necks so they couldn't move. Declan had Doina off the ground and was holding her one handed. Anya was watching impassively, arms folded. She was almost sure Declan wouldn't actually kill Doina right now.

"Anya has been very patient with you," said Declan. "But I won't be. You think I'm a monster, I'll be the monster. If you ever so much as touch her again, I will rip every single limb from your body with my bare hands. And I will do it so quickly, you'll still be alive, screaming in pain. Then, I will set what is left of you on fire and I will watch you burn. And then, I will do the exact same thing to your sons. You will be extremely lucky if I leave the rest of your clan alive after that."

Declan had no plans to touch anyone else in the family, but his aim was true. Doina had turned deathly white. "Am I making myself perfectly plain to you? You may nod if you understand me." Doina nodded and he set her down.

"I think I have made myself clear as well," said Anya. "All of you, go! You are not welcome here." She looked at Doina. "Do not ever call me again. Do not ever think about me. I have no wish to speak to you ever. Any business can be done through lawyers. I suggest you hire one if you don't already have one.

"I wish you'd never been born. I wish you'd died," said Doina through clenched teeth.

Declan snarled at Doina, who tried to flee to the car, but Anya held her. "I curse you Doina Orlova. Everything in your life will wither and die. I curse you to live in your own misery, your own people will hate you. I curse you from this moment until you die, alone and friendless. Your death will be pain and torment." She spat at Doina's feet.

Doina looked terrified at this. She backed away from Anya until she couldn't bear it and turned and ran to the car, her sons following her.

Anya watched until the car was gone and then looked at Declan and ran over to him. He caught her up and just held her.

Declan set Anya down. "Ok, the day is not over. The boys will be back with reinforcements. But let's get inside and take a look around."

"Are you ok, Annie?" Gwen asked.

"I am not thinking about it right now. I will think about it later. For now, I am fine."

"Ok. I'd like to set that bitch on fire and watch her burn. I can summon fire now."

"When the hell did you get so bloodthirsty? Have I done this to you? And since when?"

"No! Of course not! It's something I've been working on. Though I was saving it for a surprise Um…surprise!"

"Only you would think showing me fire was a good surprise."

"Isn't it?"

"Oh yes, it most assuredly is."

"Don't let Gwen fool you," Donovan said. "She enjoyed the fight at the club, she told me. She is loving all of this."

Anya unlocked the door, and they went in. When Gwen was out of earshot, Donovan told Anya and Declan he'd been giving Gwen some hand-to-hand combat lessons. "She's actually pretty good, because she's quick."

"How long?"

"Since the club attack, so not long. She wanted to be an actual asset, with more than just her magic."

"Ok. How?"

"I let her practice with Michel, and she managed to hop on his back, get her arm around his neck and cut off his oxygen. He passed out cold. I was very proud."

"Well, shit."

"Yeah. She said she didn't want to be seen as weak. I think she was afraid we'd all go off together and have adventures and leave her at home."

"As if I would."

"That's what I said. Magic is always going to be her main thing, but if need be, she wants to be able to physically throw down."

Gwen called from across the warehouse, "Anya! I found your caravan!" Anya went over and saw what Gwen had meant; her initials were carved into the back of one of them. "Yup. This one was mine. I am surprised Doina kept it." Anya looked sad Donovan and Gwen moved away to give the other two a moment alone. "I liked this little caravan. It was small, but it was just fine for me," Anya said quietly.

"Anya, come here." Declan opened his arms and Anya walked straight in. "She doesn't deserve your sorrow."

"I know." She sighed.

"Are you angry at what I said to her?"

"No. I knew she'd slap me at some point. And I knew that you wouldn't be able to not do something. Honestly, I may be evil because I enjoyed it. I thought it was super sexy. "

"You know what was super sexy? You cursing her."

"Did you like that? I thought it was inspired. I don't believe in curses. But she does." His hand snaked up under her shirt and he laid his palm flat on her stomach. "Behave!"

"No. I shan't."

"You're insatiable."

"And you're not?"

"I didn't say that. But we can't. Gwen could bound up to us at any time."

"Donovan is keeping her occupied."

"Unless they're having sex, she's not that occupied. I know her. So, stop it."

He kissed her long and deep to show her what she was missing.

CHAPTER 12

They'd been going through the inventory list for a couple of hours, making sure everything was accounted for and in good order, when Anya's brothers showed back up with reinforcements, a mixture of demons and humans.

"Oh, Vlad is not going to like that. Not at all." Declan mused. "He does not like renegade demons on his turf."

"How do you know they're renegade?"

"Because Vlad would never sanction any demon to attack you, or. me, for that matter."

"Good point." Anya sighed. "I thought it would take them longer to get this together. They must have expected this on some level when they went after Tomas."

"In here or outside? Donovan asked.

"In here. I don't want to attract a crowd. And if they damage anything in here, I can have them arrested for destruction of property." She sighed.

The foursome made a loose line and faced the door. Yuri, Nik and about a dozen or so demons and humans burst through the double doors, all quite obviously looking for a fight. "No killing the humans," whispered Anya. Declan snorted. "Ok, the ones that aren't my brothers...unless they're going to kill you. I suspect that this is just a lot of posturing and pissed off feelings for them. They're cheap and wouldn't have paid for decent help."

"How are your brother's fighting skills?"

"Well, I didn't teach them anything, so...pretty mediocre." Anya raised her voice so her brothers could hear her. "You know this is going to change nothing. At the end of the day, I still own this place, I can have you arrested, and your asses will get kicked. There is no scenario where you are the winners. So, just turn around and go."

"We could kill you, that would make us winners."

"That's cute," Declan replied. "But I don't think so."

"So, there you have it. Just turn around and go," Anya said.

Yuri, always the more stubborn of the two let out a yell and ran towards her. She sighed and as he got close, and sucker punched him in the nose. "What do I always tell you, fists up, you dumb fuck." Nik headed towards Gwen, as the demons and humans split their time between Declan and Donovan. A human got to Declan first, saw the red eyes and in the moment that he hesitated, got his arm broken. Three of the humans heading towards Donovan saw this and pivoted away. Donovan grabbed one of them and threw him into the grouping of demons trying to surround him.

Nik was trying to grab Gwen, but she was much faster than he was and kept dodging him, laughing, and mocking him all the while. A demon grabbed her from behind, but before Anya could help, Gwen had stomped his foot hard enough to cause discomfort if not pain. His surprise gave her the chance to flip him over her shoulder into another oncoming human. Anya raised an eyebrow, impressed. Another human ran out of the warehouse, but Nik kept coming. Gwen sighed. "So, Anya did get all the brains, huh?" He snarled and came after her but this time, she just tripped him. He fell on his face and groaned. She jumped on his back and with a little trick Donovan had taught her, managed to cut off his air enough for him to pass out. "Your brother can't fight for shit!" Gwen yelled to Anya.

"I know, right?" Anya called back. Yuri was a better fighter, but he was impatient, and he telegraphed every move he was going to make. Anya didn't even need to pull out a knife. She felt one of the foot solider demons coming at her from behind, spun and landed a roundhouse kick to his head, pulled a knife, and severed his jugular and he erupted into a cloud of dust.

Donovan and Declan were easily picking off the hired thug demons that kept after them. Anya was right, thought Declan, this was posturing. He and Donovan had moved above the main floor in order to lure the demons up there and away from the women so they could concentrate on Yuri and Nik, but he still heard the click. The room went still. He looked down in dread and saw Yuri pointing a Glock at Anya. She had flicked her wrists and two very large daggers extended from the spring-loaded sheaths she wore on her arms. "You bring a knife to a gunfight?" he scoffed at her.

"No, I brought two very dangerous daggers to a gunfight." Jesus, she was fearless. Which, Declan had to admit, scared the shit out of him.

"You don't think I'll shoot you?"

"Oh, you'll try but you won't hit me."

"How do you figure that? You're right in front of me."

"You won't hit me. Like everything else in your life, you will fail."

Gwen was looking on, terrified, wondering if she could do anything. Donovan caught her eye and shook his head, nodding at Declan. Gwen nodded slightly and sat down on Nik's back. The other humans were gone and the demons that were left, had stopped once the gun came out, warily watching the proceedings.

Yuri screamed. "You bitch! I'm the one with the gun! I'm the one in control!"

"You are barely in control of your own bowel movements, you little twerp. You don't scare me. You're not dangerous. You're a child, playacting." Anya knew which buttons to push when it came to Yuri. She knew his insecurities and had no problem using them against him. But Declan was really wishing she wouldn't. Theoretically he knew she could take care of herself, but that was a Glock, they weren't fully mated yet and she could still die right now. Shit, she could still die within the first year of being mated.

Yuri's face was bright red; he pulled the safety and then there was a loud roar as Declan catapulted over the side of the catwalk above. He landed in back of Yuri, grabbing the gun and tossing it in Gwen's direction. Anya barely registered what he had done. Declan had moved so quickly, that there was no way anyone would think he was ever human. Gwen raced to grab the gun and then sat back down on Nik. Declan's arm came around Yuri's neck and one very sharp claw stroked his neck, where his jugular was. "You tried to kill my mate," he said quietly. "I cannot tell you how upset this makes me." His voice was calm, too calm. Anya stood still, watching. Donovan jumped down to stand by Gwen.

"Now Declan, you did promise not to kill him," Anya said. Yuri looked hopeful. "Straight away. I mean, eventually, I know you will, but maybe not right now. Declan flipped Yuri around, holding him by the neck and lifted him off the ground. He walked over to where Gwen was sitting on Nik, who was beginning to come around. She got up and he reached down and picked up Nik with his other hand. "It doesn't mean I won't kill you another day, but today is a lucky day for you. It's not a matter of if, it's a matter of when. Just go." He tossed them lightly across the room and they fell to their knees.

"Get out," Anya said, putting her daggers away. "You'll need a head start after I tell Vladimir about today." Every single demon fled immediately. No one wanted to piss off the Demon of Eastern Europe. They'd need a head start to get out of Russia.

Anya started to turn away when she heard "Anya!" from Declan. Yuri was barreling towards her. He smashed into her, taking her to the floor. They grappled for a bit with Anya trying to gain ground, but Yuri, while not a superior fighter, was larger. And he was pissed off. She eventually managed to get her legs up between them and she pushed, hoping she could flip him off of her. Nothing. She took a fist and smashed into his side and his surprise helped her lever him off of her with the next push of her legs upwards. It was inelegant, but effective as he landed on his back. She rolled on top of him, straddling him with her knees pressed into either side of his neck. Anya squeezed some and then squeezed harder, cutting off his air. She felt not quite herself, but strong. She could feel power course through her as she began to glow lightly.

Declan was watching intently, but Anya didn't move off of Yuri. She was deadly calm, looking down at him dispassionately, while Yuri struggled for air. He could feel something wasn't quite right with her. It wasn't just the glow, which was getting brighter, but she felt off to him. He also knew as much as she hated Yuri, she'd feel terrible guilt if she did kill him.

Declan decided to try something he wasn't sure would work yet, but he hoped the blood bond was strong enough. He spoke to her silently, heart to heart. *Let him go, love, let him go. He's not worth it. He's not worth your soul, he's not worth twenty of you. Stop Anya, stop! Please, stop!*

It was the *'please'* that got to her in the end, he felt it. She stopped and rolled off of Yuri. He started coughing, as Anya just lay there, staring up at the ceiling. She heard Declan tell Nik to get his brother and go and not come back. Next time, Declan would kill them both. Gwen ran over to Anya. "Annie? Annie? Are you ok?" Anya couldn't move, she couldn't even speak right then. She felt Gwen's hands on her and then a sharp intake of breath. "Declan!" Gwen was upset. "Declan, she's shaking. All over. I think she's in shock."

Declan came running over and leaned over Anya, stroking her hair. *"Cushla machree?"* he asked gently. "Are you there?" She looked up at him and stroked his cheek, but her eyes filled with tears. "Where's the key to the warehouse, sweetheart? Your pocket?" She nodded and he went through each jacket pocket until he found them, handing them to Donovan. "Can you both lock up? I am going to take her to the car."

"Of course," Gwen said, visibly trying not to cry. Declan picked Anya up gently, whispering in old Irish to her the whole way to the car. He placed her inside gently and was gone for a moment. She heard the trunk open and close and he was back, wrapping her in a blanket. He slid into a seat, picking her up again and settling her on his lap, still quietly whispering to her. She slid her arms around his neck, leaning against him and closed her eyes. She was still shaking, but nowhere near as much as she had been moments before.

Inside the warehouse, Gwen wrapped her arms around Donovan's waist and cried a little. "What's wrong, Gwen?"

"I've never seen her like that before."

"I know it's upsetting, to see her almost kill…"

"Oh, not that. Although, that was also weird. I mean, just lying there, with that distant look, and the shaking. And the tears. I am not used to seeing her vulnerable."

Donovan smiled down at Gwen. "You would be upset about that, wouldn't you? Not that she almost killed someone, but that she's upset."

"I'd rather see her murderous than like that."

Donovan hugged her. "She'll be fine. I think…I think something was happening to her while she had her brother in that amazing chokehold. It's like…like she has power of some kind. You saw the glow."

"I did. It's a little scary though."

"It is. But she has you. And all of us, she'll be fine."

"She's my ride or die."

"I know. Let's lock up." She pulled away, nodded, and helped him lock up.

***

Declan carried Anya upstairs to the bedroom and sat her on the bed and stepped outside the door. He looked at Gwen and gave her shoulder a quick squeeze. "She'll be ok. The past couple of days have been tough. As much as she thought she dealt with all of this in the past, I don't think she did. And I don't think the power surge she felt helped. I think it scared her some."

"Is that common?" Gwen was holding onto his arm and her hand was ice cold.

He put his hand over hers to warm it. "It's not. I think Anya is...special. I am not sure how or why yet, but I think she's something new for us. She's feeling my power way earlier and way more intensely than I would have expected. Admittedly, I don't know a ton about this, but I don't believe it's common. She's safe, she's healthy, she'll get through this. I will help her with this. We all will. But right now, I am going to take care of her. *Ná bíodh imní ort.*"

Gwen smiled at him, "Using Irish to make me feel better was very sweet. I will try not to worry knowing that she's in good hands."

He smiled at her. "Donovan, feed the woman. She did well today."

"That's my plan. Come on, Gwen."

Declan stepped back into the room and Anya was sitting on the edge of the bed. She had taken off her jacket and slipped off her boots. He walked over to her and kissed the top of her head. "It'll be ok, sweetheart." He walked into the bathroom and started running her a bath. He looked around and found some lavender oil and put a little in the running water. Back in the bedroom, she looked up at him, her eyes brimming with tears. "I almost...I could have...I wasn't in control, and I could have..."

"Sssh, sssh" he said, hugging her. "You didn't."

"You stopped me."

"You would have stopped. I just helped. Let me take care of you. May I?"

She nodded. He slowly undressed her, dropping small, comforting kisses on her neck and shoulders. She sighed at his touch and his heart melted a little more. He picked her up again and carried her into the bathroom, turning off the water and setting her in the tub gently. He took his shoes and socks off, rolled up his sleeves and kneeled at the back of the tub. He began to gently soap her back, rinse, repeat. He washed her arms and her legs, quietly singing to her the whole time. A very old song that he used to sing to his children when he bathed them. He shampooed and rinsed her hair too. She sat there, letting him. Crying every so often.

She knew it was ridiculous, but she had harbored a small hope that maybe, just maybe, they could turn it around and be a family. She knew they hated her. But she had hoped time would have eased that some. The guilt she carried had lessened, but it's something she'd always have. And she cried because for a second she realized how easy it would have been to take her brother's life. To stop his heart. It frightened her.

She sighed, enjoying being touched with such tenderness, being sung to with the same. It felt nice to have someone taking care of her for once. It was nice to just have someone doing something for her. Oh, Gwen was a wonderful friend, but this was different. She felt...cherished. She also felt exhausted, too exhausted to tell Declan how much this meant to her.

He chuckled. "You don't have to tell me, I know," he said. She looked up at him. "I try not to, but sometimes your thoughts are loud."

"You talked to me in my head."

"I did."

"We can do that?"

"It would seem so. But that's a discussion for another time. You are exhausted." He stood her up and wrapped a large, fluffy towel around her. "And I do cherish you. You've had a couple of really shitty days, the least I can do is try and help." She put a hand to his cheek and blinked back tears. She was such a crybaby! "No, you're not. But I think it's beyond time you had a good cry." He toweled her hair gently. He picked her up and carried her into the bedroom.

"I can walk."

"I know. I like carrying you." He dried her and went to get an oversized t-shirt for her, but she shook her head. "What then?" She shook her head again. "I understand." He toweled as much of the damp out of her hair as he could while she had her hands on his waist. He pulled the covers back and she climbed in. He covered her and gave her a gentle kiss. She grabbed his hand. "I am not going anywhere. I am going to undress and get into bed with you." She let go of his hand and turned onto her side. A few minutes later, she felt the covers on his side get pulled back and felt a dip in the bed, letting her know he was next to her. He started rubbing her back in slow circles. She snuggled into the bed and right before she fell asleep, she murmured "I love you," quietly. So quietly, that only a demon would be able to hear it.

CHAPTER 13

Anya slept deeply for several hours and when she woke up, Declan was sitting up in bed next to her, reading that old book she had tried to read earlier. Her voice was a little hoarse when she spoke. "I am annoyed that I cannot read that book."

He looked over and smiled at her. He was so beautiful when he smiled like that, like no one else mattered. It lit up his whole face, making him look almost impossibly young. It was a smile just for her. "You'll be able to very soon." He reached over to the bedside table and poured her some water. She sat up and drank the glass down. "Thank you." He filled it again and she sipped slowly.

"Most welcome. You'd be parched."

"No. I mean for everything."

"It was my honor to be able to do for you." He closed the book and put it aside. "Come here," he said, holding out his arm. She slid in. "How are you feeling?"

"Better for having slept. Sad, for them and for me. Freaked out some by what happened."

"Understandable. I think that you, my Anya, are something amazing and new. Anaranth thinks you're going to be very powerful."

"Does he? When did he say that?"

"After you left the room. I've wanted to talk about it, this isn't how I pictured doing it, but it's here now."

"But what, exactly?"

"I do not know. We'll have to figure it out together. That's why this book. I am hoping it gives me a clue, but it's tough reading to be honest. And I am not completely focused on it right now."

"Am I going to be ok?" She chewed her bottom lip a little.

"Yes. Of that, I am sure. I just think you are going to be a powerful consort, in your own right and not just because of me. And I think someone else thinks that too."

"Could the notes and the thing with my family be a distraction?"

"That's very possible. I think a lot of this is being orchestrated to make us think it's your family. But I don't think they're the masterminds here."

"Me neither. I mean, you've met my brothers. I am surprised they can find their asses most of the time."

He laughed. "I am also surprised by this."

They lay quietly for a while, and she started running her hand along his chest. Her blood started to heat up. "I should mention that I am also feeling something else right now."

His blood answered hers. "I can pretty much tell how you're feeling right now. Are you sure you're up to it?"

She reached down and found him. "I am. And oh look, so are you."
He growled playfully at her and rolled on top of her, kissing her. Kissing her neck, her shoulders, her breasts, before coming back to her mouth, his hands gripped in her hair. "Am I too heavy?"

"Oh no." She nipped his bottom lip. "I can still do this." She flipped them so she was on top of him.

"I have never been so turned on by a show of female strength." His hands slid to her hips.

She looked down at him. "I want all of you, Declan. I want the man, the demon, all of it. I am ready to let you in completely. Are you ready to do the same?"

He looked up at her. "Are you sure? If I do this, I give up a little control…you'll see more of the demon."

"Is it like Anaranth?"

"In theory, but not so alien. You'll recognize me, but some of my features will change. And it won't happen whenever we have sex, it's just a bonding thing. I don't look like the devil or anything, this is real life…not mythology."

She rolled her eyes. "I didn't think that." Ok, she had wondered just a little bit maybe.

He smiled. "It could be off putting. Also, to be clear, the demons in the house will know."

"How?"

"Aside from your screams of passion, you mean?" She pinched his nipple. "Ow! Ok, ok! They'll be able to feel the energy we create. Just by virtue of being in the house."

"Gwen?"

He made a face. "I don't think so, but it won't matter because you're going to tell her first thing anyway."

"True. Are you not ready?"

"I am absolutely ready. But you have had a rough day and I want to make sure you're ready and it's not because of what happened earlier."

She thought for a minute, her blood a low, but insistent thrum. "I am sure. I can deal with the change. I want to be mated with you. I want to belong to you and have you belong to me. I want to get on with our lives and if someone is fucking with us, I want to figure out who it is. But mostly, right now, I just want you."

He pulled her head down so he could kiss her, her breasts were rubbing against his chest, and it was almost unbearable it felt so good. "We already belong to each other as far as I am concerned, but I am also very eager to be mated to you."

I'm staying put here, I want to be on top."

"Your wish, my command."

She grabbed some of his hair and pulled his head to her, gently biting one ear, then the other. His hands had started to turn already, and she could feel his talons on her bottom. He pinched her there and she squirmed, causing him to groan a little.

"That's what you get for pinching." She sat up, lowered herself onto him and they both shuddered. "Mine!" she said, triumphantly.

"Yours." Declan rasped out as his body slowly began to change.

Anya started moving on top of him, while Declan's hands, talons distended, palmed her breasts. "That feels so odd, but really good. Your hands are rougher too, I like it." He pinched her nipple and she bit back a scream. She looked down and his body had gotten rougher, the muscles were bigger, his incisors dropped which made her giggle. It felt very vampiric. His face also got rougher, his nose and eyebrow ridge were bigger, and his ears longer, not pointed, like an elf from *Lord of the Rings*, but not quite ear shaped either. He still looked like him though, a little odd...but she'd still know him if she saw him like this somewhere else. She leaned over and took his earlobe in her mouth and bit down playfully. She could feel his growl.

She threw her head back and began to ride him in earnest. His hands were on her hips, and he would raise his own to thrust up into her. She could feel him growling low in his throat and she had her own answering growl, which turned Declan on even more. As she rode him faster and faster, taking all of him, she started to glow that gold again. Brighter this time, not faint at all.

Declan thought he'd never seen anything so beautiful as this woman. She was the missing piece of the puzzle that was his life. Just to be able to have Anya was a gift. Yet, it didn't dull what had felt with his mortal wife. It enhanced it. His own eyes had started to glow red, but they were rimmed in the same gold as Anya's glow.

She panted. "Your eyes are red and gold. It's gorgeous. Am I glowing?"

"Yes, and it is the most beautiful thing I've ever seen."

She looked down at him and saw how serious he was. "Truly?"

"Truly. I love you and I'm glad we belong to each other. I am yours, always." His voice was rough, but from emotion this time.

She smiled and if possible, glowed more. "I love you too. And I am yours, always." And their world exploded in a shower of gold.

***

Declan was first to the breakfast room, Donovan entering two minutes later. Declan was humming to himself while he drank coffee and looked at the paper. It took him a minute to realize Donovan was glaring at him.

"What?"

"Really? Did you really have to complete your bonding last night?"

"Sorry. Anya was insistent." He smiled.

"I was playing backgammon with Gwen because she couldn't sleep and all of a sudden, I'm horny with a raging hard on."

"And Gwen?"

"No clue. But trust, she beat me at Backgammon."

"Wait? You *just* played backgammon?"

"We did."

"You're an idiot."

"It's not that simple."

"Donovan, it is that simple. I know that now. Your wife died hundreds of years ago; she would not have wanted you to shut your heart away like that."

"Look…"

"No, you look. We always joke about Matthew being a monk, but you're worse than he is. You haven't been with anyone since you became a demon."

"I should never have told you that."

"But you did. What the hell is the matter with you? You like this woman!"

"I promised!"

Declan stared at him. "What? Who?"

"My wife. I promised I'd never love anyone else!"

"You were mortal."

"No! Declan, Henriette knew what I was going to do. She knew and she made me promise to never love anyone else."

"Oh. Oh, Donovan. I cannot believe that she would want you to live an immortal life with no love in it. Not really. Had she thought about it, she never would have made you promise that."

"I know."

"Then, why?"

Donovan shrugged. "I don't…I don't know. I just need time."

"Time you have my friend. But she doesn't. You need to remember that."

"I have not made my decision about her yet."

"It's really cute that you think that's true." He poured Donovan a cup of coffee and pushed it in his direction. "But Gwen was ok last night?"

"Yes. And please stop looking so pleased with yourself!"

"I am pleased with myself!" Donovan gave him a baleful glare. "Hey, do not blame me because you have blue balls. That's your own damned fault."

"Do you think the women are discussing us?"

"Have you met a woman?"

***

"So, you didn't feel anything?" Anya asked as Gwen put her friend's hair into a French braid.

"Nope. I was exhausted and worried, and Donovan was a perfect gentleman. Damn him. I am glad you were feeling better though, you big jerk."

"I am sorry you were worried."

"Don't be sorry. It's what friends do. Remember when I had pneumonia and you came in and carried me out of my apartment, yelling at my cousins and got me to the hospital and stayed with me the whole time? That's what you do when you are friends," she said laughing. "I'm chuffed for you. Even if I went to bed all alone." Anya laughed. "Girl, don't move your head while I'm doing this."

"Sorry."

"Ssssooo...what does it feel like? I mean, you're immortal now, right?"

"Oh, oh I guess so. I hadn't thought of it. I feel good. I feel strong. Though Declan did say I still have to be careful for about a year or so. I am like a baby demon in some ways."

"Did you glow?"

"Yup."

"Do you know why?"

"I don't. Declan said he's got an idea, that's what that old book is, but he's not sure yet."

"Do you love him?"

"Terribly."

"I thought so. So, how does it work? I mean, can you feel him, somehow?"

"Yes, it's like I carry him around inside of me. I feel him in my heart and my blood calls to his. I can always feel him. We have a true blood bond."

Gwen whistles. "Donovan told me those were pretty intense. And pretty rare."

"Apparently so. It means we're connected, God this sounds so dumb, at a really deeper level than a lot of consorts. All consorts mate, not all of them have a blood bond. I can tell you that he is fine, he's happy and that he loves me. I can just feel all of that. If one of us is in danger, the other will know immediately that something is wrong."

Gwen blinked back tears but the emotion in her voice was obvious "That's really great."

"Are you crying?"

"Shut up, of course not!"

"How silly of me."

"Ok, your braid, she is done!"

"Thank you! It's lovely as always."

"Welcome. So, what next?"

"We go home."

Gwen rolled her eyes. "Don't be obtuse."

"I am going to move in with him. He has a big place; our girls' nights are going to be even more epic."

Gwen looked serious. "Are we still going to have those?"

"Are you kidding?! Of course we are. You're my best friend, nothing can change that."

"Well, you've got a new life now."

"No. I have an addition to the life I'm living. And a big part of that is you. One of the best parts. Yes, there will be big differences, Demon Council and all that, but I couldn't even imagine doing this without you." The one thing that they couldn't, wouldn't face now, was the fact that Anya would outlive Gwen. If Anya thought about it, her heart would break. She would have Gwen for as long as possible and beyond that, she couldn't handle right now. She hugged her friend tightly. "Let's go have breakfast, and then go home."

"Sounds good. I hope my cousins have left the apartment standing."

"Don't count on it."

****

Anya breathed a sigh of relief when they were finally airborne. "Better?" asked Declan.

"Yes, I am very glad to be going home. Question, do you have a lawyer?"

"I do. Why?"

"I need to deal with the warehouse and present Doina with an offer. I don't have a lawyer since I haven't really ever needed one. It would be easiest if I could use yours."

"I'll have him call you, he's a human actually. But a very good lawyer. You really want to sell it all?"

"Yes."

"Ok. I get first crack at your caravan though."

"Why would you want that?"

"Because it was yours. And we haven't had sex in it yet."

She burst out laughing. "Really?"

"Yes, really." He was perfectly serious.

"I'll take it off the list. Consider it a mating gift then."

"Excellent!" He gave her a kiss. "I have a gift for you too. It's at my place. Will you stay with me tonight?"

"I will stay with you every night, you moron. I am going to need to get clothes and such, but we can start taking care of that tomorrow."

"Sounds good." He gave her a long, deep kiss.

"This is really quick. Are we moving too fast?"

"Anya, do you want to be with me?" She nodded. "Good. I want to be with you too. It is fast. It's ridiculously fast, but I don't care."

"We still don't know each other very well."

"We know enough for now. And the rest will come. Trust in that. I am absolutely sure we're doing the right thing."

"Ok. That's good enough for me. But so you know, I don't cook."

"Me neither. I have someone who manages the house. She also cooks and she is amazing. She's a bit scary, but I can't do without her."

"Ok, whew." She bit her lip. She had a question she wanted to ask but it was kind of silly. "I have a weird question."

"Ok, go ahead."

"Are vampires based on demons?"

"What?" He choked on his coffee. He had been expecting a serious relationship type of question. This took him by surprise.

"Is the idea of vampires based on you all? Is the book Dracula based on a demon? I am assuming that vampires are not real." She thought for a moment. "Wait! Are they?"

"No, they are not." He gave her a bemused look. God, he loved the hell out of her mind.

"Didn't think so. So, are they based on demons?"

"Why would you ask that?"

"Think about it. Preternatural strength, you can be 'created' and you have a sire of some kind, kind of. You have fangs, you make vampire-like noises. You have a beast form."

"How do you know what noise a vampire would make?"

"Books and movies. Come on, you know I have a point. Oh! Did you know Bram Stoker?"

He sighed. "You do have a point, I suppose. I met Stoker, in passing. But we didn't spend any real time together and he didn't know I was a demon. Did he know other demons, I cannot say, but I think the similarities are coincidental. We eat, we don't need blood to survive, we can go out in daylight, you can't kill us with a stake. There are also a lot of differences."

"Hhmmm, all true as well."

"I can see you remain skeptical."

"It just seems that there are a lot of coincidences. Are there famous demons?"

"Demons mostly tend to not seek out fame or notoriety. When you're pretty much immortal, it's hard to just disappear over time, harder if you're in the public eye. We tend to control things in the background."

"So, the power behind the throne?"

"Yes, in many cases that is true. I run a lot of things in France that may surprise you. We have some texts on the subject. I will see what I can find for you to read."

"Thank you! So, what do you control in Paris?"

"Well…all of the major tourist sites. The museums, some churches."

"All?" He nodded. "The Eiffel Tower?"

"Yes, to the Eiffel Tower. The Louvre and the Orsay are under my auspices. Oh, and I maintain guardianship over both Notre Dame and Sacre-Coeur. Along with a number of smaller churches throughout France. My reach is beyond Paris to all of France and Belgium, but I don't oversee everything outside of the larger cities in both countries."

She was gaping at him. "Are you shitting me?"

"I am not. I have quite a number of humans and demons working for me, when you get right down to it."

"I guess the fuck so. Anywhere else?"

"I also have people, mostly demons, in government agencies. So, police, fire, the President of France's office. Etc."

"Holy shit. Man, you are kind of a hot shit, huh?"

He grinned at her. "It works the same in most of the major cities across the world."

"So, you are all way more widespread than anyone would suspect then." He nodded at her. "So, no famous demons ever?"

"There have been a few." Declan conceded. "But it never really ends well."

"Oh! Tell me one. Just one for now."

"Cardinal Richelieu."

"SHUT UP! For real?"

Declan laughed. "Yes, you daft woman. For real."

"What happened? Is he still alive? Is he on the Council?"

"He works for the Council. He has fingers in many pies, but he keeps things running. He's also quite the spymaster for Anaranth. His antics pissed off Anaranth so much that he refused to put him on the Council proper. So, he works in the shadows. Which I have to admit, suits him and his purposes. I don't think the cardinal really considers it a punishment."

Will I get to meet him? Please say yes."

"Yes, you will. He will likely be the first to greet you at the official presentation. You two will either love each other or hate each other on sight. Actually, he'll love you, I am sure of it. He may be a good ally. If something is going and he doesn't know, it will piss him off and he'll be more inclined to help us figure it out."

"That's something to look forward to!" Anya sat back, beaming.

Declan thought for a moment, wondering if it was a good time to bring up the idea that had been percolating in the back of his brain. "Anya, are you going back to teaching?" She gave him a look. "No, I am not about to tell you I don't want you working. I enjoy my balls too much to endanger them that way. But I keep getting this sense of dissatisfaction from you and the only thing I can think of is teaching. By the way you reacted to Richelieu and the myriad of questions you ask me, I don't think it's about knowledge or learning in general. You get excited about history and books but that joy never quite reaches you when it comes to teaching."

She made a face and sighed. "I don't know. I haven't missed it. I started teaching because it was a means to an end. I had all these degrees, so I figured that I may as well use them for something that would pay me a salary." He took her hand and rubbed his fingers over her knuckles.

"What would you like to do?"

"Well, I enjoy history and I still enjoy learning new things. I still love to write. I've also been thinking about going back for a medieval history degree." He looked at her. "This was before you, but yes, I admit it's more attractive now because of you. But the whole process of writing, doing the research, it's something I have always loved. I used to work as a research assistant when

I was in school, and I adored it. Paid crap though. So, I went into teaching. Still pays crap, just pays a little more crap. I mean, look how small my apartment is."

"So, you realize money is not a problem anymore."

"I can't be dependent on you. I need to be able to make my own money. I have some put away, yes. But it's modest. Especially in comparison to you."

"Understood. But there is enough money for you to do what you love, writing, research if that's what you want. That said, I could likely get the Council to hire you. Well Anaranth could and I can convince him."

"As what?"

"Archivist. Official Historian. We need a comprehensive history written. We have it in a lot of different places, but not in one place and no one is really in charge of it. This book I'm reading refers to other works quite often, but I don't have those works, or I don't know if I do because it's not like I've catalogued anything. I have a lot of texts on the subject. We should also digitize. The older Council members may not avail themselves, but they have younger assistants to do grunt work and they would use it. I mean, you could build a really great historical database." He tried not to smile at how her eyes started to shine at this.

She just looked at him. "Are you serious?"

"I am. I mean, you don't have to, obviously. You can keep teaching, that's fine...but I don't see you getting joy out of it, and if I can help you find something you love to do, why wouldn't I do that? And the Council will sure as shit pay you more than you get teaching."

"Where would I work?"

"I own buildings with space. Or, you'd have an office at my house. You could work there. You could choose staff. But it would also allow you time to go back and get your history degree if you decide to do that."

She was looking at him in a state of shock, but also wonderment. "I mean, I could officially study demons and write about you, as a career *and* go to school?"

"Yes. It would be an official title, etc. You're answerable to the Council, or Anaranth, which isn't the easiest thing. They'll yank your chain just to do it. Are you interested?"

Anya unbuckled her seatbelt and crawled into Declan's lap and started raining kisses all over his face. "So, this is a yes, then?"

"Yes!" She started kissing his jaw, his neck, his face. "I suppose I should finish out the term, there's not much time left though. I could use family as an excuse. I mean, I hate to burn a bridge, but I can't work up much guilt there. The dean hates me anyway."

"Why does he hate you? Do I have to kill him?"

"Not as of yet. He doesn't like me because I wouldn't go out with him. So, now I get a lot of passive aggressive emails about how I look or act." She started unbuttoning his shirt.

"Asshole."

"Yes. I'll call him tomorrow and set up a time to see him."

"Whatever works for you. What are you doing?"

"It should be obvious. I am very pleased and trying to show you how pleased I am."

"By stroking my chest."

"I'm hoping this will lead to you carrying me into the bathroom so I can have my way with you."

"It's not a done deal, yet."

"Yes, it is."

He laughed. "You're right, Anaranth will agree to it. Oh God, that feels good." She unbuckled his seatbelt and he stood up in one motion carrying her. He stalked past a sleeping Gwen and a laughing Donovan to the bathroom. His last words to her before they stopped talking for a while were "So far, this consort thing is amazing."

CHAPTER 14

Things were quiet enough for the next few weeks that Declan and Anya were able to sort out the living situation quickly and quietly. Her landlord was very sweet about letting her out of her lease and she paid for an extra month, so he'd have a little breathing room, as well as leaving him most of the furniture. She was sure that the appearance of several tough looking characters to help move also went a long way to his good mood about losing her as a tenant. Declan's place was huge, an entire house on the Ile St. Louis, with an amazing view of Notre Dame. Her office was huge. There was a second level around three of the sides with floor to ceiling bookcases.

The shelves were empty, but Declan assumed she'd fill them over time. All of her boxes of books were sitting on the main level of the office, along with a number of crates of books that would aid her in her job as the official Demon historical and scribe. Anaranth had approved the idea quickly and they were paying her a very tidy sum to make it happen.

All the books and texts would need to be catalogue before they could be put away. But more kept showing up every day or day. Anya was in heaven. Her window looked out on the Seine, and she loved it. The room was all gleaming dark wood and big comfy couches and chairs in jewel tones. Her desk was an antique mahogany desk with room for her laptop and two large extended monitors. He'd had a second desk set up when she'd decided to work there just in case she wanted an assistant. "I left the walls without shelves bare, so you can hang your own art. We can change any of the furniture, but I thought these would be things you'd like."

"When did you do this?"

He looked a little uncomfortable. "I had it done after the first time we slept together." She looked at him. "I was feeling hopeful."

"Confident is more like it." she snorted.

"Fine, confident then. "

"With good reason." She looked around. "And you did well. I really like the furniture. We're totally having sex on this couch at some point."

"I was hoping for the desk."

"Why not both?"

"I like the way you think."

"So, in the short term, I think I only need one person to help me start with the cataloguing."

"Anyone in mind?"

"Yes. I suspect he'll show up when I pack up my office at the university."

"Him?"

"Don't be jealous. Though he is a much younger demon." She winked at him.

"Luc." said Declan.

"Yes. Well done, you!"

"Well, he is one of mine. And you know I've had Matthew and Michel keep an eye on him." Anya stared at him, waiting. "He was already dying, Anya." He sounded pained. "There was a fire, he saved the other people in the house. He went back one last time, for a little girl's doll, and the smoke got him. Trust me, it pained me a lot that he went so young, He's demon born but I would have tried to extend his life if I could have."

She stroked his cheek, feeling how this caused him pain. Poor Luc. "I'm sorry."

"He is so painfully young. He seems way less broken up about it than I do honestly. Even Matthew is gentle with him, and he can be a real hard ass."

"Declan, he needs to be able to defend himself. If he's still young, he's vulnerable right now."

"He can, he's getting stronger by the day. I am not neglecting that aspect of things. And both Michel and Matthew are good teachers in that regard. I just don't want to rid him of all his humanity just yet." He felt the same about Anya. Her humanity was precious to him, he wanted to protect it the same way he wanted to protect Luc's.

"You care about him."

"Yeah, I do. But the oath, once taken, is unbreakable. I did give him the option though. Demon or death. He chose demon."

"How long ago?

"A little over a year. How do you know him?"

"He's a student of mine. I knew he was a demon the first time I saw him. Anyway, I think he'll show up when I go to clean out my office."

"Are you sure the Dean is going to be amenable?"

"I am sure."

"Because he made a pass at you, and you said no?"

"A pass? You are so adorable."

"Anya." His voice held a tone of warning. Declan, she had learned, was fairly jealous.

"Yes, that's all. He was drunk, it was the holiday party, he grabbed my boob. I kicked him in the balls. Trust me, he'll let me go, willingly."

"That's a bit more than a pass, Anya. You realize I have to kill him now."

"No, you don't." She kissed him. "It's fine." He growled at her. "Stop growling at me and don't kill the Dean."

Her joy at her office was only matched by her joy in the bedroom and the giant closet they would share. "Sharing is ok?" he asked.

"It is. How did you do it?"

"There was another room, a sitting room, attached to the bedroom. I just had it turned into a closet. They did it in record time, I have to say."

"It's perfect." Right down to the cabinet he had built for her knives and daggers. "I don't even know how you did this, but it's amazing."

"Open the bottom drawer."

She did and nestled in silk where two of the most amazing broadswords she'd ever seen. The hilts were gold, with rubies, emeralds and sapphires set into them. The steel just gleamed. The sapphires in the sword matched the sapphire in the necklace he'd given her their first night back. She fingered the necklace now and he remembered how she had looked modeling it for him, naked. She caught his line of thinking and glanced at him. "Down fella, it's sword time."

"Later," he promised, causing her to blush.

"Holy shit, these swords though! What are these?"

"Yours."

"Mine?" She leaned down and gently removed them from their nest. She tested the weight of one, then the other. Picked up both and twirled them. "They're perfect for me, perfectly balanced."

"They are. They were gifted to me about 500 years ago by one of the Ancients. She told me to hold them. That I would know to whom they belonged and when to gift them." He watched her go through some simple movements with them. "And I'm right. They're meant for you. I am not sure why, but you'll need them. I also had a scabbard made for you. It goes over your shoulders, and they set into it, so when you pull them, you pull them from there. I thought it would look badass. And it leaves your legs unencumbered. They are a mating gift."

"I need to learn how to use them properly."

"Matthew or I can help there. Matthew would be the better teacher though. The Ancient also gave me a matching set, weighted perfectly for me." And that, he thought, had to mean something.

"They are the most beautiful things I have ever seen. Have you ever seen anything so gorgeous?"

"Just one," he said quietly.

She looked up, set the swords down and kissed him deeply. "Thank you. I love the necklace, but you knew the absolute way to my heart would be these swords. They are perfect. You are perfect."

"I am far from perfect, my love, but I do want you to be happy." She stroked his cheek and kissed him again.

After putting away the swords, she looked through the other drawers. "Hey! These aren't mine." They were heavy daggers, with a Celtic design on the hilts and the ends were blunted.

"Ah! They are now. Gift from Anaranth. He requests that you wear them, along with the arm sheaths, to your formal presentation. Despite the fact that weapons aren't officially allowed."

She looked at him. "Really?"

"Really."

"To what purpose?"

"He's bored and he's using you to fuck with the Council. They'll get on you for wearing weapons, even if they are blunted, and he wants to see how you're going to handle it."

"So, it's a test."

"It is."

"Well, I suppose I can humor him. They are stunning and my outfit is sleeveless, and they will look pretty sweet with it."

"What are you wearing? Is it here?"

"No, it's not as of yet. And you can see it when everyone else does. Closest to a wedding dress that I am going to get to, so you can be surprised."

"Who's making it?"

"Gwen."

"Gwen?"

"Yes. Did you not know? She works for an Atelier. She's the head seamstress. She asked if she could make my outfit for the official presentation." She thought for a moment. "I am also going to buy very expensive shoes. You can pay for those."

"Naturally. I had no idea. Is that why she squints at me sometimes."

"Yes. She's trying to find a flaw in your tailoring."

"Has she?"

"You'd know if she had."

"Is she coming with you?"

Anya's eyes widened. "Can she?"

"Yes, she can. Aside from the fact she's your best friend, she's fought at your side. She's your second...that's how the Council will see it, so we've a bit of a loophole there for a human who is not a mate coming along. I just thought, once again, it would be nice to have your best friend there."

"You know, if you keep doing thoughtful things, people won't think you are a big, bad demon boss."

"Only you know my secret side and if you tell, I will take the swords away."

"Bastard!"

"Absolutely! Anyway, the Council likes a hierarchy."

"You hate that."

"I do. They like to make people feel less. I don't like when it hits my people."

"You don't make your men feel like less. I can see that and so can they. Don't worry what others think, it's not important. Stop worrying so much."

"It's just..."

"I know. It pisses you off that the Council feels that way but, change comes from within."

"They call themselves a 'Council' but really, it's like court. And Anaranth isn't any better. He will pit them against each other because he's bored."

"Then we just have to be better than all of them."

"We change what we can, we weather the rest."

She kissed his nose. "It's all anybody ever can do, anyway." He picked her up. "Where are we going?"

"To the bed, of course." He carried her over to the massive king-sized bed and flopped her onto it, bending to undo her boots.

"I have to meet the Dean."

"That's not for hours yet." He got the second boot off and reached up to undo her jeans. "We have plenty of time."

"Declan…"

"Calm before the storm my love. Once you are formally presented, I suspect our enemy is going to move quickly." He pulled her jeans down. "Have you gone commando?"

"I figured it was easier than you ripping every pair of panties I own."

"Aw, that's part of the fun." He nipped the inside of her thighs and put his mouth on her, watching her while she arched her back and grabbed his hair.

"Ah well," she said breathily. "Needs must!"

***

The meeting with the Dean went as expected. He balked for a minute, she reminded him of the holiday party and may have let it slip that her new husband (just easier that way) was the jealous type, which is why she had bodyguards outside the door and maybe they could just dispense with the formalities and let her go quietly? He agreed quickly and in return, she agreed to vacate her office that very day.

When she got to her office, there was another letter waiting for her onto the floor. She sighed and picked it up. Dougal took one look, grunted, and stalked off down the hallway to see if he could see anything or anyone suspicious.

"What does this one say?" Matthew asked peering at her over the sunglasses he wore.

"You know you don't need those in here?"

"Yes, but I can scan for danger without people catching on." He nodded towards the letter. "And they look dead cool."

She snorted and opened the letter, read it and blanched a bit. "Ummm…" She handed it to him. He read it silently.

> *You slut. You think I don't see how you act around all those men? You're probably spreading your legs for all of them. Your time will come. Whore."*

"Well, that's fucking appalling," Matthew said.

"You're not wrong. Can you…"

"I'll text it to Declan and let him know that you're fine, just pissed off. And I'll hold onto it for you."

He did that while she was packing up her office. As she had expected, Luc showed up, right behind Dougal's return.

Luc rushed in, dropped to a knee, and breathed "Consort!" at her.

She stared at him while Dougal rolled his eyes and let out a "Fer 'chrissakes lad, stand up!" in a thick Scots brogue, while trying not to laugh. Matthew had to step out because his shoulders had started to shake with laughter. "Luc get up please. You do not have to bow to me. Nor should you." God, he was so young.

He stood. "Sorry…it's just…well, Michel said that I should…oh, it was a joke."

"Yes lad, it was a joke on ye," laughed Dougal.

"I told him that I was nervous, and this is what he said to do, and I believed him. I just…"

Dougal clapped a hand on his shoulder. "Breathe, lad and let the lady speak." Matthew stepped back in, having gotten himself under control.

She gestured for Luc to sit in her visitor's chair. He took a few deep breaths before speaking again. "Are you leaving, Prof?"

Better, she thought. "I am. So, I've been asking around a bit about you. You're studying history with a concentration on the Middle Ages, though you seem to be taking some courses on the Renaissance. Yes?"

"Yes, Prof."

"So, why were you attending Literature lectures?"

"The ones I attend directly…*correlatif*… "

"Correlate?"

"*Oui!*" Correlate to the history classes I take. Your Medieval Lit class is one of those. I like to be well rounded."

"I've seen you in some of my other lectures."

He shrugged. "I enjoyed your lectures. So, I just decided, that if I could, I would go to others as well."

"Good answer. You're also good with computers I hear. You work part time in the computer lab."

"Yes, I do. Why?"

"I have a proposition for you." She looked towards the door where Dougal and Matthew pretended that they weren't listening. "I have been hired by the Council to do two things; write a comprehensive demon history and to catalogue and archive the books, tomes, scrolls, etc., that exist about demons. This will include digitizing the works so that they can be accessed easily, but also so that we can preserve the older books, appropriately." She saw it then, how his eyes lit up when she mentioned the project. "I could use an assistant. I insist you finish your degree, and you can even go on to get your master's and PhD if you want. You can quit the computer lab; this job will pay better."

He looked at her. "I am not sure I can afford to get a masters. I have….my family thinks…"

Oh fuck! She was an idiot; he had no family because they believed him to be dead. "Of course, Luc. I'm sorry," she said softly. "How are you paying for school now?"

"Computer Lab and I do some odd jobs."

"Luc, Declan would have paid for your schooling you know. You had only to ask," Matthew said.

"I…I wasn't sure. I didn't want to be a pain or bother anyone. It's hard to not have family. You don't want to be a burden to people."

Matthew saw right away that Luc's words had hit home with Anya, and he clearly saw the tender heart that she tried to keep hidden from most of the world. With one sentence, she had adopted Luc and would do anything she could to ensure his happiness. A woman like that could be dangerous for his own emotional barriers. He'd need to be careful.

"Luc, Declan and I will pay for your schooling, through a masters and PhD, if you decide to go that far. Where do you live?"

"Oh, I live with some other young demons, in a large house."

Anya looked at Matthew. "It's a house for the younger demons, it's a good place for him to be. It helps to be with demons around your own age." Matthew was looking at him with a gentle look in his eyes, his compassion evident.

"That's fine then." She pulled out a piece of paper. "Here is my email and phone number, email me your class list so I know how to schedule you for work. I'd like to start next week, after the official presentation. You'll come to that with us."

"Me?"

"Yes, you. We're family now."

Luc grasped the piece of paper like it was the holy grail. "Thank you! I really appreciate this; I will not let you down."

She peered at him over her glasses, realizing all of a sudden that she didn't need them. She could see perfectly well. She pulled them off, letting them clatter on her desk. "See that you don't. Off with you now."

He ran out of the office, beaming. "You have a soft heart for such a tough woman," Matthew said. His clipped British accent softened some when he spoke. "Declan is a lucky demon to have you. Luc is lucky to have you on his side."

"He's a good kid." She paused. "And I am lucky to have Declan as well. And all of you."

Matthew had to swallow past a lump in his throat. He hadn't expected that. So much for the vow of self-protection he'd just made. Donovan had been right. Declan's consort had been a lonely child who had grown into a lonely woman. Now, she was surrounded by people who liked and accepted her for exactly who she was. And she had accepted all of them. She was smart and tough, and she'd brought some peace to one of his oldest friends.

Dougal was laughing quietly. "That kid is going to get so much…"
Anya looked at him. "Female attention, when he's ready."

"He might not like women in that way?"

Matthew gave her a look. "Have you not seen how he looks at you?"

Anya looked startled. "Matthew! Come on, he's just a kid with a little of…I don't know, hero worship for Declan. It's just filtered over to me."

He raised an eyebrow. "You really don't see it, do you?"

"See what?"

"How people see you? That kid has a gigantic crush on you. He likes women." He thought for a moment. "Which doesn't mean he also doesn't like men. But he definitely likes women."

She shook her head. "Now that's something else I have to worry about, beating the ladies off with a stick. Or the guys too for that matter. Those big blue eyes of his are going to be a problem."

"Yes. He gets a lot of attention that he doesn't even notice."

"He is too busy thinking about you," Dougal said. "Or you and Declan." The Scot grinned wickedly.

"Jesus! Dougal do you have someone?"

"Plenty of someones."

"No one special?"

"Ah lass, they're all special."

"No one will have his ugly mug for too long." Matthew smiled. "That said, Dougal is a bastard, but he has a point."

"You guys are a real riot. Let's finish this so I can get out of here. I'm going shopping with Gwen."

<u>CHAPTER 15</u>

"So, I can really come with you?" Gwen asked. They were sitting in the Tuileries having coffee and pastries after spending way too much money shopping for shoes. The park was one of their favorite places in the city.

"Yup! It's all arranged. Do you really like these shoes?" Anya pulled one of the midnight blue silk stiletto heels from the *Galeries Lafayette* bag. They were simple, but elegant.

"I love them!"

"I spent too much." Anya laughed.

"Well worth it. Your outfit will go perfectly with it. So, the presentation?"

Anya smiled at her friend. "Yes, I am sure. And I really want you there."

"Good thing I have something to wear."

"Were you making something, just in case?"

"Mmmaaaybbbeeee."

"I know you're making mine; I don't want you to be stressed."

"Yours is almost done. You need to come and try it on."

"Will do. Do you think I should have left the purple suede boots?"

"I do not." Gwen looked her in own bag. "I should not have let you buy my shoes."

"Yes, you should have. You are a great friend. Loyal, smart, funny. I love you and I wanted you to have pretty shoes that you would never buy yourself."

Gwen blinked back tears. "Oh. Well, thank you. Or should I say thank Declan."

"Nope. Those were all me."

All of a sudden, they heard a shout. *"Oh mon Dieu! Il a un enfant !"*

"What's going on?" asked Gwen, sounding worried.

Anya stood and saw a man standing in the Grand Basin, holding a child. "Oh shit! He does have a kid! Go get Dougal!" Anya took off at a run towards the basin.

"Anya, wait!"

"I can't!"

"ANYA!" Gwen yelled. "Declan is going to fucking kill me."

Dougal ran past her. "I've got her! Get to the car!"

"Don't think so!" She said starting to run in the same direction as Anya and Dougal. She'd stay out of the way and not use magic, too many people around, but she would not abandon her friend. She was plucked out of the air by Michel.

"Oh no, you don't. To the car with you."

"Put me down!"

"Absolutely. Once we get to the car. And do not use your magic on me. Do you want Anya worrying about you? We need to contain this quickly and there is nothing you can do."

"You asshole!"

"Yes. I am following orders."

"Whose?!"

"Donovan's. And do not get me in trouble." He set her down gently when they got to the car.

She glared at him, but knew he was right. "If I behave, will you show me that jab to the windpipe move?"

"Yes, I will."

"Ok, fine. I will stay put. This time." She looked around. "Where's Matthew?"

"Went after Dougal and Anya. I'm staying with you."

The basin was in chaos as Anya charged into the fray. People got out of her way, but she didn't notice. All she saw was the demon, because he was indeed a demon, holding a small child hostage. She waded into the water, putting her hands up so he'd think she wasn't armed.

The demon saw her and grinned. "Come closer," he growled.

"Let the child go and I will."

The demon looked down, almost as if he'd forgotten he'd been holding the little one and threw the boy off to the side.

Anya looked at the boy. "Run!" She shouted in English. Hoping he understood. He did. He ran off and was scooped up at the edge of the water by his mother.

She looked back at the demon, and he snarled at her, coming towards her. She backed up as he moved forward. She wanted to get out of the water before taking him on, but he had other ideas. He reached out, lightning quick, closing the distance between them and picked her up right off the ground. She kicked out and connected with his kneecap and she got an elbow up and slammed it into his windpipe. But he didn't let go of her. He carried her out of the basin and slammed her down onto the concrete edge.

"Anya!" yelled Dougal but his scream was lost among those of the bystanders own screams. She barely heard any of it as the demon slapped her hard and then wrapped his hands around her throat. Fuck this guy was strong. Anya was stronger than she had been before, but this demon was still stronger, and she was starting to get woozy. She tried to get her knees up, but he ground his foot into her, giving her no leeway. She was beginning to lose consciousness, when all of a sudden, she could breathe again. She started coughing, looked up and Dougal was holding the demon by the neck. All of the onlookers had not made it easy to get to her. She sat and the demon landed a kick to her cheek. "Declan is going to be so pissed at you."

The demon snarled. "I don't give a shit!"

"Oh no, he's going to be pissed at her. You, he's going to kill." Dougal was grim.

"I can't die! I was told I couldn't die!"

Dougal sniffed him. "You're pretty young, he can probably tear ye apart. You messed with the consort, lad. You won't survive this."

"His...what?"

Matthew came running up just then and helped Anya to her feet. "Jesus, Anya," he said looking at her face and neck.

"Is it bad?"

"Yes. And it's not going to heal before Declan sees it."

"I suppose we have to tell him?"

"You have a blood bond, Anya. He could feel it."

"Ah, shit." She'd forgotten about that part of the bond. It was all still very new to her.

"Tell Declan I am taking this guy to Brimstone."

"Got it. I'll take her home. We're lucky we haven't had a random policeman come by." Matthew helped her up and she leaned on him on the way back to the car. Michel whistled when he saw her face. "Christ, Anya!"

"Is Declan really mad?"

"I don't think I have ever heard him make the sound he made over the phone when I called him."

Anya groaned and got into the car. Gwen said nothing, just put her arm around her friend's shoulder and held her hand, trying to give her strength for what was to come.

***

Matthew walked Anya into the house thirty minutes later, after dropping Gwen off. Anya promised to call her friend later. Declan took one look at Anya's face and roared. Very loudly. His eyes went deep red, his claws came out and his face began to change shape before he got himself under control, something that took him a good five minutes to do. Anya wasn't scared that he'd hurt her, but she knew he was furious. And she knew his control was very fine right now. He was bone deep furious because she'd scared him. The terror he had felt when she was being choked had been almost too much to bear. "Matthew, thank you for bringing my consort home. Would you please leave us alone now." It was not a question.

"Yes Declan." He gave her a sympathetic look and left quickly.

"Declan…"

"Don't say a word. Not one fucking word until we get upstairs." He stared at the marks on her neck for a long time. He then scooped her up and carried her quickly upstairs. There was nothing romantic or playful about it. Once inside, he kicked the door closed and got her a compress for her face.

"Thank you," she said quietly.

"It will heal by tomorrow, but it's got to hurt." She could hear the barely restrained fury in his voice.

She started to open her mouth and he put a hand up. She closed her mouth and bit her lip. She could see he was still struggling for control.

"What in the hell were you thinking running into danger like that?" He yelled and it was loud and deep, and she was glad her ears weren't mortal ones any longer. As it was, she winced. "You put yourself in danger. You put the people at the park in danger. What possessed you to do that?"

"I saw that he had a child and I just acted."

"You knew it was a demon?"

"Yes."

"And you thought you could handle it?"

"I didn't think. But I assumed I would be able to handle it."

Declan punched a hole in the wall. "Yes. Your face tells me you handled it beautifully."

She pursed her lips. "Now look, Declan…"

"No, you look. You cannot just run headlong into every battle by yourself without thought to your surroundings. You should have waited for Dougal or Matthew."

"You know, I did fine taking care of myself before you came along."

"Did you fight a lot of demons before I came along?"

"No, but I didn't think I was in real danger."

"He used that child as bait! Probably to get to you. You could have been seriously hurt, Anya. You are new to immortality. You can still be wounded. You can still die given the right circumstances. You ran in ready for action without assessing the situation and people could have gotten hurt. Mortals die, and they die very easily. Whoever did this knew that you were likely to act first and think later. Did you not give any thought to any of this before you decided you could handle a violent demon?"

She had scared him, badly. She saw that. But it was more than that. He was right, she had acted rashly. She should have thought things through. She could have caused more people to get hurt. Still, Anya was stubborn, and she wasn't quite ready to back down completely. "I am who I am. I am going to do what I think is right." God, that sounded stupid, even to her own ears.

"You are not fully capable of judging a situation when it comes to demons yet."

"Now wait a fucking minute, I have fought next to you."

"Yes, next to me. Not in a park, with humans around. There were children there!"

She sagged. Children. That little boy he had been holding. Fuck. Stubborn was one thing, but the mention of children broke through that. He was right, she was not an expert at fighting demons yet and they were all stronger than her. Even Luc was stronger than she was right now. "I'm sorry. You're right. I was rash. I should have made a different decision and thought it through. I don't strategize, I just act." She paused and walked over to him, putting her hand on his cheek. "And I am so sorry I scared you, Declan. It was never my intention."

He crushed her to him. "Christ Anya, I couldn't handle it if anything happened to you. I felt it when he was choking you. I was going out of my mind. I have never had my beast fight me for control like that before." He leaned back and looked at her neck, rubbing it gently. "Does it hurt, *malysh*?" He was still furious, but he would never touch her in anger.

"A little sore, that's all. It's fine. My throat is a little raspy."

"I'll have some tea brought up for you. "

"Thank you. Dougal said he could tell that this was a new demon. But that he was much too strong."

"I know. He called and told me this."

"Are you going to hurt him?"

"Oh, yes. Yes I am."

"But..."

"He not only attacked you. He attacked my city. He put mortals in danger. I cannot let that pass. The minute he grabbed that kid and laid hands on you; he sealed his fate."

"Declan…." She was coming face to face with the reality of her new life tonight, and it wasn't easy.

"Who I am can be brutal and merciless. You have seen the civilized side of me, the loving side. But I have kept control of France and Belgium because I can be brutal. And ruthless if need be. People will see you as my weakness now and they can never think either of us weak, is that clear?" He didn't like to put it in those terms, but it was the truth. He could not afford to let this slide, she could accept that or not, but this demon was going to be dealt with. Dougal had told him the demon was young, but ridiculously strong. Too strong for one so young. Declan needed to know how this was possible.

"Yes. Understood." She had to learn to accept this side of him too. He was right, she lived in a world that played by a different set of rules now. And she would need Declan's help to do that. Asking for help was not something she was used to doing. She was far more used to going it alone and figuring it out as she went along. But she wasn't alone anymore, and she had to learn how to navigate in different waters.

"You stay here and rest, please." She breathed a small sigh of relief. She honestly did not want to go, but she would have.

"Thank you. I'd prefer to do that. What's Brimstone?"

"It's a place you'd hate. It's where I deal with demons who have crossed the line."

"Can I see it?"

He sighed. "Yes, at some point. And I hope you never need to go in there again after that. That place is barely under control at the best of times."

"Ok." He winced listening to her voice. She kissed him softly, but thoroughly. "Go on now, the sooner you go, the sooner you can come back home to me. I love you."

He kissed her nose. "And I love you too."

***

When he got to the club, he circumvented the main floor and headed down two floors to a sub-basement. The rooms down here had their own kind of demon magic, so the ropes holding the demon were holding fast. Dougal was standing against the wall, his eyes had gone a light red, but he was calm. Declan, on the other hand, was barely leashed fury at the moment and Dougal held out no hope for their guest.

"Does he have a name?" Declan asked. He stared at the tied-up demon and it was clear; this demon was high on something and very much out of his depth.

"Won't give it. I don't have enough power to force him." He may have had enough, but he didn't want to tire himself by forcing the issue when he knew that Declan could do it easily enough.

Declan whipped around and in an unearthly voice demanded the demon's name. The demon tried to resist; his eyes started to bleed from the effort. It was an order from a powerful demon and any demon with less power, would feel compelled to comply. It was a power that Declan used very sparingly.

"Lad, you may as well tell him, it's no use having yer eyes bleed o'er it," Dougal said.

"C….C…Connell." The demon was American it seemed. And aside from the obvious smell of drugs in his system, he didn't feel right.

"Good lad," Dougal said.

Declan took off his jacket and began to roll up his sleeves while stalking around the tied-up demon. "You know Connell, there are things I may have been able to overlook today had you just practiced a little caution. I know what it's like to test your abilities some, I was once a young demon. But you didn't practice any caution. You caused panic and used a child as bait. You put hands on my consort." Declan's brogue had gotten thicker, his eyes had gotten redder, and his claws had extended. Declan had not gone full beast in years, but Dougal was damned sure it was going to happen tonight. "Taken together, I cannot let any of these things go. But, if you tell me who put you up to this, I may take pity and give you a quick death."

Connell looked panicked. "I can't die. He said I can't die."

"Oh Connell," Declan said sadly, leaning down and scraping one claw along the back of the youngster's neck, drawing a line of blood there. "You're very young, not yet a year, I'd say weeks at most by the smell of you. Demons can die within their first year of becoming demons. But the trick is, only another demon can kill you. So, my consort can't kill you, but I definitely can."

"I…I…didn't…don't…"

"What, Connell, spit it out. I'm losing patience." To prove his point, he sliced his claws down Connell's chest.

Connell gasped. "Ow! Fuck! I don't know who hired me. I got an envelope in the mail with the job and money. More money than I'd ever seen. Fuck, that hurt."

"And you didn't question it?"

"No. This is the kind of work I did as a human. I rarely ever really knew who was hiring me."

"Did you make a deal to become a demon with someone?" Connell looked at him blankly. "Did you find a demon, or were you approached by one because you wanted something? In return, you agreed to become a demon."

"No. I went out one night, met someone and they did it. No deal. I didn't ask for it."

This was very bad. This kid was never meant to be a demon, Declan was sure of it. Which means someone was finding humans and creating demons to suit their own ends. This wasn't done. There was an order to how things worked. Either you were born with the predisposition in your genetic makeup for becoming a demon, or you brokered a deal. That was it. To create demons from humans who didn't follow either of these conventions was forbidden. Consorts were immortal as long as their demon lived, but they were not demons. But now someone was breaking rules. The demon born lived shorter mortal lives in general, but it was also forbidden to take them before their time, unless the human agreed to it. In Declan's case, he had gotten more time. And that was highly unusual. Not even the Council was allowed to break this rule.

"Who approached you?"

"I don't know his name. He was from Russia, I think?" Declan's eyes widened. He felt a growing sense of dread as an idea formed, but he couldn't think about that just now.

"Did he force you?"

"No. He came up to me, started talking to me, things got fuzzy and the next thing I knew, I was...was a demon. Russian guy tried to tell me a bunch of things, but I was still a bit confused."

"What did the note you received say?"

"That I would be called on to cause a distraction somewhere at a certain date and time and that they'd contact me when it was time. I got another note about thirty minutes before I was told to be at the park. It told me to go there, grab a kid and if I could, bring the woman down. I destroyed the note though." Which means someone had been following Anya today. Considering the note she'd been left, it made sense that someone was watching her. It didn't take a genius.

Declan held up his hand. "You are too strong for a new demon. My consort should have been able to subdue you easily. What were you given?"

"She's human!"

Dougal snorted. "Lad, that woman could have thrashed ye with one hand tied behind her back if you weren't on something."

"Some kind of elixir, he called it. He said to take it before I went to the park. It would temporarily make me stronger so I could get the woman."

Dougal and Declan looked at each other with horror. "Declan, that's a myth."

"Apparently not."

"So, can I go now? Let me live, please!" Connell was whining now, which was just pissing Declan off more.

"No. You are going to die. Really die, this time."

"But you said…"

"I said I *may* kill you quickly. I never said you wouldn't die. I find as we've spoken that my anger has grown, not lessened. Your death is going to be very, very painful. Quick, but it's going to hurt like a motherfucker."

"How can you do it? I don't understand?"

"Oh Connell, I am going to tear you apart with my bare hands." Declan was eerily calm. It chilled Dougal. He'd seen Declan lose his shit before, he was there the last time he had turned into the beast, when he had eviscerated a group of young demons for killing a group of nuns and orphans that were hiding in the basement of a church.

Connell looked at Declan's hands. He looked confused. "Not these hands, mind you," he said looking at his own hands, long fingers with claws, still mostly human. "The full-on claws I have in beast form."

Connell went from confused to properly frightened.

"Oh lad, may God have mercy on ye, because Declan won't."

Declan's beast roared to life. And Dougal hoped like hell he had a change of clothes in the car because the ones he was wearing had been shredded with the change. The force strong enough that the demons on the main level of the club felt it and they all froze in place, the music stopping. The fear that the one who ruled the city was coming for them was palpable. Even when it became clear he wasn't, the club was much more subdued, the music started again at a much lower volume. The demons were still agitated.

Anya felt it at home, waking from a sound sleep with her blood on fire, thrumming through her veins so quickly and violently that all she could do was gasp. She could feel his blood lust and his rage, knew he had taken beast form and knew there was nothing she could do to help him. But she also felt joy, his beast was free, and that beast felt the joy in the kill. It was happy to be free for once. It should have frightened her, but she was fascinated by it. But now she had a better idea how Declan must have felt when she was being choked. Helpless, powerless, and frightened. It was a hard lesson for her to learn but learn it she did. Chances are, she was still going to fuck up, but she now knew there were serious consequences to her actions.

Meanwhile, Declan's full beast snarled at Connell, who kept looking around as if he could hide somewhere. Dougal watched impassively from the wall. He wasn't worried about getting killed. Declan's beast would know his smell and recognize him as a friend. When Dougal was a boy, he and his friends had imagined what devils looked like from looking at the pictures that the Vicar had in his books. Large, snarling beasts. No cloven hoofs or horns, but true beasts. This is what Declan looked like now. What they all looked like in this form. Declan picked Connell up and as promised, tore him limb from limb. Arms, legs, head and torso all torn apart with a quick flick of what was, a paw at this point. The pieces crumbled to dust. Declan stalked the room for another ten minutes while the man worked to take control back. Anya had collapsed onto all fours on the floor, as she felt her Declan return and she wept with relief.

***

An hour and half later Declan walked into their bedroom. Anya was sitting up in bed, watching him carefully. He had different clothes on, which didn't surprise her. He was still very angry, she could feel it, but he was in complete control. The night had taken a bigger toll on him than it had on her, she thought. "You should be asleep." His voice was gravelly.

"I was for a bit. When I woke up, I decided I wanted to try and wait up for you." She didn't need to tell him what actually woke her right now.

He nodded. "I need...I need to shower."

She heard the water turn on, and the sound of the shower door opening and closing a couple of moments later. She got up, took off her nightshirt and went into the bathroom. She could see he was just standing there, soap in one hand, other hand on the wall, just staring at nothing. She stepped into the shower. "Anya," he said.

"Sssh," she said, taking the soap from him. She soaped the back of him and then turned him around gently to rinse while she soaped his front. His eyes stayed on her the whole time. They were still a light red but were quickly fading back to the green that reminded her of Ireland's rolling hills. She hummed softly. His hand moved to the bruises, already much lighter, at her neck. He then turned to rinse himself again, and she leaned into his back, giving him her love and strength. "Are you ok?" she asked.

"It takes a lot out of me."

"I know."

He turned to her "How?"

"I could feel it. I could feel the beast when he was free, the joy he felt, that you felt, when you took that demon's life."

"Jesus I'm sorry."

"Why? It's part of you who you are. And it drove home the point that we are connected in ways I don't fully understand yet."

He put his arms around and pulled her to him so that she was leaning against his heart. "I can hear your heart. Do all demons have a heartbeat?"

"We do. Even though we're technically undead, we have heartbeats, we bleed, we're warm to the touch. It's demon magic that I don't quite understand, but I am grateful for it. We also tend to run a bit warm, which is why I sleep naked." She sighed and snuggled closer. "The thing is, the beast is part of me, he's hard to control, but you're right. We both felt joy at that kill. I don't feel shame when I kill. I feel exhilarated by it. Even when I take back over, it makes me feel strong. That's what I feel shame about, that joy."

"You shouldn't. You aren't taking innocent lives, I would assume. Killing is never easy." He tightened his hold on her.

"Anya, I spent the entire car ride home fantasizing about fucking you while I was in beast form. I couldn't stop it; the beast was still in control even though I was back in human form. I don't like that. When we got here, I had to sit in the car for twenty minutes until I was back in control. Until I was sure I would not hurt you."

"You feel different in that form, but you also still feel like you, deep down. I don't think I was in any danger from you, not really." She was stroking his back gently.

"How can you be so calm about what I just told you? It's an animal form. One I have little enough control over when he's out. The fact that he kept some control over me that long is not good."

"Because I trust you. I don't think you'd do it, come in here and try and take me in beast form. This is evidenced by the fact that you sat in a car until you could control yourself. It's been too long since you let him out, I think. He was feeling kind of frisky."

"Are you saying my beast form was fucking with me?"

"I am. It wouldn't have happened. He knew you'd assert control soon enough."

"He'll recognize your smell as something that's his though."

"But something of his to protect, I think."

"How are you so sure?"

"The compress."

"What?"

"Earlier today you got me a compress. As furious as you were with me, you took care of me first by getting me the compress for my face. Also, as mad as you are or were at me, you still don't hold a candle to how mad Doina used to get." She meant he didn't hit her like her mother had. He really was going to enjoy killing that woman. "And I am turning into a prune."

He turned the water off and grabbed two towels. He wrapped her in one and the other around his waist. "See?" she said. "You take care of me. You, or your beast, wouldn't do anything to hurt me."

"I wish I was as sure of me as you are."

"I wish you were too. Now, let's get some rest. You look exhausted."

"I am exhausted. But I can still do this." He scooped her up, lovingly this time, and carried her to bed.

"I can walk."

"I like carrying you." She slid under the covers and a second later, he slid in on the other side. She turned on her side, turning off the lamp and he nestled up next to her, sliding his arm under her head. "Declan?"

"Mmmm?"

"Was it hot?"

"Was what hot?"

"The fantasy you had in the car."

"Really, Annie?"

"Yes, really. I want to know."

"I am not answering that."

"You should tell it to me one day." Anya was far too curious sometimes, she knew this.

"Maybe." He yawned loudly. He highly doubted it though. It wasn't something he was particularly proud of.

"Go to sleep now, love." she whispered.

"Mmm…Annie." And with that he dropped off. She joined him minutes later.

CHAPTER 16

When she woke up the next morning, she could feel Declan stroking her hair. She turned to face him. "Good morning."

"Good morning. Your bruises are gone."

"Good." She kissed him longingly and he started stroking her back. She sighed and rested her head on his chest. "How are you feeling this morning?"

"I'm fine. Much calmer than I was last night."

"I'm glad. I am so sorry I scared you like that. I don't think the changes in my life really hit home until yesterday."

"That's understandable. I should have been a bit more patient with you yesterday."

"You were plenty patient really. When you changed, I felt helpless. Powerless. I could feel your fear that you might not be able to change back, or that you might hurt me. It drove the point home better than anything could have. You are a complex man, Declan O'Shea."

"Not so complex, really. But I am sorry I scared you." *Cushla machree, I would hurt myself before I would ever hurt you.*

Anya sat straight up. "You didn't say that last thing out loud, did you?"

"I did not. You try it."

Her brow furrowed. "How?"

"Just think at me. Find the bond and send me a message down it." *Declan?*

He winced. "Ooph! You don't have to yell at me."

"Well, it's not like I've done this before, you ass."

He laughed. "Ok, that's fair. Try again and just use your regular volume."

"It's not that easy."

"It's child's play. Do it again."

Child's play, huh? For you maybe. Asshole. She grinned at him and planted a kiss on his nose.

"Much better."

"So, we can just talk to each other in our heads?"

"Yup. We should also be able to pick up each other's moods and thoughts. So be careful if there is something you don't want me to know. You think really loudly."

"Again, I repeat...asshole." He laughed and rolled her onto her back.

"That's going to come in handy when we want to talk shit about people."

"Mmm..." he said, kissing her. She wrapped her arms around him and stroked his shoulders. "Do we have to get up? Can we not just stay here all day?"

"I cannot think of anything I would rather do. And as soon as all of this is over, we're going to do just that. Actually, we're going to go on vacation."

"Oh? Where are you going to take me?"

"Somewhere tropical. Where our bedroom looks out on beautiful, blue water and we're going to watch that water, from our bed, for at least a week. Probably two. All of our meals will be served to us right there. I am going to keep you naked and happy."

"No swimming or sunning or being a tourist?"

"Maybe swimming so I can see you in a bikini."

"Perv. I don't own one."

"Swim naked then, I am fine with that."

"It's a date." She laughed.

"Good." he purred at her. He sat up briefly and texted something into his phone. "I am asking Mara if she'd bring up some coffee." Mara ran the house, did all of the cooking and made the best coffee that Anya had ever had.

"My hero."

"And pastries."

"Be still my heart! Oh, we adopted Luc yesterday, I forgot to tell you." She chuckled at the notion that they'd basically adopted a college student.

He sighed. "Of course we did. What are we doing?"

"Paying for his schooling. Making sure he's ok and not too lonely. Maybe finding him a nice girl. Or boy. Or both. I also hired him to work with me. So, we're paying him."

"This is going to be a pattern with you, isn't it? You're going to find all the lonely strays and take them in. We can't do that with everyone, you know." Truly, he didn't mind. He thought it was sweet that his Anya cared that Luc wasn't lonely.

"Sure we can. Ppplleeeassee...can we keep him. He's so cute with those big blue eyes." she batted her eyelashes at him.

"You are really bad at that."

She laughed. "I know. But can we?"

He sat up. "Yes, we can. He's a good kid."

"Matthew says he has a crush on me. I think he has a case of hero worship where you're concerned."

"Oh, he for sure has a crush on you."

"Bah!"

"He does!"

"He also worships you."

Declan rolled his eyes. "Maybe."

"Declan, he's alone. He misses his family. I get what it's like to feel so alone. I know he's in a house full of people, but it's not the same thing. You're like a father figure to him right now."

He leaned over and gave her a kiss. "Then adopt him we shall. I like him and honestly, I think his looks are going to be an asset to us." He got up to get the coffee and pastries from Mara. He fixed a plate for Anya and poured her some coffee; then did the same for himself. They enjoyed a peaceful breakfast together.

She watched him walk into the bathroom, admiring that amazing ass of his. She heard the shower go on and picked up her phone to text Gwen that she was fine, Declan was fine, and she'd be by at noon for her fitting.

When he came out of the bathroom about twenty minutes later, a towel wrapped low around his hips, she almost lost her train of thought for a moment. "I've been thinking."

"God help us!" He walked into the closet, and she followed him.

"I'm serious. And you won't like it."

He had pulled a pair of pants down and was reaching for a shirt when he pivoted towards her. "What?"

"I think you know."

He looked at her, picking up on her thoughts. "Absolutely not. No fucking way!"

"You know I'm right. I have to meet your beast and he has to meet me. The beast from last night, the full animal."

"Too risky."

"We can plan for that."

"How?"

"If we have people in the room with us, they'd be able to stop you or get me out at the very least if something goes wrong."

"No. It's too dangerous."

"I trust you. Why don't you trust you?"

He sighed and sat down on a bench. "Because I don't know if I can control him around you." Last night was still bothering him.

"I don't think you have to. I think he'll be fine. He'll smell me and recognize me as his and as someone he'd never harm." She was possibly being naive about this, but it was important he did this. She trusted him, but like with any wild thing, you never knew. "And he is part of you."

"Down the line…"

"No. It has to be now. We need to do it before I meet the Council."

"Why?"

"Because one of them has to be behind this whole thing. And they could use this against us. Force you to turn or try to convince others we aren't for real because I haven't met your beast. Any number of reasons." She was grasping, but it seemed like a logical argument to her own ears.

He sighed. She was right. And that's why several hours later, he found himself in a large, almost empty room in one of his buildings. There was a couch and a few chairs, a table. But nothing else. Dougal, Matthew, and Therese were in the room. Therese was standing closest to Anya. She was the oldest of all of them, strong and fast. Her being a woman was also going to be less threatening to Declan's beast, than a man standing by her. Friend or not. And even though it seriously pissed Gwen off, she was in Declan's office at the club, waiting with Michel and Donovan. There had been much arguing about it, but Gwen, while a friend, was not going to be as familiar to Declan in beast form and could be a distraction.

Therese and Declan had known each other for most of Declan's demon existence and her scent would not confuse. Anya knew he doubted himself, so she couldn't. Not for a minute. This could go tits up, she knew that. They all did. But she also wasn't going to act like her meeting this beast was freaking her out. I mean, it was. She wasn't a moron. This was dangerous. She got that. She thought the most he'd likely try to do in beast form was fuck her, but in making sure that didn't happen, it could get dicey. She was wearing familiar clothes that had both her and Declan's scent on them. Black jeans and a black pullover sweater that belonged to him. And of course, her spring-loaded arm sheaths, each with a dagger tucked up in them.

"This is a bad idea." Declan looked like he was going to be sick.

"Declan," said Matthew. "None of us are going to let you hurt her. We promise you that."

"I just don't…"

"I promise you, as your friend, I will not let you harm Anya. Even if I have to get between the two of you," Matthew said. The others nodded in agreement.

"And I can get her out of the room quickly and subdue you if need be." said Therese. "I've subdued you before."

Anya turned to look at the tall woman with long, dark hair and dark eyes. "Really?"

"Yes. I will tell you about it another time." She winked quickly at Anya.

"Nor will she be able to hurt you. Despite the metal she's carrying," Dougal said.

"I always carry knives. And tonight wasn't going to be the exception."

"Nope, between the two of you, I am going to let her hurt you. So we're clear on that." This was from Therese. Declan nodded at her. That's why he counted on her. She understood. "Declan, it's going to be fine. I mean, it might go terribly wrong. But it might not."

"Ok, shit. Let's do this." He looked at Anya. Walked over to her and kissed her hard on the mouth. "You asked for this."

"I did." She sat down.

"You're sitting?"

"Yes. You'll be less threatened by me if I'm sitting. It's animal 101, my friend." Therese snorted behind her.

He smiled at her. "Ok, this is going to be weird."

"Do it already! Jesus!"

Declan blew out a breath and relaxed his shoulders. His hands lengthened into claws, his face changed, and he let out a deafening roar which would have for sure blown out her eardrums had she been mortal. Her ears were taking quite the pounding lately. His whole body jerked, he was still fighting it some, and with a rending sound, he was fully in beast form.

Yup, Anya thought, he's a beast. She could sort of see Declan's features, but it might have been wishful thinking on her part. He was full on, in actual animal form. He roared again and smashed one of the chairs. He then let out a long, low whine. Everyone was still, and silent. His nose twitched as he smelled everyone in the room. He turned and caught sight and scent of her.

She sat very still and remembered her circus animal training. She had never been afraid of any animal and she was not going to start now. She looked down and didn't look him in the eye. Worked on the big cats and she hoped like hell it would work on him. He came closer on two legs and sniffed around her. She felt Therese tense, so she shook her head just a little to show it was fine. He circled her, whined again, and moved away, destroying the other chair. He went down on all fours and once again roared loudly. He was highly agitated right now.

The beast was trying to work it out. She knew that he wanted to pounce on her, but something held him back. Likely Declan himself, but also, he knew he wasn't supposed to hurt her, and he was trying to figure out why.

She sighed and very quietly said his name. "Declan." His ears perked up, and the whine was high pitched. "Declan." Again. He turned to look at her and she put her hand down. He came over, on all fours, sniffed her hand. "It's ok. It's me, just relax Declan." Her voice was very soft and very calm. She could only see Matthew from her vantage point, but he stared with rapt attention, his body tense, in case he had to get to her quickly. Declan moved around the room again, but he was calmer. He went over to smell each of the others in turn. But he quickly went back to Anya. "I know you're in there, *lyubov moya*. I know you recognize my smell. Come here, come closer." Declan moved closer.

"She's a fucking demon whisperer," Dougal said quietly. Matthew shot him a dark look. But he also didn't think Dougal was totally wrong. Therese, for her part, thought that this was one of the most fascinating things she'd ever seen. And she had seen a lot in her long life.

"Come on now, a little closer. You can smell me, and you can smell yourself too, on this sweater. It's your sweater." He was right in front of her now. She reached her hand out, he sniffed at it, and she made contact with him, stroking his head and down the side of his face. He put his head on her lap and she moved to stroke down his back. He whined quietly, but there was no heat in it. She continued to gently stroke his head and back as she spoke softly to him in Russian. He wouldn't know the words, but he'd know the tone. "You're safe," she said in Russian. "I will never hurt you. And I know you won't hurt me. You're always safe with me." He closed his eyes and sighed, as close to a human sound as he could get in that form.

"Well, fuck me." said Dougal.

"No thank you." said Therese. "Been there and don't need to visit again." This caused Matthew to laugh silently, while Dougal made an obscene gesture at his friend.

They stayed that way for a while. She petted Declan in beast form, while each man tensed, ready to act.

"Declan, it's time to change back now." Whining. "I know you don't want to love, but you have to. We need the man back now. You're part of each other, you have to work together. Now is not your time." More whining, but softer this time. "Please. For me." He backed away, roared and was once again her Declan. A very naked Declan. He looked for Anya first and saw she was fine. He then made sure each of his people were also ok. He took a deep breath, then another. "Team, thank you. But can you leave us now?"

"Of course, boss," Dougal said.

Matthew dropped a garment bag onto the couch on his way out. "Your clothes."

The door closed and Anya leapt at him. He caught her easily, tumbling her to the floor gently. "You're ok. I didn't hurt you?" He didn't recall doing anything to her, but sometimes it got a little fuzzy.

"No. You let me pet you after a time."

"You were right."

"It was a near thing. I was worried you wouldn't recognize me for a minute."

Declan bent his head and nuzzled her neck, giving her a long lick, before moving up to her mouth and giving her a searing kiss.

"I think you get really horny after you turn back, don't you?"

He laughed. "Maybe a bit. But when it comes to you, I don't think I am ever not horny."

"You're going to fucking kill me with all this sex."

"Or kill you, fucking," he said, waggling his eyebrows at her.

She laughed. "We cannot have sex now."

He was unzipping her jeans and pulling them down over her hips. He dropped a kiss on her hip and replied. "Oh, really? I am pretty sure we can."

"There are people outside the door, waiting for us."

"The 'people' have gone to my office, like I told them to do earlier, if this went well." He stopped. "Wait. Sorry. Do you really not want to?"

She stared at him. "Declan, I would make it very clear if I weren't in the mood. Don't worry. But thank you, consent is sexy." She pulled the sweater over her head while he finished working her jeans off, after pulling off her shoes.

"I can't believe you didn't wear anything under this."

"I really *was* hoping for sex."

He flipped her over and entered her from behind and she screamed. He chuckled behind her. "Your wish is my command." He started pumping her from behind, whispering to her about everything he wanted to do to her. Anya wasn't sure she could form a rational thought he was thrusting so hard, ramming into her with the force of both himself and his beast. But it didn't hurt, it felt glorious. She was writhing underneath him, willing him in even deeper by lowering her head and raising her ass. He growled at her. He pulled out almost all the way and then pounded into her, doing it again and again, stopping just short of letting her come each time.

Finally, he picked up speed again, leaning over her and taking her breasts in both hands as he finally drove her over the edge, joining her a moment later. They collapsed on the floor, breathing hard. "Wow is all I can say right now."

He rolled over to her. "I love you."

"I love you back, you dumbass." He laughed and rolled her on top of him. "Again?"

"Oh yeah, again."

***

They walked into Declan's office a little later to six faces, smirking at them. "What?" asked Declan innocently.

"That took a long time," Gwen said.

"Yes," replied Anya blandly. "Yes, it did." She winked at Gwen, who grinned back.

"It went well?"

"It went just fine. Even in beast form, Declan is putty in my hands."

He snorted. "Uh-huh. You just keep thinking that." She kissed his cheek.

"Ugh. Get a room!"

"Technically, Miss Gwen, *this* is my room."

"True enough. Ok, can Anya and I go dance now?"

"Sure, go ahead." He looked at Dougal and Therese pointedly and nodded in the direction of the ladies. They nodded back and followed them.

"I have to say, that was pretty amazing." This was from Matthew. "She was so calm and easy with you. If she was nervous, she didn't show it. Spine of steel that one.

"*Merde*, I wish I had seen it."

"I am going to tell you both that I think that was the calmest my beast has ever been outside of a kill. Ever."

"I am suitably impressed," Donovan said, and Michel nodded his agreement.

"It felt odd, but good." He sat down in his chair. "Down to business. We need to discuss the presentation and security. All of you are coming, along with Gwen. And I think, Luc."

"Really? *Il est un enfant.*"

"He is young, yes. But he is not a child. He adores Anya, so he'll keep his eyes open. It will be good for him."

Donovan burst out laughing. "You are so domesticated now."

Declan growled. "Coming from the man who moons around after a small, blonde woman, that is rich. Those in glass houses, my friend." It was Michel's turn to laugh. "Oh, you can laugh now. Wait until you fall for a woman."

"I do not fall for women. They often fall into bed with me, but that is all the falling that is done." You couldn't get hurt if you never let them get close. And Michel was not getting hurt again, he thought as a face flashed through his mind quickly.

"Oh, you're missing out then."

"*Peut-etre*. But I wouldn't want to disappoint the ladies, after all. Not all of us are monks like Matthew."

"Excuse me? I'm a what?"

"A monk. You are a monk."

"Just because I choose not to wave my dick around at every female that storms the place, it doesn't mean I'm a monk. And I need to remind you that Declan was very monk like before Anya. And don't smirk Donovan. You're rather celibate yourself."

"This is true," Declan said. "Matthew is just very discreet, I am sure."

Matthew was very celibate, but no one needed to know that. He checked his phone as it buzzed. "The ladies are actually ready to go home. Apparently, the music 'sucks' and they're tired and want pizza and a movie instead. Anya says she will see you at home later and to not work too hard."

"I won't lie, I feel better about that plan. Therese and Dougal are with them tonight. Donovan will pick up Gwen when she's ready to go home and Therese and Dougal can swing by the other clubs and check in on them. You can go check back into the monastery."

"Such wit!"

"Good evening, my lord."

"Suck it, Declan." Matthew retorted without heat and left to get the ladies home.

"So, it's true then?" Michel asked. "He was an actual lord?"

"He was. And that is his story to tell."

"It explains why he is so posh. I still don't understand though, the ladies love him. But he gives none of them the time of day. Human or demon alike."

Donovan shrugged. "Who's to say? Maybe he has a thing for Anya?"

Declan's head snapped up. "What?!"

"I'm kidding. I just wanted to see your reaction."

"You're such a dick. Both of you get the hell out of here now. I have actual work to do. We'll talk about security tomorrow."

CHAPTER 17

Four days later they were getting ready for the official presentation. Declan was sitting in their living room with the team, including Luc, who looked so eager it was almost painful, going over the plan for the evening. "So, I am going to walk in with Anya. Gwen and Matthew will walk in behind us."

He leaned over, pointing to a schematic of the receiving room that was laid out on the table. "I've marked where I'd like each of you. Dougal and Therese, I need you to already be inside, second level, on either side of Anya and myself. Watch the floor and watch the Council.

"Luc, inside the doors on the main level, on Anya's side. You watch her. Michel, the other side. You watch the Council, and you watch above them on the second level. Matthew will stay behind me. Gwen will be behind Anya." He had debated whether to use Luc or not, but the kid asked if he could actually help with security. He wanted to learn, so he was being given a chance. Michel would keep an eye on him. And he knew Luc would have no problem keeping an eye on Anya.

The cardinal will be in the front of the room, behind Anaranth and next to Grace."

"Cardinal?" Luc broke in.

"Richelieu."

"No *way!*"

"Way," Declan said, as Luc looked suitably impressed.

"You've the cardinal on your side?" Matthew asked.

"We hope to, but I am counting him as an ally for the moment regardless. I've asked to meet with him before the official presentation. This is why we're going a bit early. He knows everything that goes on at the court. If he doesn't know what's going on, he's going to be pissed off about it, which will likely mean he's amenable to helping us. He doesn't like to not be in the know and he does not like any machinations that were not put into motion by himself. He is very vain in that respect.

"Ok, seriously, the actual Cardinal Richelieu?"

"Luc, yes. Do you want to meet him?"

"Absolutely not. You scare me enough. I can't imagine meeting the cardinal."

"Aw, Declan's a pussycat. Or, a bear cub, if ye will."

"Don't make me have to murder you, Dougal."

"Ye can't, laddie!"

"Dougal is going to murder us all with that cheesy brogue." said Therese drily. He narrowed his eyes at her but said nothing.

"Anyway, I'd tell you he's nothing to be scared of, but honestly, he scares me a bit too. It's always better to have him on your side. But is everyone clear on what they're doing? Your job is to keep your eyes on Anya. But I also need you to keep ears open and listen for anything or anyone unusual. Everyone nodded at Declan.

The door opened and Gwen walked in, followed by Anya, who was wearing a long, black velvet cloak. "Are ye nae going to show us just a bit, lass?"

Anya winced. "Dougal? Is your accent actually that thick or do you just put it on?"

"Anya, you wound me!"

"Therese was just ribbing him about it. It's mostly a put on." Matthew answered. Dougal glowered at him. "But really, he's right. Do we not get a peek?"

Gwen piped up. "Absolutely not! I want the shock and awe of the entire room when they see her. You're lucky I'm letting you see her face. The cloak has a hood. Declan and Matthew will see her about a second before she goes in. The cloak comes off last minute." Gwen was wearing a long black dress with bell sleeves and gold cord tied a few times around her waist. The gown itself was dotted subtly with Swarovski crystals, so Gwen sparkled when she walked. Her hair was long and curly. She looked like a faerie. A fact Donovan could not keep to himself.

"I am playing up the witch thing," she replied when he commented.

"Or the Stevie Nicks thing," Anya replied.

"Either works."

Declan was staring at Anya. Her hair was pulled into a high tight braid that was wound with clear Swarovski crystals. Her lips were a dark red and her eyes were framed by longer lashes than usual and black eyeliner. "Something's missing."

"How can anything be missing? You can't see anything."

"I can see your head, and something is missing." He pulled a box out of his pocket and handed it to her. "For you."

She looked up at him, her eyes softening. "Thank you." She opened the box and saw the most gorgeous earpieces she'd ever seen. They were delicate branches in platinum, set with diamonds and sapphires throughout the delicate branches. They were designed to follow the curve of her ear, from bottom to top. There was a post to fit into her pierced ear, and then a clip towards the top to hold them in place. "These are the most beautiful things I have ever seen. Thank you so much." She kissed him gently on the lips. "And the sapphires go with the necklace. Which I am wearing, so you know."

"They aren't half as beautiful as you are though." He pulled them from the box and attached one to each ear. "Now. you're ready."

She smiled. "Aren't we going a bit early?"

"Yes. But you and I are meeting the cardinal beforehand."

"Shut up! Really?" Her reaction was the same as Luc's, which was no surprise. They were both history nerds at their cores.

"Really."

"Sweet!"

***

The Paris House was actually on the outskirts of Paris. Matthew, Declan, Anya, and Gwen rode in one car, with Michel driving, while the others rode in a car directly behind.

"Are you nervous?" Gwen asked.

"Scared shitless as a matter of fact."

Declan squeezed her hand. "You'll be great. They'll love you." She gave him a look. "Ok, some of them will dislike you and one of them is likely behind trying to hurt us, but the rest of them, they'll like you."

"That is not helping."

"I know. Sorry."

They turned into a long driveway with large bushes on either side. As they pulled up the large mansion, Gwen whistled. The trees all had lights wrapped around them and there were torches lit outside the front door of the house. The place was lit up like a Christmas tree. "They are not trying to be discreet, are they?" Gwen wondered.

"Hide in plain sight," Matthew replied.

"Who do the people in town think own this place?" Anya asked.

"Eccentric millionaire with ties to the entertainment industry."

"Yeah. That tracks." Gwen affirmed.

Anya was having trouble finding her voice. "Um, can't we just elope?"

"No, we cannot. Come on, let's do this." A man in a dark suit was heading towards the car and opened the door. Declan stepped out and helped Anya and Gwen out, as Matthew got out on the opposite side.

"Good evening Roger. I believe the cardinal is expecting us?"

"Good evening, Declan." He looked at the women. "And to the ladies as well. The cardinal is waiting for you in the red room."

Of course he is, thought Anya. She really wanted to throw up. She felt Declan's steadying hand on her waist, Gwen's on her arm and Matthew's on her shoulder and felt better. These people were her family, she could do this. "Hey Roger!" Donovan boomed, as he exited the other car.

Roger broke into a smile. "How are you doing, big man?"

"Just fine. And you? How is Clara?"

"She is well. She's inside somewhere. Come, I will show you all in."

They walked inside and the house looked very similar to the one she'd been in in Brussels. She expected the Red Room to have gilt. They came to a closed door and Roger knocked. "Enter!" a booming voice in accented French commanded. Roger opened the door and ushered the Declan and Anya inside. Matthew took Gwen along to the ante-room next to the main receiving hall, while the others made their way into the receiving hall.

"You ok?" Declan whispered.

"I am going to throw up."

"Nerves?"

"No. Gilt."

Declan had to stifle a laugh. Richelieu came around his desk and walked over to the couple. He held his hand out to Declan, who bent and kissed his ring. Oh, for fuck's sake, thought Anya. Is this guy for real? Well. yes, he was actually. He turned to Anya and did the same thing. She tried very hard to not roll her eyes while she went and kissed the cardinal's ring. "Dr. Orlov, it's a pleasure to meet you. Natalia and Vladimir speak highly of you." His use of her title was flattering.

"It's an honor to meet you, cardinal." She even managed to make it sound sincere. "Please call me Anya."

He beamed at her. "Wonderful! Anya, it is. Sit, please. What can I do for you?"

They had agreed to let Declan take the lead because he knew the most about Demon politics and how to handle the canny Frenchman. Anya didn't like it, but she saw the wisdom of it. Declan went through what had been going on since he and Anya had met, up to the sad tale of Connell. He stopped abruptly and looked at Anya.

"What's the matter?" she said.

"I forgot something that happened that night. I'm sorry." He looked pained.

"Just tell us. I'll yell at you later about it." She smiled and took his hand. The cardinal watched them with a speculative look on his face.

"Connell mentioned that the Demon who approached him in the bar was...Russian."

"Plenty of people are Russian."

"This is true. But Anya, you're Russian and you have a dead brother. This is about you. What if…"

The cardinal broke in. "No one in Anya's immediate family is Demon born."

"I know. But Connell was made without a deal being made and he wasn't demon born either."

"So, you think someone is making demons, illegally? And one might be Anya's brother Pavel?" The cardinal knew everything and everyone, that much was obvious.

Anya hadn't said anything to this point. "We'll discuss how you forgot to mention my brother might be alive, later. But wouldn't I know if this was the case?"

"Did you see his body being removed?"

"No. I was ushered out fairly quickly."

"Were you at the funeral?"

She thought. "Actually, no. I wasn't allowed to go to his, or my father's." Declan could not allow himself to feel rage at this right now.

"We know when a demon born has died. We're there, we deal with it. The family never knows. Your family would be none the wiser."

She nodded. "What if it's my father?"

"Your father would not be the one to do this to you." Richelieu said before Declan could say anything. "He would have found an older Demon to kill him first." Richelieu had done some digging about the new consort. And everything he had discovered about her father spoke to a helpless neglect, not a murderous intent.

"I agree." Declan took her hands. "Anya, I could be totally off base, and this could just be a random Russian Demon, but something about it bothered me when Connell told me. And I am sorry I forgot about it, but I honestly did."

She nodded. "Let's put a pin in that for the moment and move on to why we're here now."

He squeezed her hand. "As you say. We believe it's someone on the Council. Someone who wants either Anya, or I gone. I'd say mostly Anya. Without her, I would never end up on the Council. In all likelihood, I would just choose to fade away."

Anya looked horrified. "Don't you dare!"

"Anya, please."

"No. If something happens to me, you are not allowed to just give up."

"Anya, please I've lived a long life."

"We're also going to discuss this later, but that is unacceptable." She was more incensed at this declaration than his forgetting to mention the possible family connection.

"What do you need from me?" Richelieu asked.

Anya spoke this time. "When it comes to the court of demons, nothing escapes your knowledge. Nothing gets by you. I doubt that everyone is aware of exactly how much you know, and that is to their detriment. We need to know if you've heard anything. But more than that Cardinal, we need your help to expose the threat."

"And what will you do when the threat is exposed?"

"Eliminate it."

Richelieu was impressed with this new consort. She hadn't said much, but she knew what to say when she spoke. He wasn't averse to a little pandering, and she did it with a certain sardonic wit that he found charming.

She and Declan were well matched. She wasn't afraid of him, and even though she was irritated with him, she didn't let that get in the way of what was important. He could see that they loved each other, and the old cardinal could be a bit of a romantic at times. More than that, whatever was going on, was going under his nose, without his knowledge and that was unacceptable. "I will help you. I find that I am offended by what is happening in this court currently. Someone is using forbidden methods to make demons AND drugging them with something that is only supposed to be a myth. It is disturbing. And truthfully, the fact that my own eyes and ears have not ferreted anything out is also upsetting. My pride," he paused for dramatic effect. "Is wounded. And I do not like it."

Anya beamed at him. "Thank you so much, your eminence. Declan was right to suggest coming to you with our problem."

The cardinal turned to him. "He was indeed." And with that, Richelieu's ego was soothed.

Declan whistled quietly to himself. She was better at this political maneuvering than you'd expect from someone not used to it. She smiled and winked at him just then, having caught his thought. *Your eminence?*

I was inspired.

Well played, love.

"Come!" said Richelieu. "I will walk you down to the anteroom before I slip into the receiving hall." As they walked down the hall, he regaled Anya with tales of seventeenth century France and the real Musketeers. Her laughter rang down the hallway, warming Declan. He'd been right, the cardinal had taken to her and she, unsurprisingly, had taken to him. He wondered if the cardinal would acknowledge her publicly this evening. Once they got to the anteroom, the cardinal kissed Anya on both cheeks and whispered "Courage!" to her and disappeared into the receiving hall.

"How did it go?" Matthew asked.

"Very well. Anya won him over."

"He likes compliments. Acknowledge his brilliance, and he's fine. I am sure his reputation is well deserved. I wouldn't cross him," Anya said.

"And he's not happy that someone is causing trouble under his nose," Declan put in.

"Oh no, he is not. But he's also very charming when he wants to be."

"Of course, he is," Gwen said. "To you, at least, I'm sure."

Anya pivoted to Declan. "So, can we go home now?"

"No *malysh*, we still have a long night ahead. I'm sorry."

"How come there are two more Council members than continents?" Gwen asked.

"Because people didn't want to give up territory. We've had a Council longer than we've had continents. It was easier to let it go."

"Good luck getting Eastern Europe away from Vladimir," Anya said.

Declan snorted. "True. And Leilani is never going to give up the South Pacific. Ever. "

Roger came in just then. "They're ready."

"Anya, are you ready?"

"No, but let's go anyway."

"You look beautiful. Try not to kill anyone."

"I make no promises.

CHAPTER 18

"Is there food or booze in there?" Anya asked Declan as they stood in front of a large set of double doors.

"I cannot believe you are JUST asking that now?" Gwen griped.

"Once the official presentation is over, yes."

"Thank the goddess!" Gwen sighed.

"Are you taking off her cloak?" Declan asked.

"Don't you worry about that." She stared at him for a moment. "Your jacket cuffs need to be about an eighth shorter. Your tailor was obviously having an off day. Make sure he fixes that."

Anya looked at Declan. "Told you so."

The doors opened and Gwen stepped onto the back of Anya's cloak so that as she moved through the doors it fell off slowly. Matthew reached down and handed it to a servant at the side and whispered, "That was brilliant," at Gwen, who beamed.

"We practiced that for an hour."

"How did you do it?"

"There are weights sewn into the cloak, so it stays in place, but there is no real hook, it's a magnet."

Matthew was impressed and he moved the two of them into the room.

There had been an audible gasp when Anya had walked into the room. Declan's breath caught when he got a good look at her. She was stunning. Her outfit was a deep midnight blue that served to make her skin glow. It was sleeveless and the front was a deep V to almost her belly button. She had just enough material on either side to support her breasts, she had a good deal of cleavage showing, but as Gwen had said 'still tasteful.' And Gwen had been smart about the outfit. The long skirt was split down the middle so you could see the underside was silver material, but the outfit also sported slim pants. She was wearing a jumpsuit with a detachable skirt. In case she had to fight, the skirt wouldn't get in the way. The back of the skirt had constellations stitched onto it with shimmering Swarovski crystals. Hidden in the design was a swirling 'A' and 'D' but you had to know just where to look. Gwen had made this outfit out of love and loyalty to her friend. She not only knew exactly what her friend would like, but she knew exactly what was needed. Nothing in that room would shine like Anya tonight, because nothing or no one else should. Gwen had made damned sure of that. The work on the outfit alone was a monumental achievement. On her bare arms were two black leather sheaths that housed the ceremonial daggers that Anaranth had given her. She looked like a warrior goddess. *His* warrior goddess.

He leaned down. "I had planned to rip your outfit off of you later, but I would never ruin such beautiful work."

She blushed. "Thank you."

"I have to know though, how are your tits staying up?"

She gave him a hard look and then smiled. "Boob tape. There are also hidden cups in here. It's a really well-made garment. And I think Gwen actually may have put a spell on them, for extra support."

They reached the front of the room where each Council member sat, with the consort sat next to them. The cardinal was positioned behind Anaranth, and he nodded his approval at her outfit.

Michel thought she was the second most beautiful woman he'd ever seen. The first, having passed his field of vision about ten minutes before his boss' entrance. Luc gaped. He saw Declan look at her and saw the love there, saw how deep it went. She had the same look on her face as she glanced over at him. More than anything, their love took his breath away. And he thought that in the end, that is maybe what he wanted. To love someone and be loved by someone, wholly.

Michel saw Therese smiling broadly at Declan and Anya. So rare a sight that she frightened some younger demons into backing away from her quickly. The consort looked fierce, as if she was ready for a fight. Michel knew she must be nervous, but she wasn't showing it, and this is something he knew Therese would respect. He did as well. He also saw Matthew giving Anya a soft faraway look and he wondered who his friend could be thinking about. Still waters, that one. The world needed more badass women, thought Michel. And Anya definitely fit the bill there.

Declan and Anya approached the dais and Declan bowed quickly. "Esteemed Council members, please allow me to present my consort, Dr. Anya Orlov." She smiled softly at the use of her title and bowed. She was cautioned to not speak until spoken to and also to keep her eyes down until then as well. There was dead silence in the room. Anaranth spoke first. "Anya, you look lovely this evening. Please allow me to present my consort, Graziela. Excuse me, Grace."

Anya looked up and replied, "It is my great honor to meet you, Grace."

Grace had long blonde hair. So blonde it was almost white. It was stick straight and hung to the top of her legs. She was wearing a long-sleeved red gown that clung to her and she had a giant ruby pendant nestled in her cleavage. Her voice though, was soft and melodic, and she still had a slight Italian accent. "It is my honor to meet the woman who has won our Declan's heart."

Anya smiled at her and felt a little better. She was in turn introduced to each Council member, with varying degrees of civility. Until she got to the Demon and consort of Western Europe, Francois, and Liliana. Francois was disdainful, Anya supposed it would piss you off to look at your eventual successor. But Liliana was a stone-cold bitch. "You wear weapons to greet the Council? What is this insult?" she fairly shrieked. Declan sighed beside her, but Anya placed her hand on his arm.

"My lady," she said quietly, amping up her Russian accent slightly. "These daggers are ceremonial, and the ends are blunted." She removed one quickly from her sheath, before anyone could touch her, to show Liliana she meant no harm.

"I would never cause anyone here harm." Except you, you bitch, she thought. "I would only use a blade in protection of the Council, if needed."

"A fine story! It is still an offense to wear weapons in here."

Which while true in theory, was also total bullshit. Half the Council were wearing either a sword or dagger. Most of the room actually had weapons, this included Declan and his people. She glanced at Anaranth quickly. "I was not going to mention it, as I wouldn't wish to cause embarrassment, but the daggers were a gift from Anaranth, and I thought it would be appropriate to wear them. I would not wish to insult him."

Adjoa, the demon of Africa spoke up. "Dr. Orlov, I am sure you meant no disrespect. That said, it was bold of you." Anya looked down and clenched her teeth but said nothing. "Can you actually use a dagger?" Adjoa sounded skeptical.

Oh fuck, thought Declan as Anya's head shot up. "I am an expert with knives. Of any kind. I have been doing it since I was a child and I have yet to meet my equal." She paused. "Among humans," she added quickly.

"Perhaps a test is in order." Rufaro, Adjoa's consort said.

"My relative is not a dancing dog, Rufaro. She doesn't have to bark on command." Natalia said pointedly.

"I would think if she's so good, she won't mind proving it." Francois cut in.

"Annechka, you do not have to do this." Vladimir told her.

Her eyes narrowed at the nickname, but she forged ahead. "I have no problem sharing my skill with others. I'm proud of it."

"Child, you have nothing to prove." This from Natalia.

"No, I don't. I know who I am, but I am happy to do this and then put the matter behind us."

"A throwing contest then. Between Anya and Liliana." Anaranth said. Declan narrowed his eyes at the old demon.

"Would I not be the better one to compete?" Adjoa said.

"You're a demon, several hundred years old and she's not. It's not a fair competition. I remember Liliana was fairly competent at one time." *You sly old dog,* thought Declan, *you meant for this to happen.* Liliana had been a thorn in Anaranth's side for quite some time and he was hoping to knock her down a peg this evening.

He's using you to goad both Francois and Liliana.

You think? It's fine. I still bet I am better than she is, the bitch. He sent her a laugh down their bond, and she relaxed slightly.

"I was more than competent." Liliana stepped down to where Anya was. "I will be happy to show the new consort a thing or two."

You don't have to do this.

Yes, I do. And I will. Liliana is a total bitch.

Just be careful, she's unhinged.

No shit.

They were to use a live target, which Anya hated. 6 throws each and the person who got the closest to the target without nicking them, won. It was a fairly simple challenge. The only thing Anya balked at was Liliana getting to use her own set of daggers. "If she does, then I will insist on being able to retrieve mine, from our apartment."

"Are you saying I would cheat?"

"No. What I'm saying is using your own metal gives you the advantage. You know their weight and their feel."

"She's right." Grace said. "We have daggers we can use that don't belong to either of you. Will that be acceptable, Dr. Orlov?"

"It is, thank you."

"Liliana?"

"Fine. Fine!'

The daggers were brought in, and Liliana was given the task of picking the target. She looked around, looked up and pointed at Luc. "Him!" Luc shrugged as if this was a normal request that people made of him all the time. Anya looked a little ill and Declan was furious.

The malicious bitch. Her choice is no accident.

Of course it's not. She knows he's one of ours. She's hoping to discomfit me. It won't work.

And he trusts you.

And he trusts me.

"I will go first!" Liliana crowed. She pulled out the first two daggers and then threw them. Luc didn't move. She threw the next 4 in quick succession. The last was thrown to land between his legs. Luc looked more affronted than anything else. "I highly doubt you can beat that."

Anya shrugged. "Your release is a little slow and you flick your wrist too much. I am fairly confident that I can beat that." Liliana turned red and Gwen giggled into her hand.

"I am several hundred years older than you."

"When was the last time you threw a knife, before this evening?"

"I don't know."

"Exactly. I practice every day. Can you please stand 5 more inches to the left please?" Liliana moved grudgingly. Anya backed up 3 inches. She spent a few minutes looking at where Liliana's knives hit. "Luc? How much do you trust me?"

"I trust you with my life, Madame."

"Do you trust me with the family jewels?"

He looked confused at first and then understood and smiled. "*Absolument!*"

"Good lad." She picked up each dagger in turn, getting to know the weight of each.

"Consort. This evening would be nice."

"This cannot be rushed, Liliana. And my name is Anya if you please." Matthew did laugh at that frosty tone of hers.

"Liliana, back off," barked Adjoa, who was beginning to grudgingly respect the new consort and the time she was taking studying the weapons.

Anya re-arranged the daggers in the order she wanted to throw them. She took a deep breath and then threw the 6 daggers in rapid succession to the gasps of the crowd assembled. When she was done, Luc was standing still, eyes wide open, on her. Calm. Adjoa walked over and whistled low. As close as Liliana's daggers were, each one of Anya's was sitting directly in front of hers, closest to Luc. "I think," Adjoa said slowly. "That it's clear who the winner is. Anya, this is very impressive. You are incredibly quick for a new immortal."

"She was that quick before," Declan said.

"Impressive. I would enjoy sparring with you some time."

"It would be my pleasure." She knew this Demon could teach her something.

Anaranth sighed. "Wonderful. Can we be done with this now? Liliana, you did well but you're out of practice. Come back and sit down next to Francois."

Liliana shot Anya a look of pure malevolence and sat back down. Declan walked over to Luc and clapped him on the shoulder. "You stayed calm under stressful circumstances. Well done. I am very proud of you."

Luc beamed at him. "Thank you, Monsieur. It's my honor to work for you." Luc walked back over to Michel, who gave him an effusive hug and clapped him on the back several times.

Anya walked over to Declan. "You are ridiculously kind." Her voice was soft and full of love.

"And you are ridiculously sexy. I want to throw you over my shoulder, take you home and have my way with you."

"Did I do ok?"

"You were perfect. I am proud to call you mine." He rested his hands on her shoulders and put his forehead to hers.

"I am proud to call you mine as well."

Donovan and Gwen walked over. "You two are making me sick. Stop it." Gwen poked him in the ribs for the comment.

"Oh my god! That was so badass!" Gwen grabbed Anya in a hug.

Therese sidled up to them, putting her hand up, Anya gave her a high five and the woman moved along.

Anya laughed. "Thank you. I still kind of want to throw up," she said to Gwen.

Matthew slid over quickly. "If I ever find a woman I want to be with, I hope you'll show her how to do that."

She gave Matthew a kiss on the cheek. "You know I will." Matthew moved away. "Does Matthew ever date?"

"Not that any of us know of."

"He's so good looking. Weird."

Declan looked vexed. "Really?"

"Not as dishy as you, of course. But he's so closed off, I wonder why."

"He's always been like that, especially when it comes to women."

"There's a story there." Gwen mused.

"He doesn't talk about it. Declan knows, but he won't say."

"It is not my story to tell."

The cardinal walked up then. "Madame, I do not remember when I have been so entertained." He took her hand and kissed it. "I hope you and Declan will grace me with your presence for dinner soon?" He said loudly for those assembled to hear.

"We'd be honored, your eminence."

"Wonderful. Bring your friends!" He leaned in. "Good job on making enemies straight off. It will be easier to uncover the threat," he said quietly. He moved off to join the crowd. Only he would consider making enemies a success.

At one end, another door was opened, and people started filtering that way to partake of food and drink. The foursome started to head in that direction when Rosamund stepped in their path with another female. "Good evening, Declan." She paused. "Anya." Anya stiffened and Declan put his around her waist, hand splayed on her hip, in a proprietary gesture, that was also meant to keep Anya from attacking the other woman. "Rosamund. Annalise," he said addressing both women.

"Oh Anya, you don't know Annalise, do you? She and Declan used to be...quite close."

Anya's eyes narrowed at Rosamund, more because this was such a ridiculously childish ploy. She looked over at Annalise. A petite demon with black hair, curled around her elfin face. "Nice to meet you." Civil, but perfunctory.

"Anya? What an interesting name." Annalise had a husky voice that made Anya think of black satin sheets. "What does it mean?"

Why the fuck did everyone want to know what her name meant? "It's really not that interesting. It's just my name. It's not important." Anya was officially, fucking over it. She wanted food and a drink, and she wanted to take her man home and fuck his brains out until he forgot this bitch's name.

"I suppose not. It appears Declan's taste in women had changed."

Gwen sucked in her breath and made a small, unobtrusive motion with her head, and blinked.

"Ow!" Annalise said.

"What happened?" Rosamund asked.

"I felt something bite me."

"How odd," Declan said, knowing exactly where that had come from. "Are you sure you're feeling well? There's nothing in here that would bite you."

She gave Declan a hot look. "Oh, I don't know about that."

"I do." said Anya. "There is nothing over here that would bite you. Now, if you'll excuse us, we really must move on. I'd say it was nice to meet you, but I'd be lying." They moved away. "Nice work, Gwen."

"The bitch had it coming."

The rest of the evening passed in a bit of a blur. She met a lot of demons and some of their human, longtime companion. Some of the demons were nice, and some were assholes. Her feet were beginning to hurt and every time she'd go to eat, someone would interrupt her. Finally at around two a.m., they managed to make their way to the car. This time, they were in a car with Matthew and Luc, while the others took the second car. She nodded off on Declan's shoulder and he folded her cloak over her and put his arm around her, drawing her close.

"She did well tonight," Matthew said. "There's an equal number of people who seem to love and hate her." He thought. "Ok, I think more people dislike her, but I think those people are women and, that's down to you being officially off the market now."

"Those two demons, Rosamund and Annalise, were doing a bit of um, what is the phrase? Oh yes...trash talking about her." Luc offered.

"What did they say?"

Luc grimaced. "They did call her a whore and a peasant. They insulted her body and her looks. They said that your eyesight must be slipping. I mean, it's typical I think of how jealous women talk. But it made me angry. I then reminded them and everyone listening that perhaps to speak ill of someone who is that good with knives is not a smart move, and that it would be a shame if it got back to Declan. Then Therese came up and glowered at them and they dispersed." He smiled. "That part was very satisfying."

"Well done." Matthew grinned in the rearview mirror. "Annalise, though?"

Declan winced. "Don't remind me. Even I get bored sometimes."

"How long were you together?"

"We were not together. We had sex, on and off, for about a year."

"I hear she's a great lay."

"See? Now you're just trying to be provocative. You probably heard it from her."

Matthew laughed heartily. "True enough. She did try and come on to me tonight."

Luc glanced at the enigmatic man beside him. "And?"

"She is not my type. I'd fuck Dougal before I'd get into that woman's bed."

"Sex is complicated," said Luc.

"No," said Matthew. "It's not. Sex is not complicated. Love is complicated. Sex is nice, often very good. But it is not the end game."

"What is the end game then?"

"Love. Sex, I would have to think, is always going to be better with someone you love."

"That's very prosaic. Michel would say differently."

"Michel is full of shit, and we all know it. He spent the night following Omala's movements with big, sad eyes. Sex without a connection does the job it's supposed to, and there is nothing wrong with that. But I feel like sex when you have a true connection with someone has to be the best thing there is." The two other men said nothing, but when he looked in the rearview again, he saw Anya looking at him, a contemplative look on her face.

***

Anya walked into their closet after showering to see that Declan standing there naked, putting his shoes away. She dropped her towel and went down on her knees in front of him, taking him in her mouth. He groaned and grabbed her hair, pushing her to take more of him in. She took his balls in her hand and squeezed causing him to clench his teeth. She raked her teeth along his cock and then took her free hand and smacked his ass. Hard. "Holy fuck, Anya! What was that for?"

She pulled away and eyed him from the floor. "*That* was for Annalise." She smacked his ass one more time and then took him back into her mouth, working him until he came on a shudder. When he could speak again, he said "Anya, you knew I'd had lovers."

"Yes. But I didn't think I'd get one thrown in my face tonight. And it pissed me off more than I can say."

He looked down at her. "You're jealous."

"Fuck yes, I am jealous."

"You have no reason to be."

"It doesn't matter. I am going to get constantly bombarded with every demon you've ever fucked, thanks to Rosamund." She knew that she was being irrational. But she was tired, she was hungry, and she was incredibly jealous of anyone he'd ever been with all of a sudden. The jealousy was the overriding emotion right now. It had been a long night, and it had tested her patience. She was all out of fucks to give at the moment.

"You're not being logical."

"You're mine, god dammit. And I am not going to put up with some undead harlot reminding me that she was there first."

"Oh for Chrissakes." He bent down, pulled up to her feet. "They may have been there first, but you're going to be last. For always. There will never be anyone else for me, but you. And let me remind you, that I am not your first, but I am your last. Anya, I am going to want to tear apart any man, or demon who even looks at you with casual interest."

"But the chances of you ever meeting any of my exes is not great. I will end up meeting all of yours. The demons anyway."

"Anya…"

"And that's another thing. I am really pissed off that you would want to hurt yourself if something happened to me. You can't. People need you. People count on you."

"Then I suggest you not let anything happen to you. Because if you think I am going to live without you, you are insane."

"Declan, stop it!"

"No. Fuck Anya! Jesus." He stopped for a minute and put his arms around her. She was shaking. She was overly tired and probably hungry, it had been such a long night for her, she was still so human, and she had been through a lot lately. He was going to kill Rosamund, as Annalise had been her tipping point tonight.

Her hands slowly snaked around his waist, and she laid her head on his shoulder. Softer now. "Anya, my Anya. I have never carried anyone in my blood the way I carry you. You are always with me. I simply cannot do without you. It would be a half-life." She didn't need to know he'd already discussed this with Matthew and Donovan. He had every faith in his Anya, but he had made his decision the moment he'd decided to give his heart to her. He would not continue without her.

She sobbed his name. "Declan. I am sorry. So sorry. I was so furious about it. I wanted to mark you as mine." She wept on his shoulder.

"You already have, *malysh*. You already have. Sssh now, my love. It's all fine. I'm here. Sssh, don't cry." He could never handle a woman crying. Anya, Alice, his daughter. It had always turned him to mush when it happened. He picked her up gently and carried her into the bedroom. By the time he got to the bed, seconds later, she was already fast asleep. "Sleep well, my warrior," he said quietly, tucking the blankets around her and gently getting into bed next to her. But it was a long time before sleep came to him.

CHAPTER 19

Anya woke up the next morning starving, with a raging headache, and no man beside her. She sat up. "The hell?" she said. No sooner were the words out of her mouth, than Declan came into the room pushing a cart with a giant breakfast spread, coffee, water, and aspirin. Bless his demon heart. He pulled it over to the window and set it up on the table that overlooked the Seine. "Declan?"

He turned and smiled at her. "I thought you'd probably need all of this."

"How do you do that?" she asked, getting out of bed, and heading over to the window. She wrapped her arms around him from behind and he turned to enfold her in a proper hug. "I told you, I carry you in my blood, like you carry me."

"You seem to be spending a lot of time taking care of me lately."

"I am sure you'll get your chance at some point. But your life is changing a whole lot more than mine is. Now sit and take your aspirin and eat your breakfast."

"Yes sir," she said and took the aspirin and took a sip of the coffee. "God, this is the best coffee ever." She looked at her plate. "Did you have Mara make all the food ever?"

"Pretty much. She likes you. You have a good appetite."

"For so many things," she said running her foot up his leg.

"Behave and eat your breakfast."

She grinned and then cleared her throat. "So, about last night…"

He held up a hand. "Completely understandable. You've been through a great deal since we met. Probably more than you expected. Definitely more than I expected. Of course, I wasn't expecting you, that's for sure."

"Oh, really?"

"Yup. It was like getting hit with a brick."

She looked affronted. "Hey!"

"A brilliant and beautiful brick!"

"That's better. But still, I feel bad about how I acted when we got home."

"I'm not. That was an amazing blow job."

"Stop joking!"

"I'm not. It was. You feel free to give me angry head whenever you want." She still looked upset. "Annie, it's really fine. You handled it better than I would have if we had run into one of your former lovers. Honestly, he'd probably be dead by now." He grinned at the look she gave him. "It was a very long night. One where you had to face a number of people whose sole purpose was to judge you and test you. You were accused of bringing weapons in when most of the demons there had weapons on them, including me, you had to prove yourself unnecessarily and then Rosamund and Annalise showed up to push some buttons. And you did it all with precariously secured breasts and in teetering high heels. How you managed to not run anyone through is amazing. Honestly, cut yourself some damned slack."

She smiled at him and took a sip of coffee. "Well, I still don't feel great about it. I just didn't want to be an embarrassment. And I also find that galling, as it's nothing I've worried about in the past."

"You couldn't embarrass me. Ever. I like the way you are. I wouldn't want you to change. Truthfully, I really wanted you to punch Rosamund. But right now, she'd probably hurt you."

"Yeah. Probably." She looked disgruntled.

"But I think if we work on some of your fight skills, and your sword skills, you could kick her ass quite soon." Anya beamed. "Oh and take Adjoa up on her offer to spar. She is amazing and she obviously likes you. She'll teach you a lot. She is not only good with a sword, but you need to see her with a staff. She's so fast, I saw her take someone's head off once with one. It was kind of a turn on." He grinned at her.

"Oh, really?" Anya raised an eyebrow.

"In a purely theoretical way, of course. This was also before Rufaro, so I felt at liberty to be turned on."

"Did you two ever…"

"Oh good lord, no! I was very young, and she was completely uninterested in me. She wanted, rightly so, an African consort and that was her primary focus. She takes care of her people; demon and human alike, and she wanted a strong consort to lead with her."

"Africa is pretty big; how come it's not split like Europe is?"

"It was, for quite a long time. But the other demon decided they didn't want to share. They were no match for Adjoa. Now she runs Africa alone, but she has demons who report into her from the different territories. It was a smart move."

He thought for a moment. "If I could pattern us on any couple, it would be them. They're equals and they run their territory together. It may not be romantic for them, but it works. That's what I'd want for us. I am not, nor have I ever been, interested in conquering my consort. Some are prone to it; Ning and Gorm come to mind. Francois tried that with Liliana and as soon as he lost interest in, well most things, she started running roughshod over him. If he sees that, he will never admit it. My father always asked my mother's advice about things. He trusted her; they were partners. That's what I want."

"What about your wife?"

"Alice would generally defer to me, even if I asked her opinion. So, I admit. I stopped asking. I never realized how well, modern, my father was about that. And now you're here and I am reminded of how he was with my mother and how I want us to be. I would be a fool to not get advice and opinions from you; you are brilliant. You're definitely smarter than me." He smiled at her.

"And you're fine with that?" She sounded skeptical. In her experience, that was not usually the case.

"Absolutely. Your brain is a real turn on if I'm honest."

She stared at him. Out of everything he could have said to her that morning, this was by far the best. That he wanted them to be partners. That he saw her as an equal to him in all ways. It had been more than she'd hoped for. When she had met him, she just hoped that he wasn't awful and that maybe it would work out ok. Once they fell in love and she realized he was pretty great, she wondered if she'd have a place by his side. A real one, and not a ceremonial one. They were two loners who had found each other and that was going to be an adjustment in and of itself. Right now, it was still the honeymoon phase, and they hadn't really known each other all that long. Eventually they'd relax and butt heads, she was sure of that, which would be interesting. She was kind of looking forward to it.

"Really, now?" she said, running her foot up his leg again.

"Yes. Stop being cheeky. Because I have papers for you to read and sign." He got up, grabbed a folder, and came back to the table. "So, I run the clubs in France and Belgium for the Council, but I only outright own the one where we met. I insisted on that. I have managers for the others, but I go to them rarely, for various reasons. I am at The Cellar the most, out of those. But that is because that is where I question recalcitrant demons. The tourist attractions, etc., have to be run by Demons. My network of people is run by me with no oversight but managed daily by Matthew and Donovan."

"Question, huh?"

"Among other things." He shrugged. "I own a number of buildings and businesses in Paris and in Brussels. I own this building as well. I own a small cottage in Ireland, in my village, as well. I'd like to add your name to the club, the buildings on either side of it and both homes, just to start with." She was staring at him in shock. "I don't want to put you on the other businesses, until you see them with your own eyes. Matthew on the face of it will have to run the public attractions because as I said, they have to be demon run. That said, you are actually the one that would be in charge should anything happen to me. Matthew will follow your instructions, unless he really disagrees with you, but even then, he will try and use logic to change your mind. In the end, he'll do it your way. Donovan does not want to be in charge, he prefers to work as he does. The others will also follow your command."

"Even Dougal?"

"Even Dougal. Therese will ensure that."

"So, are they…."

"No. I think once, a long, long time ago, but they are honestly just best friends. Dougal is great, but Therese runs that show." She nodded.

"Are you sure you shouldn't put Matthew completely in charge of all of the things? He's way better qualified for this than I am."

"It has to be you. You have to be seen as the authority in my absence. It's part of being a consort. With some consorts, it's a bad idea, but not with you. I trust you. And if I had to be away for an extended time frame for some reason, or if I were indisposed, I'd need to count on you." She opened her mouth and he held up his hand. "I know. But it could happen. Just because we're immortal, it doesn't mean we can't be hurt or imprisoned. There are ways to get to us."

"Where would you be going that I wouldn't be able to find you, or come get you?"

He looked at her a little sadly. "There are places I cannot take you, my love."

She looked down, realizing what he meant. "Oh. I see," she said quietly.

He went over to her and kneeled down in front of her. "Please know I never want to leave you. And I am never going to abandon you willingly. Ever." He knew that this was one of her fears, to be abandoned like her family abandoned her. If he couldn't be there, she'd have the family she was building around her, but he knew it wasn't the same as them being together. "But I still do work directly for Anaranth and there are times, he will have need of me and my...skills."

She put a hand to his cheek. "You do his dirty work for him, don't you?" Anaranth would be above getting his hands dirty. He'd need someone to do that for him, and Declan was his most trusted demon.

He nodded into her hand. "I do." What a toll that must take on him, she thought. Then a second thought, Anaranth could very well decide to press her into service, knowing what her skill set was. She could never underestimate that old demon. He had already sized her up and likely determined she'd be of use to him. She didn't need to poke that tiger right now though.

She kissed him lightly. "Ok then. I will look these over carefully before I sign."

"Good. Call my lawyer if you have questions." He stood and went back to his chair. "Are you going to start work today?"

"I am. Luc should be here sometime this morning. We should have started last week, but he couldn't break free from the computer lab that soon and I was loath to add another thing to his plate. He's carrying an overly full course load right now. I need to find out who his advisor is, so he and I can have a little talk about that."

"Wouldn't Luc have had some say in his own course load?"

"Yes, he would have chosen his courses. But it's his advisor's job to make sure he hasn't taken too much on, and that hasn't happened. Therefore, the advisor and I need to have a very serious talk about our ward. I am not happy. Education is important, but he needs time for work and for fun. Luc won't say anything about it, so I will."

"You're so cute when you're playing fierce mama bear." She grinned at him. "So, would I be taking advantage if I had a list of things that I was interested in you researching?"

"No, not at all." He handed her a piece of paper with a neatly penned list. "Nice penmanship." Her own was a complete disaster. She looked at the list and her eyebrows lifted. "Declan, the things on this list concern not only demon culture, but your rules. Am I correct?"

"Well, yes and no. I told you that this is the way that it is. But I don't know if it's the way it has to be. I have a suspicion about mates. I get the idea of consorts being connected with the Council. And demons can mate with other demons...."

"But demons can't mate with humans unless they are going to be involved directly with the Council. Or so you've all been led to believe."

"Exactly."

"But you and I felt it. Wouldn't other demons or humans feel it?"

"Humans could mistake it for simple attraction if they didn't know any better. Other demons may as well. There is a big difference between thinking something is 'not allowed' over 'not possible'."

"If you think it can't happen, your brain is going to parse it as impossible and move on to the next likely scenario. In this case, that would probably be sexual desire."

"Indeed. Over the course of hundreds of years, you'd be conditioned to ignore any of the signs. And demons are not encouraged to spend a lot of time with humans, romantically. Unless they are at one of the clubs. And that is a heightened environment."

"Less chance of humans thinking those feelings are odd. I mean, in my youth, even I had some pretty intense experiences in a club. All that pounding bass."

He quirked an eyebrow at her. "Really, now?"

"Yes, really. The point being that emotions and desires are going to be intensified in that environment."

"Exactly. Demons have their human groupies. But when demons feed off human energy, it's like a drug for both of them. Which is why I don't allow my team to do it."

"Like when vampires put humans in thrall."

"Again with the vampires?"

"It's a fair assessment of the situation."

He nodded. "You're right. It is. And no demon has ever done it to you?"

"It's been tried."

"By whom?"

"I couldn't really tell you. It's why we opted to go home that night I met your beast."

"So, this was in my club?" His voice was hard.

"Yes."

"What does it feel like?" He was drumming his fingers on the table, a sign that he was irritated.

"It felt like a knock, or it feels like being asked a question. That's the best way to describe it. I shook it off easily, without even really trying. Gwen is the same." Declan looked angry. "No one is going to try it now. Don't worry. I don't think anyone meant it maliciously, it's just the nature of the environment. I think it was more curiosity than anything else."

"Fine. Tell me if it happens again, though." She made a face at him. "Anya, I am not kidding."

"Ok, fine. I'll tell you!"

"This is huge though." She held up his list. "Are you sure?"

"I do. Ever hear the saying 'You can't make an omelet without breaking some eggs?'"

"This is bigger than omelets."

"Change has to come from within. I won't sit on a Council where people who live almost immortal lives are not encouraged or allowed to find happiness wherever they can. Not everyone will want a mate, but we should all have the option."

"Oooh, you're sexy when you get all righteous. But I happen to agree with you. As you knew I would." She looked at the paper again and frowned. "You also want me to look up a strength elixir and mind control?"

"You told me you thought your brother, Pavel, was being controlled."

"You don't forget anything, do you?"

"Not when it comes to you. Additionally, the demon from the park also said he was given something that would make him strong. There were rumors about a magic drug or elixir, but we all thought it was a myth. I am concerned it may not be and that it might see a wider distribution. Mind control seems farfetched, but we may as well check it out."

"Ok, I can work on these. That's no problem. I will take it out in trade."

"Oh? What kind of trade?"

"Well, obviously I'd expect you to service me. Sexually."

"If I must." He grinned at her and waggled his eyebrows, causing her to laugh.

"It's nice to think our friends could find mates if they wanted to. Even Michel."

"Michel is still in love with Omala, I think."

"True." She smiled. "So, the word 'consort' would just be for Council members?"

"Yes." She grunted. "Why?"

"Because that word refers to the partner of a reigning monarch and it makes me think of a royal court."

"And that bothers you?"

"A bit. But also because it shouldn't be a royal court. You don't 'rule' or 'preside' over your businesses. You...well, you run them like an actual business. You're like a CEO. I know it's semantics and I'll deal with it, but it just seems flagrant. "

"Oh, many of them do see themselves as a type of royal court." He poured them both some more coffee.

"That much is obvious after last night. They can call it a 'Council' but it's them holding court really. It feels like a show to be frank. Have they come together in the last several hundred years to discuss any kind of policy changes or systemic issues surrounding your world?"

"Not to my recollection, no."

"Right, because then they may have to look at sweeping reform to their territories. Change is hard and no one wants to be the one to start that ball rolling. They rule, they don't *run* their territories. You're right. They are archaic. They need new blood. Did they make the rule we have now?"

He liked her using 'we', more than he wanted to admit. "I don't think so. Francois may be the only one who was around them. Possibly Adjoa. Everyone is old and has been running their territories for centuries, but I believe most of the current rules pre-date most of the Council."

"Except Anaranth."

"Obviously. And he does not get involved in actual policy change. I doubt it's even occurred to him. He's simply the tie-breaking vote if needed. And he can lay down the law if things are getting out of hand. No one would really countermand him. But he doesn't take advantage."

"How do you think of me?"

"Naked and compliant."

She spit out her coffee. "That is not what I meant!" As she was laughing, she realized that her headache seemed to be gone.

"I know what you meant. I think of you as my mate, and my partner. Not my consort. Not really. It's easier to refer to you that way when necessary, and I like to tease. But where it counts, we're mates."

That was good enough for her. For now. "You're a born anarchist, you are."

"Maybe. And I am not saying they don't take care of their people, but the constant posturing and the fact that everyone has different rules is just bad business. It's...inefficient. Some things need to be standardized. I understand that not everything that works for Antarctica would work in the South Pacific, but we need to have some kind of cohesion."

She nodded at him. "See? To you, it's a business."

"It's efficient and much less open to the caprices of any kind of conceit on my part. If I see it as a business, my ego can't get in the way. My job is to keep mortals and demons safe, to make money and to keep things working for the good of all of us. And occasionally, when necessary, mete out punishment. When it's deserved, of course."

She beamed at him. "I really love you."

"Very much the same, *malysh.*"

"You don't hate the violence aspect of it though, do you?"

"I won't lie, I don't. I used to, but not anymore. It's a means to an end sometimes. Demons are often like recalcitrant children, and I need to make sure that my authority is never in question. Does the violence bother you?"

"Not particularly."

"You may need to mete out your own punishment at some point."

"Then that is what I'll do."

"Christ, I am so turned on right now."

She tweaked his nose. "We have work to do today! No sex!"

"You're no fun."

"I'll be fun later. I promise."

"I'll hold you to that." His eyes sparked with desire, and she caught exactly what he was planning on later.

"I am not sure how I am supposed to work now, but work is what we're doing. I want to get started on this request. Let's hope I can read those books now."

"You can."

"How do you know?"

"That list is written in the same language."

"It's English!"

"No, your brain sees it in English."

"Oh shit...just like the translation circuit on the TARDIS!"

"The...what?"

"Have you really never seen an episode of 'Doctor Who?'"

"Um...."

"Ok, we really have got to do something about your lack of pop culture knowledge."

"We do not."

"I disagree. But we will let that sit for a bit." She got up and went over to him, sitting down on his lap. "Right, now I just want to make out for about five minutes before I go get ready for work." She put her arms around him and started kissing his neck.

"Are you taking payment now?"

"Just a small partial payment. It's all I have time for."

He sighed. "If needs must!"

"Oh, I insist."

***

When she walked into her office an hour later, Luc was sitting at a desk with a book open on a book stand. He was leaning close to the book and taking notes. He was so engrossed; he didn't hear her come in. She cleared her throat and his head jerked up. "Oh, Professor Orlov, I'm sorry! I didn't hear you come in." He stood up and looked at her expectantly.

She smiled. "Luc, I am not a teacher any longer. You can call me 'Anya' now."

He shook his head. "I cannot."

"What do you call Declan?"

"I call him 'Monsieur.'"

"Of course you do. You may not call me 'Madame' though."

He thought for a moment. "Hmmm. How about 'Prof?' It's a bit more *décontractée.*"

"It is more casual. Ok, if you won't call me by my first name, you can call me 'prof' then." It was a compromise, and it would make him feel more comfortable, so she'd deal with it.

"*Bien*! What do we do first?"

"Well, let's discuss that and see where to begin." She handed Luc the request she had from Declan and the young demon raised an eyebrow. "I am showing you this in confidence and it stays between us for now." He nodded at her. Declan had not told her she couldn't include Luc in this and frankly, two sets of eyes were better than one in this case. "I am showing this to you because as we're identifying books, I want you to keep an eye out for these subjects. Do not officially note them in the catalogue, yet. Take separate notes and pass along to me for review."

"I can do that. Does the second request have to do with the recent trouble?"

"It does, yes. But the first request is…"

"Delicate."

"Yes. Very much so."

"*Aucun probleme*." He handed the paper back to her, having committed the requests to memory. "I will be discreet."

"Thank you, Luc." She looked around at all the boxes and crates in the large room. More of them had arrived from Anaranth with a note saying to do with them what she would. She clapped her hands together. "Ok, so we need to fully catalogue everything here. It's going to be a huge task because we're going to be creating a database and it needs to be as robust as we can make it. And we can make it pretty robust. We need to do at the very least, three layers of references, more is better. And of course, cross referenced.

"So, the first three topics in the index should be the main topics, then in descending order of mention and importance?" She nodded. "So, the book I've been looking at can be catalogued, so far as both mythology, weaponry and sexual practices, to start."

"Yes. That should work. Also, sexual practices? Really, Luc?"

"Yes. Really. Look." He showed her what she meant. "Holy shit! Is that even anatomically possible?" She pointed to something on the page.

"I have no idea. Michel may know, *peut-etre*." He looked totally guileless when he said this, that Anya had to laugh. He smiled broadly at her laugh. "I am teasing, but it may very well be true."

"We can ask him," Anya said, laughing again. "But it's going to entail a lot of reading, or skimming, and note taking. And we need to actually build the database itself. We will need to make it accessible to all demons, but editable only by us. So, web based? Does it need to be? Behind a secure server. Shit, we need to set up a secure server."

"The Council has one, we can use that one. I will work on getting us access. But for now, we can work locally."

"The Council?"

He shrugged. "They do not use it for much of anything, but it is there."

"Hmmm...good to know. Thanks Luc."

"*De rien*. Also, I have a few options for where to build the database. It doesn't have to be web based but needs to have a way to publish to the web. Come see." They spent the next couple of hours going over their choices, deciding on something and starting to build the database.

Anya sat back, impressed. "You gave this some thought?"

"I worked some when I got home last night."

"Did you not sleep?"

"I did a little, I don't need much right now. But I had some ideas when I got home, so I wanted to capture them."

"So, about what happened last night…."

"Prof, I was glad to be able to help you last night. Liliana is a lunatic. The only reason she didn't pick Gwen for her little exercise is because we are not allowed to put humans in danger. It stands to reason she'd pick the youngest person in Monsieur's retinue."

The fact that he had called Liliana a lunatic was both amusing and surprising. He was so sweet looking, that she had to remember that he was a demon and that the sweet was definitely going to come with some salty. "She could have mortally wounded you."

"But she didn't. I knew she wouldn't, and I knew you'd win. It wasn't the point. She just wanted to prove that she could. Her plan was not to hurt me, it was to try and embarrass you."

He sounded oddly very sure of this. "How do you know that?"

He hesitated. "I just know things sometimes."

"Luc?"

"I seem to have the sight, as my grandmother would call it. I thought it would disappear when I became a demon, but it did not. It's also not very reliable. I don't always see things, and it's mostly flashes or a feeling when I do. With Liliana, I could see it when she looked at you. She feels threatened."

She just looked at him. "Huh. That's fascinating. Is this something you'd want to talk to Gwen about, to work on honing that skill?"

"If you want me to."

"Luc, no. That is not how it's going to work with us. If this is something you want to pursue, we will. If you don't, it doesn't leave this room. Well, I may tell Declan, but that would be it. This is your decision."

He was silent for a moment. "I am fine with you telling monsieur, but for now I would like it to remain just between the three of us."

She smiled. "Done."

"*Merci*."

"You are welcome. Now, let's get back to work."

***

Anya spent the rest of the morning setting up workflows, fine tuning the cataloguing system and responding to random emails from a handful of demons and humans alike.

Around lunchtime, she got a delivery of a pretty amazing spear from Adjoa, along with a note reading, *I look forward to sparring with you and teaching you how to use this spear. This one is from the tribe I was born into and belonged to me when I was still mortal.*

She made a low whistle and asked the courier to wait while she wrote a thank you letter. She stressed that she was looking forward to meeting with her soon and that both she and Declan were appreciative of the support from the Demon of Africa. She also imparted that she was honored by such a gift and hoped that she would be worthy of it. *That's enough sucking up for the day*, she thought, getting back to work.

Later that afternoon she was skimming the book that Luc had been looking at that morning, when she noticed them on the page. Two sets of broadswords. One set were Declan's and the other set, hers. Her interest piqued, she began a more in depth read of the section and when she finished, she was in shock.

Declan? She thought, concentrating very hard.

Anya? Is everything all right? He answered quickly. Even in her head, she could hear the worry.

Yes. Everything is fine. Sorry, I didn't mean to worry you.

It is no problem. You don't have to concentrate so hard though; it comes across as yelling. Just relax.

She shook her shoulders out, blew out a breath and tried again, much more naturally this time. *Better?*

Much. Quick study. She could sense the smile in his voice. *What do you need? Or are you just saying hello?*

I found something in one of the books. I think you should see it. I think it is...important.

I will be home within the hour then. I wanted to have dinner with you anyway.

She smiled. *Wonderful, I'll be waiting.*

Declan walked into the office forty-five minutes later. And once again, Anya was struck with how beautiful he was. He was like a panther, all feline grace and power. He took her breath away. She hoped she always felt this way when she saw him. He stopped in the middle of the room and gave her a hooded look. She knew immediately he could hear what she'd been thinking. He slowly stalked towards her, like she was his prey. A feral gleam in his eye. She slowly backed up as he came towards her. The back of her legs hit the desk right as he got to her. He put his arms on either side of her, palms flat on the desk. She pushed at his chest lightly, he didn't move a muscle. He just stared at her. All of a sudden, he let out a low growl and kissed her until she was breathless. "A panther, huh?"

"I've really got to start thinking a little quieter. Why can't I hear you?"

"I am better at cloaking my thoughts. You tend to telegraph, especially if you're tired."

"Really?"

"Yes. I am mostly just catching things you seem to be thinking at me, loudly. But in general, if I'm thinking about you, you should be picking it up. It probably hasn't even occurred to you to try it. Try it now."

She took a breath and concentrated on being able to hear his blood hum with hers. It took her a few tries, but very quickly she picked up what Declan was thinking about. It was a very vivid image of them naked, on top of her desk. She blushed a little.

His voice was low. "As I said, quick study." He leaned over and gave her chin a little nip. "You can talk to me, so picking up what I'm thinking should be easy enough for you to do. And you for sure pick up on my moods, even if you're not realizing it." He thought one more thing and she smiled.

"I love you too," she said.

"Ok, what have you got?"

"You should read it; in case I'm mistaken."

"Do you think you are?"

She started to walk over to the table where the book was, and he followed. "No, I don't. But read it for yourself anyway."

She had left the book open to the page she wanted him to start reading. She could see by his face she wasn't wrong. He looked up. "Jesus Fucking Christ! The swords are demon killers?"

"It looks that way. They're imbued with real old magic. It's magic that predates Anaranth I believe, though I can't be sure. You said an ancient gave them to you?"

"Yes. Before she decided to become non-corporeal, she gifted me both sets. Why would a demon have swords that could kill their own race?"

"I do not know. And she was a demon? You're sure?"

"She felt like a demon. What else could she have been? Do not say vampire."

She scoffed. "I wasn't going to say that. I was thinking maybe she was a witch or sorceress."

"She could have been both a demon and a witch. The ancients used to have way more magic."

"Ok, we go on the assumption she was a demon who maybe had magic, until we have new information. It gets better, keep reading."

"We have swords that could kill me, and it gets better?"

"No, they can't kill *you*. Or me. Keep reading."

He read for another few minutes. "You have got to be kidding me?! A prophecy? There have been rumors of one for centuries, but this one seems to put us smack in the middle of it!"

"Yes."

"That is insane."

"Also, yes. Apparently, this book is about more than just weaponry, mythology, and weird demon sexual practices, it's about a prophecy."

"Excuse me? Where is the sex bit?"

"Later, you horn dog." She laughed. "It seems the swords are meant to be wielded by a demon and his consort, the 'chosen ones' if you will and they are fated to bring demon kind into the light. Whatever that means."

"Well that could be just getting them all on email."

"True."

"So, this is supposed to be us? Am I wrong?"

"I do not think you are."

"It imbues me with powers, which explains the glowing and that power surge when we were in Russia. But you are going to also have great power among demons." She sighed.

"And if someone else knows about this, it seems as likely a reason as any to harm us. Those swords are a true game changer for anyone that wields them."

"Yes. Though things have been scarily quiet since the department store."

"Calm before the storm. They need to rethink their strategy now that we're official."

"I don't know that I want this."

"Me neither, to be honest. But I am not sure we have a choice."

She pointed at the book. "It talks about a protected inner circle as well."

He read. "Twelve to start. I come up with nine."

"Players to be named later. New people? Someone's mate to be?"

"Makes sense I suppose."

"So those in the inner circle also cannot be harmed by the broadswords?"

"According to this, no. Old magic will protect. This right here," she pointed. "Looks like a spell. Gwen should be able to handle it. We'll need to ask her. There are a handful of what I think are spells in here. They're written in another language. I hope maybe Gwen can read them. Not sure what language that is though."

"Old Irish."

"What?"

"They're in old Irish. I recognize it. So, even if Gwen can't read it, I can and I can translate them."

"Is this Archaic Irish or just old Irish?"

"I don't think it's quite as old as Archaic, that's dating back to the 3rd or 4th century, but it's definitely Old Irish."

"I think the spells were added later anyway."

"Why do you think that?"

"The ink and lettering are different." He took a closer look and saw that she was correct. "The witch who wrote the spells was likely Irish then," she surmised.

"Likely." I wonder when it was written and who originally wrote it?

"Be assured I will be researching that. Do we tell Richelieu?"

"I think we have to. I think we have to choose to trust him and hope it doesn't bite us in the ass. I can ask for a meeting tomorrow with him. But now, we need to tell everyone else." He pulled Anya gently to him. "I knew you were special."

"Declan, please."

"No, it's true. I knew it. I knew you were going to be something different the first time I felt your blood."

"Are you sure you aren't biased?"

"I am completely biased, but I am also right." He kissed her lovingly. "The time for change is upon us."

CHAPTER 20

Within the hour, everyone was crowded around the dining room table. On the table were both sets of swords and the book. Matthew was carefully holding one of the swords and Declan made the decision that his friend was definitely the better man to teach Anya how to use the swords. Matthew was a master with a sword.

Dougal gave Matthew a baleful look. "How can you hold something that might kill you?"

Matthew shrugged. "Because it's a gorgeous piece of steel. I'm being careful and I don't plan to stab myself with it." He looked up at the irascible Scot, "But I might stab you if you aren't careful."

Dougal sighed. "So, let me see if I have this right. Those swords are allegedly demon killers, but they don't affect Anya or Declan because they are part of an overall prophecy and are protected. And we're all included in the prophecy too, so we don't need to worry because we can't die from them either? As long as Blondie here recites some damned spell?" Dougal scoffed.

Therese spoke up. "Thanks Mr. Exposition, I think we all understand that much." Dougal yanked gently on her braid and Therese grinned. "What I don't get is, what's the prophecy exactly?"

Luc, who had been studying the text spoke up. "It's kind of...um…" he searched for the word he wanted in English. "Nebulous at best. Anya is most certainly 'The Golden Guardian' mentioned here, but guardian of what? It is not clear and may well be in another book. Declan is most certainly 'The Chosen Demon' but what is he chosen for?"

"Is that really what those translate to?" Michel asked.

"As far as I can tell, *oui*." Luc paused. "This is an old language. We're giving it modern meanings and sensibilities. If there are better words out there, I do not know them as of yet."

"Nor do I," Anya said.

Gwen piped up, looking through the book and then holding it up in front of her face. "I need to chime in here. This book smells like magic. I mean, I can both feel and smell the magic coming off of it." She made a face. "In waves."

"Is it spelled then?" Declan asked.

"Not in any standard way. It's got old magic, but some of the magic is older than other parts of it. It's weird. It reminds me of a grimoire, though it has that kind of magical weight to it. I'd have to unravel that magic to say more, and I do not believe I am meant to do that. It has to stay spelled exactly as it. It's not dangerous. I am surprised it didn't put up more of a fight being read, but I suspect the book is also tied to the two of you."

"Luc was the first to read it today."

"But Declan opened it first."

"That makes sense." said Therese.

"I have my family's old grimoire, and it smells of magic, but it's nowhere near as powerful. The magic feels somewhat diluted, likely due to the passage of time. I can read Old Irish and some of these spells are elaborate, but some are pretty straight forward. Which I find odd, but part of one of the spells begins with 'what is fated to be is written in time and is tied to those with the light.' so the person who wrote the spells wanted it to be safe, but once it was in the right hands, not be too difficult."

"So, the book isn't against us, or evil?" asked Michel.

"Oh goodness no! This book intends no malice and is here to help us all find our way."

"Even the parts written in our language back that up." said Declan. "The first part of this book is some history and a weapons primer and some odd sex stuff, that's true. But the entire second half, from what I have seen, talks about the prophecy."

Anya chimed in. The first part is pretty dry reading. You'd leaf through it, nod off and put it away."

"They hid it in plain sight," said Matthew.

Gwen cleared her throat. "Annie, do you remember that night at the club?" Anya nodded. "If you recall, I said I felt like there was something I was forgetting, something that was a bit out of my grasp. It was there, then it was gone. Well, this book brought it back to me. I could smell magic that night. Old, powerful magic One of the people involved with this is very magical. A darker magic than mine. At some point, this magical person was at the club that night. They knew I was a witch though, they wanted me to forget. But this book unlocked the memory. And now I am really fucking pissed off that someone did that to me." Donovan went and hugged her.

"We can settle that score when we find the person then." said Donovan. Anya squeezed Gwen's hand and smiled at her.

"If I flip to the end of the book, there is mention of another book. We may not have that. We probably don't." She pointed. "Here's the part about Gwen."

"Me? Where?"

"Here." You're the Golden Mage, the true friend and witch for the Golden Guardian."

"The hell you say?"

"I do say." She snapped her fingers. "I bet that anything with magic or spells in it will be written in old Irish. Luc, make a mental note that we need to be on the lookout for that."

"Will do." Gwen and Luc started to pore over the book, with Gwen breaking down the spells for Luc, who pretended to be only mildly interested in the witchcraft, but in truth was completely fascinated.

Declan slid over to Matthew, taking Anya along. "Matthew, Anya needs to learn how to use these swords, quickly. I'm good, you're better. By quite a bit. Can I prevail upon you to give my mate the lessons she needs?" He looked at Anya, who was making a face at him. "If that's ok with you dear?"

She rolled her eyes at him. "It's fine with me, thanks for asking...*finally*." She looked at Matthew. "Do you have the time?"

"I do. And it would be my pleasure. Declan is right, I am better than he is." He grinned at her. "I have a couple of sets of practice broadswords we can use. Tomorrow morning, 9 a.m."

"You're not wasting time."

"No time to waste."

She nodded at him. "Ok, 9 a.m. it is then. I'll even feed you lunch."

Gwen spoke just then. "There are some nifty spells in here, but the spell that protects you, I have that down now. I know how it works. The book wanted me to learn it, it's practically dancing at me." She read some more. "These swords are so very old. The demon who gave them to you, Declan, was an ancient one, yes?" He nodded. "I would venture to guess these swords are older than that ancient. There is some real power here." Declan whistled.

"The spell protects all of us? Even you?" Donovan tried sounding casual and failed miserably.

She smiled gently at him. "Me too. It protects us all, plus three to come. The prophecy mentions there are twelve." Donovan let out the breath he didn't know he was holding. "I don't know if the number is significant. Time will tell."

"Well," said Therese, "There were twelve apostles and twelve Olympian Gods in the Pantheon. I mean, twelve is a significant number."

Dougal looked at her. "Really, lass?"

"Yes. You know, I had a life before you all. Also, there were twelve knights of the Round Table."

"So, twelve does have some meaning, it seems." This from Matthew.

"The spell won't work on just anyone though. I mean three people can't knock on the door and boom! They're protected. They are a specific three, the spell is very clear. One person is described as one who possesses color, and the other is one who possesses logic. The last is one who possesses endless night. Or that might be soul. That's a word I don't know."

Declan leaned over to look at it and made a face. "I don't either."

"I am sorry Annie; you will not be able to bring Rosamund into the fold. I know this makes you sad." The two women laughed.

"What am I missing?" Therese asked.

"Anya and Rosamund are sworn enemies, we'll explain later."

"This doesn't shock me. Rosamund is a real nasty piece of work."

"Right?"

"Back to the matter at hand." Declan cut in. "Can you work it?"

"Yes."

"Will you?"

"I already did. As I said, the book wanted me to know it and know it quickly, I was meant to read and cast it easily. And so I have." She smiled at them. "We're all safe, in theory at this point. There's no reason to think the spell doesn't work. The spells in here are fascinating. I will need to come and study them more."

Luc was still looking over Gwen's shoulder and frowned. "There is a part here, not a spell, that seems to point to at least two of the others being human mates. How can that be?"

Oops. We missed that, Declan.

We did indeed.

"Why are ye two looking at each other? Are ye head talking?"

"Declan, we're going to have to tell them, I think."

Declan sighed. "Ok, let me explain. I wasn't going to say anything until I knew for sure, and I am still not sure if I'm right. I think that it's entirely possible that demons, any demon that isn't one of the foot soldiers, can mate with a human."

"But, my lord and commander," said Donovan. "That's only for those involved directly with the Council."

"No, only Council members can call their mates 'Consort.' It's very possible that demons can mate with humans if they so desire. That it's not a function of demon genetics, it's just a rule that has been around so long that no one questions it anymore. And that most demons have been conditioned over the years to not do it."

There was dead silence in the room. Luc, Gwen, and Donovan looked hopeful. Michel, Dougal, and Therese looked interested, but Matthew looked a little sick at this news.

"Well," said Therese. "Isn't that a fucking kick in the head!"

***

Everyone started speaking at once. "QUIET!" Declan roared. The room became silent. Family or not, Declan was the alpha, and you obeyed your alpha. "Listen everyone, for now...this is all conjecture. Anya is researching this for us. If I'm right, this is going to change things for us in a very big and real way. Many of the Council would fight this as it would be their sovereignty, for lack of a better word into question. It will cause chaos. I am not sure who on the Council is even aware that this may be a possibility. I suspect that this has been in effect since long before this current group took power. Additionally, there is someone out there who probably knows about the prophecy and about us and possibly our mating rights. We may not be able to die, but there are fates worse than death. This knowledge puts you in harm's way."

"What about Anaranth?" Matthew asked.

"If anyone knows, it's him. And he's who I would approach first if we found this to be true." He paused. "I would wish, for all of you not currently mated, to find someone you love. Someone that completes you, a partner, a lover, a best friend. And if that person were human, I would want you to be able to have that person for as long as any Council member has their mate. It has never seemed fair or right to me that only someone meant for the Council could mate with a human. We live a long and often brutal existence. We serve a purpose.

We have had an extended peaceful period, for which I am grateful. But this information could bring an end to that peace. Sides will be chosen. We may need to be ready for a war." Declan knew he was being dramatic, but he wanted to hammer home the point that this was a very big deal and that they had to keep it quiet for now.

They all looked at him. Anya spoke first. "My sword, my honor and my loyalty are yours," *as well as my heart*, she spoke silently to him.

He turned hot eyes to her. *As my heart is yours, cushla machree.* In turn, each person in the room gave Declan their own vow of loyalty.

Matthew was the last one to speak. "My steel, my loyalty and my life are yours. But let's hope it doesn't come to that last one." Declan grinned at his friend. And Matthew knew. He knew that this was exactly what Declan was chosen to do. He was going to change the way that Demon kind worked. He was going to lead a possible political war in order to bring them out of the dark and into the light. And Anya was going to be there with him, protecting the humans and also Declan if need be. She was the light to his darkness. Coups were often bloody, and this would be no different and each of them would have a part to play. *Well*, thought Matthew, *it was getting entirely too boring around here anyway.*

***

Declan was sitting up in bed still later, after getting home from the club, waiting for Anya to come out of their closet. "Aaannnyyaaa? What are you doing?"

"Be out in a sec."

"Are you stroking your swords?"

She laughed. "No, I am not stroking my swords!"

"Interested in stroking mine?" He asked playfully.

She walked out wearing an old, oversized t-shirt. "Possibly."

"You look sexy in that."

"It's just an old concert tee."

"Don't care. You look sexy." He thought she could wear a burlap sack and look beautiful.

She smiled and walked over to the bed, pulling off her t-shirt to reveal a lacy black bra and panties. "How about this, then?"

"For me?"

"Yes. I got it especially so you could rip it with your claws." She smiled. "I'd rather you ruin this, then the t-shirt. I'm very fond of that shirt." He laughed.

She climbed onto the bed and straddled him. "You made me so hot earlier, the way you yelled at everyone. I could not wait to get you alone."

"Really now?" He started stroking her back. "Does power excite you?"

"Yours does." She answered honestly.

"It does?"

"Yes. Your blood heated up; I could feel it. I could feel your excitement and your power. I can feel it in my blood, and it makes me very horny. It feels really great." She leaned down and captured his mouth. She nibbled his lips and his hands tightened on her. She swept her tongue into his mouth and sent him a searing image. He groaned and went from reclining to sitting up in a heartbeat. His claws extended and he ripped her bra open. He palmed her breasts, claws still extended. She pulled back. "Oh good. You got that image."

"I did." He raked a claw across each of her nipples and she hissed. "Christ, that feels good. It probably shouldn't, but it does." He replaced the claw with his mouth, he took a light nip of one nipple and then the other and Anya screamed. He laughed, low in his throat. "You beautiful bastard." She raked her own nails down his chest, across his own nipples and laughed when he hissed. He flipped her over and shredded her panties. "Worth it?" she asked.

"Completely!" He raised her legs to sit on his shoulders and entered her. She arched off the bed and screamed his name. He drove into her relentlessly, over, and over, bringing her close to orgasm and then pulling back. Her eyes were closed, and her nails were digging into the bed. "Anya, open your eyes, I want to look into your eyes when you come."

Her head snapped up, eyes wide open, staring into his. They stayed that way, staring into each other's eyes and as they came together, "I love you Declan."

"And I love you, Anya."

***

Much later, she turned over and caught him staring at her. "What?"

"I really like you." She laughed, surprised. "I know that sounds odd, but I do. I like spending time with you and talking to you. I like how your mind works. I just enjoy the hell out of you."

She put her hand on his cheek. "I really like you too. You're smart, you have a good heart, you're tough, but fair and I enjoy the hell out of you as well."

He dropped a kiss on her nose. "You are also sexy as fuck."

She burst out laughing. "Well, thank you for that. May I also just say, I really enjoy your penis."

He laughed as well. "Well, now that we've settled that. Let's get some sleep."

"Good idea. I suspect that Matthew is going to kick my ass tomorrow."

"Oh, he is. Great with a sword, great with a gun. He was a gentleman *and* a soldier."

"Was he? Ooh, tell me."

"Nope. You have to ask him. He may tell you."

"He will. Eventually anyway. He likes me."

He gave her a look. "Does he?"

"Not like that! Just as, you know, a person. Not everyone wants to fuck me, you know."

"Well, that's obviously just bullshit."

"Declan, unlike you, who seems to have a demon fan club, men just don't fall in line for me like that."

"If you don't think Michel would be all over you if I wasn't around, you are nuts."

"Michel isn't that picky though."

"Yes, but he's also not stupid."

"He would have no shot. And then, there's Omala. Who is she exactly?"

"Another demon. Works for the Council. Very smart, very good at the politics of it all. But very diplomatic. She's someone you definitely want on your side."

"Well, thanks for the CV. Who is she to Michel?"

"An ex. *The* ex, as a matter of fact. There's something there still. For both of them. I've never met two people who work harder at ignoring each other. Michel sleeps around as much as he does to basically try and forget that he still loves this woman."

"Well, that's sad."

"It is. Don't butt in."

"Would I do that?"

"You would." He paused. "Would Matthew?"

"Would Matthew butt into Michel's love life? I mean, I don't know. Probably not."

"Don't be obtuse. You know what I mean. Would he have a shot?"

Anya rolled her eyes "This conversation is dumb. I am not interested in Matthew in that way."

"I know, but there is something about him that is getting to you. And answer the question."

"Yes, he would have a shot, but he wouldn't be interested at all in me. Nor would it be at all satisfying for either of us. I would then forget about it and still be his friend. Which is all I actually want to be anyway. But there is definitely something about him that is getting to me. His control is scarily tight, it worries me. Do you never notice that he always stands a bit separate from all of us? Even when he jokes around, he's never quite fully engaged with us. You always bring him in, bring him close." Declan looked surprised at this. "You don't even know you're doing it. But you feel it like I do. I know he cares about all of us, and I know he'd kill for you. I've caught a couple of really unguarded looks and it almost breaks me each time. He's so lonely and we're all he has, but he seems almost incapable of letting his walls down."

"You see a lot."

"I do. He's pathologically loyal to you, and by extension me and the rest of the group."

His mate had the biggest heart, he thought. "His loyalty has never been in question."

She sat up. "He's one of yours too." It wasn't a question.

"Yes. He is. I helped Donovan because it was the right thing to do and I saw his potential, but Matthew was demon born. I watched him grow up, watched the man he became because I always knew I'd be the demon there for him. We often get a sense of these things. I've known him longer than I've known Donovan." He sighed. "He's been a good friend and I couldn't ask for a better second. I'd trust him with my life. Better, I'd trust him with *your* life. But I do know what you're talking about. But what can we actually do?"

"I don't know. But he's so alone, and it makes me so sad. I am hoping I can get him to talk. Maybe it will help." She shrugged. "I am just going to be really annoying until he caves."

Declan pulled her back down to the bed. "If anyone can be that annoying, it's you."

"Hey!"

He laughed and kissed her. "Go to sleep. You are going to need your rest."

CHAPTER 21

The next morning when Anya walked into the practice room, Matthew was already there. She stopped suddenly. She wasn't used to seeing him so casually dressed. If he and Declan didn't make all the women in turn of the century Paris or Victorian London or wherever the hell, they spent their time, swoon, she'd be surprised. He was wearing loose black pants, a snug black t-shirt and he was barefoot, the outfit mirroring her own, but he looked way better in it. "Good morning, Anya," he said, bowing low, with a smirk on his face.

"Good morning, Matthew." She stopped in the middle of the room. "On a scale of 1 to 10, how much am I going to hate you when we're done this morning?"

"It cannot be measured with modern technology." She blanched. "Relax. Today will probably only be a seven or an eight. I brought along two sets of practice swords; the second set should be weighted similarly to yours. I want you to learn the mechanics first; before we start using your pretty ones. We need to practice basics; how to handle them being the first thing."

"Sounds reasonable."

"Good. We'll work with just one for now. Now, Declan tells me that you have scabbards that will sit on your back. For now, we will deal with pulling it from a regular side one." He threw her one and she strapped it on. "Which is your dominant hand?"

"My right. I can handle knives or daggers with both, but I am right-handed."

"Then your scabbard is on the wrong side."

"It's on my right."

"Yes, and for a dagger, which is shorter, that's fine. You don't pick up your sword on the side where it's sheathed. You use the opposite. Right-handed, so you sheath goes on the left. It's faster in combat and easier to maneuver the sword. Like so." He pulled his sword in one quick fluid motion. "That said, I want you to try it the wrong way, first, so you feel the difference. Now, pick up your sword and sheath it." She did. She handled the steel with care, her movements economical, which pleased him. "Now, pull it out."

"That's what she said."

He tried not to smile. "Seriously, Anya?"

"Sssorrryyy!" She pulled it and it was...clunky. Harder to get a good grip on it and it felt sloppy.

"Now, move the scabbard to the correct side, and do it again." She did and while it was still clumsy, that was just her inexperience. It was way more fluid this way, but still not quite right. "Ok, so you're used to spring loaded sheaths that will drop a dagger into your palm and then you flip to stab. I've seen you do it. It's very quick and very appropriate there. Not here. You're trying to pull the sword the same way you palm a dagger, which means you're pulling underhanded. Do not do that. Were you taught that by someone?"

"I haven't really had any sword work, beyond holding one a few times. And I never pulled it from a scabbard. Knife wise, I am completely self-taught."

"Natural talent."

"I suppose. But I worked really hard to get as good as I am." She wasn't just good with a knife or dagger, he thought, she was bloody amazing. Matthew had no doubt that she'd be amazing with a sword as well.

He nodded "Ok. I am going to show you the correct way. Re-sheath the sword." She did. "I am coming in close." He came behind her, putting his hand over hers and showing her, by doing it with her, how to pull the sword out. He stepped back. "Now, you do it."

She did. "Better. Again!" Anya then went on to repeat that one move, a number of times. Her arm got tired.

"Matthew. How many more times do I have to do this?"

"Until it feels and looks natural. Your sword is an extension of your hand, in the same way a knife or dagger is. I can still see you thinking about it before you do it." He grinned at her. "Or, until I say so."

"Maybe stop grinning maniacally at me then." The bastard was having too much fun.

"Then do it correctly." He grabbed a bottle of water and sat down cross legged on the floor.

"I don't get water?"

"When you do it to my satisfaction. Or you drop. Whichever comes first." He meant it too.

"Jesus, did you not get enough love as a child or something?"

"As it happens, no." He saw her face fall. "No. Do not give me a sad face right now. You do this correctly and then I will tell you something personal." Christ, why had he said that?

"Deal." And now she knew how she was going to get him to open up to her.

"Good. Now, as I said, you're overthinking it. You learned to throw knives as a child, children are much more instinctual than adults are. You need to find that instinct, channel it and then do it. As I said, like a knife, your sword is an extension of you. Center yourself and do it." He took a drink of water. "Then keep doing it."

Boy, he was a hardass. But she had no doubt that when he was done with her, she'd be hell on wheels with a sword. So, she did what he asked of her. She centered herself, remembered how she felt as a child when she first held a knife and knew what to do and then pulled out her sword.

"Excellent! Much better! Keep doing that." She did it ten more times before he was satisfied. "Nice!" He went and got her a water. "Sit down and drink this. A deal is a deal." She eagerly sat, took a long drink of water, and waited. She knew he didn't like talking about his family and she promised herself she would not interrupt. "My father taught my older brother and me how to handle swords. My brother, Reginald, was the eldest son, and my father loved him. Only him. Not me, not my younger brother or sister. Just Reg. Anyway, I wanted to be better at one thing and swords were my chance. The minute I held one, I knew exactly what to do. Like you, with knives. It felt right in the same way I bet knives felt right to you." He paused and she nodded at him. "My father was a hardass; I am teaching you the way I was taught. It's tough, but I learned, and I learned well. And I am not being as much of a dick as he was, trust me. He used to whack me on my ass with a sword when I didn't do something correctly. You need to learn to wield those things with absolute precision and strength, and I can teach it to you. I can see you have about a hundred questions. You may ask two." He'd be answering questions all day all day otherwise.

"What about your mother? And did you ever use a sword other than practice?"

"I will answer your second question first. Yes, I was a soldier. My father got me the commission, that's what second sons did. but I was glad of it. I was good at it. And there was always some war or conflict in those days. I was very fond of my mother, loved her quite a bit. But she was never really capable of returning that love in the way I wanted. Not to any of her children. She was shallow and vain, but she could be such fun when she turned our way. She was never cruel like my father could be, she was just absent." He spoke calmly, but she knew it cost him something to tell her this.

"I'm sorry. I know what having a challenging family can be like." They smiled at each other, each knowing a bit of what the other person may have gone through.

"I know you do. Though from what I've heard, I'd rather have mine than yours."

"You are not wrong there."

"Finish your water, we are not done yet." For the next few hours, Matthew went over the basics of holding and re-sheathing and they did a few simple moves, over and over again until she thought her arm was going to fall off. She had more strength and stamina than she did before, but it was very early days. Her strength was like that of a young demon still. He even had her practice with her left hand. Declan came in around lunchtime to see Anya giving Matthew a murderous look and started laughing. "I think it may be time for lunch."

Matthew gave him a speculative look. "Do you? I think it may be time to give Anya a look at an actual sword fight." Declan grinned and took off his jacket and then his shoes, so he wouldn't have an unfair advantage. "Shirt too, pretty boy. That one is way too snug for you to fight in."

"Oh, he of the snug t-shirt. You too. Even playing field."

Both men took off their shirts and Anya said a small prayer of thanks for it. Now, there were two finely honed bodies right there. She sat on one side of the room, just enjoying the view as they got situated. She'd never seen Declan with a sword, so this was going to be fun. The minute the two started, she was mesmerized. They were poetry in motion. So fast, so efficient, no extraneous moves or showboating. Matthew, she had to admit, was better. But he wasn't holding back that she could see. If he was at his best, it made Declan work harder, made him better. When they were done, she applauded. "That was fantastic. You are both amazing. Matthew's better though."

"Matthew is better," Declan said. "Always has been."

"Declan is better at hand to hand."

"Oh God, will you two wrestle naked for me now? Please?"

"Absolutely not!" said Declan.

"Come on...just this once."

"No, woman! Stop it. You are not allowed to see Matthew naked."

"Look, I have no problem with it. I am happy to strip for your mate."

"Matthew, I'd hate to have to kill my best friend, but I will do it."

Matthew laughed and put his shirt back on and grabbed his shoes.

"In that case, I was promised lunch."

"And you shall have it. Joining us?" She walked over and gave Declan a kiss.

"I think I'd better. Else, the Monk may well strip for you."

"I am pretty sure I could handle both of you naked." She laughed.

"I am also sure and yet, we shall never know."

"I mean, we could. We've shared women before," said Matthew.

"Holy fucking shit, Matthew! Why would you do that to me?!" Declan was turning red.

"Oh, really? Do tell. I want to know all the details."

"No! For God sakes! It was only once, and it was an accident."

"It was twice, you liar. And only the second time was an accident. You were trying to cheer me up the first time."

"An accident?" Anya asked.

"On our part, yes. Not on hers. She was a buxom lass. Much like Red, over here." Matthew pointed his head towards Anya. "I mean, it'd be like old times."

"So, a bit of role playing? Ok, I can pretend to be a buxom tavern wench."

"I dare say you could. I bet we could find you the costume and everything."

"Ok, but you two have to be in costume as well."

"Obviously."

Declan looked like he was going to burst, until Matthew and Anya started laughing. "Oh, that's really funny you guys. I was beginning to worry. Did you plan that?"

"Beginning to? You looked like you were going to explode, my friend. And no, we didn't. But your face, how could we not keep it up."

Anya was wiping away tears. "Jesus, you looked like you were going to murder someone."

"I hate you both."

She walked over to him and said softly, "No, you don't." She kissed him thoroughly.

"Jesus, get a room. I want food, not a show."

Declan clapped him on the back. "Let's go eat then. I spoke to Richelieu this morning and I can tell you what he said."

<u>CHAPTER 22</u>

At lunch, Declan relayed the conversation with Richelieu. "I told him what we discovered, and he looked far less surprised than I would have thought. Apparently, there have been rumors about a prophecy for quite a while now. No one has paid them any heed. Same with the swords. The Council definitely knows about the prophecy, at least. He's heard it discussed, but never seriously."

"Meaning the Council can't be seen believing anything so silly." Matthew mused.

"Exactly. For creatures that are somewhat mythical in nature, no one wants to believe any of the myths."

"Ironic," commented Anya.

"Very."

"Has he been able to ferret out any information though, about our attackers?" she asked.

"He said there are some very odd things happening, concentrated mostly in London, but there are some rumblings through Western Europe as well. He suspects either Francois or Liliana, or both are involved. Many of the odd happenings seem magical in nature."

"Really? Magic?"

"Yes. Francois has always had a thing for magic. You never saw a demon more entranced with magicians and witches. The rumor is that's how he found Liliana. She was also a fan of magic and was dabbling a bit. The dabbling caught Francois' eye. Though, his interest in most things does seem to be waning, maybe he is still caught in the magic trap. The cardinal has some demons that are very good at smelling magic. I am a little concerned that these demons were witch hunters, but I am trying to not ask that question. That said, I don't want them near Gwen if we can help it." Anya looked startled but nodded.

"He thinks the illegal turning of demons, and possibly the drug, is helped along by magical spells. That's just a guess, but his guesses are good ones. Additionally, he's noticed an uptick through Western and Eastern Europe surrounding the number of new male demons."

"Really? Eastern Europe too?" asked Anya

"Yes." replied Matthew. "We're not the most prolific lot in general. People live longer now, and no one wants to be an old demon. Centuries ago, it was normal for people to be younger when they died. There are always outliers. Dougal was rather aged when he died. I was supposed to die younger, but it didn't happen." He looked at Declan, who quickly looked away, and smiled. "Now, even with demon born, we try very hard to not let them go when they are young. Luc is an exception; I know Declan would have preferred to have him later after he'd lived a little longer."

"Yes. I didn't know about Luc until it was too late and that is something I am going to need to think about at some point, because it shouldn't have happened." Anya squeezed his hand.

"When we say 'young demon' we mean they're new. Most of the demons that Luc lives with were about 10-15 years older than him when he died. We can't always make it happen, but a proliferation of demons say, under twenty-five, would be unusual."

"How old was Luc?"

"Twenty-one. Which doesn't seem young and may not have been considered that young hundreds of years ago, but times change. It's not an official rule, it's just kind of an unspoken thing."

"So, this is why some of the Council members look a bit older, some look younger."

"Exactly."

"From what the cardinal says, these guys are mostly college age to twenty-five. Our demon born numbers have gone down some in the past century, but it's not alarming. The number of brokered deals though has significantly dropped off. Which makes perfect sense in a modern world. There are still plenty of demons. Interestingly, Francois' overall numbers are not declining at the same rate as the other Council members. And this, is very odd."

"Data nerd." smiled Anya.

"Oh, I am. Definitely."

"So, something I've been meaning to ask you; he's the Demon of Western Europe and Great Britain, but you run France and Belgium. How is this so? The last time I checked, both France and Belgium were part of Western Europe."

"They still are. France and Belgium have the highest concentration of demons in Western Europe. France itself attracts a very large number of demons and a very large number of humans who go looking for demons."

"Your demon groupies?"

"Yes, that's one way to put it. The clubs we have here in Paris are the oldest ones. Demons come from around the world to frequent the clubs in France in Belgium." This was from Matthew.

"Not to brag." Declan winked at her.

"They are definitely the best run." added Matthew. "And I am bragging."

"So, why do you have groupies?" Anya asked. Declan made a face. "Fans? I mean, what am I supposed to call them?"

"Demon enthusiasts," he said. Anya rolled her eyes. "So, you know demons can siphon excess energy from humans?" She nodded. "As I said, it's excess for the most part. If your adrenaline is high, your pheromones are kicking in, you're dancing, turned on, happy...you let off energy. You don't feel that. But we can make it pleasurable. And we don't do that without the human knowing, that's a no no. The humans have to want to do it and that's where the clubs come in. The only humans who go in there, know what to expect and they are for it."

"Because it feels good? Like sex?" He nodded. "What do the demons get out of it?"

"A high. It feels good to them too. It gives them an extra boost, extra energy, stamina if they're young. It feels really good."

"Do you do it?"

"No. Not anymore. None of my circle do. But we've all done it. Young demons find it beneficial, but it's not strictly necessary. Most older demons do it because it just feels like nothing else."

"But you have clubs that cater to many...interests?"

"Yes. Paris is like fetish central for demons. Michel is really the expert there."

"That is hardly surprising."

"Hah! Not like that. Or I don't know, maybe. But it's because he's in charge of making sure that things don't get out of control. Matthew used to do that."

"I much prefer dealing with the city's tourist attractions and city buildings."

"Is that how you met..."

"No! Do not say her name." Matthew turned to Anya "And don't even ask me."

Anya shrugged. "Fine. But that still doesn't explain why you're in charge and not Francois."

"Both countries need a firm hand. Firmer than Francois can handle. He does very little of the day to day because he really does not give a shit any longer. We can't have that here; we need quick decisive action when it's necessary. The demons were out of control here for centuries because no one was minding the store. Anaranth asked that I step in. I said yes, but with the stipulation was that I have complete autonomy. It looks like I report to Francois, but I report to Anaranth in reality."

"Do the other demons and Council members actually buy that?"

"No," Matthew said. Declan made a face. "Declan, it's the worst kept secret among our kind. It's why people both respect and fear you and why they come to *you* for help, not Francois. Everyone knows, no one says anything. As long as it looks good, Francois is happy. But I am betting Liliana is not."

"Agreed. She has ambitions beyond Francois'. I think Anaranth wants to separate Francois from Europe and just give him Great Britain, and give me Europe, but he can't figure out how to do it without creating huge controversy and causing a possible rift on the Council."

"Demon politics are weird." said Anya.

"Not wrong." said Matthew. "If Francois is behind this, he's jeopardizing his seat on the Council."

"Agreed. I don't think he's involved though. As I said, he just generally doesn't give enough of a shit. But if this is just Liliana, it means she is wielding more and more power. That is not good. For anyone."

"But, if that is the case, it could give Anaranth the leverage he needs to wrest territory away from Francois. Provided we can prove it."

"How would we prove it?" Anya poured each of them some more water and heaped their plates with more food. Declan raised an eyebrow at this. "Hey, I'm a feminist, but I am also polite, don't get it twisted, my friend." Declan squeezed her leg under the table.

"Jesus could you two not touch either for five minutes?"

"No." the two answered in unison.

"To answer your question, I am not sure how we'd prove it." Declan's hand was moving further up her leg to her thigh. She put her hand over his to stop his progress and he grinned. *Later.*

You are insatiable. She answered.

Yes. I make no apologies about the fact that I am, but only with you.

Matthew opened his mouth to say something to them, but Michel walked in just then. "Declan, there is a detective here to see you. Apparently, they just found a couple of bodies and both of them had cards from one of the clubs on them."

"Well, shit. This is not good. Ok, show them into my office and I will be there in a moment." Michel exited and Declan looked at his mate and his friend. "You two come with me, please?"

"Of course. Though we're not dressed for this kind of meeting."

"No matter. We may have worse problems to contend with. I do not like the timing of this."

In Declan's office, Michel stood with a tall, muscular human. He was about the same height as Declan and Matthew, with sable brown hair, gray eyes, and a decent build for a human. His aquiline nose flared a bit as the three walked in and he took them in. He was not intimidated by them, but his stance was cautious. The way he was watching them made Anya feel like he saw more than just three people standing there, like he could feel that there was something different about them.

"Mr. O'Shea?" His English was oddly accented.

Declan stepped forward and put out his hand. "Yes. And you are?"

"I am Petyr Marchand, Police Nationale." That was it, Declan thought. He was French and Russian, he sounded a bit like Anya, but his French was more pronounced, while with Anya, it was her Russian.

"This is my wife, Dr. Anya Orlov. And my business partner, Matthew Piedmont."

"Pleasure." Anya and Matthew nodded back.

"Please sit, Detective Marchand," Declan said.

Marchand sat and Declan moved to sit behind his desk, gesturing to Marchand to begin.

"Two bodies have been found, with your cards in their pockets."

"Yes, Michel just passed that information along to me. Am I a suspect?"

"At the moment, no."

"Am I a person of interest then?" Declan smirked.

Marchand smiled. "No, you are not, currently. I am simply following up on leads. But it would be helpful if you could tell me where you were last night."

"I was here."

"Alone?"

"No. Anya was here. As was Matthew, Michel, and a handful of other people. Do you need names?"

"Yes, please." Marchand didn't think this man had murdered anyone, but these people were odd and that could mean they were somehow connected to the crime.

"I'll write them all down." said Anya.

"Thank you."

"Which club did they have business cards for?"

"The Cellar, I believe it's called." Fuck thought Declan. It would be *that* one.

"*Detektiv Marshan, mogu ya predlozhit' vam kofe?*" This was from Anya.

Marchand turned to stare at her for a moment and answered in English. "No, thank you Dr. Orlov."

"Would you prefer tea to coffee then?"

"No, I'm fine. *Spasibo.*"

"Most welcome."

"Mr. O'Shea, may I show you a photo of the victims, to see if you know them?"

"Of course."

Marchand slid a photo across to Declan. Declan looked at it and sighed inwardly. Too much blood, they were human. When young demons died, there was rarely any blood, or even a body. They generally turned to dust. But they had been killed by demons, that much was obvious in the way they'd been mauled. This has been vicious and out of control. He didn't know if it was sex gone wrong or if the demons had meant to kill, but demons in his city had done this to humans. Humans who most likely were just trying to have some kinky fun and had no idea what they were getting into. Humans that were under his protection, even if they didn't know that. He'd failed them. "I don't know these men."

"Young men. They were both only twenty-one."

"Matthew? Michel? Do you recognize them?"

Both men looked and shook their heads.

"Anya," said Declan, "I doubt you would recognize them, but would you mind taking a look, just in case you recognize them from the University?" He paused. "My wife taught until recently."

"Mr. O'Shea, these photos are fairly gruesome."

"My wife is not squeamish." Marchand raised an eyebrow, but Anya came forward, looked at the photos and while she found it sad, she didn't flinch.

"They do not look familiar to me. Those poor young men. Did they not have ID on them?"

Marchand was staring at her speculatively. "They did not."

Declan took a closer look at the photo. "Their fingertips appear to be singed?"

"Very observant. They are. So, no fingerprints."

"Oh, that's so sad. Someone will be missing these boys," Anya said, frowning.

"We're running dental records, but that's very hit or miss. And we're checking missing persons reports through France to start." He paused. "Mr. O'Shea, I have heard some things about your club. I am not sure if…" He looked at Anya.

"Anything you have to say to me, you can say in front of Anya. As I said, she is not at all squeamish."

Marchand raised his eyebrows and Anya weighed in. "Detective Marchand, do you not have female detectives on the force?"

"We do."

"And do they not sometimes need to look at gruesome photos, or crime scenes? Do they never have to go into places that are dangerous or not quite up to societal norms?"

"Yes."

"Then why do you assume that just because I am female, that I cannot handle looking at crime photos or listening to you talk about my own husband's clubs?"

Marchand inclined his head slightly. "You are correct, Dr. Orlov, I apologize." Her calmness at seeing the photos though had discomfited him, he had to admit. But he wasn't sure why.

"Accepted."

"*Bien*, just so then. Your club, from what I am told caters to a very specific clientele."

"It's a fetish club, Detective Marchand. You do not have to be delicate about it. It's one of a handful of clubs that I run." He didn't want to ask this next question, but he would. "Are there any signs that these young men were…"

Marchand cut him off. "No, I can tell you that for sure. There are no signs of penetration, forced or otherwise. They have some wounds on their hands that are likely from trying to fight back, but they were overpowered by…something."

"Something?" Matthew put in.

"They look to have been mauled, by an animal." He glanced at Declan, questioningly.

"That is not allowed in any of my clubs. Fetishism is one thing, bestiality to my mind is quite another. Detective, you seem to be hinting that you think this was done at my club and the bodies were moved."

"Why do you think the bodies weren't moved?"

"Why do you think they were?"

"I asked you first and I'm doing the questioning here." Marchand's voice was mild. He was testing Declan, and both of them knew it.

"There is way too much blood for them to have not been killed there. And more to the point, this would never happen at my club. Ever."

"You're an expert on blood at crime scenes now?"

"It doesn't take an expert to know this. Forensics is pretty common among the masses nowadays."

"Fair point. But you think this couldn't have happened at your club?"

"No. I know it didn't happen at my club. I flat out know it."

"How would you know?"

"Because nothing like this would happen without me knowing about it. I trust my people. They are there because I do trust them. And quite frankly, Detective, my people would have called me before calling the police." And this wouldn't be happening right now. He or his people would have taken care of it quietly. He held up a card that looked exactly like the ones found on the young men. "Additionally, you need one of those cards to get into the club." Well, humans did if they weren't with a demon, but he didn't need to say that. "We have memberships, but those are a different type of card. We take the regular business cards when they come in. One card, one visit. If you want to come in again, you get a membership. The exception is if you come in with someone who is already a member. So, while they may have shown up, they most likely did not come in." Unless they were with a demon. And he'd check that footage himself before he turned it over.

Marchand sighed. "You are right, the two men were found up the street, in a parking lot. This is where we believe the actual crime took place. But we are assuming they were going to visit your club, or they tried to and were turned away for some reason."

"If you would like, I could provide you with security camera footage of the outside, to see if they showed up. It is possible that they came in with someone who had a membership."

Marchand raised an eyebrow. Generally, he not only had to be the one that requested the footage, but he also often got an argument about it. "That would be helpful."

"What are you approximating as the time of death?"

"We think they were killed sometime between 1 am and 3 am this morning."

"Fine, I will have the tapes pulled for you."

"Again, I appreciate that."

"I will see that it's done and delivered to you by one of my people. Unless you'd rather have one of your people come get it?"

"No, that's fine. But my people will be able to see if the video was tampered with. I am going to assume you are acting in good faith. For now. *Merci.*" Declan smiled wolfishly, knowing that a number of the Police's IT people were actually his people.

"Detective," Anya interrupted. "Here are the names and numbers of the people that were here at the house last night. I've included mine and my husband's information as well. I've also texted everyone and they'll be expecting your call."

"Very thorough. Thank you Dr. Orlov."

"You are most welcome."

"Is there anything else, Detective?"

"No, Mr. O'Shea. *Merci.*"

"*De Rien.* Let us know if we can be of further assistance." Declan motioned to Matthew, who left the room to make a call to get the footage pulled for them.

"I will. Can you have your employees be on the lookout for anyone unusual?"

"I can. And I will also place extra security in and around the club."

"You have your own security?"

"Most of the people, who work directly for me, are trained to act as security when necessary. Murders are bad for business, Detective. Therefore, extra security seems called for. When you own a number of clubs, catering to a certain clientele, you need to be prepared for anything." What Declan didn't say was that the extra security was being put in place so he could catch these murderers himself. And when he did, he was going to make the demons very sorry they had ever spilled mortal blood.

"Interesting." Marchand took out a card and handed it to Declan. "Should you need to contact me, my information is on this card."

"Thank you."

Matthew walked back into the room. "Detective? You should have the footage delivered to you by the end of the day. It will be delivered by a Therese La Pierre."

"How will I know her?"

"Oh, you'll know her," said Matthew cryptically.

"Thank you for your time, then."

"Most welcome. Michel, would you show the detective out."

"Of course." He walked to the door and held it open.

Marchand stalked over to the door and pivoted to Declan. "You are not a suspect, nor is anyone here currently. That said, there is something a bit odd about all of you and that is something I am not going to forget." Marchand strode from the room as Michel shrugged, rolled his eyes, and followed the man out.

Matthew shut the door. "Well, this is a bit of a fucking mess."

"Truer words. I want to go review the footage quickly before we turn it over. I don't think we're going to find that the men came into the club, but I want to be sure. Marchand will expect me to review it first. I am not going to doctor it though."

"He's pretty observant."

"Yes...we're going to have to watch out for him."

"Are you worried?" Anya asked.

"Not really. But we're on his radar now. Maybe he just thinks we're organized crime. I hope that's it."

"You know that's not it." Matthew retorted.

"No, but I can hope. I think he's a good man, and those are rare enough. But I will do some digging to be sure. Information is key."

"Once again, data nerd." Declan waggled his eyebrows at Anya, making her laugh.

"Is it possible that they were killed and then the cards were planted, to make you look complicit?" This was from Matthew, but Anya nodded.

"It is very possible. And the police being involved and noticing us would be an issue for the Council. It would make me look bad, as if I couldn't handle my territory." Declan growled. "Which means I now need to make sure I talk to Anaranth about it, first. Fuck!"

"He's probably going to run our names and see what comes up. Are you all going to be there?"

"Of course we are. We have to present like we're humans for the most part, which means we have birth records, tax records, etc. This is why we have people in different positions throughout different government departments. His IT people, they're mine. Eventually, your records will need to be doctored as well."

"You have people on the police force?"

"Of course. Yes, and in the municipal government, certain key positions." Anya nodded. "Smart."

"We all have to do it, everywhere. Especially because we are business owners, etc. I own and operate all of my businesses legally. Even the clubs I just 'manage' are in my name. It's just easier. Matthew's businesses are the same."

"You own businesses?"

"Of course I do."

"Wait? Are you actual business partners? I thought you worked for Declan."

"It's both. We have businesses we own together, and I have my own businesses. I work security for Declan, security wise because I enjoy it, not because I need to."

"Are all of you wealthy?"

"Matthew and I are pretty wealthy. The others are comfortable…they make their own decisions about that. Dougal and Therese don't want to own anything. Michel owns a couple of small bed and breakfasts that seem to have sentimental value to him and that's all."

"So, this one was a farmer." She gestured at Declan. "What about you then, your lordship?"

Matthew shrugged. "I realize you're joking, but you're not wrong. I was an Earl upon my death, since my older brother died young."

"Are you shitting me?"

Matthew laughed. "I am not, Anya. My father was also very good with money and passed that along to me. I like being comfortable and am used to living my life a certain way, I don't apologize for it."

"Nor should you. I am sorry about your brother though." Anya looked at him. "I bet you own a lot of art."

Matthew looked startled. "How can you possibly know that?"

"Intuition. You seem the type. So, we don't think Marchand will be a real problem?"

"I hope not. I don't want to have to deal with him. Oddly, I liked him. Well, I liked how straightforward he was."

"I did too," Matthew said, and Anya agreed.

"But I also feel like this is someone we are not going to get rid of easily."

"Is it wise to let Therese deliver the footage?"

"Probably not. But it will be amusing."

"I think we will just need to play this thing with Marchand by ear. He may prove useful at some point. But for now, Matthew I need you to go home, change and shower and meet me at the Cellar as soon as you can. I am going to go there now." He looked at Anya. "Anya…"

"I have plans with Gwen tonight, here at the house. You can let me know if you need or want my help."

"I will want your help. But today I want to check the footage and talk to staff."

"I'd be a distraction."

"Yes."

"Well, you're honest at any rate. You will be careful."

"Always, *malysh*. Always."

***

On the drive back to the station, Marchand considered Declan O'Shea and his wife. Outwardly, there was nothing wrong with them. But there was something niggling at him about them during the meeting. Declan was polite and helpful, Anya was as well...a bit of a force of nature, he thought. He'd been told off but hadn't minded it as she'd done it in a very straightforward way. Her speaking Russian had surprised him though and he suspected she had done it to test him.

He still checked them, and Matthew Piedmont out when he got back to his desk, but nothing jumped out at him. As he suspected, Anya Orlov had spent her formative years in Russia before going to school in the States and then settling here. Piedmont was from money; he had that air about him, and O'Shea was self-made.

He didn't think they had anything to do with the murder directly. His gut told him that that someone wanted him to think they did though. Marchand sucked at his personal life, but he was a great cop and his hunches usually proved to be fairly on the money. His mother said it was due to his great grandmother having "the sight" as she called it. He didn't believe that for a second. It was training, long hours and just a good working knowledge of people.

He was compiling notes and had just looked up to rest his eyes when he saw a very tall woman in the door. His first thought was *"Merde*, it's Wonder Woman!" and then laughed to himself for the fanciful thought. But she was tall, like the Amazon warrior from the comic books he had inhaled as a child. This had to be Therese La Pierre. Piedmont said he'd know her, and he had been right. He caught her eye and waved her over. She strode over to him. Lord, she was just about as tall as he was, possibly a bit taller. Dark hair and eyes and burnished skin. She looked fierce.

"Marchand?" She had a deep, husky voice with an accent he couldn't place. It was like she was from everywhere and nowhere. He was pretty sure she could kill him with her bare hands and he kind of liked that. She was the most striking

She was the most striking person he had ever met, but she was also another piece in the Declan O'Shea puzzle.

"Yes, I'm Marchand."

"Here is the video footage." She set a thumb drive down on his desk. "Since I know you need to check Declan's alibi for last night. I was at his house all evening. I left about midnight and went straight home. Here is the number of the doorman at my building. He'll corroborate that I was there the rest of the night. And if you want to press the point, you could likely ask my neighbors. I dropped something fairly heavy, and I am sure I woke someone up. I was alone though, unfortunately." She grinned at him in a way that made him wonder if she'd sensed his earlier thoughts.

"Do you all often get together with your boss?"

She raised an eyebrow at him. "Yes. He is our boss, but we are like family. The family you choose, you see. Most of us do not have much in the way of blood relations, or we aren't close to them if we do have them." Therese wasn't generally this verbose with strangers, but she considered Marchand a threat to her people right now. He was a very handsome threat, but a threat, nonetheless. So, she wanted to make him understand that they were family, and that they protected each other. She didn't want this guy fucking with any of them.

"How long have you all been family?"

"Well, Declan was always a very open boss that way. But I would say since he and Anya got together, it's really ramped up. She's big on family dinners, etc. That's what we did last night. They have not been together all that long, but she's made up for lost time." This is why Therese didn't talk a lot. She was beginning to sound like a babbling moron. She was intent on hammering her point home and she was feeling flustered by this human and his steady gaze. So, she'd answer his questions with as much information as she was willing to give up.

"Whirlwind romance?"

"For all of us. If that's all, I need to get to work." That was frankly none of his business.

"Where do you work?"

"Generally the main club, Demon's Folly. I am at Brimstone tonight though."

"Part of the security detail?"

"Head of the security detail." She smirked at him.

Ah fuck, he was doing it again. What the hell was wrong with him?

"Then I will let you get to it. Thank you, Ms. La Pierre."

"You are welcome. Most of us on the list you were given are working tonight, since we were off last night. As such, we may be harder to pin down this evening. Gwen is with Anya tonight though and so I would start with her." She knew this as she'd dropped off the mage at Anya's before she'd come here.

"Noted." And with that, Therese strode out of the precinct and likely right out of his fantasies.

CHAPTER 23

Declan had checked the security footage quickly before turning it over to Marchand. But he'd gone back to The Cellar the next day to review it in more detail, and to review the footage from inside of the club more carefully as well. He also went back a few days to see if those boys had come around earlier in the week.

The young men had come up to the club looking very unsure, but had been approached by two men, facing away from the camera naturally, and had gone off with them. Declan was sure they were demons. What else would they be? They knew he had cameras there though, so someone else had put them wise as you could not actually see the cameras from anywhere outside. He checked the footage inside, just to be sure, but the men didn't show up inside either. He had paused the footage and took a good look at their faces, alive and un-mauled. He was furious someone had done this, but he was also sad for those young lives ended too soon.

He looked at Matthew, who was standing next to him, in the security room. "Can you see if these guys have turned up another of the clubs? And while we can't see these demons from the front, we can from the back, so maybe see if we can find some kind of match. I'd also like to know if someone gave them the cards ahead of time or if the demons planted them on the bodies. But I think I may be asking too much there. And have Therese question the front door staff. They're all a little scared of her, so they'll answer her thoroughly enough."

"Will do." Matthew made a sour face. "I don't like this. I don't like it one bit."

"Me neither. I have talked to both Anaranth and Richelieu at this point, but Anaranth won't do much. Richelieu is going to install someone in Francois' house and see if that yields any fruit. For now...we amp up security the best we can, especially outside. No humans to go off with demons they do not know. Front door staff will intercede if that happens. We'll put another person on the door to make sure. No exceptions. If they let someone go, they'll answer to me. I don't care how they do it, but they'd better work it out. We'll need some people to mingle as clientele."

"Donovan is already on that, and I am texting him about the extra people on the front door." His phone dinged. "On it."

"Of course he is."

"Ok, I want to swing by the other clubs before heading off to the main one."

"I'm with you tonight. As is Michel."

"Good. Let's go." They moved through the club and went outside. Declan stopped to talk to the front door person for the night and Matthew stood by the car. Michel was already in the driver's seat. They didn't hear anyone approach or feel anything different, until it was too late.

"Declan!" shouted Matthew, but it was too late. Declan had been speared through with a large dagger. He was falling to the ground as Jean, the front door person caught him. Declan was turning dangerously pale. Matthew ran and leapt onto the assailant as he tried to get away, his claws fully extended as he pierced the man through the chest, holding him there, but keeping the wound as hidden as he possibly could in case any passed by. The Cellar was situated somewhere that did not get a lot of daytime foot or car traffic. Dougal flew out of the club, having been alerted by Michel yelling for him. Declan had gone from thrashing and yelling to still. Much too still. This shouldn't be happening to a demon of his age and strength. Michel then opened the trunk, took out a blanket and wrapped the weapon in it, putting it in the trunk. If it could do that to Declan, God knew what it would do to the rest of them.

"What the fuck happened?" Dougal yelled; half turned into his beast at this point.

"No fucking clue. This soon to be dead man here came running up, silently, likely cloaked somehow and stabbed Declan."

"Why does Declan look so…why is he still down?" Dougal was having trouble talking as his beast was taking over.

"Dougal, get back into the fucking club if you're going to do that. Not out on the street for chrissakes!" Therese came out and dragged Dougal back inside. Matthew threw the demon over his shoulder and carried him into the club, dropping him hard, onto the floor. "Throw him into one of the cells. We'll question him later. Declan is more important now. Something is wrong, very wrong."

"You can't keep me...you can't…." The man was having trouble talking from Matthew having stabbed him.

Matthew pulled the demon, young by his smell, up with one hand. "I can do whatever the fuck I want. And what I want to do is kill you. And I am going to. But first, we're going to make you wait, and think about things. You're going to tell us everything."

"But he said I couldn't die."

Matthew was icily calm. "He was wrong. Before I kill you, you are going to beg me for death." He then punched the kid so hard, he passed out.

Therese was looking at him. "I forget sometimes how scary you can be."

"Dougal, take him downstairs, revive him and rough him up if you want, leave him alive. We have to get Declan home. Will call when we know something, promise." Matthew didn't wait for the answer, he didn't need to. He ran outside and into the waiting car as it sped off to Declan's home.

***

Anya and Gwen were poring over the prophecy book when it happened. Anya stopped speaking, lost all color in her face, dropped to the floor and started screaming in pain. Something was happening to Declan, and she could feel it.

He had been hurt and he was in horrible pain, possibly dying. But that couldn't be right. Anya doubled over and let out a blood curdling scream as pain ripped through her.

Gwen turned white as Mara came running in, having heard Anya scream. "Anya, Anya? What is it? What's wrong? Tell me!"

"Declan! He's...oh...Jesus, it hurts!" She collapsed onto the floor. "I can feel...Gwen, he's dying!"

Was Anya also dying then? She needed to call someone. No sooner had she grabbed her phone than it began to ring. It was Donovan. "Donovan! Anya says Declan is hurt, dying!"

"I know! Declan is hurt, and he's on his way to you all."

"Is he dying?"

"He...he...it looks like he is." Donovan could barely say those words.

"Is Anya?" Gwen whispered.

There was a pause. "She may be Gwen. I don't know. But we need you now. It's likely that this was magic based. You need to be calm. Can you do that for us? For them?"

"Ok...ok." Gwen took a deep breath. Then another.

"I am on my way there now. Be strong." He hung up the phone. Gwen explained as Mara picked Anya up easily and put her on the couch, cradling her head on her lap. She'd never seen the unflappable cook and house manager look so frightened, but she simply nodded her head at Gwen. Anya was white, and her breathing was shallow, but she was holding on, or trying to. She was crying from the pain and being able to feel how far Declan was from her now. She tried to call him in her head and there was...nothing. No response. Gwen started flipping through the prophecy book. She was sure she'd seen a spell in there that would help. Her hands were shaking badly though, and it was hard to turn the pages.

"Breathe Gwen, just breathe." Mara leaned over and put a hand on her shoulder and rubbed gently. Gwen took a deep breath, then another and her hands steadied. She closed her eyes, opened her third eye, and asked the book itself. It answered quickly and Gwen found the right spell. "Thank you, Mara."

"Of course, Mage." Mara squeezed the younger woman's shoulder and removed her hand to stroke Anya's forehead. Gwen was seated on the floor in front of the couch and stroked her friend's arm while she read the spell. "Touch is good. It's good that she knows we are here, even if she can't communicate with us." Mara smiled gently at Gwen.

Two minutes later, Matthew and Michel burst into the room. Matthew was carrying a very still, pale Declan. He laid him on the other couch. Anya sat up abruptly. "Declan?!" she cried. Matthew gently picked her up from Mara's lap and set her down, right next to Declan. She grabbed his hand, as tears ran down her cheeks. "Don't you dare die on me." She couldn't feel him, or she could, but he was so weak that he was barely there at all. *Please don't leave me, my love. Please hang on, don't die. Please. Please....stay.*

"Anya, how are you feeling?" Matthew asked.

"I'm in pain, horrible pain. I can feel what he feels, and I can feel our bond waver, that's also causing me pain. I don't know if I'm dying as well. I don't get it. But Matthew, he is. He's dying Matthew! I can't...he can't die on me! I won't have it." She was out of breath after that speech, she doubled over in pain again, groaning from it.

Matthew couldn't answer her, he didn't know what to say. He gently took off Declan's Jacket and shirt, so they could see the wound. It was ugly and dark.

"I brought the weapon." Michel said.

"Let me see it!" Gwen commanded. Michel unwrapped it and Gwen wrinkled her nose. "Oh yeah, that thing is bursting with magic." She closed her eyes. "Dark magic. I can feel the spell and it's a strong one. Cover it up and I will deal with it later. Be careful with it! Declan is more important right now." She flipped through the book quickly, making sure she only needed the one spell that the book had shown her. "Ok. Let me see him. I have to be sure." Donovan burst into the room at that point and took in the scene. "Donovan, I am glad you're here. You're good at keeping me centered." He sat next to her on the floor. "Anya? Honey? I am sorry sweetie, but I need you to move some so I can look at him." Anya didn't move. Matthew moved in back of her and grabbed her, she shook him off. "Anya. Anya, you need to move for him. You need to let Gwen work. Come on, be strong. Be his mate." Matthew's tone was gentle, but firm and it did the trick. She moved. Matthew stayed at her back, offering what comfort he could. Mara and Michel stood over by the window, watching silently.

She looked at the wound and grimaced. "It's not really healing. Shit!" She took off the scarf around her neck and cleaned off the wound some. Gwen took a breath, closed her eyes, and placed her hands on Declan's chest. He was barely breathing, even for a demon. His heart was very still. Because of Donovan, she knew what was normal for a demon and this wasn't it. She could feel the magic, feel the poison. "He's trying to hold on. His body is in turmoil and is in a great deal of pain. He shut down for that reason. As much as you hurt Anya, he's got the brunt." She paused and looked up. "It's supposed to kill you too. I can feel the magic. It's trying to get you. He's not letting it." Gwen sounded amazed. "Christ, it takes a lot of strength to do what he's doing. That's one reason he's so weak, he's fighting the poison, but he's also protecting you."

Anya doubled over. "Well, that's fucking typical of him. Declan, I demand you stop doing that patriarchal bullshit right now." *I am going to fucking kill you if you die on me!* She sent this thought at him.

Matthew snorted. "Keep giving him shit, let him know you're here."

"Still hurts a hell of a lot though." She felt like she was going to throw up from it any moment.

It should be hurting you more though." Matthew looked at Gwen. Her powers were growing, getting stronger, he thought. He knew in that moment that Gwen would save them both, just looking at her, how determined she was. She wasn't giving up. The prophecy was true, and he believed in it with every fiber of his being. The truth of it was currently staring him right in the face. He wasn't a man, but he was as sure of it as he was of taking his next breath. He was not losing his oldest friend and he certainly wasn't losing his newest. Gwen rubbed her hands together and spoke. "Ok, I think I know what to do now that I've read through the spell a couple of times. It is a tough spell, and it is going to take time and Anya, it is going to hurt both of you like a fucking bitch."

She looked at the spell in the book and grimaced. "It's also going to hurt me as the magic, the poison needs to come out through me. That's not going to be pleasant."

"Gwen," Donovan started.

"Don't even start. I'm doing it and you are not stopping me. I'm meant to do this. I am NOT letting this man die. And I am not letting my best friend die or be heartbroken. So, as Anya says...you can take your patriarchal bullshit elsewhere." She smiled at him to show she knew he was coming from a good place.

Donovan kissed her forehead. "Yes, ma'am," he said quietly.

She tied her hair back. "Matthew, you are going to need to hold Anya. She is going to kick and scream and thrash around a lot. Anya, you have to let Matthew move you away from the couch completely and let him hold you." She saw her friend's face. "Don't argue with me. I would not ask you to move away from him if it wasn't important." Anya nodded and allowed Matthew to carry her over to a position on the floor, not too far away. "Donovan, I need you to hold Declan, he may or may not scream but he is going to thrash. As for me…" Luc took that second to burst into the room, panting. "I can help! I can help!"

"Who called you?"

"No one."

"Then how did you know?

Anya looked up from her position on the floor, her eyes glazed with pain as she tried to focus on the young man before her. "You'd...fuck, ow...better tell them now, I think." The strain of talking had been too much, and she fell back against Matthew, who tightened his hold on her.

Luc nodded. "I know things sometimes. Today was one of those times. I guess, it's the sight? I don't really know." He was a bit embarrassed. "It's not consistent. But I felt this from across town." He paused. "I got here as quickly as I could." He'd borrowed a friend's motorcycle thinking it was the fastest way to get through the traffic. He was lucky he hadn't gotten pulled over because he ran every single red light he hit.

"You have sight?"

"Yes." He exhaled. It was going to be fine; these people would accept him for who he was.

"Ok, so you have some magic then I'm betting. I need you to help me. Sit behind me. I need you to hold me steady and I may need you to filter energy to me if I flag. Can you do this?"

"*Oui.*" Luc took off his jacket, kicked off his shoes and positioned himself right behind Gwen, his long legs stretched on either side of her, his hands on her shoulders."

"What would you like us to do?" Michel asked.

"Mara, you may need to help with Anya, she can flail like mad. Michel, actually, down by Declan's feet. Get his shoes off. You may need to hold him down from there." She looked down and read some. "Ok, fair warning...when this is done, Anya and Declan are going to sleep for a long time. I will probably drop off for a bit and Luc might too. It is very draining." They all nodded at her. She turned to Luc. "Are you ready?"

"Yes, mademoiselle."

"Luc, I think you can call me Gwen after this." She looked down and read through one more time to be sure she had it right in her head. She started to speak in a low voice, reciting the spell. Luc was looking at the spell over her shoulder as well, memorizing it. Nothing happened for a few minutes and Gwen was getting concerned when she felt it. A tug of magic. Luc felt it as well as he jumped a little, but he held steady. She started speaking more forcefully and the first scream tore from both Declan and Anya simultaneously. Anya started thrashing and Matthew was having trouble holding her, without hurting her more. Mara got down on the floor and took her feet, rubbing them and quietly singing. Matthew wasn't sure who the singing was for, Anya, himself, or Mara, but it was actually making him feel better. He rested his head on top of Anya's and tried to make comforting noises. Every so often she'd get loose and get him in the face with her hand or kick Mara with her leg, but they weathered it. She was screaming and crying, repeating Declan's name over and over and Matthew thought his heart was going to break with the sound of it. Mara, always stoic, had tears running down her face. Michel had moved to the couch and was trying to hold Declan's legs, but he kept kicking out and shouting, screaming in pain. Both Michel and Donovan were laboring to hold him still. Luc shot out an arm every so often if a limb got too close to Gwen's head. Donovan made a mental note to make sure the kid got a huge bonus, for that alone.

Gwen was sweating and she would wince every so often. Luc started saying the spell with her in order to take some of the magical weight off of her. She stopped, cried out in pain and Luc picked up the incantation with as much ease as he could. Donovan looked at her questioningly, but she indicated she'd be fine. She squeezed Luc's hand as a thank you and they both picked up the pace of the spell.

It took 90 minutes for the thrashing and screaming to quiet down. And every demon in that room thought that time had never passed so slowly. It took another hour after that to get rid of the poison of the spell completely. Gwen started to feel better when she saw the wound on Declan's chest start to heal.

Luc tried to get Gwen to drink some water, but she wouldn't, so he opened himself up more so he could take more of the magic. Jesus, this spell was a real motherfucker. It was strong and it was dark, and it was poisonous. She was still doing the lion's share of the work though. He felt it when she lost the rest of her energy. She sagged against him. "Gwen, I will finish, you rest there." He removed her hands from Declan's chest and put his own in their place, and within the next few minutes, closed the spell completely. This all felt very natural to him, and he knew he shouldn't have fought his gift for so long. He had been denying who he really was, and that is never a good idea.

"Is it done?" Matthew's voice wavered and Mara had slumped some, her normally indefatigable demeanor had quite simply had enough. Anya had curled into a ball in Matthew's lap and fallen asleep, but he could still hear her whimper some in her sleep. Mara reached over and stroked her head and the whimpering stopped. Matthew considered that Mara might be magic, but then he realized that it was just that Mara was comforting her like a mother would, and that just about broke him.

"*Oui*, Matthew," Luc said. "It is. They will sleep now." He looked up. "Donovan, perhaps you can move Gwen to the other couch. She's fallen asleep." Donovan got up on shaky legs, picked Gwen up carefully and laid her on the other couch. He found a throw and covered her.

"But they are both going to be ok?" Michel asked.

"Yes. The poison is gone. Declan's heartbeat is strong and true, as is Anya's." Matthew raised an eyebrow. This was the first time Luc had used their first names. Matthew smiled and decided not to point it out, lest the young demon stop doing it. "Perhaps we can put Declan on his side and then move Anya in next to him. I think they would sleep easier together, *non*?" Donovan and Michel shifted Declan and Matthew carefully set Anya on her side next to him. As he dropped her, Anya's hand came up to cup Matthew's cheek, thanking him, even in her sleep. Matthew cleared his throat and stood. Mara covered them both with another throw. Anya immediately turned so she was facing Declan, her hand coming to rest on his heart.

"I shall make some coffee for us all," Luc said. Something had happened today with Luc; he was more self-assured. But he was now also comfortable with them, he no longer saw himself as less just because he was younger. Matthew knew that nothing was going to please Anya more than seeing Luc start to come into his own.

Mara hugged the young demon to her. "No, Luc," she said gently. "You have done a lot today and you must be tired. I will make coffee and some snacks. I think we could all use some energy." With that, she left the room. No one needed to know that the older demon was also going to go have a good cry while she made the coffee.

"I have seen a lot of things in my life," Michel said. "But I am not sure if I have ever felt so scared or so helpless. Ever." He plopped down on a chair. "I do not like this feeling. When we find out who did this, we are going to kill them. Very viciously," he said this calmly, but no one thought he was anything less than deadly serious. It took a lot to wipe the smile off of Michel's face, but this had done it.

Matthew nodded his agreement. "Luc, you were amazing today. Gwen was very lucky to have you. I am so glad you're part of our family. I am also glad that you have this gift."

Luc smiled. "I think today is the first time that I have also been glad that I have it." He yawned. "If you don't mind, I am going to stretch out on these cushions for a bit."

"Please do." Luc grabbed yet another throw, grateful that Anya seemed to have them in abundance and immediately fell asleep. "I like the man he's becoming. And I am going to go call Dougal and Therese." Matthew also needed a few minutes to himself.

He left the room for a bit, but it was going to be a long night as Matthew knew none of them would be leaving anytime soon.

***

Luc slept for a couple of hours and was famished when he woke up, Gwen slept for five hours and was also famished when she got up. Luc and Gwen then managed to remove the spell from the weapon as well, most of the magic had dissipated once the poison found its home. It had been set up that way. So that undoing had been fairly easy in comparison. Therese and Dougal had arrived sometime during the night carrying boxes of pizza. "Is the prisoner in one piece?" asked Matthew.

"Sure enough." said Dougal. "We roused him, then Therese lost her temper and threw him against a wall. He passed out again. So, I just left it. I'll kick the shit out of him later." Dougal hadn't even bothered putting on that brogue of his. A sure sign he was both upset and deeply angry.

Therese shrugged. "I got angry. He's lucky all I did was throw him."

"Speaking of scary people," said Matthew, echoing Therese's comment about him from earlier.

Declan and Anya slept for twelve hours. Gwen assured them that this was normal. She or Luc checked on them every so often. Matthew made several calls over the course of the night, keeping all of the businesses running for Anya and Declan. No one was going to feel better until they woke up. Especially not Gwen. She was pretty sure she had done it all correctly, but what if she missed something. She tried not to worry but couldn't help it. She felt better for having Donovan there.

Declan woke first, sitting bolt upright and yelling Anya's name. Hearing her name, Anya woke with a start and the two nearly fell off the couch in their scramble for the other. Something that would have been funny under any other circumstances. As it was, the room just felt a huge weight lift. They held each other for a long time until they realized they weren't alone. No one had wanted to interrupt them. Declan looked over Anya's shoulder and saw everyone staring at them, relieved looks on everyone's face. Anya turned her head. "Oh! Oh shit, I didn't know we weren't alone. I am sorry everyone." Her voice was barely a whisper.

Declan swallowed and spoke "What happened, exactly?" His voice was incredibly hoarse. And he felt weak. That was new. He put his arms around Anya and moved her onto his lap, with what little strength he had. She curled up there, patting him every so often to make sure he was truly there with her. Matthew explained everything that happened, and Anya was flat out crying by the end of the explanation. The only thing she remembered was dropping to the floor. After that, not much else. Declan was rocking her while Matthew finished speaking, his voice cracking at the end.

Declan cleared his throat or tried to. It still hurt. "There is no possible way that I can thank you enough for what you all did last night. Not just for me, but for Anya. For taking care of her when I couldn't. I am very lucky to call you all my friends." The room was silent, no words necessary.

"How do you both feel?"

"Exhausted, weak, sore, pissed off," Declan said. Anya nodded.

"You would be. You both need to rest today. In bed. You can both get back to regular life tomorrow. Though you both should take it a bit easy for a few days."

"I will take care of them, no worries," said Mara. "You will do what Gwen says and rest."

"Well, that won't be so hard," Anya said.

"No sex." Gwen admonished.

"Aw, really?"

"Really. I doubt you're even up for it."

They admitted they weren't. They stood slowly and Anya and Gwen hugged. "You are the best friend a demon's consort could have, witch. Thank you for all you did. I love you with my whole heart."

"I love you with my whole heart and I am glad you're ok. I would have been pissed if you'd died." Anya laughed and Donovan took Gwen home.

Michel, Dougal, and Therese hugged the couple and took their leave. Therese, not saying anything, but the fierceness of her hug told Anya all she needed to know.

"Luc, I'll take you home. Your friend picked up his bike hours ago," Matthew said. "Anya, you'd have been very proud of Luc. He helped Gwen with the spell and finished it once Gwen's energy went."

Anya's brow furrowed. "I kind of remember now. Luc, does everyone know you have the sight now?"

"Yes, Anya."

"Except me," Declan said. "Well, I know now. And I'm glad for it." He embraced Luc. "I'm proud of you."

"*Merci*, Declan." He moved to hug Anya. "I am so glad you're both ok."

"Thank you, Luc," she hugged him as tightly as she could."

"I will wait in the car." He left the room quickly, emotion overcoming him.

"Matthew, can you convince him to take the day off from his classes?"

"I can."

"He's calling us by our first names now." As Matthew suspected, she was delighted by this."

"He started doing it last night. We all kept quiet in case he stopped. Do you need help getting upstairs?"

"I've got them." Mara said from the door.

"Matthew…" said Declan.

"Don't. You're welcome. Both of you. You took several years off of my demon life, but you are still welcome. Don't ever do that again. None of us can take it. I will handle work until you are feeling better." He and Declan hugged. Then he hugged Anya.

"Matthew, thank you for everything you did for us last night. You are one of my best friends and I love you."

"Oh fuck Anya." Matthew was now choked up. "I guess I love you too." He kissed her on the forehead and left quickly.

Anya turned to Mara. "You sang to me." Mara nodded. "Thank you."

"It was my pleasure to be able to help you some." She turned brusque. "Now upstairs. Come." She helped both of them upstairs and over to their bed and then grabbed their phones.

"Mara!" croaked Declan.

"You are to rest. You will stay off of your phones so you can get some more sleep. If anything happens that you need to know about, I will let you know. Maybe." With that, she was out the door.

Declan looked at Anya. "We have the most amazing people in our lives."

"You are not wrong." She walked over to him and kissed him gently. "You scared the fuck out of me."

He hugged her. "I know. I am so sorry. I could hear you yelling at me though."

"You were trying to protect me! Taking most of that pain, making it worse for yourself."

"Yes Anya. I was. Because what else could I do?" He wiped away a tear making its way down her cheek. "You can yell at me about the patriarchy all you want, yes I heard that, but I am going to do everything in my power to protect you. Always." He swayed a bit and she helped him sit on the bed.

"Sssh, I'm sorry. I would do the same for you." She pulled the blankets back. "Come, get into bed." He stood and she finished undressing him, being as gentle as she could. She got him into bed and kissed the small scar he still had from the wound, something he may always have as a reminder.

"Are you coming to bed too?" He yawned.

"Of course." She came around the other side of the bed, shedding her clothes along the way, and climbed in next to him. She propped herself up a bit and put her arm out. He crawled right in there, his head pillowed on her breast. She started to stroke his hair, humming an old Russian lullaby. He was asleep in minutes, and she soon joined him.

<u>CHAPTER 24</u>

The couple slept for several more hours. It was dark again when they woke up. Declan dropped a kiss on Anya's shoulder and sat up. "Well, Mara took our phones and I want coffee."

Anya stretched and sat up as well. "She's been checking on us regularly. When she comes by again, we can ask her to bring us some."

"How do you know that?"

"I woke up briefly once and saw her sneaking from the room. Therefore, I assume she is checking regularly. Also, it is Mara." She got out of bed.

"She sang to you?" Declan remembered Anya saying this earlier.

"She did. And stroked my head. Like a mother would do. It comforted me."

"She was a mother, so that stands to reason."

"I am not surprised. I am going to go run you a bath."

"Baths are not manly," Declan said teasingly.

She rolled her eyes. "What if I get in it with you?"

"I accept those terms."

"Figures." She walked into the bathroom to start the bath and sat down heavily on the side of the tub. Head in hands, she took several deep breaths. She didn't think she had ever been so scared in her life as she was at the thought of losing Declan. She hadn't been concerned about dying, she'd only cared about losing him. She didn't think she could bear it if he'd died, leaving her here. Alone.

"You could have borne it," a quiet voice from the doorway said.

She looked up. "You weren't supposed to hear that."

"You're tired and upset. You aren't shielding your thoughts very well." He kneeled down in front of her. "And you would have been fine."

"No, I wouldn't be fine. I'd pretend to be. But I'd never be right without you. Something would always be missing."

"Anya…"

"It's true. And you know it. And you'd be the same. So, do me a favor and don't die. And I won't either." She leaned over and turned off the water. "Now, get into this tub, mister."

He gave her a soft kiss and got into the tub. She sat behind him and washed his back and then his chest. Then they just lay back and let the hot water do its work on their sore muscles.

"I may be changing my mind about baths. I think they might be pretty great."

"You're just saying that because you're lying on my tits."

"Yes. That is probably true."

There was a knock on the door. "I have left you coffee, water and food out here." It was Mara. "I have returned your phones now. But do not use them to do work." Mara paused. "Anya, you may want to let Gwen know how you're doing though as she's called me half a dozen times. I will be here if you need me."

"Mara, didn't you have plans?"

"My plans involve making sure you continue to rest. If you argue with me, I am going to be vexed by it." Her voice was firm, brooking no disagreement.

"Ok, Mara. We'll behave. We promise," Anya said.

"See that you do. And don't stay in there too long, you'll prune up. I will see you both in the morning. Don't hurry down though." They heard her walk away from the door and leave the room.

"We scared her, and she's annoyed about it," said Declan. "But she makes a good point. I am ready to get out."

"Me too, Plus, I am starving."

"Thank goodness!" Declan said.

"Are you making fun of me?"

"Absolutely not. I know things are getting back to normal if you want to eat." He kissed her. She put her arms around him. "You feel amazing," he said running his arms up and down her back.

"We're not supposed to have sex."

"We're not. I am just kissing and fondling you."

She laughed. "That's just semantics." She pulled back and handed him a towel, also grabbing one for herself. "Now, towel off and let's go eat." She wrapped a towel around herself and went into the bedroom, laughing again. "Well, Mara brought us all of the food. Per usual."

Declan walked out of the bathroom; towel wrapped low around his waist. "Christ! There is a lot here." He moved the cart over to the table by the window. "She was obviously stress cooking."

Anya followed him over to the table and poured both of them out some coffee. "Good thing she stress cooks, since I stress eat."

Declan sniffed the coffee and groaned happily. "She makes the best goddamned coffee."

"She really does." Anya fixed Declan a plate before making hers. They ate in silence for a few minutes. "Ack! Let me text Gwen quickly." She grabbed her phone, texted Gwen and sat back down again. "I asked her to let everyone know we were fine and that we were eating something."

"Good." Declan put his fork down. "So, we need to discuss this, but not tonight. We're going to eat this and get back into bed and see how we feel in the morning."

"I agree. My brain is still fuzzy." Her phone beeped. She looked at it and smiled. "I think Gwen broke the record for the number of heart emojis in one text."

Declan smiled at her. "Not surprised." He went and picked up his own phone and barked out a hoarse laugh. "Matthew texted that if I call him tonight, he's going to tell everyone on the Council that I cried like a baby when I was stabbed." He dashed off a quick text to Matthew confirming he would not call him about work, stood and stretched. "I think I'm full for now."

"Same." Anya stood and whipped off her towel, then whipped Declan's off as she moved past him.

Declan narrowed his eyes. "Now...now. We have to behave today."

"I know." Anya moved over to the bed and laid down on it. "It's just past midnight. Technically, it's tomorrow."

"Well then, we followed our witch's rules." Declan moved over to the bed and stretched out on top of Anya, who shivered at the contact. "You feel really nice."

"Nice?" Nice? Surely we can do better than nice." Declan started kissing her neck, her shoulders and moved down her chest. He took one nipple between his teeth while he worked the other with his fingers, pinching it. "Is that still nice?"

"Nice is not how I'd describe it."

"Mmm," he said. He began to use his tongue around her breast, while still tweaking her nipples.

"You know that drives me crazy."

"I do. It's why I do it." He lowered his mouth to her stomach, licking down her body. He went lower and he moved her legs apart. She grabbed his head and opened more for him. He gave her sex one long, slow lick and she cried out. "God Anya, I need you so much right now."

"Same." she breathed. She pulled him up to her and he was inside her in one stroke, both of them gasping at the contact.

"I am going to try and go slow, so we don't tire out too quickly. But fuck woman, nothing feels better than you."

She laughed and took his mouth in a deep kiss while they continued to move together, slowly at first. As Anya tightened around him, he sped up some, but he still kept up a leisurely pace. *"Cushla machree"* he murmured to her over and over. She couldn't stop her hands roaming his body, satisfying herself that he was still here with her. "Declan, Declan..." she breathed.

"Are you close, my love?" He kissed her deeply. "Come with me, my Annie. Come with me, *malysh*." He peppered kisses all over her face and when they went over the edge, they went together.

***

Matthew walked into The Cellar, navigating down to the sub-basement, where Dougal was waiting for him. "Is he in one piece?" Matthew asked.

Dougal shrugged. "I dinna hurt him too bad." Matthew raised an eyebrow. "Truly! I roughed him up some, but that was more to scare him than anything else."

"Ok, let's do this then."

"Are we questioning him first?"

"Yes. Though I assume that his story is going to come close to what Connell told you and Declan."

The two men stalked into the room and the man on the chair started whining. "You can't keep me here! I have rights! I know I can't be held like this! I have…"

"SHUT UP!" roared Matthew. The man clamped his mouth shut and started shaking from fear. Dougal's eyes widened. Matthew very rarely lost control of his temper, and strictly speaking, he hadn't, but the Scotsman could tell he was absolutely furious right now. "I have questions, you're going to answer them."

"I don't have to."

"Oh, but you do." said Matthew silkily. "What I do with you depends on it." It was shitty of him, but he knew this kid would tell him what he wanted to know if he thought he could save himself. He doubted he was going to have to use compulsion to get his answers. He would, in this case, if it was needed. But this kid was so scared, he thought he could get away with just being menacing.

The kid gulped. "I don't know anything."

Matthew's claws distended. "Of course you do. And you're going to tell me what I want to know. Every time you don't answer me, I am going to slice you open. You may heal, in time, but it's going to be painful. You're young, you aren't that strong. It will hurt, I will make sure of that." The demon paled considerably. "And just so you know that I am serious, here's a reminder that I am not to be trifled with." He slashed one claw down the demon's chest, opening it up. The young demon screamed from pain. "Now, are we clear on how this is going to go? Or do you need me to school you further?" The demon nodded his assent.

Matthew was positively frightening when he went all cold-blooded demon lord of the manor, thought Dougal. He was glad they were on the same side. For the next thirty minutes, the young demon, named Peter, told them what had happened to him. The story very much matched Connell's story of how he became a demon and how he'd gotten hired. The only difference being that this kid hadn't been a petty criminal like Connell. He'd just been at a bar, having a drink after having played the tourist all day. Why these guys? What did these young men have in common?

"Well Peter, so far you've answered my questions very well. Would you like some water?" Peter nodded and Matthew gave him some water.

You bastard thought Dougal. *You're letting him think he may live through this.*

"Now Peter, let's talk through your instructions for the attack. Take me through it."

"I…I… don't…I…can't…."

Matthew put a claw to Peter's throat. "Oh, can't you?" he purred. "You've been doing so well up to now. Come on now…tell me what happened?"

"He said he'd hurt me if I told?"

"Peter, I can actually make you tell me, I don't want to do that. It feels unsporting. Is this the same man that made you a demon? The Russian?"

"Yes."

Could be Anya's brother, but no proof yet. "Peter, I am much much older than the Russian you met. I am much stronger than he is. It's not him I'd worry about if I were you. You aren't with the Russian now, you're with me and I am really very angry at the moment." He practically purred the last sentence. Once again, Dougal got the chills watching Matthew work.

Peter gulped. "Ok, fine! He told me that I had to do a job. He told me I owed him for being made a demon, for getting to become immortal. He convinced me I should do it, or I'd be in trouble. He didn't tell me anything about your boss." Peter took a breath. "But, when he thought I was asleep, I heard him talking to someone. This person gave him the dagger. He said…"

"Peter…"

"I am trying to remember!" He thought for a minute. "He said that the dagger had a strong spell on it, that it was important that neither he, the Russian, or I touched the blade. We could die if it cut us. That's what he said. And then the Russian asked if it would work? Would it kill the demon, plus his consort? And the other person said yes." Matthew sighed. He might have let Peter live if he hadn't known the dagger could be fatal. But he had, and he'd done it anyway.

"Did you see this man?"

"No. I didn't. I was pretending to be asleep."

"What did he sound like?"

"Sound like?"

"Did he have an accent?"

Peter tried to remember. "Yes." Peter nodded. "It sounded French, maybe?"

"Did he say anything else?"

"Yes. The Russian said…and I remember this clearly, I am not sure why, but he said 'That bitch better reward me for this. I am doing all the work while she sits on her ass. She's no better than my fucking sister. But my sister will finally get what's coming to her.'" Matthew and Dougal shared a look. Well, that was as close to proof as they were likely to get. This had to be Anya's brother. "I remember that. Because he sounded so cold. But that is all I remember. I took the dagger, and I did what I was told. I didn't ask for this."

"No, but you did it anyway. Knowing it was wrong. You got hopped up on a drug you were given and decided to try and commit murder. "

"I wanted to run."

"Oh Peter, I really wish you had run."

Peter's eyes widened. "There's one other thing!" A last gambit to save his own life.

"Yes?"

"The Russian sometimes seemed…sick, or in pain? He was good at hiding it, but I saw it a few times. Like sometimes it was a struggle to talk or walk."

Matthew nodded. It was all information, but in the end it would not matter. "Peter, let me break it down for you. You stabbed a very important, powerful demon, one that will run Western Europe one day. He has a very powerful mate, in her own right. He loves her very much and you put her in danger. She also loves him, and you hurt him. Trust me, I am doing you a kindness. She would be way more ruthless with you. That Russian is her brother and he tried to kill both of them, through you. You were not supposed to be a demon, you weren't supposed to die. The Russian is the same. If you had run away, or come to us before you stabbed anyone, we'd have let you live. But you didn't, and we can't. And unlucky you, they also happen to be my best friends. And I am very very angry. But take comfort, what I do to you is going to pale in comparison to what's done to that Russian and the rest of the people behind this."

"You let me think you wouldn't kill me."

"Well of course he did, lad. He wanted information from ye."

Dougal put in. "Did ye know, lad that we can turn into beasts?"

"I…no. No, I didn't." Peter was petrified now.

"Well, now ye do."

"Is it going to hurt?"

Matthew smiled at the man. "Oh yes. It's going to hurt like a motherfucker." He took off his jacket and kicked off his shoes. "But, you were very forthcoming with information, so I am going to make it quick, more or less." Peter started to pray quietly. "May God have mercy on your soul Peter. Because I won't."

***

Anya and Declan slept very soundly, and the sun was bright when they finally appeared downstairs for a late breakfast. Mara took one look at them, nodded, and made them a huge breakfast.

"This is a lot of food, Mara," Declan said, taking a large gulp of coffee.

"It is, you're still both a little pale, you need to eat."

Anya smiled. "You take good care of us, Mara. Thank you."

Mara stopped at that. "Oh, well…you're welcome."

"Mara, sit down and have some coffee with us," Declan urged. "I am sure you know everything going on and you can update us." It was Declan's way of getting Mara to sit and relax a minute. Based on the spotlessness of the kitchen and all of the baked goods that were cooling nearby, he suspected Mara had been up either very late, very early, or hadn't gone to bed at all. Mara started to argue, then shrugged, poured herself some coffee and sat down. "Now, first question; is there anything left of the demon that stabbed me?" Declan asked.

Mara's grin was feral. "No. Matthew was apparently as furious as Dougal has ever seen him. Still pretty calm, but very scary. He did question him of course, before ripping him apart."

"Damn! I was hoping to get a crack at him." This was from Anya and Mara gave her an approving look. "I never have any fun."

"I am sure you will be able to kill a demon before too long, dear," Declan said blandly.

"Did Matthew go full beast?"

"Oh, yes. Dougal said even his beast was scary calm. He got some good information out of him, so he made it quick." Declan started to speak. "He didn't share it with me. You'll need to ask him."

"Ok, where is he now? I hope, home and asleep."

"Yes. Donovan and Michel slept last night so they could be day shift. Dougal and Matthew took the overnight, along with Therese, who went back to security detail for the clubs."

"Thank you. I will follow up with Matthew this evening." Mara gave him a long look. "I will take it easy; I promise." Declan was feeling pretty much back to normal, but he didn't want Mara to worry too much.

"Gwen and Luc?" asked Anya. "How are they?"

"They are fine. I sent food over to Gwen last night and she texted me a thank you and that she was fine. Luc is also fine. He needed some quiet and a good sleep, so Matthew ended up taking him back to his place and letting him stay in one of the apartments. I sent him food this morning."

Anya looked at Declan, who answered her unspoken question. "Matthew owns the building he lives in. He keeps a couple of apartments open in case they're needed."

"Oh, that was nice of him."

"Matthew is a bit of a soft touch when it comes to that young man, I think. Much like you Anya. He's going to try and convince Luc to move in there permanently," Mara said. "Therese informed Luc's advisor that he would be taking yesterday and today off and if he had anything to say about it, he could take it up with her, and not Luc."

"I assume it was no problem." She wouldn't cross Therese and since she knew Luc's advisor, she knew he wouldn't either.

"It was not."

"Marchand stopped by to check in and I told him you were both down for the count with a stomach flu. He said it was nothing urgent and I said you'd call when you were feeling better. I think he just wants to talk about the footage from the club."

"Thank you. Have you slept?" Mara looked down at her coffee.

"Mara?" His note held a tone of warning.

"I slept for an hour or two."

"Bed. Now. You have the rest of today and tonight off. And don't give me that face. I am pretty sure that there is enough food in the refrigerator to last for a week." Mara blushed.

"Stand down, soldier. Off to bed," said Anya gently.

Mara stood. "Well, I am fairly exhausted." She moved towards the kitchen door. "I am really glad that neither of you died." And with that, she was gone.

Anya looked at Declan. "Well, what should we do today?" Declan waggled his eyebrows at her and Anya laughed. "Aside from that?"

"Well, let's have an easy day. Let's just sit together on the couch in your sitting room, answer some emails and watch movies like normal people. I will even let you pick the movies."

"You may regret that decision."

"Probably. But I am going to let you do it anyway."

****

Several hours later, the couple were knee deep into *Doctor Zhivago* and arguing about the Bolsheviks when Matthew walked into the room.

"I'm sorry, but is Declan watching a movie made after 1945?"

"He is! He's watched several today and he's enjoyed them!"

"Is this true?"

"I'm afraid it is."

"To be fair, it was a very carefully curated list."

"*Star Wars?*"

"Working up to it." Anya stood and gave Matthew a hug. "Thank you so much again for everything you've done." Matthew hugged her back, tightly. Something she hadn't expected. She pulled back and looked at him. "What?"

He sat and looked at the couple across from him and how Declan easily picked up Anya's hand to hold and he knew they'd be fine, no matter what. "So, we questioned the demon that attacked Declan and we found out that, I'm sorry Anya, it looks like Pavel is indeed involved."

This upset Anya, even if she had expected it. Declan squeezed her hand. "It's ok, *malysh*. We thought that this could be the case."

She sighed. "I know. It's just really disappointing, upsetting, annoying."

"All true. Ok, so let's break this down Matthew, what did the conversation entail?" Matthew related the whole interrogation to them and when he got to what Pavel had said about her, Anya's eyes narrowed, and she swore in Russian. Both Matthew and Declan would much rather see her pissed off. Frankly, Matthew wasn't sure he could ever stand to see her as distraught as she was the other day. It had taken him the better part of the last couple of days to build back up the walls she'd crumbled with her crying. And he wasn't entirely sure he had succeeded completely. Emotions were becoming a real pain in the ass for him lately.

"So, Pavel is a demon? Does this mean he's illegally made, or did he broker a deal with someone?"

"He's not demon born, that's for sure. He did not broker a deal with Vlad, but I suppose he may have with someone else."

"My guess though," said Matthew, "is that whoever is behind the attacks approached Pavel while he was still alive." He paused. "Anya, Declan shared what happened with me, I hope this was ok." She nodded at him. "I am the only other one who knows though. I think that your shooting of him was arranged by our unknown demon and Pavel. I think they meant for you to kill him. They were counting on you to be able to defend yourself and not be the one to die. They were playing the long game."

Anya looked shocked, then resigned. "That makes an absurd kind of sense. But why not kill me outright and not worry about it anymore?"

"Declan. Natalia may have said something to someone about you being his consort to someone she shouldn't have, or someone figured it out from the prophecy somehow and they decided to either take both of you out of the equation, because even alone...Declan could still be a challenge. This way, the people behind this do away with both of you."

"My father, though?"

"Collateral damage, sadly. I don't think Pavel expected him to rush in. But I think he took the opportunity to double how guilty you would feel." Matthew had spent a fair bit of time thinking about this and he was pretty certain he was on the right track. "It's a really shitty aspect of human and demon nature, that penchant for cruelty. He knew how you felt about your father, and he decided to go through with it." Anya looked shattered at this, and it infuriated both men to see it.

"I am sorry, Anya." Declan put his arm around his consort and pulled her close.

Anya put her hand on Declan's knee. "Thank you. Thank you, Matthew, for telling me. We're obviously going to need to do something about him, but I don't know that I can kill him. Again."

"There are fates worse than death. But if it comes down to it, you won't have to be the one to do it if you don't want to be. Either Matthew or I could take care of it easily enough, with the right weapon."

"Which we seem to have access to," Matthew added dryly.

"Declan..."

"Anya, to be clear, if it's a choice between you and him, I am not going to hesitate to end him. Any of my people would do the same." Matthew nodded. "I know he's your brother by birth, but he is not your family. He does not deserve your compassion or your pity."

"You're right. I know you are. I just...I just remember what he was like as a kid, and it makes me sad."

"I know, my love," Declan said gently. "And I know that it's difficult. But please know that we are all here for you."

Anya kissed Declan's cheek. "I know, thank you." She looked at Matthew. "And thank you too."

Matthew smiled at her. "You are most welcome."

"Now, tell us the rest of it," said Declan.

While Matthew recounted the details, Anya got up, went over to the small bar in the room and proceeded to fix him a drink. She handed it to him, and he took a sip. "That is the most perfect vodka martini that I have ever had."

"Dated a bartender once. Shit in bed, but a great mixologist."

"Oh really?" Declan raised one eyebrow at her.

"Yes, really." She looked at him. "Don't be jealous. I said he was shit in bed."

"Must you bring up your exes?"

"As long as I am subjected to Rosamund parading yours at me, yes."

"Frankly, Declan, I think that is more than fair." Matthew was trying not to laugh.

Declan shot him an indignant look. "Finish your story."

Matthew took a sip of his drink, sighed contentedly, and finished his tale. "So, it seems that whichever Demon or consort is behind this has their own mage."

"Based on what that kid overheard, I'd say Liliana was still a good bet."

"Agreed."

"But what do we do about it?"

"We need more information, and we need to get close to where we think the source is. So, we're going to take a little side trip to London. Visit Francois and Liliana. Pay our respects, as it were."

"Right into the viper's nest, then?" asked Anya.

"Yes. Matthew, you'll stay here and oversee things. I'll take Michel and Therese."

"We should bring Luc."

"Agreed. He has a ridiculously angelic face. He can likely get some of the staff to talk to him. And it would be good for him to be more involved."

"She makes several good points."

"She does. Maybe he can pick up something with that sight of his. I don't want anyone outside of us knowing he has it, but it's a benefit for sure." Declan's phone buzzed. "Ah, it's our erstwhile detective. You two chat, I'll step out and take it." Declan left the room.

Anya looked at Mathew. "What?" he asked.

"You tell me," she answered quietly.

He sighed. How the hell did she do that? Just know when something was wrong. "I am envious of what you two have. It makes me a bit sad that I will likely never have it for myself."

Loneliness, thought Anya, was a real prick. "You don't know that Matthew."

"I am pretty sure. You have to be open to it."

"You don't want to get hurt again."

"No."

"What was her name?"

He paused just long enough that Anya wasn't sure he'd answer her.

"Catherine. Her name was Catherine Stanhope. She was my fiancée."

"What happened?"

"I was stupid. I visited her after I became a demon. She wouldn't believe it at first, thought she was going crazy, but then she thought I was an actual demon from Hell and tried to cast me out."

"That sounds pretty terrible," Anya said, her voice mild.

"It was. I mean, I get it. She didn't understand. I was naive to go there, but she wouldn't listen to me. She wouldn't stop shouting at me and throwing things at me. She had holy water and started to spray it at me. I just...she was so beautiful and everything I thought I wanted, and she seemed to love me. Not just my money, but me. And maybe I was wrong about that." He paused, looking pained at the memories. "Why didn't she listen to me?" he asked finally.

'When was this?"

"Seventeenth Century."

"Well, I think you just answered your own question. It was the seventeenth century. While demons are not well known now, they were certainly less so then. You were dead. She saw you and you were corporeal, not a ghost. She didn't know what to make of you, so her mind went the only thing you could be. An actual biblical demon from Hell. Things were so different then. You were all still willing to believe in witches at that point."

He nodded, took a breath. "That's not all. She did marry after that, but she went crazy. She started to lose her mind slowly, becoming a real religious fanatic. Declan told me not to do it, but I didn't listen. Idiot that I was. I thought I could make her see reason."

She took his hand as her heart ached for him. "You were not an idiot. You were in love, and you found yourself in a new, unknown situation. You wanted to cling to what you knew, and she was what you knew. It's not her fault. But Matthew, it's not yours either. Stop carrying the guilt around with you. You are an idiot if you let this stop you from loving someone."

Before Matthew could answer, Declan came back into the room. "Well, that was fun. Turns out that they did manage to catch someone on CCTV where the bodies were found. They ran him through facial recognition and came up with one, supposedly very dead, Pavel Orlov."

CHAPTER 25

"I cannot believe he let himself be seen." said Matthew.

"I can," said Anya. "I really did get all the brains in the family." She sighed. "But that's the final nail in the proof coffin. He is obviously the one who left me those letters, probably for spite."

"Most likely, *malysh*," Declan said gently. "Are you ok?"

Anya thought. "I find that my overriding emotion is anger right now."

"I think that makes sense."

"I assume Marchand wants to speak to me?"

"He does. He's coming over in the morning if that is fine with you?"

"It is. I wonder if Doina and the idiot twins know about this?"

Declan snorted. "I am not sure. It doesn't seem likely, but anything is possible."

Anya nodded. "I suppose you're right."

"I think we should still be able to leave for London straight after lunch though."

"Sounds good. I am a bit tired; I am going up to bed."

"Are you sure you're ok?" Declan frowned at her.

"Yes. Just tired, it's been a long couple of days." She gave Matthew another hug and kissed Declan. "Come up soon?"

"Absolutely."

Anya left the room and Declan stared after her until Matthew cleared his throat. "Declan? You there?"

"Yeah. I'm just worried."

"About Anya?"

"Yes."

"She'll hold."

"I have no doubt. But I know dealing with family upsets her. I can feel her emotions when she thinks about her family, and it's not good."

Matthew nodded. "Fair enough." He paused. "Try not to worry too much. She's a strong woman and we're all here for her."

"Matthew, if it comes down to it…."

"I will cleave that son of a bitch in two with your demon killer if need be. I have no issue with that."

"She could resent you for it."

"Better me than you. And she'll get past that too."

"I shouldn't ask it of you."

"You don't have to ask. You never have to ask."

"Matthew, should anything else happen to me…"

"It won't."

"It might. If it does and Anya survives it somehow…"

"Yes, I will look after her. But nothing will happen to you and if it does, she will drag you back from Hell itself." Of that, Matthew had no doubt.

Declan grinned. "She would do that." His look turned serious. "She's the key, Matthew. She's the key to change. With the Council, with the status quo, with a lot of things." He thought for a minute. "They're figuring out how best to get to both of us. This was just the first blow."

"You want Liliana to know that you know," Matthew said wonderingly.

"I do. I want her to know that none of us go down without a fight."

"No, Declan. None of us go down. Period."

***

The next morning, Marchand showed up at exactly 10 a.m. and was shown into Declan's sitting room, where Anya was waiting. Alone.

"Detective Marchand, good morning."

"Good morning Dr. Orlov. Thank you for seeing me on such short notice."

She smiled. "It's not a problem. Coffee?"

"This time, yes. Please." She poured him some, handed him a cup and motioned he should fix it the way he wanted it. "I am sure Mr. O'Shea explained why I wanted to see you." He took a sip of coffee and sighed in bliss.

"He did, yes. It's a bit of a shock." Anya had decided she was not even going to try to play the grieving sister on this one.

"Dr. Orlov, your father died the same day as your brother, is that correct?"

"It is. My brother shot him; I am sure that's a matter of public record."

"Yes. It was an accident?"

"Yes. He was aiming for me." That was not a matter of public record. Marchand stared at her. "Excuse me?"

"He was trying to kill me. My father got in the way." Marchand blinked several times at her. "Detective, are you all right?"

"I am, yes. You just surprised me. Why was your brother trying to kill you?"

This was trickier, but she would stick to the truth as much as she could. "It would be no secret, Detective, if you had done any research on me at all, that I am not close to my mother and brothers. A situation exacerbated by the fact that I now own the circus my family has run for years. I never really, for whatever reason, fit in. My little brother, over the years, became convinced that there was something wrong with me. I always assumed this idea came from my mother, but I can't be sure. She was often verbally abusive to me in front of him."

"What about your father? He did nothing?" He knew it was a personal question, but he was appalled at what Anya was telling him.

She shook her head. "My mother was a strong woman and she cowed him. I think he felt bad about it though. That day, he wanted to protect me, he walked in front of the gun. The situation went from bad to worse from there. In that chaos, my brother was killed."

"Did you confirm your brother was dead?"

"I was too busy crying and screaming over my father being dead. He…" she paused for a breath; it was still painful to think about. "He died in my arms. I only remember being outside with my uncle Tomas after that."

He nodded. This had all been corroborated by her uncle, whom he'd spoken to the day before.

"You will get a different story from my mother and surviving brothers though."

"We can't find them."

"Pardon?"

"Your mother and brothers have disappeared. They took all the cash they could lay hands on, it seems, and are in the wind."

Well that explained why her lawyer hadn't heard from them in regard to the circus. "Well, that's not surprising. She may be with her family. Her people are Rom and as you know, they do not stay in one place."

He noted that down. "Thank you. So, you can't confirm that your brother actually died that day."

She hated to lie but had to. "No, I can't. I'm sorry. No one told me any differently. If it were covered up, my mother would be behind it." Throwing that bitch under the bus was no problem for her.

"So, I assume that Pavel has not tried to contact you?"

"No. Not at all." She paused. "Though, I did get some threatening letters. They may have been from him," She picked up two envelopes on the table and handed them to Marchand. "I thought you might like to see them."

"*Spasibo*" He opened and read them. "What does this mean?"

"I don't know. I wouldn't have thought it was Pavel, I thought he was dead. But this was the type of thing he spewed at me, so it may be him."

"You didn't report this?"

"No. I thought it was just someone trying to get a rise out of me." She and Declan had discussed the letters that morning. Turning them over was a risk, but one they felt they should take. They wanted Marchand's trust. "I thought it might be a student who'd gotten a bad grade maybe. I didn't like it, but I didn't think it was anything serious. I wrote the dates of each letter on the envelope. So you know when I got them."

"Thank you. This is helpful." Almost too helpful once again, he thought. But he believed her. Well, he believed her about her mother and brothers. The jury was out on the rest of it, but he didn't think she was involved in this. Something in his gut told him that this group of people were hiding something, but the something didn't kill those young men, or even know about them. And they didn't feel necessarily evil, but there was just something off about them. "Dr. Orlov, may I ask you a question not related to the case?" He took a sip of coffee. Jesus, this was excellent coffee.

"Of course."

"Why do you use 'Orlov' and not 'Orlova?'"

She smiled at him patiently. "Because I believe it's an archaic tradition. I don't need an extra letter on the end of my name to let people know I'm a woman. It's one more way for the patriarchy to differentiate between men and women unnecessarily."

He gave her a bemused look. "Thank you. My mother would agree with you, for what it's worth." He stood. "One final question?"

"Of course."

"Where does this coffee come from? Because it is amazing!"

She laughed. "You know, I am not sure where Mara gets it, or if it's just her own brand of magic, but I will ask and let you know.

"Thank you!"

"You are welcome. Good coffee is important."

"Thank you for your time. I understand from your husband that you're taking a quick business trip with him to London, is this right?"

"It is, yes. Is that ok?"

"Yes, it is. I may have more questions, so may I call you if I do?"

"Of course. Detective, I hope you find my brother. Maybe he can get the help he needs. And I hope you find my mother and other brothers. If I hear from them, or anyone who has seen them, I will let you know."

"Thank you."

She walked him out and after she shut the front door, leaned against it and let out a shaky breath. Her mother would deny everything she'd just said if Marchand got a hold of her. But she was pretty sure the Detective would choose to believe Anya's story. One that was as accurate as she could make it. She took out her phone and then smiled, she didn't need the phone. *Declan?* She thought at him through their blood bond.

Malysh, is all well?

It is. Marchand is gone, I think it went fine.

Good. But how are you doing? His voice stroked her down the bond.

Better than expected and raring for a bit of a fight right now, so part of me hopes Liliana won't behave.

He smiled at this. *So fierce! I'll be home shortly.*

Good. I miss you.

And I, you.

Anya made a couple of quick calls, but no one knew anything about Doina. Them disappearing was not a good omen. How did the saying go? *'It is an ill wind that blows nobody any good.'* With that thought, she went upstairs to pack for their quick trip.

***

In the car, on the way to Francois' and Liliana's, Declan brought them up to date on recent goings on and what he expected at Francois' when they got there. "Anya will be with me, obviously. Can you be nice?" He asked Anya with a glint in his eye.

"Sincerely nice, or you know...nice enough?"

"Start with sincere."

"I'll give it a try."

He shook his head a little at her and went on. "Luc, I need you to try and keep your senses, all of them, open and see if you can pick up anything. But I also need you to use those angelic looks and see if you can get anyone to open up about the mood of the house. Additionally, Richelieu's spy is installed in the house now. They will find you and pass along any information they may have discovered."

"*Oui*, Declan. I am on it." Anya smiled at his continued use of first names.

"Michel, you have a friend in the house, yes?"

"*Oui.* You want me to see if I can glean any information from him?"

"Yes. I want you to see if you can find out about any increased security and comings and goings." Michel nodded at him. "Therese. You're one of the most observant people I've ever known. Stay with Anya and me and watch Liliana and Francois very closely. And let Liliana see you doing it."

"So, be menacing?"

"Yes."

"Hey! How come she gets to be menacing and I have to be nice."

"Because she doesn't have to be political. You do." She glared at him. "Therese, situate yourself behind Anya at all times."

"Of course."

"Is that because you're worried that I am going to go after Liliana and you know Therese will make sure that doesn't happen?"

"Yes. But also, the likelihood of Liliana sitting right across from you is very good, I want Therese in her direct eye line as well."

"Why?"

"Therese scares her."

"Therese scares me." said Michel.

Therese bared her teeth at him. "That's because you tried to get me into bed the first time we met."

"Can you blame me?" He smiled.

"No, of course not." She winked at him.

They pulled up to a large house in the Belgravia area of London. It had been separate residences at one point, but when Francois moved in, he had bought out the two buildings on either side of him. Anya let out a low whistle. "Shit, that is a lot of house. There's going to be a lot of gilt isn't there?"

"Yes, there is." Declan smiled at her.

"Should have taken some Dramamine," joked Therese.

"We aren't staying with them tonight, are we? Please say no."

"No, we are not. Matthew has a house here, we're staying there. We're not too far now, actually."

"Do I have time to go shopping tomorrow before we go home?"

"Yes, that won't be a problem."

"Good. It's been a while since I've been down to Camden Lock Market, and I'd like to go do some shopping there." Of course, his Anya wanted to go to Camden, that was very her. "They have the coolest stuff."

"Anything you want." She smiled at him. "But now, let's go in."

They all alighted from the car and walked to the front door. Michel rang the doorbell and stood braced, ready for anything, as did Therese. The door swung open and an impossibly tall, gruesome looking demon let them in. "Baines." said Declan.

"O'Shea." The man's voice was cold and hard. "You're looking well."

"Much to your eternal annoyance, I'm sure." Declan's voice was just as hard.

Baines chose not to answer that. "Liliana and Francois are waiting. You're late."

"We're not. But it's fine if you choose to think so."

Baines stared at the assembled group, who stared back. The demon sniffed and led them down a hallway, stopping in front of a ridiculously ornate door. "Are you all going in?"

"Michel and Luc have friends in the house to visit. Therese is coming in with us." Declan paused. "Baines, you've been very rude to my consort." His voice was low, but cold as ice.

"Have I?"

"You know you have." Declan's voice was hard.

Anya looked at him in what she hoped was an imperious manner.

"Dr. Orlov, may I congratulate you and welcome you to the home of the Demon of Western Europe." His voice was flat, letting Anya know what he truly thought of her.

"Thank you...Baines, was it?"

Baines cleared his throat and knocked on the door. "Come!" came the reply.

Baines opened the door. Declan ushered Anya in first and as he went in, Baines hissed at him. "Upstart!"

"Come the revolution," replied Declan softly "You'll be the first to go."

"I thought we were being polite." whispered Anya.

"Never to him." She started to say something. "We'll discuss it later." She nodded and squeezed his hand as they made their way into the room.

"Declan! Anya! It's good to see you." This from Francois. He was sitting in a chair that seemed almost like a throne, Liliana was seated next to him, in a slightly smaller, but no less ornate chair.

Is he kidding with those chairs?!

He is not. He is deadly serious about them. He had them commissioned to look like thrones. The chairs are taller, so we'll look smaller when we sit on that couch.
This is absolutely hysterical. She felt his laughter down the bond.

"Francois, it was good of you to see us on such short notice."

"Of course, of course. Anything for one of mine." If he thought to put Declan in his place, he'd need to try harder.

"We still appreciate it. Liliana, you are looking well."

"Thank you, Declan. As are you." She paused and looked at Anya, whose face was a portrait of serenity. "Anya," she looked her up and down, taking in her all black ensemble. "You look lovely."

"Thank you, Liliana. May I say that gown is stunning." Therese snorted but covered it up with a small cough. Liliana was wearing a diaphanous pink gown that was all wrong for her coloring. It had a smattering of gold flowers on it and it was very ugly.

"Thank you. Please, sit." The couple sat on the couch and Therese stood directly behind Anya, arms crossed in front. of her. As Declan suspected, Liliana was right across from Anya. She'd want to look down on her, it would make her feel powerful.

"What brings you to London, my boy?" asked Francois.

Anya took Declan's hand and squeezed it, Francois' tone was meant to irritate him, and she could tell that it was hitting its mark. It wasn't entirely personal, but Declan was a definite threat, and the old demon knew it. "I had an unfortunate incident a few days ago and I received a lead that the person behind it was in London, so I decided to check it out in person."

"Incident?"

"Yes. I was stabbed."

"Stabbed?" Francois looked sincerely confused and concerned about this. "Who would do that? You weren't hurt though?"

"Oh, I was. The dagger had dark magic on it, a strong spell apparently."

Anya was watching Francois, but Therese was watching Liliana and saw her grow pale and begin to fidget in her seat. *Gotcha, you old bitch.*

"That's appalling." Francois looked at Anya. "You would have felt it too."

"I did. It was...it was horrible." Anya let her voice break when she said that.

"Oh, my dear, of course it must have been." Francois had moved closer to the edge of the chair in his agitation, but Liliana was sitting stock still. He looked at her. "Isn't it, my dear?" There was an edge to his voice.

"Oh! Oh, yes...of course. How...how terrible." She cleared her throat. "But you're both well now?"

"Oh yes, thank you."

"But how?" asked Francois.

"Well, their little witch friend of course." Liliana said.

Anya stiffened at this. Declan narrowed his eyes. "Our little witch friend, Liliana?"

"Yes, the little blonde that seems so attached to your Anya."

Therese moved her hand to sit lightly at top of Anya's back, a warning to stay calm.

"You mean my friend, Gwen?" Anya asked.

"Yes."

"How did you know she was a witch?"

She's overplayed her hand. Declan thought to her.

Yes, she has. And now I will have to fucking kill her.

Naturally. But not today.

"Oh, I am sure someone mentioned it at the presentation."

"Hmmm. I don't recall that."

"It was a long evening."

"Wasn't it just?"

"But no, not her. She can do a few spells, but she's not that powerful really. She likes to dabble mostly." Anya's eyes were wide and innocent. She felt Declan's laughter and approval at this outrageous lie.

Liliana looked surprised, but not entirely convinced. "Really, now?"

"Really. She's one of my closest friends, I mean, I'd know. She can do some fun, simple spells, but otherwise, nothing major." She hated to denigrate her best friend's abilities, but she had to keep her safe. "We were lucky though. We had...well...we had..." She stopped and pursed her lips. "Declan?" she asked him beseechingly. Wringing her hands together and looking upset. "I don't..."

Jesus, she was good. "Anya my love, it's fine. We can tell Francois and Liliana." She rested her head on his shoulder for a moment, a single tear trickling down her cheek. Therese was trying very hard not to laugh. Neither Francois nor his consort knew Anya well enough to know how utterly comical this act of hers was. Anya continued, "We do have a witch, a mage if you will." Liliana started at this, and Therese grinned wolfishly. "They were able to lift the spell. She's very old though and she keeps to herself. Russian, so it's someone Anya has known for years."

"Oh? Through Natalia?" Liliana asked.

"Oh no! Through my mother."

"Then wouldn't she be Romanian?" Liliana was grasping at straws, and this was causing her to slip up.

"Liliana, you seem to know quite a bit about Anya." This was from Francois. "Why is that?"

Liliana's face drained of color. She knew she'd gone too far. "Well, Francois, after the presentation, I asked Natalia about her. I realize that I probably overstepped, but I found Anya so unusual, that I wanted to know more about her." Neither Declan nor Anya was convinced, but Francois took his mate at her word. "I have been remiss though. Would any of you like refreshments?"

"Sounds lovely," Declan said. *Sorry love, we're settling in for a visit.*

I know. But I really want to rip her face off.

That's my warrior.

CHAPTER 26

Michel found his friend Jack in Francois' weapon room. "Polishing your sword there, Jack?" Michel emphasized the French pronunciation of Jack's name, something he knew annoyed the thoroughly English demon.

Jack pivoted and let out a bark of laughter. "You old sod! How the fuck are you?" He put out his hand. Michel scoffed and pulled Jack into a quick hug. "Get off!"

Michel laughed. "Well, you haven't changed any."

"Never! What brings you here?"

"Declan, and his consort, Anya, are paying a call to Francois and Liliana."

"Nice work if you can get it. Swanning around, paying social calls." Jack grinned at Michel.

"Well, not all of us can be big tough guys, like you."

"Hah! That's the only reason you're here then?" An odd look passed over Jack's face.

"Jack? I recognize that look, what do you know?"

Jack sighed. "I shouldn't say."

"Jack! If you know something, please tell me. Please." Michel's voice had an urgent quality to it that had Jack furrowing his brow. "It's important, Jack. We almost lost them, please." Michel knew that Jack had no love for Francois or Liliana. He was working for them because he had to, he owed Francois a debt and it wasn't paid yet. He knew if this got back to Francois that Jack could be in serious trouble, but if Jack knew something, he had to know what it was. For his part, Jack knew his old friend wouldn't press if it wasn't important.

Jack clapped Michel on the shoulder, nodded and pulled him into a smaller equipment room so they could talk. "Liliana has a mage. She's told Francois it's just a bit of fun, but the mage is...I don't know...dark. He and Liliana have been holing up in her wing, and there's been a fair bit of activity. Young demons in and out, but they don't feel right."

"What do you mean they don't feel right?"

"Like they don't belong somehow. I don't think they're supposed to be demons. And one other really funny thing about them?"

"What?"

"They all look alike. Pale skin, dark hair, blue eyes, similar build."

"Huh."

"Yeah, it's weird."

"Do you know what she and this mage are doing, specifically?"

"No, I don't. Francois isn't happy about the time they're spending together. I think he believes she's just cheating on him."

"Is she?" Jack looked uncomfortable at this question. "Jack?"

"Yes, I think she is actually. She and Francois have had, a good relationship, but I think it's been years since they were intimate."

"How do you know?"

"Because they were very...loud when they were. It was both comical and uncomfortable. But it's been fairly quiet in that area. Francois was old as dirt when he took Liliana for a consort, so maybe he lost interest. That being said, it is obvious he's not happy with her. He definitely suspects they're fucking around, what else may suspect, I can't say. But I don't think he knows about the young demons coming in and out. Yet. He's fairly oblivious to the day-to-day workings of the house."

"Do you know the mage's name?"

"That's another odd thing, I don't. She never calls him by name, and it's never whispered."

"Is he old?"

"He feels it but doesn't look it."

"Is he also a demon?"

"He does not feel like a demon, yet, he sometimes does." Jack shook his head. "It's hard to explain unless you're around him. There's a lot of power there though."

"Does the mage live here?"

"Yes. In Liliana's wing."

"And do you see him often?"

"Not too often, but I have seen him up close recently. I had to bring them one of Liliana's old daggers."

Dread filled Michel at this statement. He pulled out his phone and brought up a photo of the dagger that almost killed Declan. "Was it this one?"

"Yes, it was. How did you get this?" Understanding dawned on Jack's face. "They used it to hurt Declan."

"Yes. And it was drenched in dark magic. The poison in the spell nearly killed Declan and Anya."

"Fuck! I had no idea they were using it for that. I am so sorry, friend."

"Jack, I don't blame you. You didn't know. But if they ask for anything else..."

"I will let you know immediately. And I'll keep my eyes and ears open."

"Jack, while I don't want you to put yourself in danger, anything you're able to pass on, will be helpful."

"I want to help. I don't forget that Declan tried to get me out of paying this debt to Francois, to work for him instead. There's one thing I want to ask you though."

"Go ahead, *mon ami*." The two were unlikely friends, but trauma often made friends of the oddest people.

"There's been talk, Liliana, her mage, of a prophecy. Do you know anything about it?"

"I do."

"Does it concern Declan and his new consort?" The servants had been talking about it quite a bit lately. Liliana and her mage were not as careful as they should be and often took very little notice of the servants around them.

"It does."

"Then you all need to be careful. Very careful. Liliana and this mage are trying to make sure the prophecy never comes true." He looked down at his hands. "I should have passed that along to you sooner, I'm sorry."

"I know what it's like to work for monsters, Jack. As do you. It teaches you to be silent."

"Francois isn't a monster. Not really."

"I didn't mean Francois."

"I know you meant Liliana. Francois is old and set in his ways. And he does not want to give up his power, but he's tired and it's weighing on him. And Liliana knows it. She's doing what she can to extend their power."

"She's going to lose this battle."

"What if she doesn't?"

"That is not an option."

***

Luc had headed down to the kitchen. He thought if anyone was likely to hear things and not be noticed, it was going to be the household staff. And he was betting they congregated in what turned out to be, the very large kitchen. His timing was off though, as the kitchen was mostly empty when he got down there.

"What can I do for ye?" an older, heavy-set female demon asked him.

"*Pardon, madame,* I am just looking for something to drink. May I have a drink of water, *s'il vous plaît?*" The woman looked at him. He smiled innocently and widened his eyes at her some. She was kneading dough and had the look of being the boss about her, he assumed from this she was the head cook. "I do not wish to disturb you; I am fine getting it myself."

"Susie!" A young girl who had been staring at Luc with a small smile on her face, jumped up. "Get the young man a glass of lemonade."

"Yes, cook!" Susie ran to get it.

"*Merci,* ma'am."

She nodded. "What are you doing down here, lad?"

He shrugged. "Not much for the fancy. Always prefer to chat with the people who actually run the house." This answer won him a grin from the woman. "I am sorry, I am Luc. I am here with…"

"I know who you're 'ere with. Mister Declan and his missus, as it were. I'm Bess."

"Bess, it's a pleasure." Susie came back in with the lemonade. She handed it to him along with a folded-up note. "Susie, get the boy one of the apple pastries I just made, he looks like he's about to waste away."

"Oh Bess, thank you! That would be lovely." They moved off to a corner of the room.

"Nice wide eyed and innocent routine. I am impressed." Susie smiled at him.

"Excuse me?" She had to be Richelieu's spy.

"You know exactly what I mean. The cardinal sends his regards." She winked at him.

"I assumed when you handed me the note, but I wanted to be sure."

"It could have been my phone number you know." She grinned at him.

"I suppose, but that never occurred to me." He shrugged.

She pulled back and gave him a long look, smiling. "No, it wouldn't. This is a detailed note for Mr. O'Shea." She served him an apple turnover. He nodded his thanks. "I do not think there will be any surprises here though. I can tell you that there is something very off about him, but I can't pinpoint what it is exactly. He's also a real creep."

"How so?"

"He keeps trying to manhandle all the pretty demons, male and female. But he's doing it behind Liliana's back."

"You?"

"Yes. But I know how to handle myself, and him.".

"So, he and Liliana are up to something. I think...I may be wrong...that they are drugging Francois, so he goes to bed early, almost right after supper. Francois is old, that shouldn't be able to happen, but it is. I managed to finally get Bess to let me help with dinner. So, I should know tonight, and I'll contact you all."

"Do you think Bess is involved?"

Susie looked over at Bess and pursed her lips. "My instinct is no. I may be wrong, but Bess is pretty steady, very old school. I don't think she has any love for her bosses, but I don't think she'd be a part of trying to weaken Francois."

"Hey, what are you two doing over there?"

Susie blushed prettily and Luc was impressed she could do it on cue like that. "Bess, you can't blame a girl for trying to give a guy her phone number, can you?"

Luc picked up Susie's hand and kissed it. "I am very flattered, *ma petite*."

"Ah yes, but will you call me?"

"I'd be a fool not to. But I can do better; come out with me tonight?"

Susie squeezed his hand in approval. "I have to work!"

"After work then." He looked over at Bess. "Surely, after her work is done, you can spare her for the rest of the evening. Couldn't you? I am just here for tonight, and I've never been to London."

Bess was smiling at them. "Susie, after you help with dinner, you're free to go out with Luc."

"Bien! Thank you, Bess! You are a true romantic!"

"Aw, go on with you!"

"I'll go for now, but I will see you later," he said to Susie.

"Yes! I will see you later." She kissed his cheek "Very well done, Luc." she whispered to him.

Luc kissed Bess on her cheeks before he left, and the old cook blushed to the roots of her hair.

***

Back at their base of Matthew's London home, the group was sharing what they'd learned over dinner. "Francois doesn't seem to know what's going on." said Declan. "But I think he's beginning to suspect. Michel, what did you find out?"

"Well, per Jack, Liliana does have a mage and they are very close. Jack thinks Francois believes Liliana is cheating on him. But Jack was able to confirm that the weapon used on you came from that house."

"What?" said Anya.

"Yes. Jack said he was asked to bring a weapon to the two in Liliana's wing. I showed him a photo and he confirmed it."

"Would he be willing to swear to it publicly?"

"He did not say either way, but if needed to, I think he would."

"Why would he endanger himself like that?" asked Anya in between sips of wine.

"Because he and I go back quite a ways and he has not forgotten what Declan tried to do."

"What did Declan try to do?"

"Jack owed a debt to Francois, for an infraction, and Declan tried to intercede on his behalf."

"Of course, he did," said Anya softly.

Declan made a face. "I didn't succeed. The infraction was really a minor one, Francois was being a dick."

"But you tried, and that made the difference to Jack. You're the first person to have done that for him."

"You did."

"But I held no power."

"But you were tortured for having done it. You paid the higher price."

"*Non*, I think Jack did. In the end." said Michel sadly.

Declan clapped him on the shoulder gently. "I think you're correct my friend. I will see if I can press the point again."

"He won't go until he knows you and Anya are safe. Wait until then."

"I will."

"I don't suppose anyone is going to tell us what you two are nattering about?" asked Therese.

"No, I am not going to tell you. Maybe Michel and Jack will one day."

Therese wondered if Dougal knew but decided to let it drop for now. "Fine. Then let's move on."

"Too right. Is there more?"

Michel recounted the rest of what Jack told him and Declan nodded his thanks. "Luc?"

"So, I went to the kitchens, figuring that it would be a good place to gossip."

"Good thinking. Was it?"

"Not today, but I was lucky." He relayed the entire conversation and gave Declan the note that Susie had given him. "We played it off, in front of Bess, like we were going on a date tonight. Susie is going to come by and let us know if indeed, someone is slipping Francois something."

"Excellent work. Also, you two should go have some fun tonight."

"Oh, Declan...no, I mean, I couldn't. She probably doesn't even like me that way."

Therese stared hard at him. "Kid, I am not really sure you have any clue how much both men and women like you, 'that way.'"

"Really?" Asked Anya, fascinated.

"Really! You should hear how they were talking about him at your presentation."

"You are making that up!" said Luc.

"Oh, I am not. You are very popular, with those eyes of yours."

"So, getting back to this," said Declan "This note is indeed very detailed. But something has struck me based on what both Luc and Jack said. Anya, what did Pavel look like?"

"Odd question."

"Humor me."

"Well, he had black curly hair, thick. Much like Doina's. He had blue eyes. Honestly, he for sure had prettier eyes than me."

"Impossible."

"Flatterer. Pale skin, cheekbones I would kill for."

"How tall was he?"

"My height. Why?"

"Well, Susie has noted that every single young demon going in and out of Liliana's wing looks alike. And Jack, through Michel, has said the same thing."

"They look like Pavel?"

"Yes. And Connell looked like that."

"So, did the shit heel who stabbed you."

"But why? What is the point of that?" Anya's face dropped.

"Because it makes it less noticeable when he goes in and out, since he's supposed to be dead."

"Yes."

"Also, I bet he was hoping I'd notice eventually. The little shit."

"That would appeal to Liliana's sense of drama."

There was a knock at the door to the dining room and they all turned towards it. It was Susie and Alice, one of the house staff. "I'm sorry to interrupt Mr. O'Shea, but she says you're expecting her."

"Susie!" said Luc. Susie smiled at him from the doorway.

"Yes, we are. Thank you, Alice." Alice smiled and left the room.

"Is this a bad time?"

"No, not at all. Please come in. I was just reading your note."

"Oh, good!" Susie pulled a small bottle from her bag and set it on the table. "This is what they're giving Francois."

"How did you get it?"

"I was a pickpocket when I was a human, I kept that skill." Luc pulled out a chair for her and she smiled at him as she sat down. Therese poked Anya in the ribs at this, Anya poked back. "As I thought, Bess has no clue. One of the maids, I think of one Liliana's personal pets, sprinkles it on his food before she brings his plate over."

"They have stopped serving themselves from platters then?"

"They have actually. It's a recent change. Liliana said she wanted to dine more informally. So, they don't dine in the large dining room anymore."

"She wants Francois to think she wants to be more intimate with him," said Anya. "But can't he tell he's being drugged? Can't he taste it?"

Luc picked up the bottle, opened, sniffed, and made a face. Closing the bottle back up again. "Magic."

"Magic?" asked Susie.

"Yes. It's probably a fairly common sleeping draught, but there's a spell on it. I can smell it."

"This mage is really beginning to piss me off," said Declan.

"You and me, both," said Anya. "And we've been rude to Susie. Susie, I'm Anya, that's Therese and Michel. You know Luc. And you know who Declan is. Are you hungry?"

"No, but thank you, Dr. Orlov. I know who you all are though." Luc sat down next to her, and she smiled at him. "I saw all of you at the presentation."

Therese leaned over to Anya and whispered in her ear. "That's where I've seen her. Someone made a very rude comment about the relationship between you and Luc after you didn't geld him. She tripped them, very covertly, then slipped into the crowd."

Anya looked impressed. "Huh. Now, that is interesting."

"It was very impressive. I liked her immediately."

"I keep forgetting we did that. It seemed so long ago, even though it wasn't.".

"Are you sure you won't have some wine?" Luc asked her softly.

"Oh, well, wine would be nice. Yes, please." He poured her some and she took a drink. "Oh, this is nice."

"Susie, thank you. Between the note and this. I think we know quite a bit now."

"Something else you should know then; Francois picked at his food tonight. I stayed long enough to watch them a bit and he barely had two bites of it. He said he wasn't hungry, but when he left the room, I heard him ask Baines to ask Bess for a sandwich. And that she should make it herself, while Baines watched."

Declan smiled. "So, Francois suspects something. It might be just about her cheating with the mage, but it may be something else."

"He was questioning her at dinner on why she knew so much about Dr. Orlov."

"Do you think he'd be on our side?" Anya asked.

"I think he's worried that Liliana is taking too much power for herself. There is no value for him to get rid of us, we do all of his heavy lifting in France and Belgium, Paris is the main seat for Western Europe. But I don't think it will translate to his being on our side per se. That said, when we expose her, I don't think he'll be too bothered. She'll have made a fool of him. Especially if she is fucking that mage."

"I can see what I can find out there." Susie said.

"Wonderful. Thank you. But please be careful, Liliana and her mage are very dangerous."

"I will be."

"And since you've made it clear that you and Luc met tonight, why don't you continue to contact Luc directly with information. He can report back to me. That won't arouse suspicion."

"Will do."

Declan cleared his throat. "Susie, are you off for the rest of the night?"

"I am, yes."

"Wonderful. Luc has never been to London before; do you think you may be able to show him some of the nighttime sights? Unless you have other plans."

Oh, well done to you. This from Anya.

I thought you'd like that. She grinned wickedly at him.

"Oh, I don't want her to waste her evening." said Luc, standing.

"Aw no, it would be great! I'd love to do that." said Susie, also standing and taking his hand. "Your boss is giving you the night off; we shouldn't waste it." She tugged at his hand.

"Well then, I'd love that." He waved goodbye to them as Susie pulled out of the room.

The remainder of the group waited until they were sure the front door closed before they broke into peals of laughter.

"Luc looked both petrified and elated." said Michel.

Anya wiped her eyes. "He really did. But I think both of them could use a little fun."

"Oh, is that what the kids are calling it these days?" Therese winked at her.

"Cute, very cute." Anya poured more wine all around and pulled out her tablet. "Ok, let's kill this wine and make a list of everything we know." She thought. "We'll need more wine."

<u>CHAPTER 27</u>

On the way to the airport late the next day, Anya looked at Luc. "You got in very late last night."

"No," said Michel. "He got in very early this morning."

"Oh, really?" said Anya. Luc was blushing furiously. "So, did you have a nice time with the lovely Susie?"

"We had a lovely evening, yes."

"And a lovely early morning apparently," joked Therese.

"*Merde!*" said the young demon. He looked at Declan. "Can you not stop these jokes?"

"I mean, I could. Sure, I could. But I really am enjoying them too much."

Luc rolled his eyes at them. "We talked. We sat on a bench and just talked."

"Oh Luc," said Michel sadly. "If I thought that were true, I'd be very disappointed in you." Luc dropped his eyes. "You kissed the girl, didn't you? Please say you did."

"I am not going to tell you that. It's ungentlemanly."

"A-ha! That's an answer in and of itself!"

"Ok, enough. Leave the poor boy alone. It's obvious by the look of both mortification and mischief he's wearing, that he did indeed kiss the girl." Luc opened his mouth and closed it again instantly. Anya winked at him. "Now leave him be. For now."

Luc smiled, leaned his head back and closed his eyes. They had spent the night sitting on a bench by the Seine, talking and kissing. To anyone passing by, they had looked just like any other young couple. They had enjoyed that. It was so rare, especially for Susie, that had it been lovely just to sit there, and be for a bit.

Stop looking like a proud mother hen. This from Declan.

But I am. He found a girl, or she found him, and they went out and I know they kissed. Like normal people. For once. He deserves that. So does she.

"So boss," asked Therese. "What are we doing about Liliana and her mage?"

"For now, nothing. I am going to talk Anaranth. Anya will talk to the cardinal, and we will wait for Liliana to completely overplay her hand."

"Will she?"

"Oh, yes. Our visit worried her. She may be nervous we're getting close. And she is definitely nervous that Francois is getting close. She's starting to get a little sloppy." He paused. "Anya, you're going to really hate this, but…."

"You don't want me going out alone until this is settled."

"Yes. But also, you need to become way more skilled with those swords. And as such, I'd prefer you to not leave the house in the future without them."

"Even though I am not, I am sorry, 'skilled' yet?" Her voice held an edge.

"Anya, I have no doubt that you will quickly become an expert with them but you're not there yet. And you know it. Still, I'd rather you have them with you than not. And I'd rather you had one of my people with you."

"What about you?"

"What about me?"

"Who is going to be with you? Are you going to have your swords?"

"I don't need…"

"Excuse me, but you do. You die, I die. We die, there's war, because if you think our friends are just going to stand by and swallow our deaths, you're an idiot."

"You may not die."

"And then it's still fucking war because there is no way in Hell or Heaven you die without me destroying everyone involved. You want to see vengeance, that'll be it."

The car had gone totally silent. Declan looked at Anya. "Anya, please, don't."

"No, you stop it. You are important for more reasons than just being the man I love. They got to you once. They know your weakness is me. You fucking protect yourself by any means necessary, *cushla machree*."

He blinked at her, realizing he'd been done in by his own endearment. "Ok," he said, putting his hand on her cheek. "Whatever you say, Annie. I won't go out alone and I will make sure I am carrying the swords at all times."

She smiled at him, and the car exhaled as one.

"I volunteer." said Therese. "I want to be with Anya."

"Really? Why?" asked Declan.

"Where she goes, trouble follows, and I like trouble."

"Of all the fucking nerve!" Anya sounded indignant. "But I also want Therese. So, just shut up and say yes."

"Shut up or say yes, which is it?" he asked with a grin.

"I don't want to have to punch you."

"See? She's a lot more fun to be around." Therese smiled.

"Fine. Try not to kill everyone you meet."

Luc's phone pinged and he looked at it. "So, Susie says that Francois and Liliana seem to be fighting."

"Not a surprise."

"Francois wants to go back to the more lavish dinner arrangements since having intimate dinners is not leading to any intimacy. And Liliana lost her shit," he said, reading. "Hah! I've not heard that phrase before. I like it. Anyway, Francois put his foot down and said as she can't come up with a good reason, it's just her being difficult. She ran out of the room and straight to the mage. And she discovered his name is Mercule. Francois shouted it after her, it seems."

"Mercule? His name is Mercule?" Declan asked.

"Yes."

"What is it?" from Anya.

"There's something about that name, something that is ringing a bell, but I can't put my finger or brain on it right now. Shit!" Declan furrowed his brow.

There was another ping. "There's more. When Francois put his foot down, Liliana ran out and flew straight to Mercule and someone was with him. Someone Russian." He read a bit, a pained look coming stealing across his face. He looked up at Anya solemnly. "It's your brother. Mercule called him by name."

Anya sighed. "Of course, it is. Which means he knows where we were there."

Luc looked down. "That is all."

"Please tell her to be careful." She paused. "I know she doesn't need to hear it, but it will make me feel better."

"Of course, Anya." He typed a message to Susie. Got a reply and smiled.

"She thanks you for your concern and will be careful."

"Is that all she said?" asked Michel.

"*Non*. But the rest is not your business!"

Michel laughed and Therese slapped Luc on the back, a little too hard as the young demon grimaced. "You tell him!" Chortled Therese. "His love life is slow, so he wants to live vicariously through you now."

"My love life is not slow!" Michel was affronted.

"Oh really? What did you do last night?"

"You know what I did! I stayed in and we played backgammon, while drinking some of Matthew's delightful Scotch."

"Right! Normally, you'd go out and pick up a woman, or three. Last night, no. You stayed in, with me. And you seemed fine with it."

"I was fine with it."

"Yes, and that's the problem."

"It is not a problem!" Michel started swearing at Therese in French, who started bellowing back at him in some language that Anya didn't know.

"All right, you all! Enough!" bellowed Declan. "Jesus, you're a bunch of children!"

The two sat back, Michel frowning and Therese smirking.

"Thank you. Ok, so we can assume at this point that Pavel is aware that Anya knows he's alive and that they are going to up their game. We all definitely need to be more vigilant. You are back to training with Matthew tomorrow, FYI. You and I will start on hand to hand as soon as we get back." This caused Michel and Therese to start catcalling. "Real mature, you two."

"This is fine by me," Anya replied.

"No sneaking out without letting someone know."

"You either."

"Me either."

"Really?"

"Yes, really!"

"We'll keep both of you honest," Therese said. "As neither of you can really be trusted in this." They rolled their eyes at her.

Anya leaned over and kissed his cheek. "Thank you, my love."

He cracked a smile. "It is impossible to stay mad at you."

"Aw, just wait until we've known each other longer. You'll manage it." She winked at him and sat back, as they pulled onto the airstrip where the plane was parked. Michel and Therese got out first, doing a security sweep.

Once they were in the air, Anya pulled Luc aside to speak with him privately. "So, I kind of wanted to talk to you about Susie."

Luc furrowed his brows. "Susie? Why?"

"I think she's lovely, but she is one of the cardinal's top spies. I just want you to be careful." Anya finished weakly.

Luc smiled at her. "Anya, we're just friends. We just talked."

"Well, I think you and I both know that's bullshit." Luc started to speak, and Anya held up her hand. "I am not going to ask you anything, it's none of my business. But it was very obvious to all of us that you two liked each other. And that's fine, that's lovely even. But the cardinal is all of his stories. They aren't exaggerations. His spies are going to be very carefully picked. Just be cautious is all. I'd hate to see you get hurt or caught up in something that you shouldn't be caught up in.

Luc smiled softly at Anya, recognizing that she was trying to protect him because she cared about him. He leaned over and kissed her cheek. "Don't worry, Anya. I promise to be careful." Anya smiled and got up to go sit with Therese. Luc had no sooner breathed a sigh of relief when Declan sat down next to him. *Merde*, thought the young man. He suspected he was about to get the same speech Anya had just given him and he couldn't be mad. It was nice knowing they cared. It was nice to have a family back, he thought.

"When I became a demon, I was still very much in love with my wife. But the minute I met Anaranth's consort, I developed a massive, well I guess it was a crush on her. It didn't last long, less than a year, because then I met a demon that I fell in instant lust with. I felt terrible. I felt I had cheated on my wife with both my crush and the woman that I slept with. There's a lot going on inside of you right now, and everything surrounding Anya and I is not helping. Whatever you are feeling for Anya or Susie or whomever you may take a fancy to is perfectly normal. It's like puberty all over again in some ways. You are, strictly speaking, a young man. Don't worry so much, lad."

Luc just stared at him. "How did you know...how...that I..."

"It's my job to know my people. And it's telegraphed all over your face. We know you, so we can see it. That is something you are going to need to work on when it comes to the outside world. But you never need to hide from us. I could see you sitting over here, over thinking. Anya saw it too. But she's not a demon, and I am. I get it. We're all here for you. If we ever think we need to pull you back, we will."

Luc nodded. "Anya told me to be careful. That Susie was still one of the cardinal's spies."

"She's right. But also, you don't need to be too careful. Do you know what Anya says about family?"

"What?"

"That family is about having a safe place to land when you need one. And she's right about that. We're family. You have a safe place to land." Luc started and Declan winked at him. "Stop thinking so much and enjoy the moment. You have so many years ahead of you, try to enjoy yourself now. You'll find your thing and I think you will eventually find your person too. And if you find a lot of people along the way, that is also all right." He clapped Luc on the shoulder and moved along to talk to Michel and Therese.

****

Declan entered the bedroom quietly, expecting to find Anya asleep. But his mate was sitting up in bed in an old t-shirt, reading. She was rubbing her shoulder where she'd landed too hard on it earlier during their sparring session. She looked up at him and smiled. "Everything in order?"

"Well, if you don't count demons trying to kill us and an open murder investigation my club is tied to, yes. Everything is running like clockwork." She laughed as he stopped to pour them some wine from a bottle sitting on the table by the window. "I thought you'd be sleeping by now. I seem to remember you were tired from having your ass kicked today."

She stuck out her tongue at him. "You're going to stand there and give me shit after I brought up that bottle for us and waited up for you?! Connubial bliss, indeed!"

He walked over to her smiling and handed her the wine. "I'm an absolute wretch."

"You are. But you're my wretch. So, kiss me." He leaned down and kissed her softly on the lips. She sighed and rubbed her cheek against his. "I missed you if you want to know the truth. I couldn't sleep without you being here."

"Aw, you do like me."

"Just a little."

He straightened. "Going to get comfortable. Wait here."

"I'm half naked, where would I possibly go?"

"With you, anything is possible," he said walking into their closet. He was back quickly, grabbing the wine on his way back to the bed. He topped up her glass and took a large swallow of his own, before topping that up as well. He slid into bed and sighed. "Christ, that's nice."

"You have a thing about beds."

"I do. And if you were born in the 13th century, you would too."

"No doubt." He lifted his arm and she wiggled into the nook he'd created, resting her head on his shoulder. "Anything more from Marchand, speaking of murder investigations?"

He texted me earlier to let me know that after examining the footage, the club and by extension, myself, seem to be in the clear."

"Well, that's good, right?"

"It is. But I get the feeling that while he believes we had nothing to do with the murders, he is going to keep an eye on us. He doesn't quite believe we're just normal people. I am pretty sure he thinks we're criminals."

"He thinks we're criminals?"

"Yes. Which is nothing new for us frankly. And it's better that way, it goes a long way to explaining odd habits."

"Why would he think that?"

"Anya, if you were on the outside, looking in, what would you think of us?"

"Ok, good point. Do we need to worry?"

"No. He's a good cop. He does his job, does it well and follows the law. But he knows there is something weird about us."

"Well, he's not wrong. He has good instincts." She looked up at him.

"What?"

"You're thinking something, aren't you? I can tell."

"Yeah...it's...well, I mean, would it be a bad thing to have a cop in our corner?"

Anya sat up. "You have demons on the force though, you told me this."

"Yes. But they're admin mostly. They can smooth out a lot of the behind-the-scenes bureaucratic bullshit. We have a few uniforms and some random plainclothes in Vice because I own nightclubs and that makes sense. But we have to cycle them out every few years. It's a pain. This would be someone we could trust. He could help us and maybe sometimes, we could help him?" He shook his head. "I haven't really thought it through, honestly."

"You want to tell him about us? That could be dangerous."

"I do. And I know. But there's something about him that I feel like we can trust. And it may be better to tell him than to have him poking around. I think he's going to find out regardless."

"Is he..."

"No." Declan shook his head. "He's not demon born, and I am pretty sure he wouldn't want to be one. I am not going to do anything right now about it. It's just something that I'm thinking about." He gently pulled Anya back down to him. "But right at this moment, I want to lay here with you, and just be for a little while."

"Works for me."

"Do you remember this morning, when you said I was more than just the man you loved?"

"I do." She wrapped an arm around his waist.

"Even if I was only the man you loved, that would be more than enough for me. I don't really need anything else."

Anya blinked back tears. "Goddammit Declan! Why do you always have to say the sweetest possible thing?"

"Because I am a miserable wretch."

She leaned up and kissed him. "Ah yes, I forgot." She kissed him again. "Now, let's just lie here and be for a while."

"Perfect."

CHAPTER 28

The next morning found everyone sitting in the kitchen, having breakfast. They were talking about what happened in London and safety protocols going forward.

"We need to be seen." said Anya suddenly.

"I am sorry, what?" said Declan.

"We need to go out. We need to be seen in public."

"Seen by who?" Gwen asked.

"Seen by Liliana's people. We know they're around. We know they're watching us. But if we go out to the theater or to dinner or walks along the Seine; we show we aren't afraid."

"We also open ourselves up to attack," Declan said.

"Yes. We show hubris. We flaunt it in Liliana's face."

"Then she'll get angry, she'll make rash decisions and she will fuck up," said Matthew.

"Exactly! And then we get her! Also, we have the demon killers, so we can take out a few demons along the way. We get to test the weapons out." He paused. "We also get to create a mythology around the weapons."

"Now that is a good idea!" said Michel.

"Should we be letting people know you have them?" asked Gwen.

Anya shrugged. "Why not? They will eventually. There is already talk about them, at least in London. And if Liliana wants them, she'll try to get them. And she will not succeed."

"You aren't anywhere near ready," Declan said.

"No, but I am good enough for this exercise."

"She is a quick study. She's naturally good, and soon she'll be great. For now, she's proficient." said Matthew.

"She needs to be more than proficient."

"These swords kill demons. Being proficient when they won't expect her to be anything will be fine for now."

Matthew cleared his throat. "And you need to train with her."

"Excuse me?"

Matthew put up his hand. "Hear me out. It's not because of a lack of skill. You'll be fighting together, so you need to learn how to actually fight...together."

"He has a point, boss." This was from Donovan.

"Ok, yes. That does make sense." He sighed. "But, to open ourselves up to attack..."

"It's the best way. We need to force them into making mistakes."

Declan threw his hands up. "You're right. I give. You and I will go out on some dates, with our swords. Like any young couple." Dougal snorted at that.

"I am sorry, do you think you two are ever going out completely alone?" Matthew was incredulous.

"They know you guys. You can't be with us. We have to be seen as just blithely doing our thing, alone. As it is, it's going to look like we're just inviting an attack."

"You are," said Therese. "They can think it's arrogance or boredom or just a way to feel out the enemy. But you're right, they need to think you're alone."

Donovan nodded. "Agreed on all counts. But I have plenty of guys I can put out there with you, that you won't know, and neither will any of Liliana's men. But if you think for one minute that one of us is not going to be somewhere nearby, you're crazy."

Anya went to argue but Matthew spoke first. "Anya, agree to the compromise. It's the best you'll get. We are never going to be that far away from you, but we won't be seen by anyone who matters. It's not open for debate."

Anya pressed her lips together in a thin line and nodded her head. "I accept your terms. But I am serious, you can't be seen. And you don't come to our aid unless it looks like we're going to be killed. We can't test the weapons or how well we fight together if one of you is always going to butt in."

"Well lass, there ye go, taking all the fun away." Dougal grumbled and Therese poked him in the ribs.

"Can't you all get those fancy ear bud talking things that they have in the movies to communicate with each other?" This was from Gwen.

Anya looked at her friend and smiled. "That's a great idea, Gwennie!" She turned to Declan. "Can we get those, huh? Can we?"

"It's a good idea, actually. This way we could actually tell you when we need help and when to stay the hell back."

Donovan nodded. "I'll get on it." He looked at Gwen. "I suppose you'll want one too."

"My idea so yeah...duh." She reached up and gave Donovan a kiss on the cheek, then blushed furiously.

Declan rubbed his hands over his face. "Ok, settled. If you're all done making me crazy and stuffing your faces, get the hell to work. Except Gwen of course. I have no control over her." He winked at her.

"I do need to get to work."

"I'll drive you." said Michel. "Donovan can miss you for a bit."

"Sounds good." She got up and hugged Anya. "Text me later?"

"Absolutely. Take care, witch!'

"Take care, demon killer."

After everyone had gone, Matthew looked at Anya. "You have ten minutes to meet me in the practice room. Don't be late." He looked at Declan. "You have two hours and 10 minutes to meet us in the practice room. Don't you be late either." With that, he strode out of the room.

"He's a little fucking scary."

"He really is. Therese says he's the scariest of all of us, and she's positively frightening when she wants to be."

"He's going to put me through it today, isn't he?"

"Oh yes. For sure. But on the bright side, he's going to do the same to me when I get there." He leaned down and gave her a quick kiss. "You'd better go. I wouldn't be late if I were you."

Anya gulped the rest of her coffee, patted Declan on the check and rushed out. Declan picked up his phone and dialed a number. "Anaranth, we need to talk. Now."

***

For the next two hours, Matthew worked Anya harder than she ever remembered working when she was in the circus. He barked orders at her constantly, correcting her stance, and making her repeat movements over and over again. At one point, she got so frustrated she sent one of her own daggers zooming in his direction.

"So, let's take a ten-minute break then, shall we?" he said, examining how close the dagger had come to his head, before landing in the wall.

"Good idea!" she said between clenched teeth.

"Let's get your energy back up before Declan gets here." He tossed her a bottle of water and a protein bar.

"I kind of want to fucking kill you right at this moment."

"I know!" said Matthew, grinning happily. "But you're going to be an expert swords person when I am done with you and that's the thing that matters."

"So, you aren't sorry at all then?"

"Not even a little."

"Asshole," Anya said mildly, sinking to the ground.

"Always." He sat next to her, and she turned to him expectantly. "I don't recall promising to tell you anything personal this time." She just waited, looking at him. He sighed. "Fine. I met Catherine at a summer ball. The family held one every year, but I never went."

"Why not?"

"Not interested. Then I was away fighting. But when I came home, I needed something light. I'd seen a lot of death before being dragged home because my brother had died. Hunting accident because I can see you're about to ask. Anyway, I thought the ball might clear away some of those dark cobwebs in my head."

"Seems reasonable."

"She was surrounded by other young men when I got there. She was talking and laughing. I couldn't take my eyes off her. It's like…" he thought for a moment. "When it's been raining for weeks, and then the weather changes. It was like that first beautiful sunny day."

Declan had come in but stopped at the door. He didn't want to interrupt. He'd heard the story, but he was surprised that his old friend was sharing it with Anya. She'd been right when she said she'd get the man to open up.

"She was beautiful." It was a statement. Anya had no doubt.

"Indeed, she was. A perfect English rose. I stared at her until she noticed me. She smiled, then just walked away from all those young men and came to talk to me. I should have gone over there, that would have been the proper thing to do. But I couldn't seem to make my feet move."

"That sounds kind of great," Anya said quietly, her eyes bright.

"It was. I thought she was my reward for being a good soldier and for now being the heir."

He sounded so sad. Declan couldn't bear to hear anymore; his friend had been so heartbroken over her rejection of him in the end. He cleared his throat, and his friend and mate looked his way, both smiled. "I believe I am right on time."

"Barely." said Matthew dryly. "Are you ready?"

"I was born ready, my friend."

"Wonderful. I had the liberty of having your swords and scabbards brought here."

"I know how to remove swords out of a scabbard, Matthew."

"I know Declan. But how long has it been since you've done it?" Declan looked at him blankly. "Exactly. So, we're going to practice." He rubbed his hands together. "But first, Anya you can have a bit more of a break while I put Declan through some paces."

"Ggggrrreeaaattt."

"Hah! Good luck, honey!"

For the next three hours and then for four more days after that, Matthew set a punishing training schedule. But at the end of the fourth day, he felt they were ready to at least venture out. "Between this and the hand to hand you've been working on; I think you are ready to venture out on your first actual date. Which feels very odd given the fact you two are pretty well mated."

"Well dear, care to go out for dinner and a walk along the Seine?"

Anya fluttered her eyelashes at Declan. "Why sweetheart! I thought you'd never ask!"

***

The first few times they ventured out, nothing happened. They were getting frustrated, but Anya would be lying if she said she didn't enjoy those dates. She liked feeling like any normal couple, eating out, getting coffee, going for walks. But the fourth time they went out, they ended up getting way more than they bargained for.

"I'm sorry, but I find it really hard to believe that you managed to just walk out of the Bastille like that."

"Believe it! Matthew and I did just that."

"I am pretty sure that you're lying to impress me."

"Is it working?"

"Possibly, but I am already a sure thing."

"I'm not taking any chances. But really, the Bastille story is true. Mostly."

"Oh, come on now! If it were true, you two would have had to…" Anya stopped speaking abruptly. She leaned in close to Declan, hand stroking his ear, but turning on the small earpiece at the same time. "We have company."

"I know. We've had them for about five minutes," he said quietly, leaning down to surreptitiously turn her earpiece on as well.

Anya gave him a baleful look. "You didn't want to say anything about it?"

Declan shrugged. "I wasn't sure if they were going to just follow or surround us. They're surrounding us now."

Anya grinned. "Well then, this will be fun."

"Aw, isn't this adorable." A voice came out of the shadows. "The happy couple taking a walk along the Seine."

Declan sighed. "Hello, Laurent."

Laurent stepped into the circle of light from the streetlamp. "Declan, it's been a long time."

"Not long enough."

"Aren't you going to introduce me to your mate?"

Declan sighed. "Wasn't planning on it."

"Tsk tsk. Don't be so rude. I'm Laurent." The demon sketched a fairly ridiculous bow.

"Yeah, I don't care," Anya answered.

"So rude. If you were my woman, I'd teach you some manners."

"If I were your woman, I'd kill you in your sleep."

"Not possible."

"Oh, I bet if I wished really hard, I could make it so."

"Enough!" Laurent gestured and a number of demons came out of wherever they'd been lurking.

"Do you want to kill Laurent or should I?" asked Anya.

"Oh, let me do it! I've been wanting to kill him for over a hundred years."

"Oh, well fine then!" They both reached back, and each pulled out just one of their swords for now.

Laurent laughed. "Swords?! What the fuck do you think you're going to do with those?"

"Why Laurent, I am going to kill you with this sword," Declan said.

"You know he's just going to disappear as soon as you start cutting down the other demons, right?" Michel said in both of their ears.

"Lad, dinnae talk to 'em while they're fighting!" that was from Dougal.

Declan rolled his eyes and made a note to speak to his people about extraneous chatter. And also, to Dougal about that ridiculous brogue.

"Declan, I think you may be getting senile."

Declan smiled. "You think? Maybe you should come closer and find out for yourself." Declan's eyes glowed red and he snarled at the other man.

Laurent grinned back, raised his hand and motioned for the other demons to attack.

"Ready, my love?" asked Declan.

"Born ready, babe!"

The two backed up some, towards the Seine, so as not to be surprised from behind. Demons coming out of the water seemed very unlikely. Two low caste demons came at them quickly and were dispatched to dust quickly. Nothing unusual there. They fought another dozen like this, handling them quite easily.

"Come on Laurent, is this all you have?" Declan called out.

"We were expecting more of a fight," Anya agreed.

Laurent narrowed his eyes and motioned to two demons standing in the shadows to come forward. Each one of them holding a sword. "You're not the only demon with swords."

Matthew, from his hiding place on a docked boat groaned inwardly. "Ok, these are two of Laurent's top swordsmen. They are very good. And they know it."

Declan looked at Anya. "Toy with them a bit?" he asked quietly.

"Oh, yes please!" Anya whispered to him, looking delighted at the prospect. "Well, these two look like they'll give us a good fight," she said loudly, so Laurent would hear.

"Your mate is very arrogant." Laurent commented.

"You can speak directly to me, asshole."

"Mates and consorts are of no consequence."

"I bet that makes you very popular with the Council."

"Well done, Anya, that's a sore spot with him," Matthew said into her ear, causing her to grin widely.

Laurent's eyes narrowed. "What are you two waiting for?" He snapped at his men. "Attack them!"

The two demons moved very fast, and Anya was just able to defend herself from the shorter one's first attack. He smiled menacingly. *Good*, thought Anya, *he'll underestimate me now*. She pretended to struggle a bit as she got her bearings. Matthew was faster than this guy and they had practiced this very thing, so she wasn't concerned. But he was very good with that sword, which was of more concern.

You ok, malysh?

I am. He took me by surprise a bit, but now I am lulling him into a false sense of security.

That's my mate. She felt the warmth of his voice through their bond.

She could see that Declan was also toying with his opponent. She dodged a thrust and rolled under him, popping back onto her feet behind him so he had to flip around.

"Show off!" she heard Matthew say.

He's right. You really are.

I was raised in a circus. I know how to tumble.

Declan sent his opponent's sword careening towards Laurent.

What do you call that, if not showing off? Anya thought at Declan.

I can't let you have all of the fun.

Both men, sensing that Declan and Anya may be a little more adept than originally thought, upped their offensive. Declan and Anya grinned at each other and upped their own game. They let the two demons push them further back towards the river. It was fine, part of their plan after all. They each removed the second sword from its scabbards and moving into offensive positions.

"I can't imagine what you think two swords will accomplish?" Laurent sneered.

"Well, it just looks cooler."

"What looks cooler?" Laurent asked, sneering.

"This!" yelled Declan as he and Anya lifted swords and using the element of surprise, moved forward towards their opponents. Acting quickly, they lunged and in perfect unison, removed two heads from two bodies. There was a faint yellow essence that was released from the bodies of both demons as they dropped like stones and the heads rolled towards Laurent. Two sets of eyes regarded him, opened wide in both surprise and terror. Laurent went pale. His demons were most assuredly dead.

Well, thought Matthew, *now we know the swords actually do work*. But there was no joy there. This was going to put a target on his two friends. On some level, they would always be in danger.

Laurent's face was white, but his eyes glowed red. "What the fuck?! What...what are those?"

"I think you know what these are."

"They're supposed to be a myth. A legend." Laurent was fast losing control of his human form, the beast wanted out. It was angry, but even worse, it was frightened, and it wanted to subdue the threat.

"Matthew!" Declan shouted into his earpiece. "Get over here and get Anya out of the way!"

"Declan?" asked Anya.

"I am going to need to turn to deal with him. He's a shit but I won't stab him while he's a beast unless he attacks you."

"I don't need Matthew..."

"You do need Matthew...don't argue with me about this! Laurent is faster than you in beast form, and much more dangerous. I need to deal with it, and I can't be worried he's going to go for your throat."

Matthew stopped short next to Anya. "He's right. He'd be on you quicker than you could thrust that sword. Don't be a pain in the ass about this."

Anya glared at both men, but sheathed her swords, while Matthew grabbed Declan's swords. Declan shrugged off his scabbard, jacket and toed off his shoes. Matthew pulled Anya back as far as he thought she was willing to go and blocked her from Laurent's line of vision. Dougal showed up just then and placed himself behind her.

"Did you all just decide to come tonight?"

"Me, Dougal and Therese only. Therese had a feeling."

"Where is she?"

"Here!" Therese buffered Anya on the outside. Her right side being next to the water. "We're out in the open, this is a very bad idea."

"I know. But it can't be helped. Luckily, this section of the river is fairly quiet this time of night," said Matthew.

"Matthew. I need you to shift so I can see."

"Anya…"

"Shift to the goddamned left just a bit so I can watch my mate fight this fucker or so help me I will run you through, you bastard!" Matthew wisely shifted a bit to the left. One of Declan's swords in his hand.

Declan faced Laurent who was still struggling for control. "Laurent. Don't do this. Walk away. Walk away now We're out in the open for chrissakes!"

"You killed my two best men! You have those…swords! I am going to tear you, your mate and your fucking lackeys apart."

Declan started to growl as his eyes glowed brighter and his talons extended. "That is never going to happen!" his voice having gone gravelly. In a flash, both beasts were present and circling each other.

"Laurent's beast is just as ugly as his human form," remarked Therese.

"Declan is bigger," Anya said.

"Bigger doesn't mean better," said Matthew.

"Says you," joked Therese as Anya snorted.

Matthew looked at Anya. "You have absolutely no doubt he'll win, don't you?"

She looked at him, surprise in her eyes. "Of course. I have absolute faith in my mate. Always. Just like I have absolute faith in all of you."

Matthew looked at her another moment before turning back to the two beasts. Declan wasn't going to attack first, he was waiting. Laurent's beast was trying to goad him, but Declan wasn't taking the bait. His relaxed attitude was pissing Laurent off though and soon, he lunged for Declan, who moved out of the way swiftly. Declan reached out a claw and drew it down Laurent's side. Laurent howled and jumped at Declan, landing on him this time. The two were locked in combat, moving as one and moving so quickly, it was hard for Anya to follow. "Declan is still a bit out of practice," said Dougal.

"Years of prolonged peace will do that. He doesn't shift much anymore," remarked Matthew.

Anya was shaking her head. "He should have been sparring with you all, not me."

"Oh don't worry. He will be from now on," Matthew said grimly.

The two beasts were swiping back and forth but missing each other by a hair. Until Laurent managed to get a hold of Declan and used his talons to run a long, angry gash down his back.

Declan! Anya screamed through their bond. She felt the acknowledgement, but he couldn't really talk to her in that form. Still, it was good to know he could recognize the bond when he was in beast form. Laurent had the upper hand and Declan was trying to throw him off. He finally managed to lift a foot and set it down, claw first, into Laurent's foot. Laurent leapt away, tripping and going down on his stomach. Laurent growled and started to rise, but at once there were two swords at his throat. "Don't do it," said Matthew calmly. Laurent growled low.

"That doesn't work with any of us," said Anya. "I do not want to have to kill you." She looked at him. She put the tip of her blade to his throat. "I know you can understand my intent, if not my words."

"Laurent! Enough!" yelled Matthew. "Turn back!" At the command in Matthew's voice, Laurent turned back. "In pack order, I am higher than he is. His beast has to follow that command," Matthew said by way of explanation at Anya's amazed look.

"Why didn't you just compel him?" asked Therese.

"If that hadn't worked, I would have."

"You can compel people?" asked Anya.

"I can. I don't though."

Laurent looked up, the gash in his side already starting to heal. He crawled over to where his coat was, stood and put it on. "This isn't over. And when I am done, everyone will know you have those swords."

"That was the idea, you asshole." said Declan limping over, naked. Dougal tossed him a coat he had over his own shoulder and Declan put it on. "You spread this far and wide. And you remember that we didn't kill you when we could have."

"You'll have targets on your back!"

"Eh. Nothing new there." Declan shrugged.

"You are going to die for this."

"I don't think so, Laurent. Now, I suggest you go."

Laurent threw them one more hate filled look and staggered off.

"Are you ok?" Anya said, moving over to Declan's side.

"Yes. It hurt like a bitch when he got me, but it's healing." He gave her a hard, quick kiss.

"Well, that worked out the way we planned. More or less."

"I think Liliana thought we might have the swords, and this was a way to prove it," said Anya.

"I think you're right," Matthew agreed. "Ok, home now. That's enough for tonight."

A voice called out of the shadows. "Just one moment, please." Out stepped Marchand. "Maybe you'd all like to tell me what the hell is going on here. Who, excuse me, what exactly are you people?"

"Oh, fuck," muttered Dougal. But Declan grinned.

"Detective Marchand, good evening. Glad you happened by." He had suspected the detective may have been following them and he was glad to see his instincts were correct. "This is going to make things a bit easier to explain. Now that you've seen it with your own eyes."

"So, you plan to tell me what's going on then?"

"Oh yes, I hope you have the time though. Long story."

"I'm off duty. I have all night."

"Wonderful! Let's all go back to the house then. I'd rather have clothing on for this."

"Of course. After you."

CHAPTER 29

Two hours later, the group looked at Marchand expectantly. Declan and Matthew had done their best to try and explain things to the detective, with a bit of an assist from Anya. Dougal and Therese stayed quiet, which was harder for Dougal than for Therese.

The detective got up, walked over to the window, and started muttering to himself in Russian.

"Detective," Anya interjected. "You know I can understand you, right?"

Marchand looked chagrined. "I hadn't thought of it actually. It's my go to when I am frustrated about something." His mother had made sure that her children were fluent in Russian, French and English. His father didn't understand why they had to speak all three languages, but Sonya Marchand had her way there.

"What's he saying?" asked Declan.

"Mostly, he's calling all of us a bunch of assholes and wondering what other fictional monsters may be real. And the answer to that, is none." She paused. "That we know of."

Declan shrugged. "I've been called an asshole before."

Anya smiled. "Good. Because you got the brunt of the insults."

Declan grinned back at her. "I'd expect nothing less."

Marchand exploded. "Do you all think this is fucking funny?!"

"Petyr," said Declan, using the man's first name. "It's just our lives. Funny or not, it is what it is. You are nowhere near the first person to call me names. You will not be the last. Things are a bit dangerous right now. Sometimes, all we can do is laugh."

"Dangerous? Does that have to do with what I saw tonight? And does this connect to my murder case?"

"Yes, and probably. Though I don't know what the end game there was exactly."

Marchand sat back down and sighed. 'Explain, please."

"Wait," said Anya. "Let's get some coffee and maybe some snacks."

"I'd rather have a drink," said Marchand.

Matthew smiled, got up and poured out a very generous serving of Scotch and set it down in front of the detective."

"Thank you." Marchand picked it up and downed it in one shot.

"That's a Russian for you!" said Anya proudly. "But I still want something to eat."

Therese stood. "Let me go. I don't need to hear the story again." She left the room quickly with Dougal following a moment later. Matthew got the bottle of Scotch, 3 more glasses and poured everyone a drink.

Marchand rubbed his hands over his face and said, "Ok now, tell me what specifically is going on with you all."

"It's also a long story. And I have to give you the backstory on mates and consorts and demon politics."

"Demons are political?"

"You have no fucking idea."

Marchand swore in French and then sighed again. "Ok, fine. Tell me what you think I need to know."

"I'll take this one", said Anya. "When he gets frustrated, I can switch to Russian."

Anya broke down the whole thing, how they met, and the series of events that had led them to what Marchand had seen that night. She moved between English and Russian seamlessly when she sensed his frustration level rising. The Russian seemed to calm him some, and Anya guessed that his mother had spoken Russian to her children often.

"*Merde!*" said Marchand. "So, my guess would be that the murder of those two young men was done simply as a red herring. And to irritate you. If you're busy dealing with the police, then you aren't paying attention to what you really need to be paying attention to. Had you gotten a different detective, this could have taken up more of your time."

"I think we lucked out there," said Declan quietly.

"You did. I am much more circumspect, than many of my coworkers. Can I assume the stomach flu was…"

"We were still recovering from me being stabbed with that magicked dagger."

Marchand nodded. "So, I am never going to get justice for those men?"

"After everything we've told you tonight, everything you've seen, that is the thing you are concerned with?"

"Yes. Because it's the thing I am supposed to be able to control. My investigation. If this was done by demons, then this will be a cold case and their parents will get no closure from knowing I put those people behind bars."

Declan responded around the sudden lump in his throat. This was a good man, and they were now putting him in danger. "Well, I can promise to get the person or persons who did this, but they cannot go to jail. It would expose us in a way we aren't ready for, and that would cause mass hysteria. Most humans don't know about us."

"But," said Matthew, noting Marchand's dour look. "We can actually provide you with two bodies."

"The men from tonight?" asked the detective.

"Yes. That would be a kind of closure." He leaned forward to snag the last spinach pinwheel and got a death glare from Anya. He winked and put it in his mouth whole.

"You bastard. You knew I wanted that."

"Gotta be quicker, Orlov." She narrowed her eyes at him but said nothing else.

"But," asked Marchand, bringing them back to the subject at hand. "How do I explain how or where I found them?"

"I could help there. Where are the bodies now?" Declan asked.

"Brimstone. Cold storage. No idea how they'll decompose," said Therese, she and Dougal having come back into the room at some point.

"They look like any other dead body." Dougal put in. "Well, mostly. They're a wee bit paler and there's a bit of a smell, you ken? But we could explain that away somehow."

"Most humans do smell when they're dead, Dougal." Therese rolled her eyes at him.

"Can you explain away the fact that they're missing their heads?" asked Anya.

"Ah shit, that is problematic. Do we have the heads?" asked Matthew.

"We do." Dougal nodded.

"Mob hit," said Declan.

"I'm sorry?" asked Marchand.

"We send around the story that these two were working for the mob. They got their hands on a new experimental drug making the rounds, went batshit crazy and killed those two men. When their bosses found out about it, they were pissed. It's heat they don't need, so they cut their heads off, and delivered them to the station as a kind of 'gift' to the police."

"Does Paris even have organized crime?" asked Anya.

"Of course it does. Me."

"You?" Anya raised an eyebrow at Declan.

"Yes. Well, everything that happens that people think is a mafia thing is really just Demon business. I got rid of all the real organized crime years ago. But it's helpful to have people think it's still here. You can explain away a lot of things by saying it's because of organized crime."

Marchand narrowed his eyes. "At some point, I am going to want to discuss this further."

"Of course, detective. I am at your service."

"I think I may be at yours, actually. But what about this experimental drug? What is that about?" "There's a drug or potion that they've been giving the demons that they're turning illegally. It makes them as strong as a demon at least five times their age. It wears off eventually though."

"Naturally. You have had run-ins with...Christ...demons on this drug?"

"Yes. One tried to choke me to death."

"Where is he now?"

"When demons are young, they can still die." This was from Declan. Marchand looked at him. "Really?"

"Yes. I protect my people, and no one comes to this city, threatens it, harms my mate and lives to tell the tale."

The two men stared at each other for a moment, until Marchand nodded. They understood each other and deep down, Declan believed that Petyr Marchand would do the same for someone he loved. "It's not an elegant solution, and it won't satisfy my need to catch these men. But it will make their parents feel better and they can take their sons home. So, I am amenable to this. I am on duty beginning at noon tomorrow."

"We'll have the bodies delivered at about 12:30 then," said Mathew.

"Can you do it without being seen?"

"That's a rhetorical question, right?" Matthew asked.

Marchand laughed. "I suppose it is, yes." He yawned. "And now, I think I have had enough information for one night. I am going home."

Anya walked him to the door. "You're handling this well, Detective."

He shrugged. "I saw it with my own eyes. I would be a fool to try and rationalize it away. That said, I do not think it has hit me yet. What I do recognize is that you two love each other very much, and that you are in danger. And that you are all very capable of handling yourselves. It makes my job both harder and easier. And it explains a lot of very odd things over the last several years."

Anya smiled at him. "You're a good man." Marchand shook his head. "No. You are. You aren't letting your ego about the murders get in the way of trying to give their families some peace. I know Russian stubbornness, and I know that could not have been an easy decision for you."

"Do you want to know why I chose to join the Police?"

"I do."

He spoke in Russian. It was easier to say it in his mother's language. "When I was twelve, my sixteen year old sister was brutally murdered. It turned out that she had been raped beforehand, repeatedly and likely by more than one person. Then they killed her and dumped her body near a ravine. A ravine that was three miles from our home, it turns out." Tears pricked Anya's eyes. "They never caught the people who did it. To this day, it is an unsolved crime. And every day I see what that has done to my parents. It's a wound that can never heal. If I can save two families from that, I will. If it makes me a shitty cop, I am ok with that. Because at least those families will have some closure. And I trust Declan to make good on his promise to make the real killers pay."

She cleared her throat and answered in English. "He will. We both will. *Ya obeshchayu.*" I promise. She leaned up and kissed his cheek, surprising him. "Good night, Detective."

"*Dobroy nochi, Anya,*" he said, walking out the door and into what was left of the night.

***

Marchand was in the shower the next morning when the whole thing hit him like a freight train. He actually had to sit down on the floor of his shower, while the water ran over him, his head in his hands.

"Fucking Hell!" he said to the wall. "Demons?! DEMONS?!" Who the fuck would have suspected that demons existed? And that they weren't evil.

Yes, they skirted the law, but as far as Paris was concerned, the city had seen a decrease in not only gangland style crimes, and the murder rates for a large city were low. He suspected that Declan had something to do with that. But what else did they have their hand in throughout the city? Or the country for that matter? He decided to do some research on the city's crime rates for the last couple of hundred years.

When he got out of the shower, he saw a text from Anya Orlov. *Detective, I have some information I'd like to send you re: history of demons. A short history that I've been working on in my spare time. Would you be willing to entrust me with your personal email address?*

Spare time? He didn't think Anya Orlov actually had any time to spare lately. Of course she couldn't send it to his work address. Though if there weren't demons somewhere on the force, he'd be surprised. He sent along the address and added *Thank you. I appreciate this. It should help me wrap my head around it.*

I figured as much. Information is always what helps me as well. Have a good day.

He smiled to himself. Being human, Anya would understand the need to sit with this for a bit, and to learn as much as he could. He really wanted to call his mother and talk to her about this, but he wasn't sure how she'd take it. Ten minutes later, his phone rang. The ringtone told him that it was his mother. He smiled. Somehow she'd known he needed to talk to her.

"*Privet, mama,*" he said into the phone.

"*Privet moy lyubimyy syn.*" He heard his mother's raspy voice. His heart still clutched when she called him her beloved son. She'd only started doing it after Nat had been killed. She continued in English, which she preferred to French for some reason. "I had a dream about you last night. Are you well?"

"I am. Very well. I just had a very bizarre night." Did he bother her with this? He still liked to bounce problems off of her. She enjoyed it too, she said it took her mind off of things it was better not to think about. "Mom, are there any old Russian folktales about demons by any chance?"

"You mean biblical demons?"

"No. Actual demons on Earth, just you know...being demons and living among us." He winced. That was a bit ham handed.

He heard his mother's sharp intake of breath and knew his instinct to ask her had been the correct one. "Petyr, why are you asking me this?"

"Mom, do you know something you aren't telling me?"

"First, I need to know why you are asking me. Are you safe?"

"Very safe. I am in no danger." Though, he wondered if that was really true now. He shrugged off the thought for the moment, there was no point in worrying his mother.

"Then I would tell you that yes, I know what you are talking about."

"But they're not evil?"

"They can be dangerous, but they are not inherently evil in and of themselves." He'd always been able to talk to his mother about the most outlandish ideas like they were commonplace. "Petyr, have you met a demon?"

"I have met a handful actually. As part of an investigation, though they aren't suspects. Do you think you met any?"

"There were some in the village that I grew up in supposedly. While we never knew for sure, we all just kind of accepted the stories. They offered protection for our little village. One of them knew I wanted to go to school abroad and helped me."

Marchand was gob smacked by this bit of information. "Mom! How come you never said anything?"

"How would I explain something like this? I had to be careful even with stories I told you. Your father is a very pragmatic Frenchman. He thought fairytales were silly. I didn't agree, but I tried to sneak one in every so often."

"I feel like there is so much about you that I don't know. One day soon, we are going to have a long chat."

"As long as you bring those macarons I like, I will tell you anything you need to know."

"It's a deal!" Talking to his mother always made him feel better.

***

At exactly 12:32 that day, Marchand was alerted that two bodies had been dumped at the back of the station with a note for him pinned to one of the jackets. The note was addressed to him, one of the officers said. There were two decapitated bodies, but the heads were in bowling bags next to them. *Nice touch* thought Marchand. He spent the next several hours clearing up the mess, talking around a few of the inconsistencies that popped up and finally, video conferencing with the parents to let them know that the men who had murdered their sons had been found and wouldn't be hurting anyone again. He felt a twinge lying to them, but they would be able to get closure and that had to be enough this time. The parents would be coming to pick up their boys and take them home. There was never going to be a happy ending here, but he was able to give these people some peace.

All in all, Marchand considered it a good day's work.

***

Declan looked down at his phone and smiled. "Marchand says the decapitated bodies were the talk of the office today. He also thanked us for helping him put the parents' minds at rest."

Matthew looked up from his laptop. "He's a good man."

"He is," agreed Declan.

"We've completely fucked his life with this whole thing."

"We have." Declan started drumming his fingers on his desk. "I thought it might be good to have an actual detective on our side. Now that it's happened, I just kind of feel a bit shitty about it. I didn't expect to actually like him as a person."

"It is a good idea though."

"Yes, it is. I am very careful about the humans I trust, for obvious reasons, and I do trust him. But I am hoping he doesn't come to resent us."

"Stop borrowing trouble, we have enough of that right now."

"You are correct there. Do we...."

"Yes, we have someone on him. Donovan took care of it this morning. And we'll cycle regularly because he's bound to notice a tail. Honestly, he'll probably figure it out regardless of how often we change it up."

Declan smiled at his friend gratefully. "Thank you. And yes, he is. I expect I'll get a call about it."

Matthew shrugged. "Assuredly."

"What are you doing? You look annoyed."

"Art auction. I am bidding on a piece, and someone keeps trying to outbid me. It's pissing me off." He paused. "Oh fuck you! Here! Here's a bid for you...top this!" He typed furiously. "Hah! It's mine!"

Declan raised an eyebrow at him. "Do I want to know?"

"You don't. It was obscenely expensive."

"Do you want the painting that much, or did you just want to win the auction?"

"I do want the painting. But really, I wanted to win the auction. I admit it."

"Thought as much."

Matthew shut down the laptop and closed it with a satisfied sigh. "I am off to check in on some of our people. 8pm, your house."

"For what?"

"Your fighting was a bit sloppy last night. You need to be sparring with another demon. It will help if...when...you take beast form."

"Are you saying I've let myself go?"

"I am saying that while it's helpful for Anya to spar with you, it will be more helpful for you to spar with me or Michel. So, we're doing that." Declan glared at him. "You know I'm right, my friend."

Declan sighed. "You're right. I could tell Laurent was getting the upper hand."

"He's a brawler by nature. You have let yourself, well not get soft, but you are so busy with business that you don't train as much as you should. Anya trains more than you. She's sparring with Therese this morning, hand to hand. And she practices with her knives every day. She's started doing that with her swords as well."

"Not to mention the work she's doing for the Council, the quick history of demons and doing research for a new book. Christ, she makes me look like a lazy bastard."

"She's fairly amazing. You're lucky I didn't see her first." Declan narrowed his eyes and growled low at his friend, who burst out laughing. "Declan! You know I'm teasing you."

"I do wonder. You two are very close."

"She's forced herself on me as a friend, I never stood a chance against the onslaught."

"You and me both."

"You are far from lazy though. Also, she's much like a new demon; all energy and adrenaline. Luc is the same. He was on the treadmill in the gym last night, while he typed research notes onto his tablet. It made me nauseated just watching him."

"Does he sleep?"

"Not much."

"That'll regulate at some point." Declan said.

"He's determined to graduate early."

"Why?"

"Get this, so he can start on his master's sooner." Matthew shrugged.

"Are you kidding me?"

"Nope. I pulled him off the treadmill to do some training and he's very good. He actually could be yours and Anya's son. It's a little spooky."

"Well, let's keep an eye on him. And Anya. I don't want them to get burned out."

Matthew gave him a mock salute and left Declan's office. Declan felt a mental stroke and knew his mate was checking in. *Malysh?*

How is my demon this afternoon?

Missing his mate.

He felt her laugh down their bond. *I hear you.*

I heard that Therese was putting you through your paces today.

She was. I am exhausted and a bit bruised. She did not hold back. But it was beneficial, and I learned a lot.

Was she too hard on you? He didn't want Anya hurt.

Stop worrying old man, she needs to be hard on me. I'm fine. When are you home?

Matthew and I are doing some training at 8, then I am yours for the rest of the night.

Good. I have plans for you. Anya sent him an image of what she had in mind.

I am so delighted that I get to run a staff meeting with a raging hard on.

She laughed out loud this time. *Sorry, not sorry. Go to your meeting, demon. Love you.*

Love you, knife thrower.

There was no denying that they were in danger right now, but he wouldn't trade having Anya in his life for the world. He hadn't realized how bored and tired he'd felt until she had stormed into his life and demanded his attention. She had given him everything but hadn't asked for anything in return. He wanted to do something special for her, he'd think on it. He went off to his staff meeting humming a tune, a spring in his step and his heart, full of love for a certain knife wielding redhead.

CHAPTER 30

"But why are they coming?" asked Declan.

"Natalia says they haven't been to Paris in a while. They want to visit, and she has something to talk to me about."

"What?"

"I have no idea. But I don't think we're going to like it."

"Are they coming here?" Declan seemed horrified by the idea. Their house was nice enough for Council to visit, but them actually visiting filled him with dread.

"Good lord, no! They've taken a hotel suite. Or, I should say an entire floor of a hotel."

"What! Why?"

"Because they travel like they're the Tsar and Tsarina. It's ridiculous. They have this huge entourage."

Declan rolled his eyes. "They aren't the only ones, but I am always kind of flummoxed by it."

"Says the man with a private plane."

"Two actually. And I use those for business mostly. It's a means to an end."

She leaned over and gave him a quick kiss. "I am totally on board with a private plane, don't get me wrong. Flying commercial is highly overrated. I am just teasing you."

He nipped her bottom lip. "Wench!"

"You know it. Anyway, I told them that yes, we'd be over for dinner tonight."

Declan made a face. "I have to work."

"No. You do not. You just don't want to go. Why?"

"I don't know. No, I do. It feels like we're being summoned by the Council somehow. And that bothers me."

"We are. I don't fool myself, Declan. I am a tool to Natalia, that's all. A means to an end. But I have questions for her, and I want answers. She's been bleating on for years about my destiny. Well, how did *she* know about my destiny? And how does it help her? It's like she's holding cards that I don't even know exist. I don't like it. And the longer I think about it, the more aggrieved I feel about it.

"She hopes to gain more power for Vlad and herself. She thinks you can help with that."

Anya scoffed. "Ridiculous!"

"Not really, *malysh*. The swords make us powerful and dangerous. You are obviously powerful, with the gold eyes and you being able to sense when people are demons. Your knife skills for a human were scary good. "

"Has there never been a consort that could do that?"

"Not in my lifetime. And certainly no human I have ever run across has had the ability."

"Ok, fine. But how does she know about me? It's very odd."

"I do agree there. However you got here, whatever hand Natalia had in it, she's invested in you, and she wants payment."

"You make it sound ominous."

"I don't mean to, but she is fully expecting you to dance to her tune."

"Well, won't she be surprised then, when it doesn't happen."

***

"Dinner was wonderful Natalia," Declan said as they sat in the living room of the hotel suite.

"*Spasibo*, Declan. The hotel is very good about letting us bring and use our own chef."

Oh good Lord! Thought Anya to Declan.

Now, now, she is family, dear heart. Anya hid her snort of laughter in her wine glass. She took a quick drink and looked at Natalia. The woman was as tall as Anya. But she had dark, almost black hair with silver running through it. She'd started turning silver at a young age and had opted to keep it even when she had stopped aging. Only Anya seemed to have inherited red hair and violet eyes, from a distant long ago relative, most likely. Natalia's aquiline nose and deep blue eyes was the same blue her father and Pavel had. She and Anya had the same mouth, but that was the only feature the two had in common. And even then, there were differences. While Anya's mouth was softer and more prone to laughter, Natalia's was hard. The woman barely smiled, and Anya wasn't sure she'd ever heard her truly laugh. She favored a much more old-fashioned form of dress, as did Vladimir. Sartorially, they both looked like something out of the early twentieth century. Despite being dressed up in a suit and a deep green silk sheath dress, Anya and Declan looked sorely underdressed next to the older couple.

"So, Natalia...why are you here? And why have you asked to see us?"

Natalia started at the bluntness of the question. "Annechka," said Natalia, setting Anya's teeth on edge. "Don't be rude."

"Natalia, you two rarely leave Eastern Europe unless it's for a Council meeting. And that's not leaving so much as just stepping through the door." Anya was referring to the portals that brought all Council members, staff, and visitors to the main Council house on the outskirts of Paris. "You must have a reason to have done so." Her voice held an edge.

Annie, try and stay calm. I know you're irritated, but it won't do any good to let her see that you're irritated.

You're right. But she's talking to me like a child.

To her, you're acting like one.

The fuck?

Think about it from her perspective. You sound almost petulant. She's quite a bit older than both of us. I sound like a child to her.

Anya almost rolled her eyes, nodding slightly instead to show she was taking it in.

Natalia looked to be having a similar conversation with Vlad. She sighed, took a sip of wine, and spoke. "You are correct. I do have a reason. We have heard a rumor that you both have the demon killers in your possession. Is this true?"

"It is," asserted Declan.

"And you have used them. And they work?" She sounded almost too eager for the answer.

"Yes, they work." Anya was not sure she liked where this was going.

"So, you could use them on an enemy."

"We have used them on an enemy. But we would need a compelling reason to do so. A Council coup," Declan sat forward, his voice hard. "Is not a compelling reason."

Vlad frowned. "We were not suggesting that."

"No? We are also not going to be your assassins," Anya said tersely. "We will not use them to wage personal vendettas."

"You would not use them on Liliana?" asked Natalia coyly.

I fucking knew it!

Calm, my love, calm. She wants Liliana dead because if she dies, Francois will likely step down from the Council. She and Vlad would be the most powerful couple on the Council.

They aren't the oldest.

No, but they control a lot of territory, and they are formidable. They have enough clout to do it.

And with a hole in the Council, we'd likely have to step up and she figures she and Vlad would have two powerful allies.

Exactly.

The bitch. Out loud she said, "Exactly how much do you know about what's been going on?"

"Enough."

"That doesn't answer my question."

"I know that Liliana is trying to harm the both of you because you have the swords."

Anya suspected she knew more. "That's all you know?" Natalia nodded. "How did you find out about the swords?"

"The same way the entire Council did. You used them."

"Well, not the entire Council. Anaranth knew I had them." Vlad made a face. He didn't like that. "And how did you know it's Liliana?"

"We know what she was like at Anya's presentation. Who else could it be?"

"That's very weak, Natalia."

"We've been keeping a close eye on her for a long while now. She's become more eccentric these last few years. While she's not an enemy, per se, it is good business to keep an eye on them," Natalia said.

Do you believe her? Asked Declan.

Not a chance.

Me neither. I think that Natalia has been using you.

I think you're right. Still, not all bad. I have you.

Declan smiled and stroked a finger across the nape of her neck, sending shivers down her spine. "Natalia, what exactly is your interest in Francois and Liliana?"

Vlad answered. "They are a powerful couple and they have been for many years. But Francois appears to be losing steam, and this seems to have caused Liliana's behavior to become a bit erratic."

This was true enough, thought Declan. "Yes. But what does this have to do with you, directly." He paused, narrowing his eyes some at the couple. "Do you have your sights set on Western Europe? Because I need to tell you that I will not let that happen." He felt Anya's surprise at his statement, but she stayed quiet.

"Declan, I thought you had no interest in Council politics." There was an edge to Vlad's voice.

"Things change. And times change. I have a consort now; I am beginning to come into my full power and it's time I started thinking about the future."

"Are you looking to depose Francois then?"

"Not as of yet. But as you say, he does seem to be tiring, losing steam. You aren't the only one watching him." Declan had no real interest in the Council, though he knew it was inevitable. But these two didn't need to know that.

Natalia cleared her throat. "It would be...uh...wonderful to have you on the Council. But Anya has not been your consort long. She still needs some grooming."

"Pardon me?" asked Anya. Her voice had a dangerous edge to it.

"You do not understand the politics of the Council. Nor do you have the polish that the other consorts do."

"Oh, so you think to polish me up, do you?"

"Declan, perhaps you could explain..."

Declan leaned back on the couch. "Oh no," he waved his hand. "You're doing just fine Natalia. Go right ahead." *Put your foot in it even more, you old cow,* he thought to himself.

"Yes Anya, I would help groom you to be a worthy consort. Much will expected of you if you are going to be of assistance to your mate. There are things you need to learn."

"So, you'd like to make me in your own image?"

"Well, you could do worse."

"So, you'd have a built-in ally on the Council. You don't want me there yet because you don't feel I'd be of help to *you* right now, this has nothing to do with Declan."

"Annechka..."

"I hate that nickname. Please stop using it."

Natalia started at that. Anya had never pushed back before. "Of course Anya. I had no idea it bothered you so much."

"Now you do."

"Just so. Anya," she tried again. "Vlad and I have been around a lot longer than Declan..."

"Natalia, Vlad has. You have not. And you would do well to remember that." Declan had to stifle a laugh at this by taking a sip of brandy.

"You are indeed correct. My apologies." She was smooth, Declan thought, but she was rattled.

They want Western Europe. And they want us to help them get it. Anya mused to Declan.

Yes, they do. And no, we are not going to help them get it.

But you want her to think you want it.

Right again. Vlad will try and convince me that I am not ready. Maybe he will even offer to...groom me. She felt the amusement in his voice at that.

Vlad took over. "Anya, your grandmother means no disrespect. But you are young, and she has been a consort for a long while."

"That is true. Also, I think it's time we dropped the 'grandmother' nonsense. She's not my grandmother. And to keep up the pretense just seems silly."

"That I do wholeheartedly agree with," said Natalia. "It does make me feel old in a way I don't like."

You are old in a way you do not like. Declan had to hold back a snort at Anya's thought.

"Fine," said Vlad tightly. "Natalia then would be a good mentor for you."

Declan stood. "That's enough. Anya is attempting a calm that I am no longer feeling. You will never bring this up to my mate again. She does not need to be groomed. Nor does she need a mentor. Anya is perfect, as she is. The time for you Natalia to have helped her is at an end." The reference to Anya's rough childhood and Natalia's neglect hit its mark. Natalia visibly paled. "Thanks to her childhood, she is quite adept at navigating piranha infested waters." He paused. "So, perhaps you did help her after all."

He let that sit a moment before continuing. "To insult her, is to insult me and I do not advise it. Don't cross me if you ever want my support." He'd never support them, but they didn't need to know that.

Natalia had the grace to look embarrassed. They'd overstepped and now they knew it. They had underestimated Declan and Anya and would not do again. To them, it was political. But the personal is often political.

"Anya, I simply want you to be your best. I see now that I need not worry about you."

"No, you don't," replied Anya stiffly. She was furious, but she was also hurt. But she'd be damned if she were going to let Natalia see that. "I'm a bit tired, so I think it's time to call it a night."

"Of course dear, whatever you want."

***

The minute they walked into their bedroom, Anya pivoted and slammed Declan against the door. "Oooph! Anya…"

"Shut up!" she said between clenched teeth. She peeled off his jacket, undid his tie and ripped open his shirt. She raked her nails down chest, causing him to growl low in his throat. She then pulled her sheath dress off and was standing before him in just a bra, panties, and a pair of shoes. "God. I am so pissed off!" She pinched his nipple and he yelped in surprise.

"At me?"

"Why the fuck would I be pissed off at you?"

"I don't know, but you're being aggressive right now, so I thought it might be me."

She yanked at his belt as he stepped out of his shoes and toed off his socks. "I am not mad at you. I am trying to get you naked. Why is your belt so stupid?" She let out a frustrated yell.

He took her hands in his, bringing them to his lips and kissing her fingers. "Let me, *malysh*," he said softly.

"Well, hurry!" She undid her bra and took off her panties as he undid his belt and slid his pants down and off. She leaned against him, taking him in one hand, and nipping his shoulders lightly. His hands came around to cup her ass, pressing her more firmly to him. He took her face in his hands and kissed her softly.

"No! No, not like that. I do not want soft from you right now."

He smiled and nipped her lip. "Better?"

"Yes! More!" She gripped him more insistently. He moved her so they switched places with her back against the door. He took her mouth in a hard, rough kiss. She moaned low in her throat and her arms came around him, pulling him closer. "More!"

He extended his talons some and flicked her nipples and she bucked against him. He almost came right then. "Is this what you want? You want it rough tonight? Hmmm?"

"God, yes, please!" She wrapped one leg around him, the stiletto digging into his ass some. He liked it, he had to admit, liked how it felt to be marked by her, this amazing woman. He lifted her other leg so it also wrapped him around the same way. He supported her, but she was strong enough to keep herself up now. He stroked his talons down one side of her, retracted the other set and plunged two fingers inside of her. She started moving against him, moaning low in her throat. He whispered to her in French, all the things he wanted to do to her and with her and she bit his shoulder making him groan. He took his thumb and pressed her clit and she screamed. He pulled back and while she was still shaking from the first orgasm, drove into her. She screamed his name. "Is this good, *malysh*? Is that what you want?"

"Yes. God Declan, please.."

"I don't want to hurt…"

"Hard. Give me everything you have."

He roared and slammed into her and the two heard a crack but ignored it. He kept pulling back and slamming into her, her legs wound around him tighter. Both grunting and moaning until finally they both came on another yell and another loud crack.

She kissed him soundly, but lovingly. "I love you. That was just what the Doctor ordered." She set her feet on the floor but when she went to pull away, he drew her closer, kissing the top of her head.

"You feel free to use me anytime. I love you too." She sighed and stroked his back.

"Am I right in thinking we broke the bedroom door?"

Declan looked up and at the door. "Christ. Yeah, we've destroyed the door. There is one large crack from top to bottom and several more branching out from there. If you hadn't come, it'd be off its hinges."

"Oh, just me?"

He laughed. "Ok, both of us."

She turned and looked. "Shit. I think we're going to go through a lot of doors though."

"God, I hope so."

CHAPTER 31

The reaction to the use of the swords was not completely unexpected, but they underestimated the breadth of it. They had all felt that there would be some challenges, but the number of demons who crawled out of the woodwork to test them was beyond what they all were prepared for. And it was beginning to take its toll on everyone, Declan and Anya most of all.

"Do these demons have a death wish?" asked Luc one night when they were gathered for dinner.

"No," said Matthew. "They just can't quite believe it. They're cocky and want to see the dangerous swords for themselves. If you live long enough, you forget what it's like to fear death. Or fear anything for that matter." Sometimes you just become numb to everything, thought Matthew. Except loneliness. That was just pernicious.

"But they must know the swords are dangerous to them now!" Luc exclaimed.

"Do they? They heard rumors but Laurent isn't really talking. As a matter of fact, no one just has even seen Laurent since it happened."

"Then how are the rumors spreading?"

"We're spreading them," Mathew answered Luc's question.

"Excuse me?" Luc looked confused.

"We are," said Therese. "But I also suspect that Laurent had a few demons hiding the night he attacked. They may be telling tales."

"Remember lad, we want people to know we have them," Dougal said around a fork full of chicken.

"Chew and swallow, Dougal. Don't talk." Therese rolled her eyes. "But he's right. We do want people to know." She paused. "Though, I think that this is more than we all bargained for."

Declan sighed. "It is. It's getting harder and harder to actually not kill these demons."

"We did kill the grunts the other night though," Anya said.

"We had to. They were starting to swarm. Whoever sent them, backed off after that."

"What happens when you kill a grunt?"

"They don't turn to dust, like they normally would if you ran them through. They just kind of drop," answered Declan. "That was unexpected. I had not realized they could actually be killed."

"It was depressing as well, *non?*" put in Michel.

"Very much so," said Anya, quietly. Declan put his arm around her, pulling her close and she put her head on his shoulder. They were grunts, created for fighting, but she didn't like just taking their lives so permanently to prove a point. "Can we maybe stop going out so much for a bit, now?"

Declan squeezed her shoulder. "Yes, I think so, Annie." She wasn't eating much and that he did not like at all. Anya got a lot of pleasure from good food and enjoyed these communal dinners a lot. But she was sitting here, picking at her food and it broke his heart a little.

Gwen smiled at her friend and created a dancing ball of golden light, which she sent spinning around the room to cheer her friend up. She made it shower sparks over Matthew, who grimaced at her and this finally made Anya laugh. Declan shot her a grateful smile.

"Annie, I am taking a little time off from work until this is over," Gwen said.

"I don't want…"

"Shut up, I am not asking you. I am telling you. I need to make sure my spell work is perfect. Both creating and undoing them. The books you have on demons and demon lore are loaded with spells I might need. I need to spend much more time studying them. Luc, when he isn't working with you, is going to help me as well." Anya opened her mouth. "Enough, Anya. This isn't just your path, it's mine too. And I plan to be as much help to you as I can be. Now, do everyone at this table a huge favor and eat your fucking dinner."

Anya blinked at her friend. Opened her mouth, then closed it again. "Yes, Gwendolyn. Ok." Anya picked up her fork and to everyone's relief and astonishment, started to eat her food instead of picking at it.

Declan cornered Gwen after dinner. "What was that about?"

"She was feeling sorry for herself, and guilty for some stupid reason. The one way I can ever get her out of that weight of the world funk is to get tough with her. If it bothers you, tough shit. I've been here longer, and I know her better."

Declan raised an eyebrow. "Stand down, Gwen. I was going to thank you."

Gwen had the grace to blush. "Oh! Oh, sorry. You're welcome." She still looked aggrieved.

Declan crossed his arms. "Out with it, Gwen."

"She's not a killer."

"Excuse me?" Declan was confused.

"Anya. She's not a killer. She has killed, I know this. But it's not natural to her."

"But it is to me, is that what you mean?"

"Well, I mean…"

"You think I kill because I like it? You think I was born this way?"

"Declan…."

"I was born a farmer Gwendolyn. A farmer. I was born into far less harrowing and cruel circumstances than Anya was, considering I was born in the Middle Ages."

"I was not saying that."

"Then what are you saying? Anya knew what she was getting into. She knew what this life was, is. This is probably nothing to the cruelty she faced growing up with that mother of hers. To be clear, I do not kill without reason, ever. I am not a murderer. But I flat out won't hesitate to kill if I need to. If someone is in danger, if someone hurts one of mine, and that includes you, I will not hesitate to rip them apart. And neither would Anya. Gwen, if someone so much as looks at you wrong, it's all she can do to not stab them."

"I'm worried about her."

"As am I. But she's strong and I have faith in her." He paused. "What is it that you're really afraid of?"

"You! All of you. I am concerned that her humanity is going to get stripped away."

"And she'll what? Become a killing machine?"

"I am worried it will stop bothering her."

"And you think it's stopped bothering us?" Gwen had no reply to that. Because that is exactly what she'd thought. And once she said it, she realized how awful it sounded. Declan continued. "I see. So, in your mind you still equate demons with evil then? You think Donovan is evil, do you? Or Luc? You want to be our conscience, Gwendolyn? You worried about our immortal souls?"

"I'm sorry."

"I am sure you are. Do not mistake me here. This life can take its toll. I surround myself with people that know right from wrong. We will kill. We do kill. We have beasts inside of us that delight in the kill, so the person has to balance that out. My people are soldiers, we may have to go to war at any time. It is not for the soft, but we are not evil. I'm by no means a saint and I would even hesitate to call myself a good person. Balance, Gwen, balance. For you to think that I would ever want Anya to change or be any less than she is, is appalling to me."

Shit. She hadn't made him angry. She'd hurt him. "I hurt your feelings."

"Damned right you did. Because you know how much I love Anya and I've come to think of you as a good friend. I would never want harm to come to either one of you." Declan took a breath. "That said, I know this is because you love her, and this is still all very new to the both of you. I do get that."

"I am glad it came up, but I didn't handle it well."

"I didn't handle this as calmly as I should have. I shouldn't have said what I said."

"No. You absolutely should have. I insulted you and your friends, and you had every right to get pissed off about it. Obviously, my subconscious decided to take over my mouth and my brain for a minute. I trust you. I trust them, but I worry, and I have worried since she first told me all of this. The fact that I play a part now doesn't make me worry less. But hurting you was wrong."

He smiled softly at her. "Well, you're only human after all."

She threw her arms around him. "Am I forgiven?"

"Absolutely." He kissed the top of her head. "Am I?"

"Oh, definitely!"

"Good. Because I have an idea that I want to run by you at some point. Not now though."

"Something for Anya?"

"Yes. And I think you will love it; I just hope she will."

"Hey now, what's this? My best friend and my mate!" Anya said with a smile.

"We were talking about you."

"Naturally." Anya wrapped her friend in a hug. "Oh, you're just so cute! I just love you so much!"

"Anya," Gwen sounded muffled. "My face is getting smushed by your breasts." Anya started to laugh. "Now I am smushed in your vibrating breasts."

"Lord help me," murmured Declan.

Anya squeezed Gwen a little tighter and then let her go. "Sorry, wee witch!"

"Ok, it's bad enough that your mate calls me that. Do you have to as well?"

"I do." Anya turned to Declan and gave him a look. He kissed her lightly and walked away.

"I wanted to thank you for what you did at dinner. It helped."

"Sometimes you just need someone to tell you that it's enough. I am glad I can be that person."

"You are. And you are in a way that Declan won't ever be, just so you know."

"I know. I am concerned though, you just look...tired."

"I am. My body is going through massive changes. Declan and I are sharing energy and power, and I am not used to that. Plus, all the fighting. Not much used to that either. Not really. It's taking a bit of a toll. I will be fine."

"I know this too. But...ugh. I just, I am winging this, and Donovan is being weird, and my powers are being weird..."

"Wait, what? Not that I don't care about Donovan, but your powers are being weird? How so?"

"It's like...I can't describe it." Gwen thought for a moment. "It's not really weird. It's...more. I seem to be growing in power and I am not used to it. It acts up sometimes if I am not paying attention."

"How so?"

If I am washing dishes or paying bills or anything I don't use magic for, sometimes a ball of light will just shoot out of my hands. Or I'll move something without touching it. But things I want to control, I can't always control. Some things are easier, some are not."

"Any premonitions?"

"Nope. That is still purely Luc's territory it seems."

Anya thought about it a moment. "Well, your power is growing, that's for sure."

"Can it somehow be tied to yours?"

"No idea. I am not sure prophecies work that way, but I am no expert."

"I wouldn't want to be contributing to your tiredness."

"I don't think you are, don't worry about it. Now, what's going on with Donovan?"

"Both overprotective and standoffish."

"I mean, there's a lot going on. Maybe just kind of put aside the romantic stuff for now, and let's get through the immediate threat. Then, we can figure out how to deal with Donovan."

Gwen nodded. "You make a good point. But the overprotective shit…"

"So, and I can't believe I'm saying this, go easy with him there too. I am not saying bend over backwards, stop looking at me like that. I am saying try and listen to him. I think he's acting from a legitimate place of concern. He is way more familiar with demons and what they're capable of than you are. Or I am for that matter." Gwen raised an eyebrow at her. "I know I'm fighting them, but I'm doing it with Declan. When I'm out, it helps him go about his day if he can have someone shadowing me. It's a small price for me to pay right now based on the situation. It will help Donovan do his job if he knows you're safe. And right now, his job is to help Declan with the day to day so he can concentrate on other things. Like the threat to us to all of us." Anya wondered if Gwen realized that there was a very real threat to her as well. Just because no one had tried to get to her yet, didn't mean they wouldn't at some point. It filled Anya with a cold dread.

"But Annie…" Gwen stopped. It was a reasonable request, truthfully.

"Gwen don't change your habits. Don't do anything differently than you already do. Just let him do what he needs to for now. He's basically doing his job, but he's likely bungling it a bit. Once this is over, you can tell him to knock it off. These people are dangerous. And quite frankly, I feel better knowing someone is keeping an eye on you."

Gwen sighed. As much as she wanted to, she couldn't argue with her friend's logic. "Ok, fine. I'll let it go for now."

"Choose your battles, my friend."

"Do you?"

"I mean, not always. But mostly because the making up is really good."

"Bitch," said Gwen with affection.

"You bet, blondie. So, you going to tell me what you and Declan were talking about? He looked very serious."

Gwen blushed. "I'd rather not. I feel stupid about it and I just kind of want to forget it. But we're good."

Anya smiled gently at her friend. "Fine. I will let it go. But let me know if I need to kick his ass."

"No. He was fine."

Donovan walked over then. "Are you ready to go Gwen?"

"Sure. Are you going to work after you drop me off?"

"Nope. Therese is taking my shift tonight. Thought we might…uh…watch a movie."

Gwen looked at him. "Sure. Sounds nice." She was going for casual, but Anya didn't think she quite succeeded.

"Night Annie." Gwen hugged her friend.

"Night. Remember that compromising doesn't mean rolling over."

"I will." The two left and Anya wandered over to the window, looking out at the river and Notre Dame in the distance. Matthew wandered over to her.

"Are you sure you're ok?" he asked her.

She gave him a small smile. "I am. Just worried."

"And tired."

"Yeah. Well, the guy who trains me is working me hard."

"I'm sorry," said Matthew quietly. "I forget sometimes that you are human. You fit so well."

She looked at her friend's face and saw that he was harboring some major guilt. "Matthew, you have nothing to feel guilty about. These are things I needed to learn. As for fitting in," she shrugged. "When you've been manipulated your whole life to lead a certain life, when that life comes, it's easy." The more she thought about it, the more bitterness at Natalia grew. She loved Declan, and the family she now had, but she was keenly feeling how manipulated she had been. How she'd let herself be. She was also pissed at herself if she was being honest.

"Don't do that."

"Do what?"

"Firstly, feel sorry for yourself. Or be angry at yourself." He saw the two emotions warring within her so clearly right at this moment. "Secondly, don't act like you fit because of someone else's machinations. You fit because you and Declan found each other, and you found us, and you decided to make us a family. Sure, you found each other because of Natalia, but you two falling in love, that was never a sure thing. You know that. That was fate as far as I'm concerned, and I am not prosaic by nature. You could have easily walked away from this. You're that strong. You could have chosen a different life. You chose this. Why?"

"Because I didn't just fall in love with him. Though that would have been enough; I fell in love with all of you as well. Every single one of you made it impossible to walk away. You all just accepted me for me. And you made it possible for me to finally be that person with Gwen. I've never had that before. So, how could I do anything but fall in love with you while I was falling in love with Declan. You bunch of assholes." She gave him a mock punch on the shoulder.

Matthew had to clear his throat before he spoke again. "You didn't give us much of a choice."

She barked out a laugh. "That's true I think. But it's all been such a whirlwind, that I think the reality is finally hitting me. Even with the danger."

"Regrets?"

"Absolutely none. It makes me sad to think about losing Gwen one day, but I wouldn't change my mind for the world." She'd miss the hell out of Gwen, but she'd never be alone again. And she hadn't realized how that idea had terrified her, until it was no longer an issue.

"Well, if Donovan gets his head out of his ass and if what Declan thinks is true, is actually true, you may not lose her."

"Big ifs."

"They are. But what else do we have right now?"

"You're saying I should have hope? You?"

"Yes, I am. Try not to look too shocked. I am not completely a morose bastard." He thought for a moment. "Ok, maybe I am. Still true though. And don't be too hard on yourself. You've been feeling guilty about dragging her into this."

She started. "How the hell…"

"It was written all over your face as you were watching her leave. But she also has free will and she could have left at any time. Walked away. Just like you could have. You are not, as the kids say, all that." She playfully punched his arm again. "She made a choice. Respect that choice."

"I do."

"But you don't, not really. Because you want to push her away and it's all you can do not to. Respect the choice."

She sighed. He was right. She was constantly fighting the impulse to have Donovan send her away, for her safety. She had to respect Gwen's right to stay, to be involved and to fight alongside them. "You're right. I'll try."

"Good girl," he said, smiling. He kissed her forehead. "And now, I have to go keep the city safe."

"Keep yourself safe too, Batman. Please."

"Always." He walked out and Anya couldn't help feeling that as far as families go, this one was pretty great.

<u>CHAPTER 32</u>

Marchand sat at his desk and sighed. He'd just spent the last couple of hours with the parents of the murdered men. It had been hard, but they had thanked him profusely for getting justice for their sons. One of the mothers said she'd always wanted to see Paris, but she hadn't expected it to be under such terrible circumstances. He suspected none of them would visit again, and he could not blame them. It was sad those boys were dead, sad that Paris would never be a place of happiness for that mother, sad that those four people outlived their children. For one of the sets of parents, this had been their only child. Marchand knew he should be used to it; but getting used to innocent deaths were not something he ever wanted to be used to. His phone pinged. He blinked. It was from Therese. *Good afternoon detective, Anya would like to know if you want to have dinner with all of us tonight? She thinks you may have questions for us. But honestly, I think it's because Mara is trying her hand at Russian food, and she thought you'd like that. So? You coming or not?*

He smiled to himself. *Russian food is the way to my heart.*

Well, your heart is a start anyway. Bring vodka.

Anya wants vodka?

No. I do.

His heart stuttered at this. Was this...was she flirting? No, she couldn't be. Not with him. *Vodka it is then.*

Good. 7pm.

See you then.

Well, he'd probably hung around with worse people. And they certainly weren't boring. He was wary, but also excited if he was being honest. To find something so unexpected in the world, something new and something to learn about filled him with anticipation, even as he weighed the danger. Also, there was Therese. But that way was madness. But maybe it would be worth it to be mad for just a little bit.

***

"Are you adopting the detective now, too?" Luc asked. Therese had just loudly, a bit too loudly, reported that Marchand was coming for dinner, before announcing she had things to do and would be back later.

Anya shrugged. "He seems a bit lonely. And having to deal with two sets of grieving parents cannot be easy." She paused. "And what do you mean by 'too?'"

Luc grinned. "You know you did the same to me."

"Yes, because I needed someone who knows how to do research."

"*Mais bien sûr*, that is the reason." He shrugged. "I think you have a knack for finding lonely people. And you collect us, like figurines."

He was right, but she couldn't help it. She knew what lonely looked like and she hated it. Anya balled a piece of paper and threw it at him. He caught it easily and sent it flying back at her.

She laughed. "Get back to work!"

His phone pinged and he looked down at it, then up again.

"What's wrong?"

"It's Suzie. Liliana's mage is gone. As of this morning."

Anya's eyes narrowed. "Mercule? What do you mean he's gone?"

"Most of his stuff is gone. Susie heard plans being made today and then all of a sudden, gone. She saw a car driving away with him in it. A larger car with his things following right behind."

Anya's eyes narrowed. "Was anyone with him?"

Luc typed quickly and waited for his phone to ping again. He read and turned a bit red. "Umm...."

"What? Just say it."

"Yes. Your brother was with him." Luc gave her a sympathetic look.

Anya nodded. "That's what I thought." She sighed. "He and I are going to come face to face at some point."

"Are you going to be ready for that?"

"Ready to face my dead brother who hates me?" Luc winced. "Probably not. But it is what it is." She stood and walked to the door. "Chat with your gal for a bit if you want, I'll be back shortly." He nodded at her and she left the room.

Declan?

Malysh? Are you ok?

Eh. Where are you?

Upstairs. In my office.

Do you have time for me?

Always.

She took the stairs two at a time until she reached the door, gave it a quick knock and went right in. She made a beeline for Declan who just held out his arms for her. She jumped at him, he caught her, and she wound her arms and legs around him and kissed him with everything she was. Her pent-up frustration, her anger, her sorrow and her love. He fisted one hand in her hair and rubbed her back with the other, giving her what she needed just then. His love. The kiss ended and she rested her head on his shoulder, while he sat in his chair and arranged her on his lap. "Better?" he asked gently.

"Yes. Thank you."

"Anytime. And I do mean that. But can you tell me what brought this on?"

"Mercule has left Liliana's. With my brother, and it finally, truly hit home that a confrontation is inevitable. And that I might have to kill him...again. This time on purpose."

"Anya, I am not going to let that happen. Neither will Matthew. Or any of us, for that matter." If it came down to it, one of them would kill her brother so she didn't have to. It would piss her off, but he didn't want her to live with having done it a second time.

"Neither of you should have to…"

"No, don't. It's not about that. If I can spare you the pain of doing it, I am going to. Period. You'd do it for me."

"Yes, that's true. But if it comes to it, I will do it."

"No one doubts that." She had enough courage for it, he knew that. But he was still going to do everything he could to make sure she didn't have to. They could fight about it afterwards.

"Are they headed here?"

"Probably. There's a Council meeting coming up. They're coming early, and Liliana and Francois will follow soon."

"We'll need to be even more careful I suppose."

"Hmmm…yes." His hand slipped under her shirt and started caressing her nipple through her bra.

"Declan! This is important!"

"So is this." His hand moved to the other nipple and she moaned softly.

"I invited Marchand for dinner."

"Of course you did." He unhooked her bra and moved it out of the way, palming one of her breasts.

She nipped at his neck. "What do you mean by that?" Why did people keep saying that to her?

"Our detective is lonely. You are befriending him.".

"Luc said the same thing. That I collect all the lonely people."

"You do. You found me, after all." He lifted her top and she flipped around so she was straddling him. He palmed both breasts now.

"It's because I recognize lonely people when I see them."

"I know, *malysh*." He leaned down and laved one nipple, then the other. "I have a meeting in 30 minutes, but I am at loose ends until then."

She smiled at him and leaned back. "Well then, we'll have to find a way to keep you occupied." She pulled his head back down to her breasts and sighed in contentment.

***

By 7:15, everyone had gathered and were sitting around the dining room table. Marchand had brought a bottle of Vodka that a cousin had sent him from Russia. It was homemade in the man's own still and Therese's eyes lit up when she saw it. Completely worth it, he thought to himself when she smiled at him. He thought he would feel out of place and that he'd mostly get ignored, but he was wrong. They'd made him feel welcome. More welcome than any of the people he worked with, anyway.

He loved what he did, and he worked with a good group of people, but he wouldn't call any of them friends. Maybe that was on him. It probably was. He'd always had a hard time getting close to people and he just didn't connect with most of the people he worked with. He was standoffish, he knew it. And he was ok with that. These people felt more like friends already, then his coworkers. Life, it seems, had taken one weird turn for him.

Declan was in the middle of explaining to him, and to everyone else, what was going on with Mercule and Pavel and that they'd need to be ready.

"Is there anything I can do, from my end?" Marchand asked.

"Keep your ear out for anything that seems strange. Someone else may think it's nothing, but you've met us now. You know what's going on and something that may not strike anyone has more than passing strange, may stand out to you. The more eyes, ears and hands we can put on this, the better, I think. I'd like to try and get in front of this."

"Declan, the boy is human." Dougal put in.

"The 'boy' is no boy and I am right here."

"You're a boy to me, lad. Like Luc is."

"I do not like to be referred to as such either, to be honest," Luc replied.

Dougal started to argue, and Donovan interjected. "We're all grown ass people here, despite ages. Frankly, we're lucky that Therese doesn't refer to all of us as children."

"Are you older than everyone, then?" Marchand enquired. He realized that this may be considered rude.

"I'm older than everyone here combined," Therese answered.

"No shit?"

"No shit." She looked at Marchand. Jesus, those grey eyes of his. Feelings, ugh.

"Then how come…."

Therese anticipated the question. "Because I am a warrior, a soldier. Through and through. Playing politics is of no interest to me, nor would I be any good at it. Declan does not enjoy doing it, but he is very good at it. Do not make that face at me, Declan. It's true."

"I am only making a face because this is one of the longest speeches that I've heard you make. The look on my face is shock."

"You tell yourself that, son," she replied. She turned to Marchand. "And no offense, while you are an adult, you are human, and you are much more breakable than most of us are. Dougal's point is a good one." It would be a shame if anything happened to him. And if that thought was borne out of an appreciation for both his face and his build, so be it. Therese was no nun.

"True. But look at his build," said Declan. They all did, and Marchand shifted uncomfortably. "Now, look at his eyes." Again, they did. "You all see it, yes?"

They all nodded. "See what?" asked Marchand.

"You're not just a cop. You're a fighter. You have hard eyes. In another time, you would have been a warrior."

Marchand shook his head. "Not me. My father was a farmer. I am a cop, with a farmer's heart."

"You're fooling yourself there, and you know it. I was a farmer," said Declan. "So was Dougal. Michel was a monk. Your point is not valid." Declan hadn't gotten to where he was by not being an excellent judge of character. "You're a fighter. Trust."

"Against other demons though?"

"Not a demon of any real age. You'd have luck with a younger demon. And many demons use humans as well when it comes to fighting. We're less obvious that way. We take care with the humans though."

"Why?"

"My job is to protect them, not harm them. Being forced to do so is distasteful. I am careful with how I use humans because unlike many of my kind, I do not think humans are expendable. I don't think you'd have a chance with Mercule though."

"Is he not human?"

"I don't know. He's not a demon."

"What else is there?" Anya asked.

Declan shrugged. "We aren't aware there is anyone else. But most of the world doesn't know about demons. Or think that magic is actually real. I try not to make assumptions. So, we're going with him being human like. I even wonder if Mercule is his real name. He probably thought it sounded magicky."

"I have some contacts, who could tell me if anyone has been looking for muscle, off the books." Marchand paused a moment. "I don't like to hurt people unless I have no other option. I'm better with a gun, but I can handle a dagger. I own several."

Anya's eyes lit up. "Oh, really? Do tell!"

"Darling, can your curiosity wait?" Declan asked.

"I suppose so." She looked at Marchand. "We'll chat later."

Declan continued on. "Thank you. Again, another pair of eyes or ears never hurts."

"I am not sure I can beat Mercule," said Gwen. "From what I have seen, his magic is very strong."

"So is yours."

"Yes Donovan, it is strong. But not as strong and as, well, old as his."

"His magic is old?"

"Yes. Which means, he may be human but he's really old. And it's likely through magic. That's part of the reason that Luc and I slept so long and so hard after we healed the dynamic duo here." Anya stuck her tongue out at her friend. "It wasn't just how strong it was; it was how old it was. It took me until about an hour ago to figure that out."

"Well, fuck," said Donovan.

"Exactly. I can do some damage. Enough to either incapacitate or block, briefly. But I can't beat him. I can't win."

"You shouldn't try to win," said Anya. "Just incapacitate him or hog tie his magic temporarily. Whatever you can do."

"Then what?"

"We can figure it out then. Maybe he can actually die if we can figure out the spells keeping him alive."

"Annie, I am not sure he can die, and I am not sure we can undo the magic keeping him alive."

"Of course you can't, right now. Gwen, there's only so much we can solve for ahead of time. He's an unknown, we're going to have to wing it probably."

"Then you can slide in and whammy him. Or Anaranth could take care of him. Would he?"

Declan shrugged. "Possibly. But again, there are other ways to take care of him."

"You always say this, and yet you give me no details on that."

"You don't want them."

"I do, actually."

"You don't, quite actually." Declan held up a hand. "Later, please." She nodded grudgingly. "Anaranth may not interfere though, unless it's in his own best interest to do so."

"Are you not in his best interest?"

"In theory perhaps. But in reality, no one knows what makes him tick."

"I mean, I don't think he's spent eight hundred years on you to let something happen to you."

"I'm a means to an end. He could decide at any time that I am no longer worth it. Eight hundred years is a drop in the bucket for him."

"This is true. As old as I am, Anaranth makes me look like a child." Therese put in. "I think Declan is right though, Anaranth is a wild card, we can't plan on him."

"So, we don't know if we can kill or even stop Mercule. So, we have to stop Liliana. Mercule has no toehold in our world without her. Is that a fair assessment?" Declan nodded at Anya's statement. "Ok, so, what's our game plan then?"

"I have an idea, but you won't like it," put in Matthew.

"On a scale of 1 to 10, how much am I going to hate it?" asked Declan.

"It can't be measured with current technology."

Marchand sighed. He had a feeling he knew where this was going. "You want to use Anya as bait."

Matthew nodded. "I want to use Anya as bait." Declan straightened up, walked around to Matthew, and punched him square on the jaw. Matthew's head snapped back, and Declan raised his arm to do it again, when Donovan's hand shot out and caught Declan in mid punch. "Hear him out. Then if you want to hit him, you can have a proper fight." Matthew nodded and rubbed his jaw.

Declan tried to wrest his arm away as his eyes went red. Anya leapt up, rounding to the other side of him and looked up at him, putting her hands on his chest. "Declan. Declan calm down. Just listen to him. Matthew is on our side. *Lyubov moya*, please." She rested her head against his heart, which was beating too hard and just petted his back, until she felt him calm down. His beast was very close to the surface. Matthew was standing very still. He'd fight back if he needed to, but he didn't want to. "Honey, just listen to him. He doesn't want me harmed, we're friends. You know this."

Declan dropped his head to Anya's and pulled her closer to him. "I can't bear the thought that something might happen to you," he whispered.

"I know love, I know."

Matthew had heard him as well and put an arm around both of them. "Declan, I love Anya like she was my own sister. I love you like a brother. More than a brother. You have to know I have a good reason to suggest this." He was gripping Declan's arm tightly. "You're new mates, I understand that this is sending you and your beast into a tailspin, but you have the best control of anyone I've ever known...calm down. Please" It was the 'please' that got to Declan in the end. He took a couple of deep breaths and settled. He took one arm and pulled Matthew in, putting his head against the other man's, brow to brow. "I am so sorry I hit you. I know you'd never do anything to harm us, and I know you wouldn't suggest this if you hadn't thought it through."

Matthew smiled. "Honestly, I thought it would be worse."

Declan looked up at everyone. "Sorry, all."

Dougal put up his hand. "Lad, not one of us needs ye to explain yerself to us. We get it."

"But let's hear the plan." Marchand put in.

"Right. Then we can all take turns punching Matthew," Gwen joked.

Matthew took a steadying breath and dove in. "They've been playing cat and mouse with us. Even the attempt on your life."

"What attempt?" asked Marchand.

"Remember when you wanted to talk to us but were told we were recovering from a stomach flu?" asked Anya. Marchand nodded. "We didn't have the stomach flu. Someone tried to kill Declan and by association, me?"

"How?"

"Magicked dagger."

"Who was actually stabbed?"

"Him. We're connected through a blood bond because we're mated. If he dies, I die."

"Wow. That's hardcore."

"You ain't kidding," said Anya, looking at Matthew. "Sorry, continue."

"It's fine. I think they knew Declan had the swords and everyone knows he collects books on demon lore. And if they know about Anya, they knew she was friends with Gwen and that she was a witch."

"They know about the prophecy. Because every Council member does it seems."

"Right. Which means if Francois knows, Liliana does, and she told Mercule. She doesn't like Declan's power."

"That's an understatement," put in Donovan. "She despises it. I have been doing some digging and man, she fucking hates you."

"Well to know me is to love me," said Declan.

"Unless you're a threat. You are a prime threat. And so is Anya."

"What? Why me?" Anya looked surprised at this.

"You have a relative on the Council, that is a very unique position to be in."

"But..." Mara walked in at that moment and cleared her throat. "Mara?"

"The cardinal is here to see you."

Declan stared at her. "I'm sorry...come again?"

"Richelieu is here. In this house. Now."

"You are kidding me!"

"She is not, Declan!" Richelieu swept past Mara into the room. "I am here."

They all stared at him, not really believing he was there. Anya recovered first. "Your eminence, you honor us with your presence. Please, sit." She gestured to a chair, smiled, and sat down.

Marchand leaned over to Therese. "Richelieu? *Vraiment?*"

She smiled at him. "Yes, indeed. The man himself."

"Jesus Christ!"

"He certainly thinks so!" She said with a sardonic smile.

"Cardinal, may we offer you some refreshments?"

"I have heard much about Mara's baking." Mara paled. "I would not be averse to something sweet. And coffee."

That felt so normal that Anya was dumbfounded. Declan shrugged at her from behind the Cardinal. "Mara?"

"Right. Yes. Something sweet. Back in a moment." Mara raced from the room.

The cardinal looked around the table, his eyes alighting on Marchand, who started to shift uncomfortably.

"You are?" he asked mildly.

"It's an honor to meet you. Your...eminence." Therese stifled a laugh at this. The cardinal nodded. "Should I go?" Marchand added.

"Oh no, if the others have trust, I shall trust you as well." He smiled. "For now."

"Cardinal don't frighten the man. He's a friend." Anya winked at Marchand.

"For you, my dear, of course." Mara came back in with a large tray with a silver coffee service and a selection of pastries on a very fancy plate.

We have things that look like this? Anya asked Declan.

It seems so. But I could not tell you where it came from.

Richelieu spent the next few minutes sampling some pastries. "Mara, you are quite the talented baker. I don't suppose..."

She cut him off quickly, but politely. "I appreciate that, your eminence, but I would prefer to stay with Declan and Anya."

"Ah. It was worth a try. I do appreciate loyalty, in all of its forms."

"I can send you home with some more baked goods though."

"That would be lovely."

"I'll bring them down to your driver." And with that, she was gone.

Richelieu sighed, brushed some crumbs away and sat back. "I suppose you'd like to know why I am here."

"It had crossed my mind," said Declan.

"Firstly, I wanted to see for myself that you two are well, after your unfortunate mishap." Only Richelieu would refer to almost dying as a 'mishap.' "Secondly, I assume you are aware that Francois, Liliana and that obscene little magician are now in Paris, yes?" Declan nodded. "*Bien!* I thought as much. They are planning something, most definitely. But what I find very interesting, and it is the third reason I am here, is that Liliana's first visit when she arrived here was to Natalia." Anya started at this news.

"Natalia? They never talk. Natalia made a point to tell me that she doesn't like her and does not speak with her outside of Council gatherings."

"Yes. And even then, their dealings are rather frosty. As you, yourself witnessed."

"Do you know what they spoke about? I assume you have a spy there."

"I did have a spy there, but they were not able to glean what was discussed. They are young and sadly, not as ready as I thought they were. They've been recalled." The smile that crossed his face didn't reach his eyes, sending a chill through Anya. "I do know that Mercule was in there with them."

"Excuse me? What?!"

"Yes. I quite agree, Anya. What indeed."

"So, Natalia is aware of Mercule's existence."

"More than that, I am afraid." The Cardinal looked almost embarrassed. "There is one thing I did manage to find out."

"What is it?" Anya crossed her arms in front of her, looking tense. Declan walked over to her, putting his arm around her, and whispering, "Courage, *malysh*."

"Natalia is the one who introduced Mercule to Liliana."

<u>CHAPTER 33</u>

"The hell, you say?" This was from Gwen.

"It is true." Richelieu gave an elegant shrug.

"How long have you known."

"I only found out about two hours ago. Again, this spy was young and didn't report this to me until today." Anya knew that Richelieu's spy was going to pay a heavy price for not passing along that information. She felt for the person, even though she was furious that they were just finding out now. She wasn't going to insult him and ask him if he was sure about this. If he had made the effort to see them, he was sure.

"Who is Natalia and what does this mean?" Everyone turned to look at Marchand when he asked the question. "*Ya proshu proshcheniya*, but I am still new to this."

"No apologies necessary, Petyr," said Declan as he explained who Natalia was and the connection to Anya. He then realized he was going to have to explain the Council quickly as well. He did not feel the need to explain how Richelieu fit in; he knew it would be glaringly obvious to the detective.

"So, what do we think is happening, then?" This was from Therese.

"My guess would be that Natalia is playing all sides to see who comes out the winner here," Matthew mused. "If it's Liliana, she can say she helped her with the Mercule introduction. But, if Anya and Declan win, she can share in that too, while denying her involvement with the other."

"But win what exactly?" Anya fumed. "Declan and I aren't trying to win anything. Liliana is forcing our hand." She stopped. "No. Natalia started this whole thing years ago. She was grooming me."

"For what though?"

"For you, Declan. And to feed her own ambitions, something that is family legend. Even when she was still human. She found the prophecy, or a version of it, read it and decided to watch me. As I got older, it started to fit. She talked to me about you, without really telling me anything about you specifically. She encouraged me to study demon lore, using my own love of learning and study against me. She talked to me about her own life and how full it was, using my own loneliness against me as well. She led me to water, and I just drank it all up. Then, when I am fully primed and the Council was nagging you about finding your consort, she told me where to find you."

"And she coordinated that with introducing Mercule to Liliana."

Anya nodded at Matthew. "That has to be it. The thing is, did she really think the prophecy was about us, did she force it, or did she just get lucky?"

"Lucky?" asked Dougal.

"Yes. There's no way she could have known or predicted how Declan and I would feel about each other. That didn't really signify. She counted on me going through with it, regardless."

"Which says she only sees what she wants to see when it comes to you. and doesn't really know you at all. Had I been an asshole, or you hated me, you'd never have gone through with it."

"Yea think ye're not an arsehole?"

"Cute Dougal, cute."

"But she even said it before we went into the club that first night," Gwen put in. "If you hadn't liked her, or she hadn't liked you, Anya was fully prepared to walk away. Plus, you did say something about it all was bothering you."

"I did say that." Anya nodded.

"How could you think I wouldn't like you?"

"How could I possibly know what you would like? You might have hated me on site." Declan scoffed. "You can be that way now, hindsight. But we might have hated each other. It was pure chance that we are true, blood bond mates.

"And thanks be to chance," Declan said, kissing his mate soundly.

Anya took a breath. "So, did Declan and I bring the prophecy to life by getting together? Are we all part of it because that's just how it worked out?" Anya started to pace. "Also, I never told her Gwen was a witch. So, did she actually know, or was she watching me? Or was she going to try and get Mercule away from Liliana and shove him at us?" She stopped. "I have so many questions and none of them are going to get answered right now, I know this."

"How do prophecies actually even work, really?" asked Petyr. "They're generally written hundreds or thousands of years before they are actually read. Which means they are open to interpretation. You could likely pick any two people in this room and fit the prophecy to them in some way."

"Petyr has a really good point., said Therese. "Things are never black and white, and neither are prophecies."

Anya nodded. "You are right. The prophecy fits us really well because we're reading it that way. But there's no telling if it actually is us."

Richelieu held his hand up. "Let us not dismiss it out of hand though. It could mean you. It could fit you because it is supposed to be you and Declan."

"So you believe in predestination, cardinal?"

The man gave a little laugh. "I know that must seem odd to you. But I have lived a long time and have seen a lot in that time. There are indeed things that cannot be explained easily. Demon kind itself is one of those things."

"Also true. And at this point, we've embraced the prophecy, so the conversation, unless we're presented with new information, is academic."

"Exactly, Anya."

"I have a question though," said Matthew. "Does this mean Natalia may have groomed others in case you didn't work?" They all turned to him, varying degrees of shock showing on their faces.

"Oh well fuck me!" Anya let out a stream of curses in Russian that caused Marchand to both wince and laugh.

"What is she saying?" asked Therese.

"It would lose something in the translation. But this Natalia would need to be a contortionist for a lot of it."

Therese snorted. "I'd enjoy seeing that."

"You do not care for her?"

"Never have. Now, never will." He looked at her. "You don't mess with my people. She's messed with my people." This, he thought, was a good person to have on your side.

Anya let out a final curse that had Marchand flat out laughing. "My mother used to use that one sometimes. When she thought we could not hear her."

"Doina, my mother, used it too. Usually at me though." She shrugged at the memory of it. "It never occurred to me that Natalia might have done that. You know, I never quite trusted her, but I didn't think she'd go that far." She turned to Richelieu. "Is there any way to find out if that is the case?"

He smiled at her. "Of course there is, Anya." He paused. "I am already on it."

"You are a wonder, cardinal."

"Of course I am."

"What other news have you come to impart?"

"There is going to be a Council meeting in the next two weeks. I am not sure why though. Supposedly it was at Francois' request."

"But..." Declan started to interrupt.

"This is a falsehood. It was actually at Liliana's. You are going to be summoned," Richelieu said.

"The reason?"

"Those swords you are in possession of."

"What about them?" Declan asked.

'I believe that Liliana is going to cite them as a danger and that they should be destroyed."

"I mean, they are, to be honest."

"But if they are part of the prophecy..." Anya started to say.

"I do not think she truly plans to have them destroyed though," Richelieu finished.

"Ah. She wants to keep them for herself." Anya's brow furrowed. "But Natalia believes in this prophecy, why would she help...." She stopped. No, she wouldn't, would she? Yes, she would. "Natalia also wants them for herself. She feels sure she can steal them from Liliana, but not us. Which means..."

"That Mercule is really working for her." Declan's eyes started to go red, but he pulled back the anger. For now. "Which also means..."

"That in actual fact, she's responsible for the attempt on our lives."

"Had we died, she would have swooped in here before anyone was the wiser and spirited out the swords."

"And she would not have needed Gwen, as she has her own witch. Or Sorcerer."

"Would she have killed me?" Gwen moved closer to Donovan, who squeezed her shoulder reassuringly.

"She would have killed us all, I think. Or had us killed. She's not the type to do her own dirty work." This was from Matthew.

"Staging a coup and taking over Declan's territory in the process. Thereby ousting Francois from Western Europe."

"Yes, *malysh*, exactly. So, Liliana is really her puppet, but she does not know it." Declan could feel the ice coming from his mate over this. Her anger was usually hot, but this was different. It was a frosty rage, and it was scary. Not that he was scared of her, but it was a good thing Natalia wasn't there now.

"So, I was basically her sacrificial lamb."

"Yes. It would seem so." Richelieu's phone pinged and he looked down. "Ah, another situation has reared its ugly head and I must go. I will call as soon as I know anything about Natalia grooming anyone else."

"Thank you, cardinal."

"Of course, my dear." He squeezed her hand and lef them with these parting words. "Be careful and think carefully were you planning to ignore the summons. If for some reason, you were not to show up at the Council meeting, even after being summoned, you'd be hunted as a renegade demon and his mate." With that, he was gone.

Anya sighed. "And what would happen to us then? If we were declared renegades?"

"Remember the thing I won't tell you?"

"Yes."

"It involves that."

"You really need to tell me."

"I really don't."

This isn't finished, Declan.

I am not going to tell you.

You will. One day.

You are impossible.

But you love me anyway.

I do, at that. She felt the mental caress he gave her just then and smiled.

"I hate when you two head talk."

"You are just jealous."

Matthew grinned. "Yes. That's true actually. I am." He clapped his hands together. "So, my guess is that Liliana is planning to make sure that one or both of you does not show up to the meeting. And yes Anya, you both have to show up if you are both summoned."

"Well, balls."

"Crude, but true." said Matthew.

"So, we'll need to be even more careful," sighed Anya. "We have to make sure we both show up at the meeting."

"Liliana is playing the long game," said Donovan. "But Natalia's game is even longer. We need to be on our guard about both of them."

"Ye spake true," said Dougal, causing the room to roll their eyes at him and the brogue. "Arseholes!"

Declan chuckled. "It's late, we have the beginnings of a plan. We can talk it through further tomorrow. I suggest you all get some rest. I am taking my mate to bed. Or to punch something. I am not sure which she'd prefer yet."

"Both."

***

The summons, along with a note from Adjoa to Anya, arrived the next morning. Declan handed the summons over after he read it.

"That was quick. Why is Anaranth letting this happen?"

"He's likely curious how this is going to play out. He's the tie-breaker vote if he needs to be. But it's rare."

"So, he's the head of the Council, surely he has some sway."

"Any member can call a meeting and does not need to say why."

"That's really stupid. It means you can call a Council meeting because someone annoys you. The Council needs to be above that."

"I agree. But it is so. It is possible that Anaranth has no idea why the meeting is called."

"He knows about the swords though?"

"He does. Yes. But I mean, he's older than old. I have no idea how he really feels about them."

"Is he likely to let Liliana take them to be destroyed?"

"Well, he'd be letting Francois do it, officially. But it is possible, even if it may not be probable."

"And Francois isn't going to be pissed that Liliana did this?"

"Oh yes, he is. But to show it in public would be like admitting that he is weak. And that he will not do. No one wants anyone thinking that their mate was the one in control. They'd have to be dealt with." That sounded ominous.

"Has that ever happened?"

"Not to my knowledge. And not in my time. So, Liliana is really ballsy to be pulling this."

"Why do you think she's able to?"

"She's wonderful at manipulation, she's likely convinced him that she's helping him as he begins to tire."

"Bitch."

"And how. I've seen her try and sway him at Council meetings. When you think he's going to agree with her, he doesn't. And often when you think he hasn't been swayed...he agrees with her and votes her way. It's a real crapshoot. I suspect Anaranth had been wanting me to find a mate, because he wants to replace Francois, and Liliana caught wind of it, with the help of Natalia."

"She fed Liliana information about me."

"Yes, I believe so. Liliana will explain this to him ahead of time and hope to convince him like she has in the past. The thing is, she'll only tell him about the swords, not the rest of it. That he would not agree with."

"No?"

"No. Francois was a brutal man in his day. But he preferred open warfare over all this behind the door kind of nonsense. I have always respected him for that." He looked at the other note in her hand. "What does Adjoa write?"

"Oh!" She opened it and scanned quickly. "She is going to be here at 11:30 today for a sparring session." She looked a little pale.

"You'll be fine. She probably won't hurt you. Much."

"Funny. She doesn't ask though. She just assumes I will be free."

"And this sums up the Council."

"Ok, I guess I am sparring with her today. Matthew ought to love this." She looked at him. "You are frowning. What are you thinking?"

"I am going to call Richelieu. If he can find someone to work on Francois, to put the idea in his head, ever so subtly, that something bigger than swords is going on behind his back, it may help us."

"That feels sleazy."

"It is. It's also politics. Well, demon politics."

Anya stood and walked over to Declan and gave him a light kiss. "You don't like doing it, I can see that. But I also understand that you believe it to be necessary. I trust your opinion on this. I am going to shower and get dressed." She walked into the bathroom while Declan made the call.

When she emerged, dressed for the day, he was sitting at the window, drinking coffee. He poured her a cup as she sat across from him.

She sipped the coffee and waited. He didn't look happy. "Declan? What is it?"

"You are going to hate most of what I have to tell you."

"Is there anything I am going to like."

"There may be one silver lining."

Anya took a healthy swig of coffee. "Ok, hit me with it."

"So, your brother visited Natalia and Vlad."

"Which brother?"

"Pavel."

"Are you kidding me?"

"No, I am sorry."

"Well, fuck! So, she knows he's alive. And somehow she's involved in that too."

"It would seem so."

"And I can't kill her?"

"We'd have to kill Vlad as well."

"Ok."

"You want to run Eastern Europe?"

"Ugh, no. Fine. Never mind." She poured them more coffee. "What else?"

"Richelieu also confirmed that Natalia had a handful of other women, demon and human, that she was grooming if you didn't succeed."

The thought of any other woman with Declan made her see red, but the fact that Natalia was playing God with people's lives pushed her over the edge. "And are we sure I can't kill her?"

"Yes. Rosamund was one of them."

Anya's eyes narrowed. "Can I kill her, then?" This must be her silver lining.

"Yes. Her, you can kill."

Anya raised her coffee cup in a mock salute. "Well, it's a start."

***

By 1pm that day, Anya was wishing for death. Adjoa spent the first forty minutes teaching her how to hold and use the spear. She taught much the same as Matthew did. But once she got Anya comfortable, she attacked, and Anya had no choice but to go on the defensive. Matthew sat against the wall, smiling broadly every time that Anya hit the floor or didn't get out of the way in time.

"Uncle!" she finally yelled. "Adjoa, seriously! Declan is not going to be happy if you kill me." She looked over at her friend. "You can stop laughing Matthew. Really." This caused him to laugh even more.

Adjoa started laughing. "You are right. That is enough for today. You did well though." Anya just eyed the woman. "You did! Not many new demons would have been able to keep up like you did. I am impressed."

Matthew stood. "This has been utterly delightful. I have not had so much fun since Therese knocked Anya on her ass the other day. But I have to go now."

"I fucking hate you," Anya said.

"You don't!" He turned to Adjoa. "Adjoa, *Hamba Kahle*."

"*Sala kahle*," she said to Matthew. He bowed slightly at the two women and left, still laughing to himself.

"He does not laugh enough. I am pleased to hear him do so," said Adjoa.

"Agreed. Even if I have to be the butt of the joke." She rubbed her sore ass, speaking of which, while she walked over to the small fridge and got them both a water. When she turned, Adjoa had sat on one of the mats, so Anya joined her.

"I take it that this visit is not just about kicking my ass with a spear."

Adjoa smiled. "It is not. But it is a good way for me to visit without the Council breathing down my neck. Everyone heard me say I wanted to spar with you."

"This is about the Council meeting."

"It is. And the swords."

"Of course."

"You have them, you admit this?" Adjoa asked mildly.

"Of course I do. You know we do, or you would not have bothered to come right now." She took a sip of water. "Do they bother you? Their existence?"

"Not at all. I have suspected that they existed for many years. Some say they are African in origin. On this, I cannot say for sure. But I need you to know that Liliana, for it is her, is planting stories about how you and Declan are out to not only unseat them but use the swords to murder them."

"That's ridiculous!"

"Agreed."

"If we were going to kill them, they'd be dead already. And I'd be dancing on Liliana's grave."

Adjoa choked on her water, laughing. "Oh, you are a formidable mate! Not everyone is convinced. Neither Valentina nor Isabelle is convinced. Gorm is erring on her side, but he's very old and it's possible the cold has addled his brain."

"Gorm is Antarctica?" Adjoa nodded. "And Valentina is South America, while Isabelle is North America."

"Just so! I cannot say for the remainder of the Council. Val and Izzy are the only two I speak to regularly."

Anya was charmed by her use of nicknames for the two women.

"Astrid, Gorm's consort, let slip to me about how he feels. I don't think she agrees, but she can do nothing about it."

"Good to know, thank you."

"You are going to have to fight her," said Adjoa.

Anya sighed. "I know."

"You do not wish to?"

"Oh, I do. But there are layers of complications that do not make that the easiest path."

"Ah! Do not tell me, I wish to be surprised." Anya shot her a look. "I get bored as well and if there is going to be drama, I wish to see it unfold." Adjoa stood and her braids tumbled down. She secured them atop her head again and spoke, "I came to warn you that you will have to do some convincing and I want you both to be in top form. Not me, I am on your side. You are going to attend?"

Anya also stood. "Of course. We have no real choice."

"This is also true. Now, is it possible that I may see the swords?"

Anya laughed. "I think that this may be the true reason for your visit."

"You may be right."

"Well then, will you join Declan and I for lunch? I can ask him to bring them to us."

"Yes, of course. I do love Mara's cooking!"

"Does anyone not know about Mara?"

"No. We've all been trying to steal her for years!"

CHAPTER 34

The next week and half was fairly quiet. Declan had men posted where Natalia and Vlad were staying, but Pavel didn't show up again. Whenever Natalia's name came up, Anya had taken to throwing a dagger at the wall. Gwen thought that maybe a gal's night would help, even though Therese was sure that violence was the answer. But like most people, she wasn't able to tell Gwen no.

Which is how Therese found herself at Anya's house one evening, eating pizza and drinking wine. She'd sooner die than admit it, but she found she had missed having women friends and this was nice. Unusual, but nice. And Anya was relaxing a bit, so Gwen's idea was a good one.

"So, Therese," said Anya. "Boudica died around 60 AD yes?"

"Yes. 60 or 61. I think it was 61 though. Long time ago."

"You fought with her?"

"Yes. I did." Therese knew where this was going, and it was fine. If Anya was asking her questions, then she wasn't upset or angry. Declan implored them to make sure his mate had a nice evening.

Anya poured her friend more wine. "So how old were you?"

"Is this your way of asking me if I was human or a demon then?"

"Aw man, you saw through my clever ruse! Yes, it is."

"I was a demon by then." Therese smiled. "Do you want to know what year I was born?"

"Oh my God, I am sorry, but I really do."

"150 BCE. Or around there."

Anya and Gwen just stared at Therese, their jaws hanging open. "That means, you're about…" Gwen couldn't begin to figure it out. "Really really old."

"She's about 2,171 years old," finished Anya.

"I am."

"And Anaranth is older than you?" asked Gwen.

"Yes. I suspect he may pre-date time itself."

"Is that possible?"

"Sure. Why not?" Therese didn't know, but she thought anything was likely possible.

"Are angels real?" asked Gwen. The women just looked at her.

"What? I'm curious."

"That I do not know. But I suspect not."

"What about Fae?" asked Gwen, grinning at Anya.

"Oh, the Fae are absolutely real." Anya made a face. "I am not kidding Anya. They are and like all the stories, you do not want to mess with them."

Anya rolled her eyes and asked Therese a question. "How much do you remember?"

"A lot. There's a lot I've forgotten. But once I learned to read and write, I started journals from when I was first born, to when I became a demon. I still do it." She saw Anya's eyes light up. "I am not sure what ancient languages you read, but if you can learn the language, you can absolutely read them."

"Oh no, they must be really precious. I couldn't ask you to do that." Anya wanted nothing more than to do just that, truth be told.

"I've taken good care of them. And I am happy to let you read them."

"Thank you so much!"

"You are welcome. At some point, I started writing in French and then English. But the older ones, you may have some trouble with."

"I can learn!"

"I've no doubt. But for now, how about if I tell you some stories about my early years?" The other two women started applauding and Therese did think that it was really nice to have female friends again.

***

About an hour later, Anya sat up straight and stared into the distance.

"Anya?" said Gwen, worry in her voice.

"He's...gone," Anya said quietly.

"Who's gone?"

"Declan. Declan is gone."

Therese jumped up, pulled out her phone and punched in a number. "He can't be dead. Or you'd be dead too. Probably." She shrugged. "Who even knows at this point."

"He's not dead, I don't think. I just don't feel him anymore."

"The bond is gone?" asked Gwen, while Therese started muttering for someone to pick up the phone.

"No. Not exactly. I can still feel it. It's there...but then it ends. It's just quiet."

"Dougal! Took you bloody long enough! Where is Declan?" She waited. "He can't be in his office." She waited as Dougal said something to her. "Well, fucking find him! Now! And call me back immediately."

"They won't find him. He's just...poof. He's just gone." She looked shocked. "I don't understand. It's like, it's like he's hidden from me."

"Ok, honey. Ok, we'll find him. Don't worry." Gwen looked up at Therese, who looked back and just shrugged. This was beyond her.

Therese's phone rang just as Michel ran into the room. "Is Declan here?" he asked as Therese yelled "Well?!" into her phone.

Gwen shook her head. "No. He's not. Anya says she can't feel him. She doesn't think he's dead, but she can't feel him."

Therese yelled something into her phone and then threw it onto the couch. "He's not in his office and he's not on the floor of the club. They saw him in the back at one point and then he was just gone. They thought he'd gone back up to his office. They're searching the club for him now. I heard Matthew shouting and cursing a blue streak in the background." And Matthew losing his cool like that was not a good sign.

"Who was supposed to be with him?" asked Michel.

"Dougal." Therese spit the word out. They all looked at her. "What? He's my oldest friend, but he's not always the most dependable person in the world. He can be a vicious bastard though, great in a fight."

Anya saw it then. Dougal was always accompanying the other demons, the second. Declan didn't quite trust him enough to give him something of his own to run. Interesting, but not the time to think about this.

Michel nodded and looked at Anya. "Can you not feel him at all?"

She shook her head. "No, I can't. And it's kind of freaking me out."

Michel nodded. "Ok I am going back to the club to see if I can be of some help." He left quickly.

"Don't freak out. Let's wait for Dougal, or Matthew to call us back."

In the end, the two men, along with Luc just showed up at the house. "We searched everywhere in the club. We called the other clubs; we searched the area. It's like he went up in a puff of fucking smoke." Anya let out a sob and Matthew looked pained. "God Annie, I'm sorry." Matthew pulled her into a hug. "I wasn't thinking."

"It's fine," She pulled away some and laid a hand on his cheek. "I know you're just frustrated. Ok, we need to think. What is the most logical explanation?"

"He was taken."

"I'd still be able to feel him."

"He was taken by Mercule. And he's someplace you either can't feel him, or something has been done to him so you can't feel him."

"Magic would be involved," said Luc.

"Right. That is the most logical explanation. And the why of it would be the Council meeting is in a couple of days. Liliana doesn't want us to show."

"Why not take me? We all thought it would be me this time."

"You've barely been out of the house, and when you go, Therese is with you, and you have the swords." said Gwen. "Declan while not vulnerable, has been at the club a fair bit."

"How does Natalia fit in?"

"She's the puppet master here, so she has a plan for either outcome. The wily bitch. That said, she probably does know something."

"How can we be sure?" asked Luc.

"We need to see if we can get someone in there. If there isn't already."

"I'll call the cardinal," said Matthew, stepping into the corner of the room to do just that, as Luc raced out of the room.

"What's with him? I mean, aside from the Declan going missing?" asked Gwen.

Dougal shrugged. "No idea, really." The Scot looked over at Therese and held up his hand. "I know what you think of me," he said, no trace of that comical brogue. "We were up in his office, and he was looking at the cameras and saw something going on downstairs. It was between two higher ranking demons so he asked me to go down and see what I could do." Therese raised an eyebrow. "Well none of you were there, so it fell to me. I am not completely useless. I put two men on the door. Donovan's men. Declan told me he wouldn't leave the office, but I insisted the men stay anyway. When I got downstairs, I saw Christian and I asked him to go up and sit with Declan."

"Christian?"

"He's not us, but he's not without skills." She nodded grudgingly at him. "When I got back up there, after your call, all of them were gone. No sign of a struggle."

Therese glared at him. "No sign at all?"

"None. You know what Therese? I really resent you assuming that I am not reliable."

"Well, you often aren't," she sniffed.

He stalked over to her, barely keeping control on his temper. "Have I given you, or anyone else, cause during any of this to doubt me?"

"No," she conceded.

"In the last few decades, have I given you a reason to doubt me?"

"Dougal..."

"Answer the fucking question!" he shouted.

"No, you have not."

"I made one mistake. One. And I am still paying for it. It's been centuries, Therese. You say you've forgiven me, but I don't think that's true. If you don't, just say it and I will leave. But I am done with this."

Matthew cleared his throat. "Perhaps you two can handle your personal issues later?" The two had the good sense to look embarrassed. "Thank you." He looked at Anya. "Natalia does not seem to know anything about this, per Richelieu. He already had someone in there. He really is very good. His spy said they were discussing seeing you both at the Council meeting, and that it's possible that Liliana was getting a little too arrogant and comfortable."

"So, they were likely thinking of pulling Mercule back, maybe?"

"It seems so. But it's one less thing to be angry with her for, Annie." Anya knew he was using her nickname to try and comfort her, and she thought it was very sweet of him. "So..."

Luc burst back into the room, a large book in his hand. *"Ici! je l'ai trouvé!"*

Anya stared at him. "Found what, Luc?"

He waved the book around. "It's a spell. It uses something that the other person has or can do to bind them somehow. It basically turns back your own magic onto you."

"Ok. So?"

'So, demons usually form a special…umm…the word…trick, I guess that they can do, yes? More than just a usual glamour."

Matthew nodded. "Yes, true." He hated his. It was compulsion and he thought it was appalling. "Declan's is…" he and Anya just stared at each other.

"What is it?" asked Gwen.

Anya cleared her throat. "He, um…he can pull himself, and someone else out of time. By just a hair, but he can exist slightly outside normal time. But he can't sustain it for very long, well I don't think he can."

"He can't really, but only because he doesn't like using it so he's never honed it."

"He used it accidentally when we first met. When he first touched me."

"Interesting. So Luc, what do you think is happening?"

"So, the enchantment gives the spell weaver access to whatever power or magic the other person has. Mercule can then weave a spell around it. So, he could be holding Declan on the roof, and we wouldn't know because he's pushed Declan out of time a little. Anya can't feel him, so she can't find him. Mercule is using Declan's own power against him."

"So, if we can't use the bond to find him, how do we find him?"

"Old fashioned detecting," said Matthew.

"Ok, Scooby, how do you plan on doing that?"

"Therese, you know who Scooby Doo is?" Anya asked.

"I'm over two thousand years old, I know a lot of things."

"Well, we need to find Christian or any of the guards first. Find out what happened. Donovan has already mobilized a search party. Michel will be helping with that. He is really good at finding people. Not sure how he does it."

"Maybe that's his demon thing?"

"Maybe. So, there's nothing we can do right now is what you're saying?" Anya was wringing her hands.

"I don't think so. I know you want to get out there but trust me, there are a lot of people out looking. And I think you need to stay put and stay safe for now." She nodded. "Do you want to work off that anxiety?"

"Ew, lad!" this from Dougal.

"Mind out of the gutter you ugly sod. I was thinking that maybe she'd like to do some fight training right now."

Anya nodded. "I'll meet you and Therese in the training room in twenty minutes." Anya left the room to go change. Gwen looked quickly at Matthew, who nodded, and Gwen followed Anya out.

Dougal raised an eyebrow. "What was that?"

"I don't think Anya will sneak out, but just in case she is thinking about it, Gwen is going to keep an eye on her. "

"I'd sneak out," Therese said.

"Aw, you'd sneak out to find me, lass?"

Therese snorted. "No, Declan. You're on your own."

Matthew rolled his eyes. "I am going to change. You two; work your shit out. And don't bring it in here again." With that, Matthew walked out of the room.

***

Gwen knocked on the bedroom door and opened it slightly to see Anya standing in the middle of the room. "Anya?"

"You sent up to make sure I don't do a runner?"

"No, of course not!" Gwen said unconvincingly.

Anya cracked a small smile. "It's what I would have done, sent you up after me."

"Were you planning on it?"

"I admit that it occurred to me. But Matthew is right, I am not needed right now, and I would be in the way. I can't feel him, so I can't find him." She looked pained. "Gwen," she whispered. "I can't feel him."

Gwen went over and wrapped her arms around her friend. "Oh Annie, I know. He's ok. He's smart, he's tough, he'll survive until we find him."

"We'll find him?"

"Yes. We absolutely will find him!"

Anya squeezed her friend and pulled back. "Ok, then. Come with me while I change."

"Of course. Not for nothing, this bedroom is cool as hell." She followed Anya into the closet and gaped. "Holy fucking shitballs! This closet is enormous! I could live in here."

"No thank you. We have sex in here sometimes and you'd be in the way."

"Right. Is there any place you don't have sex though?"

Anya shrugged. "I mean, have you seen him?"

Gwen barked out a laugh. "You have a point. Ok, change. I want to watch you kick Matthew's ass."

"Not Therese?"

"Oh girl, I love you. But you are never kicking her ass!"

***

It was 5 a.m. when Michel showed up with Christian. He strode into Declan's sitting room, where Gwen was sleeping on a couch, her head in Anya's lap. Anya was mindlessly stroking her friend's hair and staring into space. Michael strode in with Christian over his shoulder, the club manager swearing a blue streak. "Shut up!" yelled Michel as he unceremoniously dumped the demon onto the floor. Christian immediately shut up and winced as his back hit the floor. "Michel, I told you…" Michel lifted his foot and hit Christian square in the solar plexus.

Matthew raised an eyebrow at his friend. "He ran from me. You know how that infuriates me. I hate when they run." his French accent was very strong at present, and Anya suspected it was from keeping a lid on his temper. Anya finally saw how Michel had gotten his reputation. She could feel how close he was to letting his beast out.

Gwen was awake now and rubbing her eyes. "That's quite the way to wake up."

Mara, also in the room, spoke up. "I will go make coffee."

Anya stood and walked over to Christian and looked down at him. "Consort," he said in a small voice.

She just looked at him. "His eyes are glassy. Did you give him anything?"

"All he gave me was a swift kick before he decided to carry me here. *Paysan!*"

"Watch who you call 'peasant'. You may have some skills, but you are still no match for me. The revolution was over two hundred years ago, perhaps it's time to put it to bed."

Ah, that explained a lot about Christian's overall attitude. "Bourgeoisie?"

"I was a member of the Royal household!"

"A minor member." Michel scoffed.

"Nonetheless, I was still a member."

"Yeah, I don't really care, Christian." This was from Anya. "Hoist your royal ass onto a chair and start explaining yourself or I am going to let Michel have you."

"I do not take orders from you." Christian's pupils were very dilated, thought Anya. That can't be good.

Matthew marched over, pulled his foot up and stomped right on the demon's ribs. "You disrespect the consort again; I will tear you apart with my bare hands and then dump you in a cell until I get permission to end your existence." He pulled him up and dumped him in a chair. "Now, talk. Or we'll just start by removing body parts."

"Matthew Is this usual behavior from him?" Anya asked.

"His disrespect? No, it's not. It's damned odd actually."

"Look at him, glassy eyes with the pupils dilated. Behaving in an unusual way, something isn't right."

Gwen muscled between the two and stared at Christian. "Anya's right, his eyes are glassy. It might be the dregs of a spell and it may explain why he's so pissy." She stared at him a moment more. "Or he's just kind of a prick."

"Prick," said Michel and Dougal in unison.

Matthew cut them a look and then focused on Christian again. "Christian, were you drugged?"

Christian opened his mouth, closed it. They could see the struggle. "I don't have to tell you anything," he finally bit out, then gasped at what he'd just said.

Matthew looked at Gwen. "Smack him. Really hard." she suggested.

"Will that work?"

"Not sure. It may just be really satisfying to us, but it also might clear the last of the spell out. Otherwise, we have to wait, it would take longer to unpick the magic at this point."

"I'll do it, Matthew. You'd probably take his head off right now," said Anya.

"Oh, I am going to enjoy this." said Matthew and pulled Gwen back to give Anya room.

Christian glared up at her, as Anya brought her hand back and connected with his face. Hard.

"I really wish I had filmed that," said Luc.

Christian grunted. His pupils were almost back to normal size. He nodded at her and she smacked him again. Christian shook his head. Gave himself a couple of more smacks, took a deep breath and looked up. "Ah, there you are. Clear eyes," Anya said.

"Consort, I am so sorry for what I said to you." He looked around the room. "And you as well, Michel and Matthew."

Matthew put a hand on the man's shoulder and squeezed gently. "First off, I am impressed and astounded that it worked. Secondly, that wasn't you. I mean, you are a prig, but not this big of one." Michel muffled a laugh with a cough. "Coffee is coming, but can you tell me what happened?"

"Give me a minute. I need to work it out in my head, I am still a bit fuzzy." Mara came in with the coffee just then and Anya brought him a cup. "Thank you consort. I do not deserve it. I have failed Declan."

"My name is Anya. Please try not to be so dramatic and you are welcome."

He nodded and took a healthy drink of the coffee. "I was out back, smoking a cigar and a fog came in." He stopped. "No. It wasn't a real fog. Just a mist and I thought it was odd and then a man appeared out of that mist. I kept shaking my head and he told me to stop it, that it wouldn't help." He took a breath. "The rest is going to be disjointed, that's how I remember it. He told me I needed to go in and get Declan and bring him out, make some excuse. I said he wouldn't be alone, and the man said that was fine, they could all come along. But I was to bring him outside. I saw Dougal and he told me to go sit with Declan for a bit, he needed to handle something."

They all looked at Dougal. "A dark club is not a place where I can tell someone's pupils are dilated and he was acting normal. For him." Anya nodded and motioned Christian to continue.

"I went up to Declan and told him exactly what the man outside said. It was important and he had to come. But I cannot remember...no, I do. I was told to tell him it had something to do with the consort."

"Smart of them. Anya is the only thing that would cause Declan to abandon reason and caution."

"Well, I don't like that," Anya said.

"Continue Christian," this from Matthew.

Christian shrugged. "I remember nothing after that. Well, until Michel found me. And I barely remember that."

"Where did you find him?" Anya asked Michel?"

"A few blocks west of the club. No sign of the two guards though."

"Can you recall what the misty guy looked like?"

"I only remember one thing. When I got back outside, there were two mist guys. Maybe there had been two before I do not know. But I remember something about the second man, his accent. He was Russian."

Anya stiffened. "Annie?" asked Gwen. "You ok?" Anya nodded.

"Do you need to punch something?" asked Therese. Anya nodded again.

Christian stood up. "You can hit me again. I deserve it."

"No. You don't. This isn't your fault. And I suspect the guilt you're going to lay on yourself is worse than the guilt any of us could lay on you." Michel went to speak but Anya stopped him. "No, Michel. Enough now."

"*Bien*. You are right. Christian will beat himself up enough over it. But you need someone to punch. You can punch me."

"I am not going to punch you. I am not punching any of you. It will hold until I actually get to punch someone who deserves it."

"Are you now imagining punching Liliana over and over again?" asked Therese.

"I am actually." Anya steepled her hands under her chin and thought for a moment. "Ok, we need to rest. All of us. So, that's the first thing that needs to happen. Gwen, I'd like it if you'd stay here with me." The blonde nodded. "No one goes anywhere alone. That includes me. No lone wolf shit. Christian, you're going to run the club and Dougal, you are his shadow. You stick to him like glue."

"You don't trust me," said Christian.

"I do, as it happens. But Liliana is going to know you told us what you could and that puts you in danger. And I trust Dougal to protect you." She looked at both Dougal and Therese pointedly.

"As you wish, consort."

"Jesus, please stop calling me that. My name is Anya, call me that."

"Yes Anya."

"Good, thank you. Michel and Luc, you're on Natalia and Vlad. Keep watch and see who comes and goes out of their suite. And Michel, make sure Donovan does another sweep for the two missing demons. I do not think we'll see those demons again, but I'd like to be sure. Have him double the eyes we have in all of Declan's clubs. They will report directly to him as usual. If we do not have eyes on Liliana and Francois, that needs to happen now. Matthew will run the day to day as Declan normally would and have sweeps done of the usual haunts and tourist attractions. Matthew, also please alert Marchand as to what's going on and have him keep eyes and ears out. You will not have time so please have any demon on the force report directly to him as well."

Christ that was a good idea thought Matthew. Marchand would firmly be in their circle from that point on.

Anya continued, "All the other clubs that includes the rest of France and those in Belgium need to be swept. I don't think we'll find them, but we need to make sure nothing odd is going on in them. Everyone outside of this room reports to you. Otherwise report to me." She took a breath. "Matthew, you do not go anywhere alone. Take a demon you trust, Donovan or me. It is not up for debate. Donovan will have the same rules and I will explain them myself. "She looked at Therese, who stared back. "I assume you're just going to stick to me then?"

"You assume correctly...consort."

"Therese, do not make me stab you." The other woman barked out a laugh.

"Mara, you do not leave the house alone either. I am going to be going through the books I have to see what I can find along with Gwen. The three of us will also conduct our own search. Not up for debate." She took and breath and noticed everyone staring at her. "What?"

"The way you just gave everyone their marching orders was amazing."

"Oh. Oh, I hadn't really thought about it. Matthew..."

"No. You did as you were supposed to do. You are acting in Declan's stead, as his mate. Your orders are good ones. We'll all follow them. I will talk to Donovan and let him know you'll be contacting him later."

"Now, everyone needs to sleep. I am tempted to keep you all here, but that would alert those watching us. So, everyone goes home, but be safe. I know Matthew and Luc are in the same building, so watch each other's backs. Where does everyone else live?"

"Christian lives in Matthew's building as well. I have a house, and Michel and Dougal can stay with me There's room and that's not all that unusual," said Therese.

"And my security is great. But I will add extra men and review all the protocols before I get some rest," added Matthew.

"Well, that makes me feel a lot better."

"Michel? I know you're going to hate this..."

"Yes, I will call Omala and see if she's heard anything." And he'd be cautioning her to also be careful. If anything happened to her....no, he couldn't think about that now.

"Thank you! Ok everyone, go rest." Anya would see that Gwen and Therese were settled and then get some rest. She didn't think she'd sleep, the bed was far too big and too lonely without Declan, but she did need to take some downtime, or she'd burn out. *Just hang on lyubov moya, hang on.*

CHAPTER 35

Two days later, they were no closer to finding Declan. Anya wasn't sleeping or eating, and this was causing Gwen to hover, which was increasingly irritating to Anya, though she knew it came from a good place. She was trying to choke down some food so her friend would leave her alone for a bit when Michel and Luc showed up. Anya's head snapped up. "Anything?"

"*Oui!*" said the older demon. "I do not understand why Natalia needs the entire floor of a hotel! It is absurd. And not just because it makes our job difficult. But this one, *visage d'un ange*, managed to get up onto the floor today."

Luc made a face. "I do not have the face of an angel!"

"Ah, my friend, you do though."

"I'm afraid you do Luc." Anya smiled wanly at him. "It's part of why I sent you with Michel. He is very handsome, and charming. But I thought this might also need a gentler touch. One, or both of you were going to be able to charm your way in. And for you, all you need to do is widen those brown eyes at people and boom! You look guileless."

"*Merde!*" said the young demon.

"One day, you will be grateful for it." And she hoped it would help keep him from getting too cynical or jaded. Like Michel was, underneath that charm. "But tell me what you found out."

"Natalia very well may not know that Declan is missing. But she knows something is wrong. I managed to snag a uniform from one of the bellhops, this is how I got onto the floor."

"How did you do that?"

Michel snorted. "He may look innocent, but the boy can spin a tale. He found a bellhop around his size and told him that he wanted to surprise his grandmother, whom he hadn't seen since his mother took him to America when he was small, after a terrible fight with her family. His mother had just died….and here, he managed to squeeze out some tears….and he was afraid that the familial bad blood would cause his *grand-mere* to not let him in. So, if he could borrow a uniform to get in, he was sure to get in and he could make it right. There was more, but that was the gist of it. The bellhop was openly sobbing at this point and let him borrow his extra uniform. I have never seen a performance like it and I sure as hell couldn't have done it."

"Where the hell did you learn that?" asked an astonished Gwen.

Luc shrugged. "I have always been able to do it."

"He's a reader. I can do it too. We let our imaginations run away with us." Anya winked at him. "Continue."

"Michel had swiped a keycard, so once I got the uniform, it was easy to get up there and I just stayed as hidden as I could. There is a small utility closet that abuts their suite."

"Really?"

"Yes. But it is full of all of their own personal linens, etc. There is one supply closet for the rest of the floor and one for them."

"I suppose they don't want to wait when they want things."

"I think you are correct. I saw Liliana and your brother get off the elevator and jumped into the closet. They stopped near it before carrying on to the door of the suite. Mercule was not there, and I heard Liliana tell Pavel to not say anything about Declan, that Natalia didn't know. And that she didn't need to know. Pavel said he wouldn't say anything, but that Natalia may wonder where Mercule is. Liliana said that Mercule wasn't Natalia's any longer and that the old woman had better know her place."

"Wow. Let's just pocket that little piece of information for now. We may need it later."

"Pavel seemed unconvinced. I think he is playing both sides to see who comes out the winner."

"That seems right." said Michel. "Natalia may have had a hand in bringing him back, and Liliana has promised him the moon I am sure. But he hasn't really placed his loyalty anywhere. He wants to see how it plays out."

"You've just described my brother in a nutshell. Whenever our parents fought, he'd always wait to see who would win the fight before he decided where he was siding."

"There's a bit more. The walls in the closet are paper thin and everyone seemed to be using their big booming 'I am important' voices, even your brother. Which was kind of funny actually."

"How do you mean?"

"He's no you. He couldn't command a room if it were full of toy army men."

Anya smiled and gave Luc a kiss on the cheek. "That's very sweet of you."

"He just called you formidable and scary, and you think that's sweet?" asked Michel.

"Have you met Annie?" asked Gwen.

Michel nodded. "Point."

"Anyway, Natalia and Lilliana were basically trying to get information out of each other about whether you would both be there tonight. Liliana said she wasn't so sure that you had the stomach for it. Natalia bristled at first but did say…" Luc stopped.

"Go on, Luc. Nothing she can say will hurt me."

The young demon cleared his throat but continued. "Natalia said that you were still young and undisciplined. But what could anyone expect from someone who has half Romany and was left to grow up wild. That she could mold you into a true consort. Liliana scoffed and said it was doubtful. Better to get rid of you. Natalia didn't exactly agree, but she also didn't disagree."

A knife whizzed by Luc and Michel, embedding itself in the wall behind them. "I thought you said…"

"I said I wouldn't be hurt; I didn't say I wouldn't be angry."

"Fair," said Michel.

"Ok. Get everyone together. The Council meeting is tonight, and we need a plan."

***

Anya was taking a few minutes alone in the bedroom before heading downstairs and working out a plan for that night. She had no desire to be considered a renegade, but she also didn't want to lay all of her cards on the table. Doing that might put Declan in further jeopardy. She was sure he wasn't dead, even though she couldn't feel him. The hole he left was a sharp ache, but she felt hollow at the same time. She missed him; his touch, his smell, the solid weight of him. Ugh. Love was just stupid and there she'd gone and fallen right in it. She rubbed her face and felt a faint beat. She sat up straight and silenced her brain as much as she could. *Are you there, Declan? Is that you?* It could very well be nothing, or an echo, or everything.

Malysh

There! She'd heard it, felt it. Very very faint. Almost too faint, as if from very far away.

Declan? I'm here. Where are you, my love?

So tired. Can't think straight.

She tamped down her spike of rage. *I know, love, I know. We're going to find you, but can you help?"*

It was a full 30 seconds before he answered again, and it was the longest 30 seconds of her life.

Paris. Club

Which club? He owned a handful, and they'd all been searched.

Hate it. Spell...hard to.... Get...through. Don't...you here. She knew which club that was. It was the one he didn't want her near, he didn't like going there either. But the club was necessary to keep the worst of demon behavior at bay and out of the general human populace. t was the same club that housed the basement interrogation rooms and had been the first place they had looked.

We searched all of the clubs. Are you saying there's a spell where you are?

Another long pause. *Yes.* That was so faint. *Spelled...room.*

I'm coming, Declan. We're coming to get you.

Not...worth...

It is. I know where you are, and I'm coming. Rest now, lyubov moya...you will need your strength.

Malysh....

Gone again. But she knew where he was here. She flew downstairs and into the dining room, where everyone had gathered, including Marchand. "I know where he is!"

"How? Where?" Gwen asked.

"I felt him, briefly. He managed to get through to me. He's very weak and it's likely taken him the two days to get up enough juice to do that. He's at Brimstone, God that name is dumb, there's a spelled room there. That's where he is. Gwen…"

"If it's a fancy glamour, I can break it. I can break any damned glamour they can throw at us."

"Ok, Gwen, Matthew and I go to the club, break the spell, get Declan and get to the Council meeting. The rest, head to the meeting. Try to stall as best you can."

"Is there anything you need from me?" asked Marchand.

"I don't know what to expect at the club. Is there a way to make sure people stay away from it?"

Marchand thought. "Actually, yes. Now that your people in the department know me, I can work on diverting traffic and setting up some detours. I will go do that now." He stood up to leave.

"Be safe." This was from Therese, and everyone turned to look at her. "What? He's human and I want him to be careful because… he's human."

"You said that already." Dougal pointed out. She glared at him.

Marchand looked at Therese and smiled broadly. "I promise to be careful." He sketched her a quick bow and left.

"I will murder the first person who says anything about that."

"Ok, moving on then!" said Anya.

"If the spell is really strong, I may need Luc. He's a good conduit."

"Fine. Luc is also with us. But know that it is not going to be safe and punches at minimum, will be thrown."

"Fine with me," answered Luc.

"Good. Gwen weapon up. Matthew, you take Declan's Demon Killers until we get him, and he can handle them. I'll take mine."

"Could we just go to the Council meeting and tell them the truth?" asked Gwen.

"No. First off, I think that would end up being death for Declan, and myself. Mercule could manage that quickly enough. Secondly, I am not sure I want to out Natalia yet. I am going to let her know, privately, that I know, but I am not excited about exposing her and Vlad to the Council. Who's to say we'd be believed anyway. And Declan does not want to run Eastern or Western Europe right now. If we were believed, that's exactly what would happen. I don't want Declan seen as weak because two old ladies decided they could play him. But Liliana is going to get a challenge from me, and I am going to show Natalia what an undisciplined wild woman can really do. We can't say we're strong, we have to show it. And I don't want anyone else on this Council pulling this shit in the future."

"They might."

"But if both Declan and I show up together, Liliana will see that we aren't so easily beaten, and it may cause others to think twice before screwing with us."

"You'll create enemies this way."

"Big deal. My mother was my first enemy and I survived that. I can survive this, and so can Declan."

Matthew smiled at her. Damned if she wasn't a natural at this. "Works for me."

"Great! Everyone knows what they need to do. Now, let's do it."

***

Back upstairs in their closet, Anya peered at herself in the mirror. Dressed in black leather leggings, a long-sleeved black top, black boots, and her hair pulled back into a tight braid, she looked every inch an assassin. She had rimmed her eyes in black kohl and gone with a lipstick that was so red, it was almost black. It was a look, and she knew she was going to need to look hard in front of the Council. She had knives up arms, in her boots and the demon killers strapped to her back. She had more knives in her coat. She was not fucking around. She had picked out an all-black outfit for Declan as well, he'd need to change before they walked into the Council room. She held his jacket up to her face and took a sniff. Smelled like him and she buried her face in the fabric and let out a small sob.

Straightening up, she sighed and said, "Glad that's out of my system now...enough of that nonsense." She put the outfit in a garment bag and grabbed the other set of swords and carried the whole thing downstairs and out to the car. Matthew was driving and Gwen and Luc were in the backseat. She put the weapons and clothes in the trunk and got into the front seat.

"Clothes?" asked Gwen.

"He's going to need to change." said Matthew. "He can't walk in there looking like he's been held captive the last few days."

"I can also glamour him a bit, so he looks in peak health."

"Good. Anya, you look pretty great, but scary as fuck," said Matthew.

"I enjoy hearing you say 'fuck' in that pretty accent."

"I did it especially for you." Matthew winked.

Anya snorted. "Ok, what's the plan?"

Matthew looked at her. "Oh, am I doing the plan this time?"

"You know the club better than I do, including the layout. Where's the most logical place for a hidden chamber?"

"The basement where the interrogation rooms are would be the most logical place. But I don't think they're there."

"Why not?"

"Because it's the most logical place."

"Good point. So, where?"

"The club has a main floor. There's a bar on either side, banquettes, and a dance area. There is a floor above that has another bar and more banquettes that are set into alcoves. But there is a network of rooms below the main floor, private rooms, and I think if it was going to be anywhere, it would be there. We did search it, but we weren't looking for spelled rooms."

"Did it feel weird down there?" This was from Gwen.

"Yes, but it always feels weird down there to me. And to Declan. It caters to darker demons, most of them very old and the energy is very weird. It's frightening and tempting at the same time. Those demons have some old magic. Upstairs is a lot of your basic kinks and fetishes. Some more exotic stuff, which is why the dark alcoves on the second levels...but the basement levels are the real reason for the club."

"How many levels?"

"Five. Four cater to the dark demons."

"Shit. Are those demons connected to the thing that Declan won't talk to me about it?"

Matthew's hands tightened on the steering wheel. "Yes. And neither will I."

"Ease down, champ. I am not asking you to."

"Sorry. The thing is, it's the temptation. Most of us hate it because we can see how we could very easily succumb to that level of depravity. Don't get me wrong, I have no problem with what goes on in the upper levels of the club as long as people don't get really hurt and it's all consensual, neither does Declan. But the lower levels are different."

"Are we safe?"

"These swords will kill those demons too. We're safe enough. Gwen will likely not feel anything beyond weird energy. I am not sure about you. Luc, please take care down there." He looked at the young demon in the rearview and while Luc looked pale, he nodded. "And no one should actually bother us. But all of you, eyes straight ahead, no matter what you hear. You two, walk between Anya and me. They love unsuspecting humans and young demons."

"What do they do with them?" asked Anya, not sure if she really wanted to know.

"Declan will kill me..."

"I am walking in there to get my mate back and if there is a danger to the two people, I am bringing with me, I have a right to know."

Matthew sighed. "They feed on them."

"Fucking excuse me? Like a vampire? I mean, I know demons feed on energy..."

"No, they feast on them, their bodies and their souls. We don't officially allow that, but we also can't find a way to stop it completely, so we try to get them to focus on other outlets, it doesn't always work. We do our best."

"That is appalling and barbaric and we should really just kill all of them."

"I agree. But we are not allowed to unless they pose an actual threat. If someone comes after Angel Face or Blondie back there, that is a credible threat, and they die."

Anya turned around to look at her friends in the backseat. "Maybe you all shouldn't..."

"Feck off, Anya." Gwen looked affronted. "I am going in and that's that."

"Same," said Luc. "Well, not the...um...'feck off' bit. But I am going in."

"But..."

"Leave off, Anya! I mean it."

Anya shrugged and turned back around. "Fine. Fine. Just do what Matthew says. I am not trying to kill anyone today."

Matthew grinned. "Not even Liliana?"

"I am not actually planning on killing her. I am just going to weaken her in front of everyone. I am going to make her as much of a laughingstock as I can."

"Evil."

"Yup."

They pulled up in front of the club and got out of the car. "If Declan and I were going in together. He'd take the lead, with me almost next to him, just a bit behind. Anyone else, in back of us. It's safe enough to do it that way upstairs. Downstairs, we do it as I said in the car with Luc and Gwen in between us, and I go first."

Anya nodded and pushed open the doors, into chaos.

"What the actual fuck?" yelled Matthew.

"This isn't normal?" asked Anya.

"No. It's not." He grabbed one of the servers. "What's going on here?" he growled at the youngish looking man.

"Oh, Mr. Piedmont, I have no idea. I don't think anyone does. Everything was calm, then all of a sudden it was pandemonium."

Matthew let the man go and he stumbled out of there. "He is too young to be working here. I am going to need to reassign him. Also, someone knows that we're here. This was designed to pull our focus."

"Agreed. We need height. But not upstairs," Anya said.

"The bar."

They worked their way over to the bar and Anya divested a demon of the pistol he had just drawn while Matthew berated him since firearms weren't allowed in there. "We can't really keep knives out, though there's an honor system. But guns are a clear no-no. The little fucker."

There were no stools at the bar, so Matthew jumped onto top of it and reached for Anya, pulling her up easily. "You two stay down there. You don't need to be easy targets. Eyes on the ground are good as well," said Matthew.

"Well, this is a real shit show. Ready?" He nodded. Anya checked the gun, fiddled for a moment, and then fired a shot into the air. Most of the action stopped. Matthew let out a loud roar and the place fell silent. "Now that I have your attention; is there anyone here that does not know who I am?" She saw people shaking their heads. "Wonderful. Now, who wants to tell me what the fuck is going on in here?" No one spoke up.

Matthew's eyes went red "The consort has asked you a question. I would suggest that someone answer her. IMMEDIATELY!" The last word, shouted.

Anya winced internally and hoped that Matthew was never that angry at her. Someone stepped forward, towards the bar. "Consort, I think I can help."

"Good. Go ahead."

"Someone started yelling that Mr. O'Shea was dead and someone new would be taking over and then...there were some pretty nasty things yelled about you. Other people jumped in with opinions and then, well, a fight broke out."

"As I am standing here before you, I think we can rule out Mr. O'Shea being dead don't you?"

"It's just that someone said he was taken…"

"Who said? Who started this?" From Matthew.

Three demons stepped forward holding a squirming man. "Here! Here he is! He's the fecking one!" The man had one of the thickest brogues that Anya had ever heard.

"Oh! A countryman," breathed Gwen quietly. "So nice to hear."

"I am not going to tell you anything! You fucking…."

Gwen put a hand to the man's forehead and said, "Calm yourself now." The man instantly stopped squirming. The big Irish demon looked at her. "I've a way with the lads." she winked at him, and the man blushed.

Anya hopped down to the floor. "I am going to ask you this once. Just once. Why did you do this?" Anya pulled her swords out, eliciting gasps and murmurs of 'is that them?' from all over the room. "And I had better like the answer."

"I was paid to do it."

"By whom?"

"I don't know who it was."

"Did he look like me? Speak like me?"

"He did."

"How did you know?" Matthew asked quietly, landing on the floor next to her.

"Who else would cajole someone else into saying shitty things about me? It wasn't enough to start the ruckus, he had to make it personal. I am not sure I believe him though."

"Fair point; well made. Let's see if he can tell us anything else."

"So, you were paid by my brother. Loser like you, where did he pick you up? The gutter? You can't be worth much. What did he promise you? He's lying, he'll never give you anything."

"*Russkaya suka!*" he spat. Russian bitch. "I'd do it again! I know you. I saw you when you were younger. Miss high and mighty, you'll get what's coming to you." Yup, Russian. She should have known.

"And so will you," she said calmly, jumping down off the bar and raising her sword. "*Dasvidaniya!*" With one clean sweep of her arm, she removed the man's head from his body and watched as he fell. Matthew gestured for someone to come remove the body, and the head.

"Fucking hell, that was sweet!" said her new Irish friend. "Just don't use it on me."

"You're safe enough." She turned to the crowd. "Does anyone else have anything to say about me or mine right now? Because quite frankly, I am in a mood." The place was silent. "Good!" She looked over at Matthew, who nodded.

"You all go back to what you were doing. But if another fight breaks out, and we have to come back up here, I am going to rip the place apart. "Understood?"

The entire club nodded. Matthew made a couple of gestures for the music to start and the bartenders to get back to work.

"You, who are you?" demanded Matthew.

"Sean Donnelly, sir."

"What are you even doing here?"

"Oh aye, this one," he pointed at his friend "Thought it would be fun. We just landed from Ireland. He is an idjit."

"Can you all stay for a bit and make sure things stay calm. If not, call this number and help will come. Also, take these cards. They're for Demon's Folly and I think you'll be happier there."

"Will do, boss. And thanks!" He turned to his friends. "Ok, lads...you heard the man, keep a watch now!"

CHAPTER 36

Once they made it to the entrance to the catacomb of basement rooms, Gwen spoke up. "I'm not judging, but why?"

"She had to, Gwen. She had to make a point that betrayals and disloyalty are punished. She can't be seen as weak." This was from Luc.

"Exactly. She had to take and keep control of that room. Additionally, insults to the consort are not to be tolerated. If Anya hadn't done it, I would have."

"I don't like that I had to do it. And when I think about it later, it will bother me, but I can't think about that right now. I just know it was necessary."

Gwen thought for a moment. "Fair. Thank you all for explaining."

They started down the stairs and hit the first level and Anya could feel it. It was a pulsating menace. It was frightening, but it also did tempt her. It was a dark caress against her skin, and she knew why Matthew and Declan hated it down here. It was altogether way too tempting to just succumb. She cleared her throat.

"Gwen, what do you feel?" asked Anya.

"Menace."

"Nothing else?"

"No. It feels old and dark. There's powerful magic here, but the spelled room is not on this level."

"Nothing else?"

"No," said Gwen.

"Just checking." Anya swallowed hard.

Matthew leaned over to Anya quietly. "You feel it, don't you?" She nodded. "It's the connection to Declan."

"It is putting some very, um...erotic images in my mind."

"Are they of you, me and Declan?"

"Fuck, yes." she was gritting her teeth. She did not want these images and she knew Matthew didn't either.

"Same."

"Are you two ok?" Gwen looked at them. They nodded.

Anya looked up. "Luc, you good over there?"

"*Oui.* But it is not easy, I have to say."

"What isn't?" asked Gwen.

"The space is putting ideas and images in our heads to tempt us. I am mated to a demon, so I can feel it too. Gwen, count yourself lucky on this. Ok, Luc and Matthew, breathe in very deeply and then breathe out slowly." She did it with them...Jesus, was that position even possible? Ok, no, stop it Anya. "Again." Breathe in, breathe out. "Good, again...make it count." And a third time. "Manageable?" The two nodded. "Great. Gwen...thoughts?"

"So, I think it will be on the lowest level, but I should be able to feel it. How many levels?"

"Four."

"Ok, let's roll." With each level, the images flared in her mind anew and she had to grit her teeth and work through it with some deep breaths. Matthew looked fine. His control must be ridiculous. Luc looked green, but was keeping up. Luckily, no doors opened. Anya wasn't sure she'd be able to do anything if they had. This was mortifying. They were getting the same images and they were going to have to look at each other after this. She wanted to torch this whole lower level and the demons in it. She got the sense they thought this was funny, it's how they were amusing themselves right now.

They finally got to the fourth level. "Yup," said Gwen. "It's here. Turn left." They walked for a few minutes before she called out again. "Stop! Here!"

Gwen was facing to the left. All Anya saw was a blank wall. That was the point, she supposed.

"Luc, do you feel it?" asked Gwen.

"I do," he said. "This is definitely it."

"Can you break it?"

"I can."

"Great. But we don't know what's on the other side of the door. We think, we hope that it's Declan. But it may not be, or there may be something else with him."

"He's there." said Anya. Matthew looked at her. "No, I can feel him a bit more now that we're here." The images seemed to have eased off, she thought with relief.

"Could a spell have amplified what we just experienced? Because I seem to be ok now. You two?" The men nodded.

"Yes," said Luc. "It probably was a spell. This one, instead of turning the power back on the actual demon amplified what happens down here anyway."

"Well that's fucking insidious," said Anya.

"Yes. But as soon as we got here, the spell abated."

"Yes, the malevolence I felt did back off some as well," said Gwen. "Luc, let's do this."

Anya and Matthew stood back to let them work. "Declan doesn't ever need to know about the images," said Matthew.

"Would we have seen them without the spell?"

"I don't think so. It used the close bond we all share. Even though that bond is platonic, it's still very strong." He sighed. "The images don't usually show you what you want or have thought about, but what you can have, what is possible, if you just give into it."

"That's fucked up. Have you ever given in?"

"No. Neither has Declan. It was something neither of us could help." He smiled at her. "I got Dougal once. I suspect someone just thought that was funny. It was horrifying."

Anya smothered a small laugh. "I felt that. Like they do it for their perverse amusement."

"In a way, that is very true."

"Ok! Broken!" Gwen shouted.

Matthew and Anya stepped up. "Thanks you two! Stand back!"

"God, you two look like really sexy cops!"

Matthew winced. "Don't say that. Please don't." He closed his eyes. When he opened them, Anya was smiling at him. "Kick it in, sexy!" she said. He rolled his eyes but did as she said. In the middle of the room was a chair and tied to that chair, head hanging down, was Declan.

"Declan!" she ran to him. "Declan?! Can you hear me?"

"This room feels wrong. Very wrong. He should be able to get out of those ropes."

Luc walked over to the chair holding Declan. "Also spelled. But an easy one, I can do this one myself. I have been practicing. But there *is* something wrong with the room." He leaned down. "Anya. He should wake up once I take care of the spell." He squeezed her shoulder.

"Thank you." She whispered, trying not to cry. She smoothed Declan's hair back and kissed his forehead. "I might kill that bitch after all." She stood. "So, Mercule's spell uses his magic, and it boomerangs back at him. So, I am going to assume that because of that, his use of it is nullified. But I wonder about someone else's demon magic. Matthew, what is yours?"

"Compulsion."

"Try it on me."

He blanched. "I don't...."

"Do it, please. It's a theory."

"Fine." He stared at her. "Kneel!" She remained standing. "Kneel down!"

"Nope." Anya shrugged.

"So, the room is also spelled so you all can't use your special demon magic trick. Mercule had to make sure that Declan couldn't get out of here or overpower him."

"I could have told you all that." said Gwen. She created a ball of light. "Oh, but he screwed up. He didn't set the spell in here to nullify another witch's magic. The fool!" she said with contempt.

"Is it worth unpicking the one on the room?"

"Nah. Once we get Declan, we can just get out of here."

There was a groan from the chair. "Anya?"

She leaned down. "Declan?" He raised his head. His face was bruised. "Couldn't heal himself either. Fuckers!" She stroked his face gently.

"*Malysh*, are you really here? I kept imagining...but then you weren't here."

"I am here. Really here. You talked to me; do you remember? You told me where to find you."

"I tried so hard to...wasn't sure."

"The spell isn't self-sustaining. It has to be reset, so Declan got through when it was at a weak spot."

Gwen walked around, wrinkling her nose. She said a few words and writing appeared on the wall opposite Declan. "Um,I think we're going to be getting some company any minute."

"Protect Declan!" yelled Matthew to Luc and Gwen, as a door appeared on the other side of where they had come in. It burst open and a number of grunt demons streamed in. Matthew pulled out the swords as Anya did the same. "You ready?"

"Oh, I'm ready!"

Luc and Anya pulled Declan over by the door they had come in and flanked him as best they could.

The demon at the front cackled at them.

"Jesus...does he think he's scary?"

"I think he does, yes." Matthew laughed. "You know this is another delay tactic?"

"Yeah. Let's kill who we can while we head towards our door. Gwen…"

"She's spelling the other door so we don't get more visitors and these guys can't get out. She'll spell this one once we get through it." said Luc, as Gwen was concentrating.

"His magic is a real fucker, but I think I am getting somewhere. But hurry up!"

The cackling demon headed towards Anya. "Shit! Fast!" She said as she just managed to avoid getting knocked down by him. She spun as he hurtled past, shoving one broadsword in his back, while she took off his head with the other."

"Show off!" said Matthew as he used the swords to behead two demons at once.

"One to talk!" she ran at the fourth demon, slicing him in half. "Why are they so fast? Spelled?"

"No. They're just very old and some of the foot soldiers get really fast."

"Great! That's super!"

Matthew and Anya made their way towards their door as Gwen finally managed to stem the tide of Demons coming in through the other one. "We have the spell for this door ready, but we'll need to be quick."

"Pull Declan out." Luc picked up his boss gently and carried him out. Gwen backed out after him.

"Anya, go!" yelled Matthew. Anya stepped through, and Matthew followed. He shrugged and yelled "STOP!" into the room. All the demons stopped. "KNEEL!" They all kneeled. And he slammed the door shut. Matthew and Anya re-sheathed the swords. "I thought I'd try it, just on the off chance it worked."

"Lazy spell work if your magic works from out here," muttered Gwen as she set a spell on the door to keep them in there and then reset the spell to hide the room. Declan raised his head and touched the wall and flicked his wrist.

"What did you do?"

"He pulled the room out of time, so it'll be harder to find," answered Matthew

"I thought he could only pull himself and other people out?! That's a fun addition," said Anya.

"Yup. Should hold for a while. But he's still weak and shouldn't have."

Matthew turned around and picked up Declan and put him over his shoulder, fireman style. He continued down the hallway. "There's a back exit this way, we won't be seen." He tossed Luc his keys. "You go up first and bring the car here." Luc took off.

"We couldn't have come in this way?"

"It's only an exit. You can't get in that way. You can't even see it from the outside." Gwen and Anya followed Matthew up the hallway to another set of stairs, climbing until they hit an unmarked door. The car was waiting and no one else was about. Gwen opened the door while Anya got Declan's clothes out of the trunk, took off her jacket and shrugged out of the back sheath with her swords in them and wrapped them in the silk she had also brought for this. That done, she climbed in the back with her mate. Gwen climbed in front and Luc moved to the backseat.

"Gwen, please text Donovan and let him we're on our way. All of us."

"Will do." Gwen let out a shaky laugh. "Shit, we actually did it."

"We did," said Matthew warmly, squeezing her hand.

"Declan? Honey, how are you?"

"I'd be better if I had a kiss," he said softly.

She smiled at him and touched her lips gently to his. As she went to pull away, he raised his hand to hold her head in place, deepening the kiss. "Declan, you're still weak," she said, pulling back.

"Getting better all the time. Also, you look really hot."

Matthew snorted. "Yeah, he's going to be fine."

"Am I in all black too?" Declan teased.

"Red pocket square, more or the less the same color as my lipstick."

"Jesus, you're good," he said. "Ok, I am going to need some help here."

Matthew drove like a bat out of hell while Anya and Luc brought Declan up to speed and got him ready, trying to be as gentle with him as they could. Once dressed, Gwen took care of the bruises.

"They're fading already, but I want you to look…Christ, Matthew, don't kill us…perfect. I also bumped up the color of your eyes."

"Thank you, Gwen."

"We're going to just make it, I think. Maybe a few minutes late. Fucking Paris traffic!" he said, laying on the horn out of sheer frustration.

"Well, Mercule didn't kill me, let's hope Matthew's driving doesn't either." Declan laughed.

Matthew glared at him in the rearview mirror. "See if I carry you up four flights again."

Declan smiled and put his hand on Matthew's shoulder. "Thank you, my friend. Thank all of you."

"No problem, boss," said Matthew. "Glad you aren't dead. Now try and rest a bit. You need to walk in under your own steam."

"Don't crash the car."

"No promises."

***

They pulled up five minutes late, to see Roger and Richelieu waiting impatiently. "I told them that you had phoned and that there was traffic," said Richelieu. They are waiting. I hope you have a good reason for being late."

"We do. We can tell you on the way." As Anya and Matthew pulled everything they needed out of the trunk, she quickly told the cardinal what had been going on.

They finally stopped in front of the entrance to the Council room and Anya took the time to fix her hair and lipstick quickly. "*Mon Dieu!* It is amazing you are all here. My respect for you all grows. Declan, your mate is a rare find."

"She is. I am so glad she decided to keep me." He nuzzled her neck.

"Declan, we're going through the other door. See you in there."

Declan nodded and shared a look with the other man that Anya couldn't work out.

"I shall go with you. I wish to see you both walk in." He kissed Anya's cheek. "*Courage, ma fille!*" The others went in the side door and Declan gestured for the other doors to be opened.

"Declan, the idea of consorts…"

"No, that will wait. Tonight, we need a show of strength. I shall follow your lead."

She took his arm. "I love you."

"I love you more."

And with that, they entered.

***

"As you can see," Liliana's shrill voice carried. "They are not here. Can we not have them declared renegade now?"

"I'm sorry, Liliana. Were you discussing us?" Declan's own voice boomed through the room.

Luc snuck up on Michel and whispered, "Now, that is an entrance!" Michel pulled the young man into a side hug and grinned.

All color drained from the Liliana's face as Declan and Anya stood before the Council, whole and hearty. Adjoa smiled broadly at the two of them and winked at Anya. Natalia clapped her hands. "I knew you'd come! Come, give me a kiss, Annechka!"

Anya walked over to Natalia and leaned down. "I know everything," she said, close to the woman's ear. "So, if you know what's good for you, you will back everything I say and do tonight. If you don't, we will destroy you."

Natalia remained composed and gave her relative a small nod to show she'd understood.

Anya walked back to Declan and took his arm again.

What did you tell her?

That I knew everything and that if she didn't back us tonight, we would destroy her.

God, that's sexy.

You are so weird. I don't see my brother, but I know he must be here.

I am sure our people are circulating, looking for him.

Indeed.

"Well, I am so glad you decided to show up", fumed Lilliana, not glad at all.

Francois put his hand on her arm and if possible, she got paler. A smackdown, thought Anya. Liliana is out of line. "Pardon my consort. She's been under some...stress lately. We thank you for coming."

We need to find Pavel and Mercule.

Agreed.

"Of course. But may we know why we are here."

"As if you don't know!" Liliana shouted. Francois pressed harder on Liliana's arm.

"That is quite enough, Liliana. Please sit and compose yourself." Liliana sat. But she gave a quick, almost imperceptible look to up to the left side of the balcony. Declan squeezed Anya's hand and she squeezed back to indicate she'd seen it. Declan found Matthew, but the man had already melted into the crowd having seen the look. Donovan was soon to follow.

Could be Mercule.

True, but I doubt it. I think she's likely going to try and spring your brother on you, so she's making sure he's here.

This is a good point. You're so smart.

Yes. I am. She felt him laugh through their bond and there was never anything that felt better than knowing he was back where he was supposed to be, with her.

"Again," he said out loud. "Why were we called here?"

"It has been brought to our attention that you are in possession of two fairly extraordinary sets of swords." Valentina, demon for South America, sounded bored. Lucia, her mate had her hand on Valentina's shoulder and was rubbing it lightly.

"We are in possession of a number of swords that could be considered extraordinary; could you be more specific?" If Declan had still not been feeling the ill effects of being spelled for so long, he'd almost be enjoying this.

Valentina sighed. "Declan, I like you, but please don't be tiresome."

Good to know she likes you.

It can't hurt. She does not suffer fools and I suspect she thinks Liliana is a fool. "I apologize Valentina. It's been a trying time, as there have been several attempts on my life and the life of my mate, and it's made me a bit churlish."

Well played.

I know I said I'd follow your lead, but I saw an opportunity.

We're a team. If something feels like it will work, we pivot.

"Pardon me?" Valentina sounded surprised.

"Attempts on our lives. So, if I am not entirely happy to be here discussing weaponry, you'll have to excuse me."

"To answer the question at hand," Anya added, "Yes, we have swords that can kill demons. We haven't exactly been hiding them. We've been using them to dispatch the demons sent to cause us harm."

There were several gasps throughout the room.

"So!" said Liliana "You don't deny it then!"

"Obviously not, Liliana." Declan was disdainful. "It's the only way, without magic, to kill demons that we know of."

"Magic?" asked Adjoa.

"Oh yes, magic. Maybe we should ask Liliana about that."

All eyes turned to the consort and Francois was looking coldly contemplative as he eyed his mate. "Liliana? I have suspected you were up to something. But magic?"

"Dark magic at that." added Anya.

"Liliana, you have been acting very suspiciously lately. Especially when you visited me the other day," added Natalia. *Thanks, grandma,* thought Anya. *You toe the line, and you might survive this.*

"As you know, my mate is still new and she can, like a young demon, still die."

"And if Declan dies, I also will die. He was stabbed with a dagger laced with dark magic. It almost killed both of us."

"How did you survive?"

"We have a witch." Thankfully, Gwen had insisted that they out her as a witch at the meeting.

"A witch?" asked Adjoa, fascinated. She was clearly enjoying this.

"Yes. She saved us."

"Wait, let me see if I have this straight. You have two sets of supposedly mythical broadswords that can kill demons and you have a witch."

"Yes."

And that's when the whispers of 'prophecy' could be heard through the room.

"SILENCE!" said Anaranth. The room immediately quieted down. "I have some questions about the swords, to start."

"Of course, Anaranth," said Declan smoothly.

"You received these when and from whom?"

"The when is a bit fuzzy, but I think it was five hundred years ago. It was from an Ancient who told me that I would need these one day and that I would know to whom the second set belonged when they appeared." *Which you well know, old man.*

"Who was the Ancient?"

"I do not know, she never said. She did say that she knew you when you first became a Demon."

"Well well, that is ancient." said Anaranth "So, was this when you were down in…"

"Yes." answered Declan shortly and Anya could feel the tension in his body ratchet up.

"Hmmm, fine then. And you knew when you and Anya mated that she was to have the second set of swords."

"Yes. No doubt in my mind. The Ancient was insistent that I would know, and I did."

"What do you plan to use them for?"

"Protection," said Anya. "To protect ourselves if we're attacked, or those we love. And to protect any demon who needs it if they are being hunted, hurt or abused."

Bold, my love.

I'm sorry for that. It popped out. But now that I've said it. I mean to keep that promise.

Do not be sorry, my avenging angel. It's a noble purpose and I am quite fine with it.

"What if someone makes you angry?" asked Valentina.

"Rosamund makes me angry every time I see her, but she's still alive, is she not?"

"Fair point," laughed Valentina.

"Of all the fucking nerve!" they heard Rosamund say.

"You are quite a handful, Rosamund." Anaranth chided her.

Anya snorted and had to cover it up with a cough. She wouldn't apologize for the statement though.

"So, these swords exist, and they work. That's a sobering thought, but it does not appear you have used them egregiously. So, *Liliana,*" he placed emphasis on the naming, knowing this was her idea. "What exactly is the purpose here?"

"I want those swords!"

"Oh?"

"Destroyed! I want them destroyed!"

"Well, I would like to prove that I can use them in a fight, with a demon or consort. And not kill them," said Anya.

"Really?" asked Anaranth.

"Yes. With Liliana actually." Anya smirked at the other consort.

The room fell silent again.

"Declan!" Matthew called from the balcony. Everyone looked towards the voice and Liliana's eyes widened. "Found him!" Matthew and Donovan were holding onto Anya's brother. The Russian was squirming and swearing, but his eyes were frightened.

"Wonderful! Send him down."

"Affirmative!" Matthew picked the man up. "Incoming!" and threw Pavel over the side. He landed close to Anya. He went to move, and Anya lifted a foot and dug her heel into his stomach.

"Pavel! *Moy brat! Vosstat' iz mertvykh!*" Back from the dead, indeed!

"Just in time! So, somehow Pavel here was turned into a demon, illegally. We think Liliana had something to do with it and has been using him and this magician to try and destroy us," said Declan. Not quite the truth, they actually thought it was Natalia, but they weren't ready to throw her under the bus at this point.

"Anaranth…" Liliana started.

"SILENCE!" Once again, a hush fell over the room. "This man is not supposed to be here. He should be dead." Anaranth glanced at Natalia and Vlad, giving them a hard look before he shifted his gaze to Francois and Liliana. Interesting, thought Declan.

He knows it was Natalia and Vlad, but he's going to ignore it.

It would seem so, malysh.

Why?

Natalia and Vlad are very powerful. Anaranth must want to hasten Francois stepping down, which does not delight me.

No, it wouldn't.

"Explain." One word from Anaranth.

"Anaranth, I didn't...I wouldn't..." Liliana stammered.

"I had nothing to do with this," said Francois. "But it seems like my mate may have."

"Francois, no! I said I would never, and I would not!"

Francois sighed before continuing. "It's possible you didn't bring the young Russian back." Anya stomped on her brother's hand for good measure, he yelped in surprise and pain. "But I fully believe you've been trying to harm these two and I know you believe in this foolish prophecy. I am not as much of a fool as you seem to think." He looked at Anya. "What do you want?"

"I want to fight your wife. If I win, she disappears from public life. For good. I never see her face again. She is kept under virtual lock and key. No visits from anyone, that includes Natalia. No more magicians, no more scheming. I want her gone."

"Magicians?"

"Yes. She has one. You should talk to her about that."

"I don't have a magician!"

"Woman, if you do not shut up, there will be no need for you to fight Anya. I will take care of you myself." Francois still had some teeth it would seem.

"She's been using him to harm us through magic. Without the swords, it would be her only avenue. Therefore, she is NOT getting these swords."

"They should be destroyed!"

"We can discuss that later. Anya, do you require anything else of Liliana?" This was from Anaranth.

"No."

"Francois?"

"Done. You do not want me to step down?"

Declan spoke up. "No, Francois. It is inevitable that I will be taking over for you. But Anya and I are newly mated, and it is not the right time to take our place on the Council. I also do not believe you have done all you can for your territory. But your mate is a danger. There is a further step I would request. I believe you know what I am asking."

"Done."

"Francois...you can't..."

"Liliana, let me be clear; I could repudiate our bond and then kill you. I'd still live that way. I am not going to kill you, but if Anya wins, you will be banished. Should you find a way around that banishment, then I will ensure your death." He swung to look at Anya. "If she wins? She may very well beat you."

"She gets to keep her place. For now."

"She would not be punished though," said Francois.

"If you want to devise a punishment for her, I will not stand in your way there."

Francois nodded. "That is fair. What of your brother?"

Anya looked down. "Oh, he's going to die."

"You will kill him?"

"Again? No. Once was enough. My mate will. If he chooses not to, in order to not upset me, his second in command will."

Matthew had made his way downstairs and was standing by Declan. "Well, hell. She knew the whole time what we were planning," said Matthew.

"No. I think she just knew we'd be willing to do it for her," Declan said quietly. "There are 4 swords total. I think both Matthew and I would like to dispatch the brother for her."

Anya looked over the two men and smiled broadly. "I accept that. I would like to give my bastard of a brother a chance to say his piece though. He's gone to so much trouble to try and kill me and my mate, that I'd like to hear what he has to say."

"It will not upset you?" asked Valentina.

"I would have to care about him to be upset by anything he has to say." She did care. But no one really needed to know that.

"Oh, I really like you," said Valentina. "On your feet then, Anya's brother. Come on then!"

Pavel took his time getting to his feet. Once there, he went to attack Anya, but was grabbed from behind by Therese.

"Today," said Valentina. "Is turning out to be very interesting indeed."

CHAPTER 37

"Valentina," said Therese.

"Therese! It's good to see you," said Valentina warmly.

"And you!" Therese grinned broadly.

Well, that's interesting, thought Anya. Something to follow up on at another time. "Thank you, Therese. Can you hold onto him for now?"

"Be my pleasure," said Therese as she picked up a steel toed boot and slammed it down on Pavel's own sneaker clad foot. "Oh sorry. Accident," she said as he let out a yelp.

Anya coughed to cover up a laugh. "Well, you little shit. Spit it out. You may as well have your say before you die. Again." Pavel just stared at her. "Pavel, I actually don't care one way or the other. You're dying today. And this time, I am not going to feel bad about it."

"For all of my life, I have had to listen to how wonderful you, how smart, how talented, how capable. Always being compared to you."

"By whom?"

"By our father. By...her!" he spat the word out, pointing at Natalia.

"By Natalia? Oh, well that's interesting."

"You don't even know. You don't know her part in this whole 'prophecy' bullshit!"

"I do, actually." She and Declan looked at each other and the whole thing became quite clear. Anya's original plan to not deal with Natalia flew out the window. "Good fucking God, you groomed both of us for our parts in this, didn't you? Me, to fulfill this prophecy, but you also used my brother. You wanted to create a scenario that would cement the prophecy idea. You put him in my path, so that killing him became probable. My brother was an expendable commodity to you in order to get me where I needed to be. You monster."

Pavel paled. "No...no, that's not it. Natalia, tell her! TELL HER!"

Natalia paled and started playing with the pearls at her throat, she didn't say anything. She didn't have to. The look on her face said it all. Anya all of a sudden felt very sorry for her brother. "You helped plant those seeds of hate. The only brother who ever loved me and you made him hate me. Why?" Still nothing from the old woman.

Declan stepped up and roared. The room stilled and Natalia paled even further. "Answer my mate immediately old woman or so help me God, I will pull you down and rip you apart."

Natalia looked at Valentina who looked back dispassionately. She'd get no help here. "Anya, there's...that's not true. He's delusional."

Vlad stood. "Natalia has been nothing but good to you. How can you say all of this?"

Anya pivoted to Pavel. "What were you promised?"

"Power was all I ever wanted. This is what I had to do to get it."

She turned back to Vlad. "Did he ask for this?"

"No. He didn't. We went to him with the deal."

"Vladimir, that is not done," said Anaranth. "We do not make demons for our own gain."

"It is a grey area."

"It's unethical. Not quite illegal, but you know better." Anaranth shook his head.

Anya was not convinced. She was pretty sure they used the drug on him but didn't want to admit it. She'd let that go for now. She wanted to keep it in her back pocket for another time. She caught Declan's eye and he nodded at her, thinking the same.

"How did you know that Declan had the swords?" Anya asked Natalia.

"Educated guess by Vlad and myself." Anya didn't believe her, but let it go.

"She had others you know? In case you didn't work out. You're not so special." Natalia sucked in her breath.

"I know, Pavel, I know." She turned to Natalia. Since it was out in the open, she might as well go for it. "Why?"

"Because you are your father's daughter. You are willful. Stubborn to your core. Groom you? There was no grooming you! You have always done what you want. Feeding you fairytales is all I did."

"But they weren't fairytales to you," said Declan. "You set this entire situation up; including getting Liliana involved."

"It was a win-win for us. Either you or Pavel would have Western Europe. Family." said Vlad. "Natalia does care about Anya though."

"But she cares about herself and your power base more," said Declan. "What you did to these two is unforgivable." He smiled at his mate. "I am very glad to have Anya. But you manipulated them. You warped an innocent boy. You took away someone she loved, and that loved her."

"That is very poorly done," said Adjoa, showing where her loyalties were currently. "The ends do not justify the means, Vlad. We cannot do anything more than give you an official censure. But this we will do."

Anya pivoted to Adjoa and mouthed a 'Thank you' at her. Demon politics were such bullshit.

"But look at Anya now!" said Natalia.

"Don't you dare try and take credit for this, old woman. None of this has anything to do with you. You can't say you didn't groom me then take credit when I do something right." She turned to Pavel. "So, we've established that you're jealous of me. Great. But it does not explain why you hate me so much. It can't just be jealousy. Is it our mother?"

"She's not your mother!" said Pavel. "Ah! That you didn't know!" He said, seeing the lock of disbelief on her face.

"What do you mean Doina isn't my mother?" It would explain why Doina hated her.

"Father fell in love with someone else after he married mom. You were the product of that love. Doina hated you because you were a constant reminder." He laughed bitterly. "Do you know how I eventually came into the picture? She got him drunk one night and she was lucky enough to get pregnant with me. Out of spite! I was born out of spite! If you hadn't been born, I would have been special! You're the mistake, not me!" His voice faltered.

Anya cleared her throat as Declan moved closer, offering her silent support. It made no sense. She was the oldest, that couldn't be the way that it had happened. "She poisoned Yuri and Nik against me. But not you. Not at first. Do you remember before Doina and Natalia got their hooks into you? Do you remember when you used to love me? I was your big sister, and I took care of you. When you hurt yourself, you came to me. Not Doina, me. Do you remember that?"

Gwen gripped Donovan's arm and her eyes filled. Her heart was breaking for her friend. Luc was standing next to her and put a hand on her shoulder.

Pavel's eyes clouded with confusion. "No. No, I always hated you."

"No," Anya said softly. "You didn't. Something happened and you started to turn against me. You weren't...right. Like you were being drugged. Was it Doina or Natalia?" She could see he was struggling. It must mean Mercule was close by.

Declan, I think he's being spelled.

Yes, Michel and Dougal are looking for Mercule right now.

"No, it wasn't *my* mother." He sneered, getting a hold of himself. "It was you. You were born a monster. You were born wrong. Once I grew up, I knew that. You made me kill our father! IT WAS YOUR FAULT I SHOT HIM!" He went to lunge, but Therese tightened her grip and yanked him back.

"No." said Declan. "No. Blaming Anya for things is at an end. It's done." He stalked over to Pavel. "You shot your father. Under the influence of something or not, you shot him. You killed him. You attacked your sister and he protected her. Because he loved her. He loved her in a way that he never loved you or your brothers. Because he loved her mother and not yours." It was so clear to him then. Jealousy coupled with drugs and magic was a definite poison. He was suffering, but Declan was not letting his Anya be hurt by this.

"MONSTER!" screamed Pavel.

"No. I am not the monster, you are. And not because you're a demon. Just like me. But because you turned on the one person who loved you unconditionally. She would have done anything for you. She's beaten herself up for years over you. And despite how much you say you hate her; she still loves you. And because she loves you, and I love her, I am going to give you one final chance to save yourself. Come clean, tell us what really happened, all of it, and make amends with your sister. If you do this, you can live."

"Oh, my," murmured Valentina quietly.

"I will never stop. I will keep going until she, you and all of your friends are dead." Pavel was calm when he said this. "There is no turning back. So, you'd better just get on with it and kill me." Declan looked into the young man's eyes and saw the truth there. Pavel wanted to die. He had no more real fight left in him, he wanted out. He looked up at Anya and saw she had figured it out too, in the way she was looking at her brother. She looked sad, but resigned.

Declan nodded at Matthew. Matthew handed him one of the swords, as people began to gasp at the sight of them, and then grabbed Pavel from Therese. Matthew pushed the Pavel to his knees. Declan took his place on the other side of the young demon, someone who would have been a brother to him under different circumstances. "I have one final thing to say, but it's for Anya's ears only," Pavel said.

Anya walked over, sat down on her haunches, and looked at her brother. She expected more vitriol, but she saw the pain in his eyes. "Ok," she said very quietly. "What do you need to say?"

He took a breath and let it out shakily. "*Sestra, ya proshu proshcheniya. Prosti menya.*" Sister, I am sorry. Forgive me.

Anya would not cry. "*Brat, ya proshchayu tebya.*" Brother, I forgive you. Anya stood and stepped back.

Therese moved up to stand behind her, hand on Anya's shoulder. "I know it will be hard, but you need to watch," she whispered. "To look away would be a sign of weakness. And since you still need to fight Liliana, you need to appear strong. She'll exploit this otherwise." Anya nodded slightly to show she understood. Therese squeezed her shoulder. "I saw my brothers killed, so I understand how difficult this is for you. I cannot remember the last time I met a braver person."

"Thank you," Anya whispered back, moved by the woman's words.

Matthew and Declan looked at each other, raised a sword and struck at the same time. Declan removed Pavel's head from his body and Matthew struck him through where his heart was. Within seconds, the body turned to dust. Anya let out the breath she'd been holding. Therese squeezed her shoulder. "Well done, Annie," Therese said, using her nickname for the first time.

The Council was watching them closely as well. Valentina held her hand up for silence. "These are the swords?"

"Yes. Those are Declan's. Mine are still sheathed."

Valentina nodded. "They are works of art. Later, I would like to see them up close," she said.

"Of course. We'd be honored to give you a closer look."

She looked at Liliana. "Well, now that's over, I believe you are up next."

"I don't think…"

"You don't think, what? That you should have to do this? Don't think you'll win?" Valentina was definitely enjoying goading Liliana.

I really like her. Anya thought at Declan.

I thought you might. She's very good at this kind of thing, which is why she's running the meeting tonight.

"I have not prepared for this."

"Liliana, you didn't think you needed to prepare last time you challenged Anya. Now, she is challenging you. Surely, the same rules apply." Valentina looked the other woman up and down. "What's more; the way you are dressed would signal to me that you indeed expected to fight this evening. Please don't lie to me. It's tiresome." Liliana was wearing leggings, boots, and a loose top. Top was a mistake, thought Anya. Something closer to the body would have been better.

Liliana nodded her head. "I suppose so."

Donovan had gone to help search for Mercule, so Gwen turned to Luc. "I need to get up front, close to Anya. If Mercule tries anything, being close to her will help."

Luc nodded and muscled Gwen up the front, placing himself directly in back of her.

Valentina noticed and raised an eyebrow. "Who is this?"

"That's Gwen. She's with me," said Anya. "She's my friend."

"She's a witch!" yelled Liliana.

"Is she? Come forward Gwen." Gwen looked wary as Valentina beckoned her forward. "I promise that no harm will come to you, you have my word."

"Go ahead. It's fine," said Luc.

Gwen walked up to stand next to Anya, who grabbed her hand and held onto it. "Hello, thank you for welcoming me." Anya had to stifle another laugh.

"Thank you for coming. Are you a witch?"

"Yes. I am. I am not as powerful as Liliana's witch."

"Are you a light or dark witch?"

"Magic is what you make of it. Any magic can be used for either light or dark. But I do not use spells that will harm or kill people. At least I haven't had to. But to protect, I will do what I have to."

"Irish?"

"Yes ma'am."

"Charming. Why are you here tonight?"

"Anya asked me to come with them. To help, in case Liliana's magician showed up and tried to do harm while they were fighting."

"To make it a fair fight?"

"No. To protect Anya."

"If the prophecy is to be believed, you'd be the Golden Mage then."

"I am Anya's friend. If people want to label me a Golden Mage, cool. It sounds badass."

Valentina laughed. "Did you save them from death?"

"I did."

"How?"

"A spell that I found in one of Declan's books. He has a lot of demon lore and many of the books have spells in them. This particular book had the spell I needed. It was just lucky I remembered seeing it. Still a bit of a novice" Gwen was being purposely cagey about the book and her skill level.

"You did this alone?"

"Yes." And she wouldn't out Luc either. It was not her place to do so.

"It seems odd that you consider yourself a novice and yet you did this alone."

"It does, but…"

"No. She didn't do it alone." Luc stepped. "She did most of it herself. But I have some magic and I was able to act as an energy conduit for her."

"I appreciate loyalty. Well done both of you. You both may step back now." They stepped back to the edge of the circle everyone had created.

Anya shrugged out of her jacket, reached back and unsheathed her swords.

"This is hardly fair. She has the Demon killers." said Liliana.

"Oh not to worry." said Declan. "There are two sets of these swords, you will get to use Anya's set, she will use mine." Anya spun around to face him. He winked at her. She grinned back at him and palmed the two swords: holding them out to Liliana. "Come on now, Liliana. You're good…show me."

Liliana walked down the stairs from the dais slowly and took the swords, wincing a bit at the weight. "I need to warm up."

"Go ahead, take a few minutes. Won't help." Liliana gave her a hateful look.

Anya stepped back to Declan and took his swords from her and raised an eyebrow at him. "These are mine," she said quietly. "I can feel the slight difference in weight."

"Yes. I asked Matthew to switch them when we got here. I thought you might not notice since your adrenaline was so high," he said into her ear. "I would never send you into this with a disadvantage. She has the heavier swords because I would send her in with one."

"Isn't that cheating?"

"She tried to kill us. Fuck her."

"I am not sure I could be more turned on right now."

"I bet you could be, but later." He looked at Liliana. "Are you ready?"

"Yes."

Valentina stood. "Will a scratch kill either of you?"

"No. It still has to be an actual killing thrust. A mere scratch wouldn't do it."

"Fine. You fight to first blood then. When I say stop, you stop. If you don't, I am going to be very put out."

"Magic?" said Liliana, sparing a glance for Gwen.

"Mages may protect. That is all. To do more is cheating. Liliana, if yours is here, I hope they understand that."

"He is not here."

"We shall see. We shall want to speak with him if he is." Valentina clapped her hands together. "Are we ready?" Both women nodded at her. "Wonderful! Begin!"

"This is the most fun that I think Valentina has had in years," whispered Therese to Matthew and Declan.

"Agreed. Valentina is very likely bored by the Council for the most part."

"Oh, absolutely. I'd forgotten that Val could be fun." Declan turned to look at her. "What? I've known her for many centuries."

Therese walked over to Anya, a serious expression on her face. "One final thing before you do this."

"Yes?"

"Remember the most important thing when it comes to a sword fight?"

"And that is?"

"Tits out! Swords up!"

Anya barked out a laugh as Therese winked, grinned at her and stepped back.

Anya loosened her wrists up by swinging the swords a few times. She still felt fairly limber from earlier.

"Stop showing off!" Liliana hissed.

"You are such an idiot. I am loosening up." Anya rolled her eyes.

Liliana lunged forward and Anya sidestepped her easily. She held up the swords in a defensive posture. She wanted Liliana to be the aggressor. She wanted the woman to lose her cool. Liliana parried and Anya met her, sword for sword. They fought that way for the next several minutes. Liliana was good. Not as good as Anya, but very decent.

"Anya is so relaxed and loose," said Therese. "Matthew, you've trained her well."

"She has amazing natural talent. I just fine tuned it."

"She's definitely fighting differently. And staying on the defensive is really smart."

They'd been fighting for several minutes when Anya felt a twinge. It caused her to stumble as the room gasped and Liliana smiled. Anya shook her head clear, but the spell was a good one. Gwen had turned to where she felt the magic and threw a counter spell at it, releasing Anya, who came very close to drawing first blood, but Liliana danced out of the way.

"Why doesn't Mercule help Liliana?" asked Gwen.

"It would be too obvious that Liliana was improving all of a sudden. But mostly, it's more humiliating for Anya to lose because she fucks up. And Anya would ONLY fuck up if she's spelled," Declan said to Therese.

Omala stepped up next to Declan. "Michel said they are tracking the magician based on where the magic comes from. But he moves quickly. I am going to let your mage know as well." Omala sidled off to deliver that message.

Malysh, they can track Mercule when he uses his magic. Gwen will just need to look to the spot. Can you maybe…

Talk some trash?

Yes, that.

Be my pleasure.

"You ok there, Liliana? You look a little winded."

"I am fine!" the other woman bit out.

"Too bad your magician can't help you."

"I don't need him!"

"Oh. come now. Mercule could help you if he wanted to. Still wouldn't beat me though."

"You fucking bitch!" said Liliana. She lunged and Anya managed to knock one of the swords out of her hand.

"Go ahead and pick it up. I am not done playing with you yet. And yes, I outed your little magician."

"Mercule?" she heard Anaranth say.

Another stumble from Anya. Gwen pivoted, shot light into the balcony, which broke the spell. They all heard a loud yelp. And then a "Come the fuck back here!" from Michel as the magician disappeared again.

Valentina's eyes narrowed as she looked towards the balcony. She looked down, caught Declan's eye and he shook his head slightly. Val nodded and sat back. She would put a stop to it if they wanted her to, but she was also happy to let Anya play with Liliana a bit longer.

Gwen and Luc moved closer to Declan. "I am going to see if I can find him before he strikes again. But I need to concentrate to do it. Poke me if you need me," said Gwen.

The two women started another bout of swordplay. Anya measured her moves, taking her time, letting Liliana come at her. Mercule hit twice more with Gwen breaking the hold each time. But the wily bastard kept disappearing.

"Dammit!' said Gwen.

"Let me try," said Luc. "Maybe my sight will kick in." He shrugged.

"Ok, try it then."

Luc closed his eyes, took a steadying breath and reached out. It took a couple of minutes, he let the sound of the swords become an almost rhythmic chant for him. He popped his eyes open, looked at Matthew and whispered something to him. Matthew slunk off into the crowd and in another couple of minutes, he showed back up with Donovan, who had a man slung over his shoulder.

"Hold!' said Valentina. Anya stopped immediately, but Liliana lunged again. Anya just tripped her this time.

"Valentina said to hold. So, fucking hold." Anya moved out of the center of the circle to go stand closer to Declan. Liliana stayed where she was.

"Thank you, Anya," said Valentina. "Is that him?"

"Yes. Surprised him. He's out cold now."

"Gwen, can he be kept under until the fight is over?"

"Now that he's out, I can keep down."

"Thank you. Well done finding him Luc." She winked at the young man.

Luc blushed. "Merci, madame."

"Now, let's conti…." Liliana let out a bloodcurdling yell and ran at Anya, who had no time to prepare. The two women went down, and Declan's heart stopped. His claws extended and his eyes turned red, but he held. Anya's swords had fallen from her hands and scattered. Anya was flat on her back with Liliana straddling her and holding one of the swords to Anya's neck. "What do you have to say for yourself now?"

"This!" Anya lifted herself some and head-butted Liliana, hard. Liliana went flying back, tumbling away from Anya; her swords scattering this time. Anya bounded to her feet and grabbed Liliana by her hair. "You want a dirty fight?! I will give you a dirty fight! GET UP!" she said, throwing Liliana away from her. Liliana started to get back up, reaching for her sword. "Don't you dare touch that fucking sword!" Anya's head was pounding from the head butt, but the adrenaline was carrying her through.

Liliana stood. "We have to draw first blood."

"Valentina didn't say how we had to draw it." Valentina barked out a laugh at this statement.

"You wouldn't hit me!"

"Oh no?" Anya stepped up and punched Liliana in the stomach. As she lurched, Anya lifted a leg and kicked her in the same place she'd just punched her. "You know where I learned that one? My mother! Yeah, she did that to me when I was twelve. Not that she's really my mother, it seems. I'll unpack that one later. But the woman who raised me used her fists on me quite often when I was a child. And Natalia," she landed another punch, to Liliana's back this time. "Knew and didn't do a fucking thing about it."

Natalia stood. "Annechka!"

"I HATE THAT FUCKING NICKNAME!"

"Anya…"

"SIT DOWN!"

"Perhaps Natalia, you need to sit down." This from Adjoa. Natalia sat.

"Doina hit me until I learned to hit back. Then she found other ways to hurt me. So, Liliana, when I tell you that I learned how to fight dirty from an expert, I am not kidding."

Declan was going to kill Doina very slowly and very painfully. And he was going to enjoy it. Every minute of it.

Gwen shot out a bolt of white light. It hit the wall harmlessly. "I am sorry. I got angry."

"It's fine Gwen. I find I am angry myself." Valentina sounded fairly furious.

Liliana was hurting, but she stood. She raised her fists, but it was too late. Anya pulled her arm back and with a crunch, broke Liliana's nose.

"I'd say that counts as first blood, wouldn't you?" asked Anya.

"I would say so." said Valentina. "Well done. Do you feel better?"

"I do, actually." She turned and started walking over to her family when she heard a yell and "Anya!" Anya turned on a dime, a dagger appearing in her hand one minute and then in Liliana's leg the next, sending the woman to the ground in pain.

Francois stepped down from the dais and walked over to Anya. "You won, fairly. I am so sorry for what happened to you and Declan. Is there anything else you would like?"

"Jack," Said Declan. "I want Jack to come work for me." Jack was standing with Michel and went stock still at this.

"Jack? Is this something you are amenable to?" This from Francois.

He cleared his throat around the lump there. "Yes. Yes, it is. I'd be happy to go work for Declan." Michel squeezed his friend's shoulder.

"It's done. Jack, I free you from your obligation to me. You may go work for Declan." He turned to look at Lilliana. "I will deal with her now." He held out his hand to Anya and then to Declan. He walked over to Liliana, stared at her and then ruthlessly ripped the knife out of her leg and handed it back to Anya as Liliana started to crumple. "I suggest you not fall again. You may want to save a little face by walking out of here of your own free will." Liliana rose to her full height and without another word, limped from the room, Francois and his own men close behind.

CHAPTER 38

Anaranth stood. "Declan and Anya, you have acquitted yourselves honestly and Anya, you have proven that you have a true and strong heart."

"As well as a very decent right hook." This from Valentina.

"As well as that. You may keep the swords; my word is final on this. Whether you're part of a prophecy or not, I am convinced you are not going to go on a killing spree with them. I would ask, though, that they be removed from the premises now." A noise from Valentina. "After they have been fawned over."

After the Council had inspected the blades, with Adjoa sighing with envy over them again, Donovan removed them.

"What about Mercule?" asked Anya.

Anaranth answered. "We are going to take care of Mercule. He is not...unknown to me. I have ways of getting answers from him. I will pass along any pertinent information I receive from him, through Richelieu. Is that something you can live with?"

"I will leave it up to my mate." said Declan.

She thought for a moment. "At some point, Declan and I would like to question him. But for now, I am satisfied to let you all handle it."

Are you sure, Anya?

Yes. I don't love it, but it's not a battle we need to fight right now. Mercule won't break easily. Richelieu will have to torture him. And I find I really want that to happen before we talk to him.

So sexy when you're bloodthirsty.

Flirt.

"Thank you for your trust," said Richelieu, who just seemed to appear out of nowhere. "I will enjoy convincing him to talk." Anya shot Declan a look and winked. One large demon came in and threw Mercule over his shoulder and marched out of there. "How long will he be out?"

"Another hour or so."

"Oh good! Time enough to set up his new accommodations. Anya, very well done. If matters were different, I'd recruit you." Richelieu winked at her.

"If they were different, I'd accept." He kissed her hand and was gone.

"Anya, about Natalia…" said Valentina.

"Valentina, Council members, you have been more than fair with us this evening. If it is all the same to you though, I would like to deal with Natalia, her part in this and my true parentage as a personal family matter. For now."

"I am with my mate on this. Neither of us feels it's necessary to upset the current power structure. And this rift is intensely personal."

Valentina looked impressed. "I think that's a perfectly reasonable request and I commend you on this decision."

"Thank you."

Valentina stepped down to speak with Anya. "Anya, I would very much like to get to know you better. Adjoa and I are friends, and we often have dinner together. We'd like to invite you to join us sometimes." She looked at Declan. "Just the ladies."

"I'd be absolutely delighted."

"Wonderful! Now, what else can we do for you this evening?"

"Is there a private room we could borrow? I would like to have a conversation with Natalia and Vlad now if I might."

"Of course." said Valentina. "I will show you all to one myself.'"

When they got to the room, Anya was the last to go in and Valentina held her back. "For what it's worth; I do believe in the prophecy, and I do think it is most likely you and Declan. I know this seems odd, but I am very old, and some things defy explanation. You are new blood and we needed that. We need more of it if I am honest. Not everyone on the Council will be on your side; but Adjoa and I are. I am not sure where Francois will end up on this, and Vlad and Natalia are going to be very careful going forward."

"Do you know what their end game is?"

"I believe it's to unseat Anaranth." Anya let out a low whistle. "I do not think I need to tell you not to trust her. I also suspect that you held some information back to use at a later time. That was smart. Your mother, your real mother, is important to all of this somehow. Take care. Anya. After this, you can all go home, no need to come back in. You all deserve a rest."

"Thank you!"

***

Anya walked into the room. Natalia stood up. "Anya…"

"You don't talk right now. I will talk. When I ask you a question, you will answer. Are we clear?"

Natalia nodded. "I know that you introduced Mercule to Liliana. I know you had other women that you were grooming for Declan, human and demon. If one of the demons ever gets in my way, I will kill her. A human will have nothing to fear from me, they are likely innocent dupes in all of this. You set Liliana on the path that led to her downfall. You knew she was weak and foolish. You did it because it didn't matter whether she succeeded or not, you both had a plan for both outcomes. You put my life, the life of my mate and the life of my friends…my family on the line. You also put Tomas and Irina in danger, tangentially, because your machinations are what caused Tomas to get hurt. Did you use drugs or magic to turn Pavel?"

"No Anya, we did not. That would be illegal." This was from Vlad.

"What we did was a grey area, and I will admit it, unethical. But we did not turn him against his will like that." Natalia looked desperate for Anya to believe her.

"I am not sure I believe you."

"So, you also are aware of a drug that gives new demons super strength?" Declan asked.

"No."

"Did you know that other demons were being made illegally by Mercule?"

"We had heard, but no proof of it was forthcoming."

"I could provide proof. But I tore him apart."

Anya cleared my throat. "Do you know who my real mother is?"

"No, Anya. You must believe me." Natalia was pleading.

"I do not believe you. But I will find out the truth eventually, with or without your help. To be clear, you are not welcome in my home. We are not family anymore. You let me live in a home where I was hated and abused. I will never forgive you for that."

"And if you step one toe out of line," continued Declan. "We will tell the rest of what we know, and have you unseated."

"Declan. Anya. You must see that…"

"No. We are done here. There is nothing you could possibly say to me right now that I would want to hear. This is goodbye." Anya and Declan left the room.

***

Back at the house, they had settled into Anya's sitting room and had relayed the story to a very relieved Marchand. "I am so pleased you are all still alive! I wish I could have been there though!"

"We snuck one human in, I am not sure if we could have gone for two. Maybe next time!" laughed Declan.

"My friend, I am very glad to see you well. Anya was very worried."

"I am glad to be home, thank you."

"It seems though, that you have handled Liliana and hopefully the magician. Natalia and Vlad will behave, for now. But they should be watched."

"Already on that."

"But there are more questions now. Anya's mother, who turned her brother, did Mercule invent the drug himself or did he just exploit it?"

"Oh, I hadn't thought of that. Huh. Well, all of that can wait for another day. We are all exhausted, and we are all going to go to our respective homes and go to bed now."

"You just want sexy times with your mate." said Michel.

"Do you blame me?"

"No. Glad you're feeling better."

"Thank you. Now, everyone get the fuck out."

Upstairs in their bedroom, Declan grabbed Anya to him and kissed her deeply. "Anya, *malysh*, my Anya. I knew you'd come for me. I never doubted."

She started undressing him. "I would never have stopped looking." She ripped open his shirt and started pressing kisses to his chest. He grasped her hair and pulled her head up to his, so he could kiss her again. He grabbed the bottom of her shirt and tugged up, pulling it over her head.

"You still have your sheaths on. I think it will be quicker if you undress yourself."

"Ok, fine. You do the same." In minutes they were naked, and he lifted her. She wrapped her legs around his waist and pulled his hair. "Declan. I need you!"

"I know, I need you too." He got to the bed and tossed her gently onto it, following her. She lunged and toppled him, so she was on top.

"Do not get kidnapped again!" She leaned down and bit his nipple gently. He sat up, taking one breast in his mouth, while he roughly palmed the others. "Claws!" He extended his claws and pinched her nipples, causing her to arch her back and moan. He switched his suckling to her other breast and did the same pinching move to the other nipple. He then took his hand ran one claw, gently down her back, causing her to shiver. "New move!" she gasped.

"I have plenty of them." He pulled back some, lifted her and set her down on his cock, but didn't enter all the way. He eased in and out at her head a few times while she gripped his legs. "How does that feel?"

"Oh God, so good...but I want more. I want all of you."

"All of me?" He pumped in and out slowly. "Are you sure?"

"God, yes! Please!" With one hard thrust on a low laugh, he was inside her fully. He started to move slowly, rhythmically, drawing out the pleasure, as he took her mouth. She was gripping his shoulders and moving with him. He took one hand and touched her clit. "Aaaahh!" She said. He started roll it slowly between two fingers as his pumps picked up speed. "Declan! Please!"

"Please? Please what?"

"I want…..please…don't make me beg." She bit his shoulder and he laughed again. He picked up speed with both of his thrusts and what his fingers were doing and soon she went over the edge, him right behind her.

They fell back onto the bed, laughing. "Well, that was a stress reliever!" she said.

"And how!"

She edged up to look at him. "I know that this isn't over. Not by a long shot. But, for a little while...can we just be a normal, or normal adjacent, couple?"

"Sounds good to me." He kissed her. "Ok, time for a bath."

"Man, you are a convert."

"Baths, *Star Wars*, you're opening me up to new things."

"Guess you can teach an old demon new tricks."

"Cheeky. For that...I am going to dunk you." She laughed and for now, all was right with the world.

EPILOGUE

Six months later.

"A wedding?!" Gwen squeaked.

"Ssshh!" said Declan. "I don't want Anya to hear. I know she said she didn't care, but I think she does. Do you think she'd like that?" They were on the roof of the house having a cookout. Once Anya discovered how elaborate his set up was, she insisted on an outdoor party.

"Yes. She would. She'd be fine without one, but I also know that you legally being hers, would delight her."

"So, I want it to be a surprise. I don't want her stress about anything. I want her to show up in something beautiful. Will you help me plan it?"

"Oh my God, yes! I will!"

"Great. It's going to be you, me, Matthew, and Luc. Therese will run interference, as necessary." It had taken Declan six months to get back to this idea. But it hadn't let go and the longer he spent with Anya, the more he knew he wanted to marry her. He knew they'd need to renew the paperwork every so often, but that was no problem.

"This is going to be amazing!" Gwen started pulling on his arm in her excitement.

"Hey! Stop manhandling my man!" Anya said laughing and plopping down on Declan's lap.

"What are you two talking about?"

"Just how great it is up here." Gwen spied Donovan. "Oh, let me see if I can wrangle a kiss out of that man." She jumped up and sped across the roof.

"She's a whirlwind," said Declan.

"Yup. What were you really talking about?"

"How great it is up here."

"Hmmm." She didn't buy it, but she let it go. "So, I think we should call Richelieu soon, to talk to Mercule."

"You ready?"

"I think so. I don't think he's going to tell us anything, but it's time."

"Ok. I will make the call."

"Thank you." She gave him a quick kiss and then looked across the deck "Marchand is lonely I think. Less lonely, since he found us, but still lonely. He likes Therese, but I am not sure how she feels about him."

"He's a deep one. I kind of wish he were demon born. He'd make an excellent one. Also, butt out."

"What? I am just saying…"

"I know what you're saying, and no. Leave him be. He does not need your help here. The female demons at the station LOVE him."

"Not surprised." Anya nuzzled Declan's neck.

"He's in charge of that whole contingent. Takes something off of Michel's plate."

"So, what were you and Gwen talking about?"

"*Star Wars* and how much I like the original movies."

"It's because you think you're Han Solo. Also, I still don't believe you." He kissed her soundly and she decided to change the subject. "Now, about Michel and Omala…" she said, catching sight of the two of actually talking.

"Really, stop it. Let them work it out."

"Hmmm."

"Anya, I mean it."

"Fine!"

Anya looked at Gwen and Donovan talking with Marchand. Dougal was trying to show Luc how to throw a punch while Matthew looked on. Michel and Omala chatting, while Marchand tried to pretend that he wasn't looking at Therese. "Look at them all, Declan."

"Family," he said simply.

"Family," she replied happily. "They make me happy." She gestured to their friends. "You make me happy."

"You make me happy, love."

"I love you."

"And I love you." He paused. "Anya, do you want to know?"

She knew what he meant. "I do. I don't like unanswered questions. And my biological mother is one. I think Natalia knows more than she's saying. About a lot of things."

"Agreed. This is not over."

"Not by a long shot." She leaned down to kiss him quickly. "And we'll see it through together."

"That my love, is a promise."

"And a warning to those that stand in our way."

"Absolutely!" Whatever came next, they'd be ready.

ACKNOWLEDGEMENTS

In 2017, I lost my mother to a very quick moving cancer. During those three weeks that mom was in the hospital, my friends supported me, listened to me, gave me rides and made sure I ate.

So first and foremost, I want to thank Sarah, Caitlin, and Liz for being there whenever I needed them. There are bits of them throughout the book, I hope they recognize themselves. When you find your tribe, it's a wonderful thing.

To Dally, who gave me some really good words of wisdom that I still share with people who are in the same situation.

To Lane, who is the worst sister an only child could have and while the reason we bonded was sad; I am so glad we did, and I enjoy the hell out of our podcasts! We're very entertaining.

To Erin, Jackie and Jennifer who checked in on me daily to see how I was holding up. Suzanne, thank you for looking at margins with me and telling me that I was not crazy.

To my group of friends who I met through a Duran Duran message board so many years ago (there are too many of you to name and we really need a group name), who were supportive and didn't complain about my really long posts once.

I could flat out not have done this without their support and love and acceptance.

To my beta readers, Liz, Erin and Anya (who also did a fair bit of editing) for graciously reading a very rough draft because quite frankly, I was winging it and had no clue what I was doing. I appreciate all of the feedback. Even the bits that I…cough cough…may not have used. Any grammatical or style mistakes are mine because I finished this during a pandemic, and we all are doing our best.

To all of the authors I have read over the year for inspiration and motivation. They'll never know how closely I paid attention to their publishing stories.

I also want to acknowledge all of the front line workers who toiled every day to make the rest of our lives safer and easier. From the health professionals to grocery store workers to the food delivery people; thank you all so much for your bravery and dedication.